I'M NOT THERE

I'M NOT THERE

I'M NOT THERE

ROB GITTINS

This edition produced in Great Britain in 2022

by Hobeck Books Limited, Unit 14, Sugnall Business Centre, Sugnall, Stafford, Staffordshire, ST21 6NF

www.hobeck.net

A CIP catalogue for this book is available from the British Library.

ISBN 978-1-913-793-82-1 (ebook)

ISBN 978-1-913-793-83-8 (pbk)

Cover design by Jayne Mapp Design

The hearts of small children are delicate organs.
A cruel beginning ... can twist them into curious shapes.
Carson McCullers

PRAISE FOR I'M NOT THERE

'Everything is cleverly brought together in a thrilling climax.'
   Sarah Leck

'It had the feel of one of those books that gets a plug and then suddenly takes off to be a top ten best seller.'
   Pete Fleming

'Dark, gritty, well crafted characters and some gut punching shocks, first rate crime writing.'
   Alex Jones

ARE YOU A THRILLER SEEKER?

Hobeck Books is an independent publisher of crime, thrillers and suspense fiction and we have one aim – to bring you the books you want to read.

For more details about our books, our authors and our plans, plus the chance to download free novellas, sign up for our newsletter at **www.hobeck.net**.

You can also find us on Twitter **@hobeckbooks** or on Facebook **www.facebook.com/hobeckbooks10**.

For Jake, Xavier and Henry

PROLOGUE

MY NAME IS LARA ARDEN. I'm twenty-six years old. Twenty years ago my mother vanished on a crowded train.

I still don't know exactly where we were going that day. We were travelling to the mainland; that's all we were told. It was going to be a treat, an adventure. It didn't turn out to be much of a treat, but I suppose she was right about the adventure.

She'd gone to the buffet trolley in the next carriage to collect some crisps and drinks. She told us she'd only be a few minutes. For the first five of those minutes we – that's me and my sister, Georgia – drew in the books she'd bought for us on the station platform as we'd waited to board the train. Georgia was two years older than me and better at colouring in the pictures. For those first few minutes we were silent as we both tried to out-do the other in the neatness stakes.

Then I realised Mum hadn't returned, which meant we still hadn't had our crisps or drinks. I looked down the carriage, then turned back to my book. A minute or so later I looked up again, but she was still nowhere to be seen.

'Where are you going?' Georgia hissed at me as I stood up. Across the aisle a man with a laptop in front of him smiled at us.

I don't know why. It's just one of those details that are fixed in my mind from a day I'll never forget.

My stomach was beginning to grumble now, and I gestured to Georgia to stay where she was and walked into the next carriage. The buffet trolley was immediately ahead, a press of people around it waiting to be served. I relaxed, expecting any moment to see Mum waiting with them, gesturing at an overly impatient daughter to get back to her seat. But as I scanned the line of waiting customers she was nowhere to be seen.

'Do you want something?'

A kindly face swam before me, a middle-aged woman in a dark suit with a badge on the lapel that read *Customer Services*. I told her I was looking for my mum and she smiled, much as the man with the laptop in front of him had smiled a moment or so before.

'She's probably just in the toilet. Why don't you go back to your seat? She'll be back before you know it.'

I nodded at her, but didn't move. For a moment the woman with the kindly face kept eyeing me, then she reached out her hand.

'Come on. Let's go and find her, shall we?'

Instinctively, I took her outstretched hand and we approached the toilet nearest to the shuffling queue. She tapped on the door but there was no reply. She opened it gently, in case anyone inside had forgotten to lock it, I suppose, but it was empty. So then we moved onto the next toilet down in the next carriage, the woman with the kindly face still smiling all the while. By the time she'd tapped on that door too and there was still no sign of Mum, that smile was beginning to fade a little.

'OK, now what's probably happened is she's seen someone she knows, and she's stopped to talk to them. She's probably sitting next to them, which is how we missed her, so what I'm going to do now is walk you through the train until you stop me and tell me you've seen her, all right?'

I nodded again. We started where we'd been seated, in the

first of the carriages. The man with the laptop was still there but he was absorbed in something on the screen by then. We collected Georgia from her seat before walking through every carriage on that train, which didn't take long.

By now the woman had been joined by a large man with a badge on his jacket that read *Train Manager*. Snatches of their hissed conversation reached mine and Georgia's ears as we waited in a space between two carriages that the tannoy announcements called a vestibule. If we moved even a fraction, the door to the carriage ahead would open. Move back and it would close. We did that for the next minute or so as we heard fragments of that urgent exchange before we grew bored and the door closed fully and their voices were lost.

Looking back now, all these years later, the situation was simple, of course. The train hadn't yet made its first stop and it wouldn't for another few minutes. The train had been in motion all the time with the doors locked, so no one could have got off. But according to the two small girls the Customer Service host had just walked the length of the train, their mother, who'd boarded with them that day, wasn't there now.

Through the glass door ahead I saw the Train Manager check his watch. Within a few moments the train would be arriving at its first stop. Then the doors would open and the first of the passengers would get off. He had no idea what was happening here, but he knew that once that first stop was made it would be a lot harder to find out.

We saw the Train Manager make a phone call. The woman with the kindly face took us into a small room next to the driver where she gave us the drinks and the crisps we'd been promised. As we started to eat, the train stopped at the station and the Train Manager unlocked just the one door at the front. An officer from British Transport Police embarked via that single unlocked door. Then, apologising for the delay over the tannoy, but without explaining it, the Train Manager collected us from that small room next to the driver and walked us through the train for a second time, this time with the police officer as well. We checked every seat in each carriage, each of the toilets again, and even the luggage racks at each end of the carriages and the ones over the seats.

Nothing.

Still no sign of her.

After that second and equally fruitless sweep, the Train Manager finally opened the doors and a few, now-impatient passengers exited onto the platform. We'd been taken to the ticket barrier a moment or so before and had been told to watch as they left the station. Still we didn't see the one person we wanted to see.

The rest of that day passed in a blur. The next few months passed in a blur as well. Our dad had walked out on us soon after I'd been born and Mum had had no contact with him since. If she'd had any other sort of family, we'd never met them. With Mum remaining missing, we were both taken into care and a few weeks later were placed with the first of the foster families who'd look after us from that point on.

They never found her. The mystery of how a woman could vanish from a locked train like that was never solved and Georgia and I grew to adulthood resigned to the fact it never would be.

Needless to say it all very much cast its shadow, and it was a shadow that seemed to eclipse Georgia in particular. I turned my life round to some extent, professionally at least, and became a cop. Georgia hasn't done anything with her life, as she's always been the first to acknowledge, and I love her dearly, but she's right. She drifted into drugs in her teens, flirted briefly with pros-titution and is now a recovering addict in rehab. Hopefully recovering, anyway.

What do I think now? I've had years to think about it, after all. Now, I think Mum just snapped. I think that having two small daughters to look after all by herself suddenly became too much for her and she had some kind of breakdown. Whether she meant to abandon us – whether it was part of a premeditated plan or just a spur of the moment thing – we'll never know. But now I think she just walked out of that train carriage that day and couldn't face walking back in again.

So why wasn't she spotted? How could everyone have missed her? I've thought a lot about that too. Now I think maybe that on-board search wasn't as forensic as it might have been. Maybe the Transport Officer who boarded the train that day simply missed her and perhaps that wasn't totally his fault. I've been on hundreds of train rides since, and every time I see potential hiding places. If someone was determined enough they could have evaded those few pairs of searching eyes.

But yesterday – the reason I'm writing all this down – a call came in. I was in Comms at the time, checking another shout, part of an ongoing inquiry into a spate of attacks on members of – of all things – a local S&M club. This call was from a railway station just over half an hour away, which had a situation with one of their arriving trains. A single woman travelling alone with her small child seemed to have disappeared.

Leaving the colleague I was with at the time, I drove down to the station and went on board with two Transport Officers who were already there. I took personal charge of the small and frightened child, a boy this time, called Milo. I didn't tell him or the Transport Officers why I'd made this sudden dash to be with them.

I escorted Milo along the length of the train, taking in each and every one of those hiding places I'd identified on all those train journeys over all those years, ignoring ever more vocal demands from ever more impatient passengers that they be allowed to get on their way.

At the end of what became an exhaustive trawl I stood on the platform, a small child at my side, passengers finally disembarking all around us. Wherever Milo's mother was right now she was not on that train, and I knew that for a fact because I'd just carried out the search for her myself.

All of which meant that twenty years on, history seemed to have just repeated itself.

And standing by a small child with a look on his face I knew only too well, all my neat little theories about what might or might not have happened to my own mother that day had just gone up in smoke.

PART ONE

Prepare for his sons a place of slaughter
Isaiah, 14:21

CHAPTER
ONE

THE LIVING ROOM was in its usual state of chaos. Toys, kids' drawings and discarded pieces of Play-Doh and Lego were everywhere. Only one thing wasn't usual about the room right now and that was the handgun being held by the stranger. The handgun that was pointing straight at a seventeen-year-old boy.

Ben Turow had let himself in a minute or so before. For a moment he stood in the hallway, savouring the silence from the other side of the living room door. His parents, Phil and Kate, ran a childminding business, and usually a deafening cacophony of noise greeted him the moment he came back from school, followed by at least three or four small bodies launching themselves at him, demanding that he play.

But today there was nothing, meaning the kids being cared for today were most likely down in a park a couple of streets away or at some softplay centre somewhere. Or asleep.

Ben called out a soft greeting, then pressed on into the living room with its view across the Solent, to find his mum and dad huddled together across the room, their bewildered faces staring back at him.

And that stranger, a young-looking woman, with that gun in her hand.

Ben just stared at her for a moment. They'd moved there six months before from a small links house a few miles down the coast in Shanklin. Drugs had been a problem in their old neighbourhood, sometimes being dealt openly on the streets. Burglaries were less common but hardly unknown. But guns were unheard of.

'Stop this, please.'

His mother stepped in, responding instinctively to the fast-developing panic on her elder child's face. Her only other child – a daughter, Jools, two years younger than Ben – wasn't home yet. She often lingered to talk to some of the boys from school, and for the first time since she'd passed puberty her mother thanked God for teenage hormones.

But then she stopped. What could she say? She was as much at a loss as Ben in all this and had been ever since they'd let this young woman in through their front door.

In her phone call that same morning the woman had told them she had a child who needed looking after three mornings a week while she returned to work, but that she'd like to take a look at their place and – by implication – them first. That much was expected, indeed both childminders would have been wary of any parent who simply dropped their child off without checking the carers out first.

What happened next, the almost casual way she took the gun out of her bag, had been anything but.

Phil had been the first to respond. He thought this must be some kind of robbery and gestured across to a small collection of notes and coins on the table – that week's money left by a couple of the parents just an hour before – but the young woman with the gun didn't even look at it, just told them again to go and stand by the window.

Kate had just stared at her, hadn't moved for a moment.

'I don't understand.'

The woman with the gun eyed her back, coolly.

'If it isn't money you want…' Kate tailed off, which was when the woman spoke for only the second time since they'd let her in.

'Wait.'

'What for?'

'Just wait.'

And they had.

Because they had no choice.

They waited until they heard Ben's key in the door. They kept waiting as he called out from the hallway, then came into the sitting room. That was where he'd remained, half in and half out of the doorway, staring at the woman with the gun much as they'd stared at her a few moments before, which already seemed like a lifetime ago.

For one terrible moment, a dark suspicion suddenly assailed Kate. Was this some sort of gang feud? She'd never imagined Ben to be the type to get involved in things like that, but she wouldn't be the first mum to mis-read the character of a teenage son. The woman looked to be years older than Ben, which made it even more unlikely, but was she the leader of some local outfit or other, someone he'd fallen foul of in some way?

The woman with the gun turned an almost lazy eye back onto them, making sure she kept Ben in her eyeline all the time. Her gun moved in her hand, hovering over first one of Ben's still-staring parents, then the other.

Kate willed herself not to look at her son, to keep her eyes on the young woman instead, desperately trying to make some kind of connection. She had no idea why that suddenly seemed the safest course of action, but she did it anyway.

'Please, just tell us what you want?'

But the young woman just turned the same, almost lazy, eye back onto Ben, still standing by the door, the escape route clearly open behind him. He wasn't going to take it, though; Kate could see that only too clearly. He simply seemed rooted right now.

Then the woman nodded, and now Kate could see there was almost the ghost of a smile on her face.

CHAPTER
TWO

IN THE OLD days all this would have been taking place on some badly lit street corner with both nervous parties to the illicit transaction constantly looking over their shoulder. The product would be impossible to assess until later, and if there were any problems the dealer would almost certainly be impossible to trace.

This was much more civilised. A warm apartment. A glass of wine in one hand and a laptop open on the table. Not to mention a refund policy with detailed terms and conditions and close to two thousand feedback entries over the previous six months averaging around 4.8 out of 5. As well as the occasional negative review just to add that reassuring touch of authenticity.

Dark markets can't be accessed using a normal browser. They're found on an encrypted part of the net where URLs are just a jumble of seemingly meaningless numbers and letters, usually accessed via a special browser called Tor.

The most famous of the dark net markets, or infamous, depending on your viewpoint, was Silk Road. It had been busted years before, but had spawned immediate copycat replacements including Pandora, 1776 Market Place, 30 and – perhaps inevitably – Silk Road 2.0, the latter alone soon boasting more than nine hundred vendors selling everything from heroin to opium and cocaine to acid, as well as the specific and highly restricted drug the young woman in front of her computer was particularly interested in right now.

It wasn't just drugs she could have accessed, had she the inclination. All the sites offered a market for just about anything and everything from stolen art to fake birth certificates, each complete with a product description, photograph and price. All the vendors, without exception, were unfailingly polite, as evidenced by the site she'd just clicked on, a site she'd first used a few weeks before, beginning then with a deliberately low-key request by way of a test.

Hi. I'm new here. Do you think I could buy just a tiny amount of marijuana?

Try saying that to a guy in a blacked-out Beemer, the young woman silently reflected as she took a sip from the wine glass next to her keyboard.

Hi there and thanks for the email, came the immediate reply. *My advice is that starting small with any new transaction is the smart thing to do so no problem if you want to start with just one gram of marijuana or anything, I would too if I were you. I hope we can do some business.*

The price was more variable than could be obtained out on the street, and in some cases a lot more expensive. The average price for marijuana itself was about a third higher, while heroin could weigh in at over twice the normal street price. But there were other considerations to take into account. Cocaine out on the street, for example, had an average purity as low as two per cent. Those two thousand individual feedback entries averaging around 4.8 out of 5 provided a reassurance of quality.

The payment method was equally innovative, with Bitcoin the crypto-currency of choice. Easily exchanged for real world currency, it had the advantage of being completely anonymous, and if that still raised alarm bells an even more secure payment method called multi-seg escrow had recently been launched, with money only transferred when both parties signed off on any transaction.

The young woman's fingers clicked on a series of keys on the keyboard. A message appeared on the screen confirming the transaction and thanking her for her custom. The product would be delivered within the next two days, and it would be, she knew that; there'd be no delay and no excuses.

Then the young woman put the print-out of her now-adjusted Bitcoin balance back in her credit card holder, next to her Police ID.

CHAPTER
THREE

KATE KNEW that none of this was real.

How could it be? They ran a small childminding service from a modest maisonette in a seaside town. Their days were spent clearing up after minor domestic accidents and playing games with occasionally fractious and always excitable young kids. The highlight of the day for those kids was an excursion to the local park, just visible across a small patch of scrubland from their sitting room window. The highlight of the day for her and Phil was the quiet time after lunch when the children they were looking after that day would settle in front of a DVD and hopefully drift off into sleep for an hour or so, just like the two charges who, thank God, were currently tucked up in their cots across the hall.

Their days did not and could not include being held hostage by a strange woman with a gun, which was why she had to be hallucinating in some way.

Except it was happening.

And there she was.

Holding that gun.

The young woman herself didn't seem crazy or angry. She seemed ultra-calm, in fact. Apart from that gun in her hand.

Phil hissed at her.

'Just answer the question will you? What the fuck do you want?'

Kate stole a quick sideways glance at her husband, his face a living study in frustration and fear.

Then Ben spoke too.

'I don't understand.'

But he did. Kate could see it in her son's eyes. And it was the same realisation she could see slowly dawning in Phil's eyes now, too. For some reason too twisted to even begin to comprehend, this young woman had decided that they were all going to die on this totally normal and hitherto-uneventful afternoon.

Then, as the woman glanced quickly towards the window of the flat, taking in the clock on the wall at the same time, another and equally terrifying possibility suddenly assailed her.

Was she waiting for Jools? Is that why they were all living through this strange sort of suspension? Was this woman waiting for her to appear as well to complete a family execution?

Which was when, from across the hall, one of the two children they were looking after that day began to stir.

The woman with the gun glanced – almost involuntarily – towards the hall, then back at the window again, taking in the wall-mounted clock again at the same time.

Ben spoke. just a single word this time, but his voice was higher now.

'Mum?'

Kate knew what he was saying and it was lacerating.

Stop this.

Please.

Just tell her to stop.

'Look – let's all just calm down, shall we?' By her side, Phil made another belated effort to try and wrest back some sort of control, but the young woman just kept staring at them as the toddler in the next room now began to protest his imprisonment more and more volubly.

Still by the open door and still seemingly unable to move, Ben stared wildly at his mum, then at his dad. The whole room felt as if it was on fire. The young woman's eyes were fixed only on Ben now, and for a moment Kate didn't understand what she was seeing. Then it became only too obvious, as the large stain that had suddenly appeared on Ben's school trousers spread wider, turning darker all the time, as the terrified young boy pissed himself.

Kate stared back at the young woman again. Then the world exploded in front of her eyes as a shot rang out and Phil crashed back, blood spraying geyser-like as the bullet blasted through his body and embedded itself in the wall behind.

Kate looked at her son as he stared at the twitching body that had been his father, and anger suddenly rose inside her, immediate and massive, the rage of a lioness confronted with a threat to her cub, and all she could think was why hadn't it come before, why hadn't she been able to ride that rage until now, until it was too late for Phil at least?

Which was when, equally suddenly, the world turned black for her too.

Across the room, Ben stared as the young woman turned back from the second of the bodies that was now lying on the floor, his mum's life ended as efficiently and brutally as his dad's, while all the time the toddler in the cot in the next room yelled even louder.

And Ben kept staring as the young woman approached.

CHAPTER
FOUR

LARA CROSSED a small bridge traversing one of the inlets that fed into the nearby Medina, a few apartments hewn from converted warehouses looking down on it from all sides.

Night was falling by now, but lights were visible in only one or two. Most were owned by speculators, used occasionally by them or their families but empty for the rest of the time. It seemed to make no sense until those same speculators sold those same apartments for up to five times the price they paid for them, usually within just a couple of years and often to other speculators.

Five minutes later, she was passing small garages and storage outlets, even the occasional modest mosque. Those five minutes took Lara from one world to a different world completely, which was quite appropriate in a sense. The man she was going to visit had also been living in two very different worlds, and for perhaps too long now.

Lara had first met Rollo as a lowly PC on the beat when she'd been called to the scene of an assault. A panicked neighbour had called it in, a female immigrant from Sudan who spoke little English. From her halting report it seemed some kind of major siege was taking place next door. Lara had been on probation at the time and attended along with a couple of uniformed patrol officers. As they neared the address one of the officers recognised it. They'd been called to that same house the previous week and other officers had been called there the week before as well.

Briefly, both officers flirted with the option of turning round and leaving the family inside to sort this out themselves, and if Lara hadn't been there maybe they would have done. The expression on their faces said it all. Nothing was ever going to be gained by any sort of intervention in this ongoing battle between the desperate and the damned.

But the presence of the new recruit demanded otherwise, principally because that new recruit wanted to know what the flying fuck they were talking about. They could hear the shouting and screaming from a hundred metres away. How the hell could they just turn round and pretend they hadn't?

The officers looked at each other, the same battle-hardened weariness on both their faces, but then they exited the patrol car and approached the small house on the well-kept street. Two minutes later, Lara first met Rollo.

———

The first Rollo's parents knew something was wrong with their son, Corporal Rory Adams of the Princess of Wales's Royal Regiment, also known as the Tigers, was a night or so after he'd returned from his latest tour of duty in Basra. They'd gone out for a meal to celebrate him coming home, but the table they'd been allocated at the far end of a restaurant with a view over the nearby marina had to be changed. At Rollo's insistence they were all seated with their backs to the wall in clear view of the door instead. Rollo spent the whole of the evening scanning the faces that entered for any kind of threat, the food he'd ordered largely untouched.

Rollo himself didn't understand at the time why he'd suddenly flipped into what might be called battle mode. The only thing he could put it down to was another diner being served his steak at a nearby table as they were waiting to be seated. The smell of the meat had suddenly brought into his head the aroma of burning arms and legs.

Over the next few weeks the smallest thing would trigger the same switch, spiking Rollo's anger along the way. A pair of shoes left out by his father sparked one particularly violent and mystifying outburst. It was only later that Rollo's parents discovered that his staff sergeant, who went on to become a renowned paralympian, had lost both legs courtesy of an improvised explosive device. Rollo himself had clamped the man's wounds to try and stop the blood loss, reassuring the yelling casualty that he would play football with his son again, which was the only thing that seemed to concern him at the time. As the helicopter flew the injured man away, Rollo had picked up his discarded shoes in the hope he'd collect them one day and that Rollo would make good his promise.

On another occasion Rollo's mother came home to find him smashing the ringing phone. The next night his father tried to restrain him from haring out into the street and confronting a teenager charging his car over a newly constructed speed bump just outside their house. Rollo lashed out at him instead and his father lost three of his front teeth.

What happened to Rollo was a depressingly all-too-familiar story of soldiers returning from conflict zones, and many other families had been torn apart by it too. But his family was close; they stuck together. By doing so, Rollo's PTSD was transferred as if by proxy to his parents, and soon there were three casualties in need of help instead of one. And this latest battle royal would most probably only end, as those patrol officers had wearily predicted, with one party or the other actually killing the other.

Rollo didn't kill anyone that night. He left the family house instead. He dropped out of sight, and his parents slowly began to recover from the madness that had returned to them one of the walking wounded, even if his wounds were invisible to most.

For the next six months his mother read reports of bodies being washed up on various beaches around the island with a leaden feeling in her stomach, convinced they were going to be called on to identify one of those bodies as her son.

———

A couple of years later, Lara found Rollo. Or rather she found a sodden collection of rags that turned out to be Rollo. It was August and the height of the annual invasion of sailing folk. Everywhere she looked it was wall-to-wall upturned collars and Pimms. A large crowd of them had gathered outside a gastro-pub converted from a former dispensary. Further down the same street an equally large crowd had gathered outside an orangery attached to an old stately home. In between was the collection of rags underneath which slumbered, or attempted to slumber, the frail figure of Rollo, formerly Corporal Rory Adams of the Princess of Wales's finest.

Lara was off duty that night, walking back to a flat she was renting after a session in a local boxing gym, one of many she'd tried out back then and found wanting. She turned the corner to find eight giggling weekend sailors pissing over the collection of rags that concealed the now-writhing figure of Rollo as he tried to divert the steady stream of urine from his mouth and ears.

Lara didn't associate the broken figure clad in rags with the ex-soldier she'd seen in that house a few miles or so away on that probationary night. She just saw the grinning faces of the occasional sailors, grins that very much faded a few moments later when Lara produced her warrant card and arrested all eight under the Sexual Offences Act. Rollo had been camped under the window of a budget hotel, and several families had seen them turning the street outside into a makeshift toilet and Rollo into a human urinal.

It hadn't a hope in hell of standing up in court, but once the duty sergeant in the capital's nick heard the circumstances of this most unusual of arrests he had little hesitation in banging all eight up for the night. They'd be released in the morning with little more than a caution, but it was going to give them a massively uncomfortable few hours at least.

Rollo was pretty uncomfortable by now himself, so Lara also oversaw his transfer to St Mary's, where his still-sodden and evil-smelling clothes were peeled from his body. Then the assorted termites and parasites that had taken up residence on, and in some cases inside, his skin were removed too. Once Rollo was returned to a condition that might be regarded as almost human, he was given clean clothes. At the same time he began to enjoy the simple comfort of decent food and heat on a cold night. It was then that Lara finally recognised him.

After his stay in hospital, Lara referred him to a PTSD counsellor, who tried his best, but couldn't really get through. A couple of other counsellors had tried before, with much the same result. It seemed that once his time in hospital was over, Rollo was destined to be delivered back to the streets, where fairly soon he'd be in much the same sort of state that Lara found him in that night – until Rollo himself tentatively mentioned the only thing that had helped up to that point.

As Lara subsequently discovered, PTSD could be treated in many ways, but some people were resistant to them all and the reason was simple enough. When people revisit traumatic experiences – a necessary pre-condition to confronting them – they often become emotionally flooded or numb. Any meaningful therapy usually becomes impossible after that. But a couple of clinics had tried a different approach, giving patients controlled doses of the restricted drug MDMA.

When Rollo had first been given the drug it had been like the sun breaking through the darkest of clouds, until the clinic in question lost its licence for flying in the face of conventional counselling in that way and Rollo's supply ended overnight. And in his current condition, sleeping rough with no money, Rollo had no means of accessing any more.

———

Lara knocked on the door of the rented flat that had been home to Rollo for the previous few months. A smiling Rollo answered and she moved inside, handing over the drugs sourced from her unknown vendor on the dark net.

It was a regular ritual. And over the course of the following months and courtesy of that same ritual, Rollo had changed out of all recognition. He now had a part-time job helping out in a local DIY store and so far he hadn't assaulted any of the customers or staff. But that evening, there was to be some even more welcome news to report.

'I've got visitors this weekend.'

'Who?'

Rollo struggled for a moment. In a life that had enjoyed more than its fair share of big deals lately, including finding a fairy godmother where he previously believed none existed, this was on the large side of enormous.

'Mum and Dad.'

Lara looked at the shyly smiling Rollo for a long moment.

'I called them. Last week. We've talked a couple of times since.'

Lara let herself out of Rollo's flat a few moments later on something of the same high that was now infusing Rollo too. A few years before, the only contact Rollo had with his parents was of the blunt and brutal variety. Now he was treating them to tea.

Lara could still not offer herself the same hope of any kind of happy ending when it came to members of her own fractured family.

But she'd managed at least the promise of it for him.

CHAPTER
FIVE

MOMENTS after the double killing of Phil and Kate Turow, Celia Edwards came out of a convenience store a short distance from their maisonette, having spent roughly four times the amount of time she expected to spend inside. But there was a deeply serious transaction to ponder. Her four-year-old daughter, Tolula, had been promised a lolly from the display by the till. There must have been fifty or more on offer and they all looked identical to Celia, but Tolula had solemnly examined each and every one before finally making her choice. All of this meant Celia was now running late for the bus that would take them to meet her mum for a late afternoon shopping trip where the choices, hopefully, wouldn't prove anything like as tortuous as the one she'd just endured.

Celia turned up the street, barely seeing the party of girls who'd disembarked from a school bus a moment or so earlier. Briefly she caught snatches of their excited conversation, all of which seemed to be about an upcoming Prom. One girl's mother was fixing up for her to ride there in a limo. Another had already booked herself in to an upmarket hair salon. A third was gloomily wondering whether her dad's promise of arranging a

Del Boy-style Reliant Robin as her transport for the evening was a joke or whether he was actually serious.

As a second bus turned the corner ahead and began to approach along the street, she heard another of the girls call across to a boy who'd just emerged from a maisonette opposite, asking him to leave the door open because she'd forgotten her key.

Instinctively she glanced across the road in his direction as the girl turned back to her friends.

Then all movement seemed to stop and all sound seemed to cease as she saw the gun in the boy's hand.

The bus was now passing the group of girls, cutting the boy off from sight. By the time the bus had gone, the girl was already moving on without giving the boy, presumably her brother, a second glance, and also without waiting for a reply. From the concentrated expression on her face, thoughts of the upcoming Prom were still all consuming.

With the boy still in her eyeline, Celia remained frozen, her hand gripping her daughter's, desperately trying to send out to her a silent signal to stay still, to not draw any attention to themselves. Maybe then the boy with the gun in his hand would simply move on. News reports of mass shootings swam before her eyes; images of innocent bystanders being gunned down by crazed gunmen for no reason at all. And so Celia stood statue-like, praying that her daughter would remain fixated on her precious lolly.

Then, slowly and with Celia watching him all the while, the young boy with the gun in his hand moved out into the road. At about the same time, another bus – Celia's bus, although she barely registered it – turned the corner ahead. The boy, who seemed to be moving as if he was in some sort of trance, began to cross in front of it, and the driver, who was still some good few metres away, hit his horn, impatient. The boy stopped dead at the sudden sound and stared, uncomprehending, at the fast-approaching vehicle. By the time the driver realised he wasn't going to move – which was at around the same as he also saw the gun in the young boy's hand – it was too late to stop.

Celia saw him wrench the steering wheel to the side, but the bus still hit the young boy at almost exactly the same time as an ever more horrified Celia heard a piercing scream from across the road.

———

Some people just couldn't help it, could they?

They couldn't help taking the piss.

Lara had been circling the small car park for five minutes in her Mini, waiting for a gap to open up. Lara's Mini, derivative Cooper, was one of the originals, not the later Rover incarnation or the bloated landcrab with the same wheelbase as the original Range Rover that somewhat shamefacedly boasted its name. Lara's Cooper was a Mk 1 hailing from 1965 with windows that wound up and occasionally wound down, sporting four forward gears that usually went forward when selected and one reverse gear that went backwards if it felt like it.

But when a Chelsea tractor began to reverse out of one of the spaces ahead, another car tried to nip in. Blasting her horn, Lara barrelled forward, missing the Chelsea tractor by inches as she squeezed into the newly opened space ahead of the wannabe-interloper. Locking her car a moment later, she heard a second blast of a horn as the aggrieved driver – a female, aged around forty – protested her presence in what she clearly regarded as her parking spot. Lara just flipped her the middle finger and moved on.

Lara walked into her home nick less than a minute later. The CPS were due back that morning with a decision on the exact charges to be laid against a drugs dealer she'd banged up some few weeks before. His particular speciality was raping young girls picked up from one of the island's numerous ferry stations before force-injecting them with heroin. Sometimes the routine varied: the heroin came first followed by the rape, but the result was always the same. Within weeks, young girls who'd come to the island hoping to find holiday work or adventure found themselves servicing punters on the prowl for cheap sex.

But as she walked into the main open plan office that housed the Serious Incident Team, one of her team, DS Jordan Banks, approached.

'Lara.'

Jordan handed his DI a report from Comms that had just come in. There were no 'guvs', no 'ma'ams' in Lara's department. She was actually surprised to see him; he was meant to be taking that day off to see his teenage daughter, a rare treat following his recent divorce. Something had obviously gone wrong with that eagerly anticipated arrangement, and for not the first time too, but there was no time to pursue it. The expression on Jordan's face told Lara there were more pressing priorities than teenage treats right now.

Lara scanned the report, and less than one minute later she and Jordan, in a police pool car this time, were heading for a small maisonette with a sitting room window boasting a view across the nearby Solent.

Inside were two dead bodies, a mum and a dad just discovered by their daughter.

———

A few moments before, all that had been on Jools Turow's mind had indeed been that upcoming Prom. She knew that no limo was going to call for her and there'd be no upmarket hair salon for her to visit either. Mum and Dad's childminding business was doing well, but not that well. But she had seen a retro dress in a vintage clothing store in Ventnor that might mean she could still make something of an entrance.

Now that dress, limos, hair salons, as well as the prom itself, were banished. They were the preserve of the girl who'd walked into her home a short time before. The girl who was now being looked after by the badly shocked neighbour she'd run to was someone different and from that point on always would be.

Dimly, Jools was aware of two police officers, both plain-clothes, a black man and a white woman, moving past her. Scene-of-crime tape had been erected outside the door and they'd had to duck underneath to get inside, but she barely took any notice. So many people had gone in and out of that house since she'd run back out that they barely registered anymore. All she could see in her mind's eye now was her brother, Ben.

Dimly too, a picture was beginning to form inside her head. In one sense it was a relief – anything to try and blot out those other pictures she knew even now she'd never be able to erase of the bloodied bodies of her mum and dad on that sitting room floor.

But this new picture brought fresh horrors in its wake.

Jools, almost involuntarily, reconstructed her walk from the bus stop. Once again she saw Ben before that bus passed between them and cut him off from her view. She hadn't thought anything about it at the time, hadn't even registered the fact that he hadn't replied to her as she'd shouted out to him. She'd just pressed on inside, through a door he had indeed left open. But now something was registering, something about the way he was walking – or maybe something else.

Something in his hand, maybe?

Jools, almost involuntarily again, circled round the image that still obstinately refused to solidify into shape.

All she could think was, what was it?

What was it she'd glimpsed, for just that fraction of a second, in Ben's hand?

CHAPTER SIX

So this was heaven.

A soft bed.

And curtains shielding everyone from view.

Ben dimly recalled an ambulance and paramedics checking him over as he lay in the road after being struck a glancing blow by that violently swerving bus. He dimly remembered lights overhead flicking past as he was wheeled down a corridor. He thought he could remember voices asking if he was in pain, and if so where? But he hadn't answered because – and like his now-dead mum before him – Ben knew that none of this was real.

Because if this was real then everything else was real, and that couldn't have been, so this couldn't be either.

Instead, Ben zoned in on his comics. They'd been a passion of his for the last year or so. He had the usual collection – *Sandman*, *Tank Girl* and *Swamp Thing*. But his absolute favourite and the one he was immersing himself in right now inside his head was *The Preacher*.

The Preacher himself was Jess Custer, who came from a small town in Texas called Annville. At some point in the past Custer had become possessed by a supernatural creature called Genesis, the infant product of an angel and a demon. So Custer possessed both pure goodness and pure evil and he spent his days attempting to find God, who he believed abandoned Heaven the moment Genesis was born.

Ben heard voices from the other side of the curtain but once again banished them, journeying instead with The Preacher and his constant companions, his girlfriend, Tulip O'Hare, as well as a hard-drinking Irish vampire called Cassidy.

'Ben.'

The curtain was drawn back and now a woman was standing there, mid-twenties by the look of her and white, as well as a tall black man who looked to be a few years older.

Ben burrowed back inside his head, focusing again on the latest adventure of The Preacher he'd read, involving a confrontation with The Saint of Killers, an invincible, quick-drawing Angel of Death answerable only to a mythical figure known as He-Who-Sits-On-The-Throne, a disfigured suicide survivor turned rock star.

But the same voice broke in again.

'Ben, I'm Detective Inspector Arden, this is Detective Sergeant Banks. We need to ask you a few questions.'

Frantically, Ben kept his mind fixed on The Preacher as he took on not only The Saint of Killers but also The Grail, a secret organisation that sought to control the governments of the world at the same time as protecting the bloodline of Christ.

Then Ben sensed pressure on his bed and felt, rather than saw the young woman sitting down next to him.

For one last desperate moment Ben struggled to keep focus as figures from The Preacher's own family swam before his eyes, including The Preacher's nasty Cajun grandmother as well as her bodyguard Jody and the animal loving T.C.

Then the woman spoke again and her tone wasn't harsh or angry, even though she quite clearly knew she was being ignored. There was an understanding note in her voice instead, almost as if she could see the pictures he was trying to banish right now.

'Ben, come back to me, please?'

Ben, finally, looked up at the woman. Behind the woman and the tall black man he could see nurses moving backwards and forwards outside his cubicle, and a moment later that was all Ben was left with. Not The Preacher, not The Saint of Killers and not The Grail. Just himself and this woman and the man standing behind her, his two visitors making it only too clear that, unlike the world that had just vanished before his eyes, they were going nowhere.

Which was when everything changed.

Because this wasn't heaven anymore.

This was hell.

———

'Where did you get the gun, Ben?'

Ben struggled for a moment, but he knew that silence wasn't an option. This woman and this man were going to keep asking him questions and he was going to have to answer.

'I didn't.'

Jordan eyed him.

'It was found on the street by the paramedics just a few metres away from where they found you. We've got at least one eyewitness, a woman who was on the street at the time with her daughter, who saw you carrying it.'

Lara kept eyeing him too as Ben just shook his head. It was an hour on from their arrival. Now there was a duty brief with them, the brief doubling as the regulation appropriate adult, but he was staying silent for now too.

Ben looked like a frightened young boy. Totally lost and completely alone. In any other circumstances he might have been an object of pity. The two dead bodies on his living room floor made him anything but.

By Lara's side, Jordan cut in again.

'We've already had the gun examined. There's no other prints on it, Ben. Only yours.'

Ben just shook his head.

What were they doing?

Why were they asking him all these questions?

'Your sister – Jools – she saw you walk out of your house as she was getting off her bus. She called out to you, but you didn't answer. She went in, which is where she found your mum and dad on the floor, where you'd left them.'

Suddenly, Ben spoke.

'I didn't leave them.'

Then he stopped as he blinked back tears, and for a moment all he could hear was the sound of blood roaring inside his ears.

What could he say?

That a total stranger had approached him after killing both his parents, the gun that had killed them still in her hand?

That she'd pressed that gun into his own hands, presumably after wiping it of prints, before she'd walked out, leaving Ben looking down at the still-twitching bodies of his mum and dad?

It didn't make any kind of sense to him; how could it make any kind of sense to anyone else?

There was only one thing he did understand right now.

Mum and Dad were dead.

They were dead and he'd watched them die.

Jordan kept looking down at the young boy in the bed.

'Did you have a difficult relationship with your parents, Ben?'

Jordan knew all about difficult relationships with teenagers. He sometimes felt as if his daughter, Coco, was from another planet, but since she'd moved out of his house and gone back to live with her mother, relations had turned even more alien. But never – in a million lifetimes – could he imagine his daughter doing something like this.

Lara kept looking at him too. Ben was no saint, they'd already established that. He'd been in trouble at school, nothing even remotely on this scale admittedly, but there'd been the occasional fight, some talk of drugs. Some of the neighbours they'd spoken to so far seemed to have been more than willing to come forward with some juicy little titbits about the local teenager. Ben wasn't exactly unpopular, but he seemed to have fallen in with some bad company lately.

'Did you get the gun for your own protection? Or just to flash it round a bit?'

Ben stayed silent as Jordan leant closer.

'You probably didn't mean to use it; most people don't. But then something happens, someone gets at you, gets to you, and suddenly there it is, and you don't mean to pull the trigger either, but the next thing you know you have done and then it's too late.'

Jordan had every right to be saying all this and Lara knew it. The minds of most of her colleagues back in their home nick would be running on exactly the same lines right now too.

Lara glanced across at the still-silent duty brief. He looked out of his depth and for good reason. He'd never come across anything like this before, and the expression on his face said it all. He didn't want to ever again.

Then Lara stood, Jordan standing too. They wouldn't get any more out of Ben right now. The question was whether that was because he'd erected a protective shell around himself and was determined nothing would penetrate it.

Or because there was no more to find out anyway.

————

'Bullshit.'

Jordan's verdict was unequivocal. Lara remained silent, but she wasn't contradicting him. All the evidence they'd collected so far pointed to the conclusion that had just been summarised so pithily by her junior officer as they collected coffees from a small Costa outlet on the ground floor of the hospital. Ben Turow wouldn't exactly be unique. Unusual, yes, but he'd still take his place in a well-established clique of kids who'd killed their parents.

———

Just a year before Lara had arrested a sixteen year old from Sandown, David McLean, who'd argued with his dad over his choice of music. His dad had snapped one night, confiscating David's entire collection, and David snapped in turn, stabbing his father to death as well as visiting the same fate on a hysterical sister who'd tried to intervene. When the mother returned from her late-night shift at a local convenience store she found both bodies, each with upwards of fifty knife wounds, and her son gone.

Lara and Jordan, acting on CCTV sightings, had arrested David an hour or so later after his mother's almost incoherent call to the emergency services. Where he was actually going he didn't say. Maybe he didn't know. He didn't even seem to know who he was by then, but if it was all part of some early defence ploy it didn't work. His later plea of temporary insanity was rejected by a jury who convicted him of murder.

———

'No evidence of any forced entry, no eye witnesses placing anyone else at the scene, no sightings of any stranger either entering or leaving that house and no prints on that gun apart from Ben's.'

Jordan shook his head as Lara stayed silent, another past case swimming before her eyes.

———

Esme Asunta was a year younger than David McLean. She was also from a very different background and class. Her parents were Chinese immigrants who, according to her blog, were in the habit of setting almost impossibly high standards for their daughter. She'd already been grounded once during that school term for only scoring ninety-six percent in a routine test.

On her next test, a music practical, Esme fell short of the straight 'A's they demanded by scoring two 'A's and a 'B', so the mother put Esme's prized piano up for sale.

It didn't seem to be a serious threat, as other family members subsequently told the investigating officers. It was probably just a warning to her daughter to improve. But Esme clearly took it ultra-seriously. She became manic the moment she was shown the online notice advertising the sale and attacked her mother with a hammer from the kitchen that the father had used the previous evening to tenderise some steak. By the time Esme had finished she'd broken almost every bone in her mother's face. Then she'd called the police, seated herself down by her mother's lifeless body and waited for them to arrive.

At her subsequent trial she pleaded guilty to manslaughter, a defence tactic that was accepted once the jury had reviewed the evidence. After that score of ninety-six percent in the previous school test one of her friends told the court that Esme had been forced to strip naked and stand in a corner of her bedroom for the whole of that same evening. It seemed to many at her trial that Esme was as much a victim as a villain in all that subsequently unfolded, but it didn't alter the fact she was still a kid who'd killed a parent.

It happened. Teenagers, hormones raging inside them, occasionally lashed out, and the combination of fully formed bodies and unformed minds could sometimes be lethal.

It happened the other way too, of course. Parents killed their children as well. Like all police officers, Lara was well aware of the uncomfortable truth that a young child was on average killed by a father or mother in the UK every ten days. Statistically, and incredible as it always seemed to Lara, it could actually be more dangerous leaving a child with a spouse than with a complete stranger out on the street.

Lara looked across at the Koan – or the *Land Sea Light Koan*, to give the brightly coloured cylindrical sculpture that stood defiantly outside the main entrance its full title. Despite the assurances made on its installation, it had never fulfilled its promise to rotate, and its coloured lights only ever seemed to work intermittently.

Jordan sipped at his Americano, the biggest size available.

'Everything he's saying might be true, in his head. Everything he's telling us might just be how he sees it, the only way he can see it, because it's the only way he can deal with it.'

His coffee was almost gone and they'd only been sitting there a minute or so. Not for the first time Lara marvelled at her junior officer's asbestos-lined stomach.

'I heard this voice. It told me to do it. Someone else was there with me. They'd taken over—' Jordan broke off, abandoning the mimicry. 'You've heard it yourself, all the shit they come out with.'

He shook his head, sour. 'Just take some fucking responsibility.'

As Jordan drained his outsize coffee, yet another face mixed across Lara's vision, that of Hasib Hasan. Hasib was seventeen and again, according to his friends, had been at odds with his parents over his sexual orientation for at least two years, Hasib's problem being that in the family's native Bangladesh, homosexuality didn't officially exist. So, and as Hasib's stern father had told him on numerous occasions, they might as well talk about little green men from Mars; they bore as much resemblance to reality as the kind of practices with which Hasib was attempting to sully the ears of his long-suffering parents.

The gun that Hasib had used to kill first his father and then his mother was real enough, though. As were the words picked out in their blood on the wall.

To the kids who are dying inside, you are strong and you are beautiful and you are worth more than you can ever know.

No one knew if as a confession it would have stood up in court, because the case never came to trial. Hasib hanged himself one month later while on remand.

———

Suddenly, and without saying a word, Lara turned and made for the nearest lifts. Jordan stared after her for a moment, then followed, reaching her just as the lift doors opened.

Lara strode back into Ben's room a few moments later. Ben himself was now turned to the wall. The duty brief was long gone and Lara shouldn't have been seeing Ben without him there, but she only had one question for the young boy anyway.

'When she pressed that gun in your hand, how did she look – happy – excited – as if she was enjoying herself – what?'

Slowly, Ben turned. Then he looked at Lara for a long moment as, unable to help himself, he re-lived another moment that would now haunt him for the rest of his life.

For a moment Jordan didn't think the young boy was going to answer, but then, finally, Ben spoke.

'She looked sad.'

Lara and Jordan stared back at him.

'She looked as if she felt sorry for me.'

———

Lara leant back against the corridor outside Ben's room a few moments later. Jordan stood, silent, beside her. Lara didn't speak but she didn't need to. Jordan had worked with Lara for three years now and he could see it in her eyes.

It was early days, very early days. But Lara believed him.

And Jordan was right. All Lara's instincts were telling her that the killing of his parents was nothing to do with Ben Turow.

CHAPTER
SEVEN

CHRISSIE ARCHER KNEW it wasn't Harper's birthday, but she couldn't help it. Today, and not only today but for the last few weeks, she could refuse her six-year-old daughter nothing.

Chrissie swung the unfamiliar bulk of the old Jeep into a parking place well away from any other cars. She could have parked a floor down, but that would have meant squeezing in between the vehicles of other shoppers, and complicated manoeuvres like that were beyond her at the moment. One day, if this relationship continued, and she hoped more than anything she'd hoped for in a long time that it would, she was going to have to persuade her new boyfriend Kieran to buy something more user-friendly by way of transport. But for now it was a small price to pay for a man who was making her feel as if she was walking on air.

Chrissie looked at her daughter and smiled. And Harper could have few complaints right now either. All she'd had to do lately was mention some movie she wanted to see, some activity she'd heard about in school, and her mother, who always seemed to be smiling these days, would grab her hand and take her.

And that's where they were going today, after trawling the nearby shops. To a trampoline class in a local community centre.

Chrissie had never been to a trampoline class in her life, and a few months ago, before Kieran came along, she'd probably have pleaded all the usual excuses of the single mum – not enough time – the classes cost too much – why couldn't Harper find something to do a little closer to home etc etc?

But now here they were, mother and daughter giggling over Chrissie's fumbling efforts to steer Kieran's Jeep inside the white lines of a parking bay, with Harper already wondering if this afternoon's treat might run to a pizza as well.

Chrissie and Kieran had met on the fast ferry service out of Yarmouth. Chrissie had been working on the coffee outlet ever since her husband, and Harper's father, Adam, died. Adam had earned good money up to then as a builder, but a sudden and fatal heart attack had put paid to all that and had forced Chrissie back to working for what was little more than pin money once she deducted child care. But it was still better than nothing at all, which was just about what she would have if she hadn't opted for her new life on the water.

It brought with it some fringe benefits, including free travel for herself and Harper whenever they wanted it. And it had brought other fringe benefits too.

Most notably, Kieran.

Chrissie had noticed him on what was quite obviously his own first day in his new job too. He was part of a small team helping secure the ferry to the docking station using the simple technique of throwing a rope, lasso-style, over a mounting on the platform.

The first time Kieran had attempted it, the rope ended up in the water. The second time it had ended up over the head of a waiting and startled passenger. The third time he'd managed to fix it to the mounting, to the ironic cheers of just about everyone on board. The shyly smiling Kieran had turned and bowed his head to his makeshift audience, and in that moment Chrissie had lost her heart.

She'd read somewhere of a man who'd fallen in love between

standing up and sitting down. He'd walked into a restaurant, and as he'd taken his seat, he'd looked across at a male waiter coming in from the kitchen, a plate in hand. And that was that. The same proverbial bolt from the blue. The man had stayed in the restaurant all afternoon. That same night he moved the waiter into his flat. They were together ten years until the Grim Reaper selected yet another heart to break by taking his lover in one of the first round of deaths following the AIDS outbreak in the eighties.

Chrissie didn't move in with Kieran that night. But they did talk, then talk again, then talk some more. Chrissie even helped him practise his lasso-type throws. A couple of the other female staff gave her knowing looks as she and Kieran laughed and joked their way through the rest of the shift, but there were smiles too. Because somehow, right from the start, these two just seemed to fit.

Harper was the potential deal-breaker, of course. How would her six-year-old react to a new presence in her mother's life? Oddly enough it had been his Jeep that had brokered the break-through. It was the most avowedly uncool car Chrissie had ever seen, being over thirty years old and looking as if it had never seen a bucket of water. But Harper had loved it from the moment a nervous Kieran turned up outside their house. She'd driven around in it looking down on all the other cars they passed, feeling as if she was the Queen. Kieran hadn't needed to do anything else, just play chauffeur all day. Every treat they'd planned, every conversation they'd rehearsed suddenly become redundant. And Kieran slotted into Harper's life as smoothly and as naturally as he'd slotted into her mother's.

Chrissie exited the car and pressed the key fob to lock it. But nothing happened. Chrissie pressed it a second time, and this time lights briefly illuminated as the doors locked into place. Then Chrissie took Harper's hand and they headed away.

———

Motor manufacturers long ago worked out how to thwart electronic code-grabbers that replay the wireless codes embedded in vehicle security devices. They simply moved the ISM radio signals used by those key fobs to a system of rolling codes with the numbers changing with every use. Any code that was used twice was rejected.

But the device that had just been used on Kieran's Jeep was ultra-simple in turn. Chrissie's first attempt to lock the car had been jammed. At the same time the hacking device that had been used to do so picked up the fob's signal and recorded its wireless code, a code that hadn't actually been activated. Like most drivers, Chrissie tried again and thought no more about it when the second attempt worked.

Using the initial and still-usable code the shadowy figure watched as mother and daughter disappeared. A quick check around the rest of the car park was made next, but most drivers had elected to park on levels closer to the actual shops. The figure waited a few moments longer just in case the woman and her child had forgotten something and reappeared.

Then that same figure walked up to the old Jeep, activated the wireless code intercepted from Chrissie's first attempt to lock the vehicle and smiled as the lights flashed back their customary welcome.

CHAPTER
EIGHT

Both safe houses were typical of the breed.

Both were small and anonymous units on new build estates. Both were home to a floating population, the vast majority of whom never even saw their neighbours, so were hardly likely to take any interest in anything they did. Both were tidy but not overly so, with gardens that were well maintained but wouldn't win any prizes in a TV makeover programme.

And both were quiet. Very quiet. The two protection officers who looked after the various charges housed there made sure of it. But as those charges themselves were usually frightened souls who just wanted to shut out a world that had suddenly turned hostile and cold, they didn't normally have any interest in making too much noise anyway.

The two protection officers in question were a man in his early forties, Tony Stone, and a woman around her mid-to-late thirties, Beth Quinlan. To the outside world they presented as partners. They occasionally seemed to host relatives who'd come to visit, if anyone cared to ask, but so far no one had. But not everything that took place in those houses was always played totally by the book.

Protection officers, for example, aren't supposed to get

involved in the lives of their clients – and they were always called clients too, never witnesses. But it was inevitable they'd get to know some details, at least. Those details usually came from the clients themselves, because they were often desperate to talk, obsessed with trying to make sense of whatever seismic event had precipitated their flight into the protection programme in the first place.

So far Ben, in the first of those two safe houses, hadn't said a word. But his sister, Jools, who'd been taken into the other safe house a few miles away, hadn't stopped. Most of it had been incoherent, even hysterical. But Tony and Beth had still tried to made sense of it, even if what Jools was saying really didn't make any kind of sense at all.

Crime was changing day by day, and the two protection officers knew it. Criminals were getting younger all the time, and Tony and Beth knew that too. But the double killing in broad daylight of two parents, apparently by a son who'd suddenly turned into an assassin, was still sufficiently out of the ordinary to give both officers pause for thought.

Beth had taken primary care of Jools. Tony was looking after Ben, and it was Tony who was now liaising with Lara and Jordan as Ben remained in the next room.

'Any special instructions?'

Lara shook her head and for good reason. She was still very much feeling her way on this one.

Then she hesitated. 'But if he says anything…'

Lara tailed off. She didn't know Tony well, but he did have a reputation for not suffering fools – or interference – gladly. By her side Jordan looked at him, also trying to gauge his reaction. In the past they'd been told to take a running jump when they tried to lean on protection officers with a veiled request to act as their eyes and ears.

Lara hesitated again.

'I'm not asking you to spy on him. Just give us the heads-up if he comes out with something.'

Tony hesitated too, but only for a moment. Then he nodded, but looked at them, curious, unable to help himself, it seemed.

'So did he do it?

'We don't know.'

'He's not been charged yet?'

'No.'

'And how long will he be here?'

Then Tony stopped, as he and the other two officers heard something. Ben had been left in the next room watching a DVD. What they'd just heard was the sound of that DVD being ejected from the machine. It was an innocuous enough sound in any other circumstances and with any other individual. But not in these circumstances. And not with Ben. Which maybe explained why the atoms in the atmosphere had suddenly seemed to rearrange themselves, at the same time as the air seemed to be sucked from the whole of the house.

Lara was the first to reach the door, Jordan a second or so behind. By the time they'd arrived in the sitting room the DVD was already in Ben's hand, and he was using it as a makeshift blade to slice into his throat.

Ben had managed three incisions so far. The fourth might have achieved the desired effect, but before the bloodstained DVD could do the damage a young boy who just wanted his world to end intended, Lara and Jordan had wrestled it out of his hand.

CHAPTER
NINE

THE AMBULANCE WAS at the safe house in under five minutes. That by itself would render the property useless for its present purpose from that point on. Even the most incurious of neighbours would wonder at the sight of paramedics rushing in from an ambulance flashing blue lights up and down the street. It would only take one of them to register the different characters that the house seemed to host from that point on for its cover to be well and truly blown.

Not that accommodation was exactly the main priority at present. All that mattered right now, after making sure Ben Turow hadn't succeeded in his attempt to separate his head from his neck, was that he hadn't caused any lasting damage along the way.

Ben was intubated, on a stretcher and out of the house within thirty seconds of the paramedics arriving. He'd lapsed into unconsciousness by then, blood still pouring from his self-inflicted wound, but it wasn't pumping out as Lara and Jordan would have expected had Ben severed an artery. With luck they were looking at just a few stitches. What they'd have been looking at had they not heard that faint whirr from the machine as Ben ejected that DVD neither wanted to think about.

But as they accompanied the paramedics and the blood-stained stretcher outside, a car pulled up, immediately behind the ambulance. A woman who seemed vaguely familiar to Lara exited and strode up to the safe house. She looked confident and calm, as if she had every right to be there.

'Just a minute—'

Then Lara stopped. Suddenly she'd placed her. It was the woman from the car park, the woman who'd protested Lara's sudden appropriation of what she obviously regarded as her parking spot and had been flipped the finger as she'd blared her horn.

Jordan stepped in, quickly.

'You weren't at this morning's briefing, Lara.'

Lara looked back at him, bewildered. There'd been a meeting that morning while she was settling first Jools and then Ben in their safe houses, but she'd still have expected to be updated had anything significant come out of it.

Lara looked at Ben, now being loaded into the ambulance by the paramedics. Then again, it had been something of a busy morning.

Jordan cleared his throat nervously and nodded at the woman who was still just eyeing Lara.

'Our new DCI.'

Lara turned to see a pair of steel-blue eyes looking back at her. For a moment neither officer said a word, but then the new Detective Chief Inspector broke the silence.

'I think the word you're looking for is, fuck.'

Lara kept looking at her.

She was right.

———

Twenty minutes later, Lara, Jordan and DCI Paula Davies were in a greasy spoon, two streets away from the scene of Lara's impromptu rescue of Rollo all those months before. But all that, and Rollo, was far from her mind right now.

'Why a safe house?'

Paula had started immediately on a debrief that was sounding more like an interrogation, and Lara couldn't help it. Already her shackles had begun to rise.

'What should we have done, given his parents' house a quick rub down and tell him to bunk down there?'

By Lara's side, Jordan shifted uncomfortably. From out of nowhere came an image he'd once seen on some wildlife programme on TV; two scorpions facing each other, only one about to get away from the upcoming encounter alive.

'What I mean is, why was Ben Turow put into the protection programme at all? He was found in the street outside his murdered parents' house with a gun in his hand, for Christ's sake.'

Lara finished it for her.

'So why isn't he already banged up in Young Offenders?'

Across the chipped and worn table Paula Davies eyed Lara, who held her stare. She'd clearly taken the words right out of her mouth.

'Number One. If all he's saying is true, if there is a lone female killer, could she return for Ben and his sister? On that count alone, these two need protection. Number Two. Ben's not going anywhere. Not 'til we say so. Whether he's in custody or the protection programme makes no difference to that. But custody would be one more massive shock for him, maybe on top of too many already, meaning he'd close down and then we might never get him back. The protection programme's our best chance of making things as normal as possible right now, so maybe then he'll start telling us the last normal thing he remembers. That's either just before this woman he insists killed his parents, or just before he had some sort of meltdown and did it himself.'

Lara nodded at Paula and continued, 'Either way, we gain nothing by treating him as a killer until we know for sure he is.'

Paula stared back at Lara for another long moment. Jordan could almost see the raised and hovering tails about to sting. Then, suddenly, Paula nodded and stood, this impromptu debrief over as quickly as it had started.

Jordan watched her all the way to the door, then turned back. For her part Lara didn't speak. She just kept staring after her new senior officer, well aware she'd just been set some sort of test.

The problem was that she was totally unable to decide whether the simple nod she'd just received was an acknowledgement she'd passed, or silent confirmation she'd failed.

CHAPTER TEN

An EXECUTION-STYLE MURDER is defined as an act of criminal intent in which the perpetrator kills at close range a conscious victim who is under the physical control of the assailant and who has been left with no course of resistance or escape.

In that respect it resembled a judicial killing of the type outlawed decades before in the UK but still practised in the US, only in those cases the taking of life was by the due process of law. But in all other respects the M.O. was exactly the same.

Lara looked at the two bodies on the mortuary slabs in front of her.

Ben Turow's parents, Phil and Kate, were together in death as they had been for most of their lives. Childhood sweethearts, they'd married when they were both eighteen, having first Ben and then Jools two years later. They were only in their late thirties at the time of their deaths, and they must have felt as if they still had their whole lives in front of them.

Lara looked at the two lifeless bodies again.

They were wrong.

Lara looked across as the door opened and the pathologist came in. She was one that Lara had worked with before and the one Lara had hoped would attend this double-killing now, firstly because she was good and secondly because she always went the extra mile. It had been something of the story of Maisa Abdulkader's life up to that point.

Maisa had first come to the UK as a refugee from Damascus some eleven years before, although for a time it seemed unlikely she and her family would ever leave their temporary refuge in Preservo in Serbia. After weeks of enduring temperatures approaching almost 100 degrees, the family managed to get to a refugee camp in Kanjiza, at which point they were told that not only would they not be going any further but that they'd be returned to Syria.

Maisa, a teenager at the time, was the youngest of three siblings. One day, while her mother was standing in line at the makeshift offices of one of the hard-pressed refugee border agencies, desperate to avoid the repatriation they all now feared, her elder brother took matters into his own hands.

Spotting a UK news crew making a live broadcast he'd approached them, seemingly keen to add his testimony to the others they'd amassed so far. Then, with the cameras rolling, he ruined the lunches of countless viewers back home by producing a knife and calmly, almost clinically, slitting his throat.

One day later – and with media interest in this particular family now at fever pitch – Maisa, her mother and the rest of her siblings landed in Gatwick as the now-panicked border agency fast-tracked their case. Three years on and Maisa began her studies as a doctor. Five years later she graduated, dedicating her new qualification and new life to her elder brother.

Three years on from that graduation she was in a windowless room, the overhead lights focused down on two dead bodies, determined – as with everything she now encountered in both her professional and personal life – to make the next few moments count. Nothing escaped Maisa's forensic attention, particularly where the loss of innocent life was concerned. Her brother's sacrifice meant cases like these attained something of the status of a crusade.

'Single gunshot to each of the heads.'

Maisa rattled off her findings, as efficient as ever. There was no gallows humour and she never wasted time, which was another thing Lara liked about her. She knew better than most that life was short.

'Cause of death was cardiac arrest in both cases, directly linked to the force of the impact.'

Lara kept looking at the bodies on the slab, trying to square all this with the broken boy she'd seen just a few hours before trying to remove his head from his shoulders with a DVD.

Maisa kept talking all the while.

'Before we left home in 2011 a fundamentalist clique rounded up some insurgents. They paraded them through the streets before lining them up in the main square. They got them to kneel, then a single gunman walked in front executing each one as he passed. Their bodies fell backwards in front of us. Everyone stayed to watch because no one dared leave. Each of those victims had exactly the same sort of entry and exit wounds.'

Lara kept staring at the bodies of Phil and Kate Turow, Maisa's words echoing inside.

Insurgents.

Fundamentalist cliques.

Lara shook her head, increasingly convinced that all her first instincts were correct. Ben Turow was a schoolboy, for fuck's sake. The closest he would ever have got to execution-style shootings would have been on a Sunday afternoon on his PS5.

An hour or so later, Jordan was waiting for her as she used her key pass to access their large open-plan office.

Behind, a small team of officers were already working on the Ben Turow case, including an officer acting in a strictly temporary capacity as Media Liaison, a twenty-something female, Mairead Devonald, who was fielding calls from the press, both local and national. It was too late to put a lid on the story – Ben's appearance out on the street with that gun in his hand had already put paid to that. Too many shocked eye witnesses had already unburdened themselves to relatives and friends, including Celia, mum to the lollipop-loving Tolula. But Mairead, as Lara could already hear as she passed her temporary desk, was doing her best to choke off some of the wilder speculation.

Jordan handed her a coffee from the Unit's ancient moka pot that some not-so-bright number cruncher had once tried to replace with a vending machine. That had very nearly turned their Serious Incident Unit from murder investigators to suspects, particularly when they discovered that the new efficiency initiative, as it was called, extended to dispensing with the services of the Unit's legendary tea lady, Peggy O'Riordan, as well.

The moka pot worked, so Jordan had once attempted to explain to Lara, by forcing hot water through the ground coffee, the uniquely shaped pot then coaxing the resulting syrupy liquid up into the top chamber through a chimney. It produced a strong, bitter, sometimes thick but always wonderful concoction from something that looked like a discarded piece of scrap metal, showing that appearances were deceptive. On that count alone, Lara would have fought tooth and nail for it to stay exactly where it was. Call it a constant reminder.

'Update from the hospital on Ben.'

Lara looked at him. She'd been waiting for this.

'He'll have trouble swallowing anything more substantial than ice cream for the next few days.'

Jordan shrugged. 'But as he's probably not much in the mood for eating right now anyway…'

Jordan didn't finish. He didn't need to.

'We've also managed to have a first proper interview with Jools, his sister. She's still badly shocked, but she did tell us a little about the relationship between Ben and his mum and dad.'

'And?'

'There'd been a few rows lately. Ben wanted to go to some gig on a school night; they said no. He wanted some comics that had just been released in the States, collectors stuff apparently, but what do I know? They said yes to two of the comics, but told him he'd have to wait 'til Christmas for the others.'

Lara nodded.

'In other words, the usual sort of stuff.'

'They weren't the Waltons. What family is? But...' Again, Jordan didn't finish. Again, he didn't need to.

The moka pot was now directly in Lara's eyeline, her original conviction firming up inside her all the time, and from the look on his face Jordan was clearly coming round to the same view too.

They had a sole female gunman in their sights. And, for now anyway, not a single clue as to who she was or why she might have targeted Ben and Jools's parents like that.

'Lara.'

Lara looked up as Mairead approached, having just taken another call.

'You'll want to see this.'

Which usually meant it was the last thing any reasonable person would want to see, and so it was to prove.

'A mother and her daughter. Mother's in her thirties, the daughter's six. This is probably coincidence, but they live a couple of streets away from Phil and Kate Turow.'

Mairead paused. 'They went on a shopping trip yesterday afternoon.'

Lara kept looking at her. Like Jordan before her, Mairead really didn't need to finish, but unlike Jordan she did.

'Haven't been seen since.'

CHAPTER
ELEVEN

TRAMPOLINING WAS SIMPLE, right? Chrissie and Adam had bought one for Harper when she was three, a small self-assembly unit that stayed out in all weathers. Harper had bounced on it for hours at a time.

Up.

Down.

Then up again.

Nothing to it. And nothing like the class Chrissie and her daughter had just attended either, although maybe it should more accurately be described as endured.

They'd arrived as two giant metal-clad beds were being carefully unfolded in the centre of the hall before being bolted into place. Harper wanted to start straight away, but they were first escorted across to a smaller safety net where they had to warm up with some shoulder and leg rolls.

Chrissie had stared at him. Warm up? What for? They were going to be pretty warm doing all this anyway.

A short time later, she had her answer. No, they were going to be hotter than an oven ready turkey on Gas Mark One Thousand. Or at least Chrissie was. Harper, of course, took the whole thing in her stride.

'Just bounce lightly in front of that red line while you stare straight ahead.'

That had been the instructor's first instruction, and it had sounded simple enough until the first time Chrissie tried it and she'd catapulted at least a metre forward before landing on the floor.

Then came the seat drop.

'It's all in the hips.'

That was the instructor again. Dan was his name, or at least Chrissie thought it was. By then she was beginning to forget her own.

'Attack it as if you're on an assault course. If you're too tentative, you won't push back up properly.'

Harper once again mastered it effortlessly, spurring Chrissie on in turn, but her body obdurately refused time and again to return to anything remotely resembling a standing position.

But then, suddenly, she managed it. A perfect manoeuvre. By her side, Harper clapped her hands in genuine delight. And Chrissie's heart, as it always did when it came to anything to do with her daughter, almost broke in two.

Harper had helped Chrissie through more than trampolining. In the dark days and even darker nights after Adam's death, the little girl had clung onto her, never leaving her side. At the beginning, and Chrissie was ashamed to acknowledge this even to herself, Harper had felt like another burden at a time when she had too many already. It was only later she'd realise that Harper hadn't been a burden, but a rock.

Chrissie hadn't intended to hurt herself. Yes, there were dark days, but even in the darkest she hadn't sunk that low. That didn't alter the fact that she'd nearly turned a little girl who'd recently lost a father into an orphan.

———

'Your daughter's here.'

The words swam through what seemed like a veil. Shapes floated in front of her eyes, brief snatches of conversation meandered across her consciousness, but that was the first thing that actually registered.

Then Chrissie opened her eyes to see Harper standing by her hospital bed. Chrissie just looked at her for a moment, then Harper leant close, bringing her mouth up to her ear.

'I'm going to look after you, OK?'

Harper's hair smelt of shampoo and ketchup. Suddenly, as well as her words, which were the most wonderful Chrissie could imagine, it was the single most magical smell in the world. And she felt her body fill with guilt.

She'd already taken that day's dose of powerful anti-depressants. How could she have forgotten? How could she have doubled her intake like that?

And what would have happened if Harper hadn't spilt orange juice on her dress while she was playing at her friend's house a short way along the street and insisted on being brought home to change?

Chrissie knew that everyone would have thought she was a selfish cow who'd decided to take the easy way out, uncaring of the effect a double bereavement would have on her small child. The fact it simply wasn't true would have made no difference. If it hadn't been for that simple accident to a little girl's dress, Harper would have walked back into her home later that day to be confronted with a corpse.

Harper kept looking at her, her small face solemn.

'I don't want you to hurt anymore.'

Back it had come, instinctive.

'I don't want you to hurt either, sweetheart.'

Harper had frowned for a moment as her brain absorbed that. Then she nodded. 'So we've got a deal?'

What Chrissie heard next was like an actual voice in her ear. If she'd been religious she would have said it was God, but the truth was it was probably her own befuddled and drugged conscience.

Live, you selfish cow.

Live and be grateful for what you've got, never mind grieving over what you can't get back.

Look what's here, right now, right in front of you.

Just fucking live.

Chrissie held out her arms and Harper moved into them. All Chrissie could think about was her beautiful daughter doing deals at her tender age. What would she be doing at fourteen, at twenty-four? Chrissie didn't know, but all she did know was that she wanted to find out.

––––––

Chrissie levered her aching limbs into the driver's seat of the Jeep. Harper threw herself into the passenger seat without so much as a twinge. Immediately Harper began unwrapping an outsize chocolate bar Chrissie had hidden in the glove compartment and which Harper somehow just knew was there. Chrissie put the Jeep into gear just as Harper asked the very question she herself was debating right now.

'Can we go to the Super Hero café?'

The Super Hero was a new café that had just opened a mile or so away, a street front eatery stuffed full of life-size replicas of just about every Super Hero you could think of. Harper bit down on her chocolate, then looked at Chrissie again as she didn't answer.

Chrissie couldn't.

Because all she could see were a pair of eyes reflected in the rear-view mirror, staring at her from the back seat of Kieran's Jeep.

CHAPTER
TWELVE

JORDAN DIDN'T GO with Lara to interview the partner of the missing woman and her daughter; Mairead accompanied her instead.

Partly that was for professional reasons. Jordan had been deputed with the ongoing task of liaising with Beth, the second of the protection officers, about the other surviving member of the Turow family, the still-deeply traumatised teenage daughter, Jools. But partly it was for personal reasons too.

Jordan's latest update from Beth didn't amount to much. After her outpouring in her first interview, Jools had simply closed down. She was just seeing pictures now, the same pictures she was seeing before she went to bed each night and the same ones she was seeing as she woke the next morning.

The sitting room of a home that was never going to be any sort of home again.

A room that had been turned into an abattoir.

The strong likelihood was that Jools could add nothing to the investigation into what exactly had happened there that day, but Jordan had still been tasked with making regular checks on her just in case.

That assignation over, it was time for another. A more

personal one this time, and the reason Lara had cut him some slack that afternoon.

———

Jordan was halfway along School Lane when he got the text. Kids in their regulation orange and black uniforms were pouring out from the nearby primary into the care of waiting parents, and for a moment Jordan smiled as he remembered his own days on similar pick-up duty, standing at those same school gates exchanging anecdotes with the long-serving and much-loved school caretaker as his excited daughter approached brandishing some drawing she'd just done, or updating him breathlessly on the all-consuming class gossip of that day.

Then Jordan's mobile beeped. In strict contravention of all good practice he opened the message displayed on the screen. Ten seconds later he pulled over, fighting all-too-familiar feelings of frustration and rage.

Jordan put the car back into gear a minute later. Then he resumed his journey, pulling up at the end of a small street of old links houses by the side of an inlet where various riverboats – mainly weekend pleasure craft, but the occasional working boat as well – would moor. He remained there for the next hour.

This had been Jordan's old home before his divorce and move out to a small rented flat overlooking one of the island's whole-sale meat markets. Edie and his daughter still lived there. Coco had initially moved out too, and the original intention was that father and daughter would set up in a larger flat while Edie retained their old home. But within six months, Coco had moved back in with her mum.

If Jordan and Edie had split up a year earlier everything would probably have been fine. A year later and they might have weathered the storm. It was just sheer bad luck it all coincided with Coco's sudden transformation from sweet little cherub who adored her dad – to the point of electing to go and live with him after the break-up – to a nightmare teen, a transformation that must have taken a few months but which seemed to Jordan to have happened virtually overnight.

Jordan tensed as the door to his old home opened and Coco herself appeared. She didn't even glance towards Jordan's parked car, just turned the other way, and it was Jordan's shrewd suspicion that she wasn't making for the local library. Coco was heading for bars and for boys, and she'd have no problem getting into the former or attracting the latter. Coco might still only be sixteen but she could easily pass for ten years older. If she'd walked out of Jordan's flat like that she'd have been called back immediately. It was a school night, for one thing. Jordan's ex-wife, Edie, had probably lent Coco her make-up.

Edie's relaxed attitude to just about everything was a character trait that Jordan had found irresistibly attractive at eighteen, but a bit more difficult to take at twenty-five when he'd come in from his shift at six in the morning to find a house party that wasn't even remotely in danger of winding down, drink and drugs everywhere – and in the middle of it all a small girl who clearly hadn't been to bed.

Even the fact that Coco had been afflicted with asthma from birth and would have to rely on her ever-present inhaler for life, hadn't dissuaded Edie or her friends from shrouding the house in smoke from just about every substance Jordan could imagine and some he never would.

Jordan grew up, in short. Edie didn't. At least that was his verdict on the breakdown of their marriage. Edie had her own. Either way it led to the same ultimatum. Put up or bale out. Jordan baled out and took Coco with him. Initially a perennially stoned Edie hardly seemed to notice. Then Coco left Jordan and moved back in with a mum who continued to let her do anything she wanted whenever she wanted, which sounded, as it would to any young teen, like paradise.

Jordan watched Coco as she turned the corner ahead, his phone with her text curtly cancelling his latest visit still in hand.

What was he supposed to do? Run after her, stop her, demand she return to a home and a mother who might not even have realised she'd gone out in the first place? Jordan kept watching long after the daughter he still loved with all his heart vanished from view.

Then he started his car, turned round and went back to his flat. And then, and because he wasn't so totally as whiter-than-white as Edie had increasingly scornfully come to paint him, he took his usual refuge in the first of several lines of coke.

CHAPTER
THIRTEEN

KIERAN WALTERS LIVED in a small terraced house one street away from the best pie and mash shop on the island. It was run by an exile from East London who'd learnt her trade at the legendary Maureen's in Chrisp Street Market and had named the shop after her. Like the original, there was no choice of pie filling, but there was a choice of liquor or gravy, although anyone who chose the latter needed their heads examined, in Lara's view.

Lara looked out from the front room window of Kieran's house at a steady stream of customers ferrying takeaway versions of the café's finest back home as behind her Mairead coaxed what information she could out of him.

'She went off for a shopping trip. Her and Harper. I told her to take the Jeep – she didn't want to be hauling shopping bags back on the bus. They said they'd be back for lunch.'

Kieran leant forward.

'An hour or so, I didn't think about. There was nothing that wouldn't spoil anyway. Then it got later and later. I tried calling but her mobile just went straight to answerphone, so I got a mate of mine to give me a lift round to their place. Nothing. I tried looking in through the windows but the place was all locked up.'

'And no sign of your Jeep?'

'No.'

Lara looked back at him. Kieran seemed genuinely worried. He was saying all the right things in all the right places and his call to the emergency services had the mark of authenticity too. Not too quick in signalling something wrong, which would have been suspicious, but he hadn't been tardy in reporting it either. Everything matched the figure he was currently presenting; a boyfriend waiting for, and becoming increasingly worried about, the new love in his life and her small daughter.

'What happened just before Chrissie left?'

Kieran looked at Mairead, seemingly genuinely puzzled by the question.

'I don't understand.'

'How was she, how was Harper?'

'Just...'

Kieran struggled for a moment, again at a seemingly genuine loss for any sort of response for a moment.

'...normal.'

By the window Lara stayed silent, letting Mairead continue the gentle probing. So far she was doing well. She wasn't saying anything that would cause any shutters to suddenly slam down, because if they did so under this sort of routine questioning they both knew that would very much continue down at the nick.

Lara looked at Mairead. She had a difficult home situation, Lara knew that. No romantic entanglements, just a father to whom she acted as unpaid and – from the little Lara had been able to glean – largely unappreciated carer. Occasionally it made absences from work unavoidable. But when she was there she more than made up for it, just as she was doing now.

Mairead continued. 'I've got a friend, she has a kid about the same age as Harper. She leaves him with me now and again. After a few hours I'm like a rag doll. How do parents do it, and day in, day out too?'

She smiled warmly, but her eyes were far from warm. If Kieran Walters had anything to do with the disappearance of

Chrissie and Harper, he hadn't put a foot wrong so far. But he would have had hours, maybe more, to plan his story. He could have rehearsed every step of this from the initial call to the emergency services to this very first interview and beyond

Kieran didn't respond. Strictly speaking, he didn't need to. Mairead's observation might have invited a response, but it wasn't actually a question. Kieran just looked more and more haunted. Whether that was because he was tormented by what might have happened to his girlfriend and her daughter, or because he already knew, was still to be discovered.

'What's Harper good at in school?'

Kieran continued to look at Mairead, increasingly puzzled.

'Has she any special interests, anything they might have gone off to do?'

Kieran cut across, getting really agitated now.

'What the fuck is this? Something's wrong, really wrong. It's been a whole day since Chrissie was supposed to have come back and you're asking me what lessons Harper likes?'

Mairead couldn't work him out. Across the room the still-silent Lara couldn't either. They'd run a background check on him on the way over and nothing had come up, no form of any kind, the occasional speeding and parking fine aside. But they were still treading very carefully here. Both officers had seen too many men take up relationships with single mothers in order to get close to their kids.

Then, suddenly, he came out with it.

'Frogs.'

Mairead stared back at him.

'She loves frogs.'

Kieran nodded outside.

'There's a pond at the bottom of the garden – she always goes out there when she's here. She squats down on her hands and knees, lifts up all the stones 'til she finds some. She can watch them for hours.'

Lara looked behind the wracked Kieran and saw a familiar

looking white takeaway bag on the worktop. Then she spoke for the first time since they'd arrived.

'Liquor or gravy?'

Kieran and Mairead looked as puzzled as each other. Lara nodded at the takeaway bag.

'The lunch that you got in for them.'

She gestured out of the window towards the café at the top of the street. 'It was from Maureen's, yeah?'

Kieran hesitated, then nodded back.

'Chrissie's favourite. And Harper's. Always have to get double mash for her, though.' Kieran stopped suddenly, that simple detail seeming to pierce him.

'So?'

Kieran shot Lara a momentary, pitying, smile. As if he felt sorry for anyone who even had to ask the question.

Lara moved back to the window and stared again at the steady trickle of hungry punters carrying those exact same bags. It was hardly what you might call scientific. And she wasn't going to quash Mairead's totally legitimate line of questioning because a man preferred one accompaniment to a pie and mash dish over another.

But, and even though the two cases were radically different, one a killing and this a disappearance – she was still beginning to experience the same feeling she had when faced with Ben Turow, and it wasn't just due to the close proximity of the respective addresses. That, as Mairead had already pointed out, could just be coincidence.

Something was wrong here.

Something was badly wrong.

But her instincts were already telling her it wasn't anything that was going to be laid at Kieran Walters's door.

CHAPTER
FOURTEEN

ALL HARPER COULD FEEL WAS something pressing into her back.

They'd driven a mile or so away from the car park. All the time her mum's eyes had been darting almost continuously from the road back to the rear-view mirror and she hadn't stopped talking either, just variations on the same few phrases.

What do you want?

What are you doing?

I don't understand.

Harper didn't understand either. She had no idea who her mum was talking to or who was in the back of Kieran's Jeep right now, but she knew that someone was there, because of the ever-present pressure in the small of her back. At first she'd tried squirming away from it, but she couldn't so she stopped.

Harper looked out of the window. Everything looked the same. The usual shops lining the same streets, children walking along the pavements, with parents, with friends. Everything seemed totally normal, on the outside at least.

Inside Kieran's Jeep, it was anything but.

'Left.'

The voice in the back of the car spoke again. It was only the second word they'd said. The first was drive, and Harper still couldn't decide if the voice belonged to a man or a woman.

But there'd been a delay before that first word. Harper sensed rather than saw something being held up behind her, and she saw her mum's eyes widen as she looked through the rear-view mirror. Which was just before she felt the pressure on her back.

Harper had seen enough action movies in her short life to realise it was probably a gun. Nothing else could really explain why her mum was doing everything the voice in the back told her to do.

They'd turned off a lane into a small alleyway at the back of some shops. Harper had seen a hardware store she vaguely recognised as they turned off the main street, with some ladders and buckets outside. They'd been there once when their shower had started to leak and they'd needed a new connector or something. The back of the hardware store and the other shops in the row lined one side of the alley, a couple of lock-up garages lined the other, and at the end stood a small warehouse unit, its door now open, just enough room inside to take a car, or in this case a Jeep.

'In there.'

But now her mum hesitated, and no wonder. Driving on into the dark space ahead suddenly looked so forbidding.

'Whatever you want, just open the door and let Harper go, yeah?'

Her mum was staring now into the rear-view mirror, her eyes pleading, but there was just silence from the back of the car.

'She can find her own way home. We've been to these shops lots of times.'

Still just silence behind.

'Whatever this is all about – whoever you are – this is nothing to do with her.'

Suddenly Harper gave a small yelp. Now it wasn't a dull pressure she felt in the small of her back, but something harder, almost like a jab.

By her side Chrissie pressed the accelerator and Kieran's Jeep moved into the small unit ahead.

––––––

The figure in the back stared at Chrissie as light was eclipsed by dark, her words from just a moment before echoing inside.

Whatever this is all about – whoever you are – this is nothing to do with her.

The figure activated a button on a remote control held in one hand, closing the doors to the unit behind them, making sure not to release the gun that was being held with the other, the gun that had been pressing into the back of the passenger seat and Harper's spine ever since they'd started off.

This was nothing to do with her?

Didn't she understand anything?

The woman's small daughter was the only reason this was happening at all.

CHAPTER
FIFTEEN

JORDAN STOOD at the door to the Serious Incident Room taking a moment to try and compose himself.

Last night he'd been so wired he felt he'd never need to sleep again. At one point he'd even contemplated a midnight visit to his old home to read his estranged wife and daughter the riot act. But even in the middle of a coke-induced high he'd been aware that it probably wasn't such a good idea.

But he felt very different now.

On the other side of the door he could hear two members of the team checking CCTV images, trying to trace Kieran Walters's Jeep. It had been spotted leaving a car park, but despite the tech boys massaging that single image from all sorts of angles it hadn't been possible to see who was actually inside.

And from that point on all sightings ceased. Either the Jeep had simply vanished from the face of the earth, or it had negotiated a route away from all neighbouring cameras. That could have been just good luck on the part of whoever was responsible for its disappearance but was already looking likely to be something much more sinister.

Jordan took another moment. Frantically he tried to remember some details of the file he'd been sent the previous evening updating him on all that was known of Chrissie, Harper and Kieran. There was to be a brain-storming session with Lara and the rest of the team starting in just a couple of minutes' time and everyone, himself included, would be expected to be fully up to speed. The problem was that Jordan felt as if he was in the grip of a full-blown flu. He actually had the runny nose and the headache, as well as aches and pains in most of his joints. But it wasn't any sort of flu.

Last night had been the up, the high. This morning was the come-down, the low. No one had witnessed the former. Now he only had willpower and some fairly rusty acting skills to make sure no one realised he was in the grip of the latter.

The door opened in front of him and Jordan tensed, but it was Mairead, not Lara, who came out into the corridor. Jordan didn't know Mairead that well; no one did, she always seemed to hold herself at one remove from the rest of the team. But this morning she was to surprise him.

Mairead took one look at him, then took him by the hand and steered him into the nearby Ladies toilet. Then she ripped off some paper from a nearby dispenser, scrawled on it for a moment and handed it across.

'It's basically a crib sheet. Five points I came up with last night.'

Jordan looked down at the single piece of paper, a few key points from the file he'd been sent the previous evening picked out in red.

Mairead nodded at him.

'You can have numbers two and four. Leave me the other three.'

Jordan stared at her. She hadn't once referred to how he looked or the fact he was already in danger of running late for the upcoming meeting, and she hadn't begun to explain how she seemed to instantly know that he hadn't even scanned the file that was the subject of that morning's brainstorming.

Was he really that fucking obvious? From all that had just

happened in the last thirty seconds the answer seemed to be a resounding yes.

'Mairead—'

Jordan tried mustering some inadequate expression of thanks, but nothing came out. Mairead just crossed to the door and exited. Jordan looked down at the crib sheet, trying desperately to memorise the two points he'd been allocated by his unexpected saviour, then he looked in the mirror as some sixth sense kicked in.

Reflected there, standing in a cubicle door that had just opened behind, was Lara.

Lara didn't say a word, just looked at him.

Jordan didn't say a word either.

He just looked back at her.

———

It was as if a conspiracy of silence had descended. Not a word was said by Lara as the brainstorming session got under way. The focus was on one thing and one thing only. The present whereabouts of Chrissie and her daughter, Harper.

Yet more background checks on Kieran Walters had still failed to produce anything even remotely suspicious. The same background checks on Chrissie had yielded the same result, or lack of it.

Yes, there'd been a single hospital admission to St Mary's to treat Chrissie for an overdose a year or so before, but from all that the attending paramedics and doctors had recorded in their notes, that seemed to have been a genuine accident.

A few friends and work colleagues had also been interviewed, and all seemed mystified by what seemed to be a totally out-of-character disappearance too.

Chrissie's parents were both dead, so there could be no further information forthcoming from that quarter.

'Chrissie's just snapped.'

That should have been Jordan's contribution to the session. Or, more accurately, Mairead's contribution handed to him. Point two on the crib sheet. But when it came to his turn to speak, Jordan just couldn't do it. He gave a small silent shake of the head as all eyes had turned to him, and Mairead, after hesitating a moment, took over.

'Maybe it's been building inside, ever since she lost her husband. Maybe she's tried playing the perfect mum, being strong for her daughter; she's even managed to start a new relationship, fooled herself life was on the up.'

Mairead shrugged. 'But it was all a sham. Underneath she was falling apart.'

Jordan kept his eyes fixed to the floor as Mairead continued. 'Maybe that overdose last year wasn't the accident everyone seemed to think it was. Maybe that was an early warning sign. Now, suddenly, everything's just come to a head.'

All Jordan could feel were Lara's eyes on him. And suddenly he realised just why he hadn't been able to speak. It was that one simple word from Mairead in amongst all those others.

It would just have been a sham.

'So what are we talking about?'

Jordan was in another toilet, the Gents this time. It was an hour later. He'd just swilled his face with cold water for the fifth time in as many minutes, but his head still pounded and his arms and legs still ached. He raised his head and looked at Lara, now reflected in a different mirror behind him.

'Three? Five? Eleven?'

Jordan hesitated as Lara kept eyeing him. It was a test and Jordan knew it. Three was Coke, Five was Ecstasy, Eleven was Ket. It was a code developed so punters could hold up the right number of fingers in a club without even the mention of any kind of drug passing their lips.

Jordan stayed silent.

'Don't tell me. It's not a problem.' Lara nodded at him. 'Not yet anyway.'

Jordan didn't know if that was a question, a statement or a prediction. If it was the former he wouldn't have been able to answer. If it was a statement he wouldn't be able to contradict it. If it was a prediction, maybe it was all too prescient.

Jordan knew he must be fast becoming a villain's wet dream in Lara's eyes. A cop with a problem. A problem that could be exploited. Meaning a favour that could be called in.

Jordan kept his face poker still. Lara did the same. For a moment the Gents toilet positively reeked of cordite as the two officers played out High Noon.

Then Lara paused.

'We've worked together for what – two years now?'

'Three.'

Back it had come, instinctive. And there was something in Jordan's tone now too – a note of pride, and the reason was simple. They'd been the best three years of his professional life, even if his personal life had been falling apart throughout, and he wasn't about to have a single minute discounted through being misremembered.

Lara nodded as if a point had just been made. Maybe it had.

'One week. We don't talk about this for one week.'

Jordan bristled. *This*? What the fuck was *this*? He'd told her nothing, nothing at all.

Lara rolled on.

'Then you come to me – this time next week – and you tell me everything's fine.'

Jordan maintained his poker face as Lara nodded at him again.

'One week. The clock's ticking.'

And with that she turned and was gone.

———

From the window of the Serious Incident Room, Mairead watched Lara as she emerged from the Gents toilet and headed back along the corridor towards the stairs.

A moment later she watched Jordan emerge from that same door before heading along the corridor to a water cooler.

Mairead knew that some would call what she'd just done, or attempted to do, an act of charity. But it was more than that. Or maybe less than that; she scarcely knew anymore. She rested her head against the window as she watched Jordan drink the first of a number of large glasses of ice cold water.

All she did know was that she'd lived with human frailty for too long now.

And she really didn't know how much longer she could keep on doing it.

CHAPTER
SIXTEEN

'*ALLAHU AKBAR, ALLAHU AKBAR.*'

'*Ashhadu al la ilaha illa-llah.*'

Harper could hear the words dimly through the wall. She recognised them too; they were the same words she'd heard sounding from inside a mosque they'd pass sometimes on their way home.

Mosques were always depicted as ornate domed buildings in the picture books she'd read in school, but even at her tender age Harper knew the outward trappings didn't matter. All that mattered was a place to congregate and pray and give thanks to God. And Harper was now hoping against hope that even though the God she could hear that congregation praying to right now wasn't her God or her mum's God, some God somewhere might be hearing those prayers. Because she and her mum were in dire need of help from someone right now.

'*Assadu anna Muhammader Rasulu-llah.*'

Harper still couldn't see who was behind her and she still didn't dare turn round to look. So Harper did the only thing she could do. The only thing she could control right now.

Harper fell asleep.

———

'*As-salatu khairum-min-an-naum.*'

Chrissie could still only see a pair of eyes. But she knew the figure behind her still had that gun in their hand and she knew it was still pointing at Harper from the way her small child kept stirring uneasily in her sleep next to her.

Meaning it must still be pressed into the small of her daughter's back.

Chrissie knew her home island had a reputation on the mainland for being sleepy, but the reality was it was anything but. It not only had its fair share of the usual burglaries, car-jackings and knife attacks, but much more violent crime too. Like anyone, Chrissie knew she could suffer the simple bad luck of being in the wrong place at the wrong time.

But this was different. She could understand what might be called those everyday horrors because they were motivated by impulses she could comprehend. Money. Sex. The twisted imperatives that in a lot of cases had replaced previously simple faiths of the kind she too could hear being celebrated just a few metres away.

But she was no nearer working this out than she had been those minutes before when she'd first seen that pair of eyes in the rear-view mirror.

Chrissie should have done the safest thing she could do right now. She should just have kept quiet as those chants sounded even louder through the nearby wall.

But suddenly she couldn't. Because if she could hear them, they had to be able to hear her. And suddenly Chrissie started to yell, feeling Harper stir beside her again as she did so, not even knowing what she was yelling – only to feel a strange pressure on her eardrum a single second later as the figure behind her pushed a flick knife into her left ear and pressed the button.

The six-inch blade shot out, embedding itself in Chrissie's brain. For a second there was silence as Chrissie writhed in her seat, the knife twisting inside her skull, tearing through her brain tissue. Then she was still.

By her now-dead mother's side, and splattered with her blood, the stirring Harper lapsed back into sleep. Through the wall the chants grew even louder as the prayers next door reached their climax.

'*Allahum-ma Rabba hadhihi-d-da 'wati-t-tammati wa-s-salati-I-qa'imati ati Muhammada-ni-l wasilata wa-l-fadzilata waddarajata-rrati'ata wa-b'athhu maqqmam mahmudan-illadhi wa'adta-hu.*'

'O Allah! Lord of this perfect call and ever-living prayer, grant to Muhammad nearness and excellence and raise him to the position of glory which Thou hast promised him.'

CHAPTER
SEVENTEEN

THE RENT WAS RIDICULOUS. The neighbours might as well not exist for all she saw of them. Maybe they didn't. The on-site concierge was pleasant enough, but on some days, particularly at weekends, his was the only face she saw.

But as Lara stood by the long floor-to-ceiling window that looked down onto the water, she told herself, and not for the first time, that it was worth it. To come home to this ever-changing pageant of life outside her window more than made up for the financial struggle required each month to finance it.

Maybe that was also the reason why, even if she could sometimes go the whole of a Saturday and Sunday without speaking to a single living soul, she never felt alone. At any time of the day and night she could watch pleasure cruisers, barges and yachts all passing within metres of her window. It might be life experienced vicariously, but it still made her feel part of some larger community.

But today there was something else on her mind than simple sight-seeing. Something other than the new boxing gym she'd seen open its doors a few streets away too, which she'd promised herself she'd check out at the first opportunity she could. And something other than the work that had consumed almost every moment of the last few days as well.

Some of that had been difficult enough, and in unexpected ways. Despite their confrontation she'd effectively turned a blind eye to all that was happening with Jordan and she knew it. No, correction, she'd stared directly, if not forensically, at all that was happening and had chosen not to take any action. She just hoped the next week would justify that decision and her faith.

Jordan was a talented officer. She could go into any situation knowing that if she had him at her side he wouldn't bale out, that he'd make the extra effort she demanded of herself when it came to more than usually tricky investigations. The downside was that Jordan had an unusually complicated personal life that seemed to be wreaking its perhaps inevitable effect.

Lara glanced down at the small pile of papers on the clear glass table that had remained in the same place for the last few weeks, untouched by her and unread by anyone else.

An unusually complicated personal life?

Who hadn't?

Lara looked up towards the window again.

Lara had never even thought about joining the police when she was growing up. For a time, especially in her teens, she roamed the same hinterland as her sister, traversing terrain that seemed to threaten disaster at every turn. Georgia embraced drugs; Lara embraced something potentially even more dangerous. Even today her arms and legs were criss-crossed with scars, an all-too-visible legacy of years marred by self-harm.

Then, one day, she'd witnessed a car crash, or RTA, to employ police-speak. One minute it was a totally normal day. The next moment the world had been plunged into chaos, car horns blaring, people screaming, smoke rising from twisted metal. Within moments again – meaning the local police and ambulance crew really must have been close that day – the world had been restored to order once more as paramedics treated the injured and patrol officers separated and moved the damaged cars.

All the time Lara stood a few metres away, watching. She'd spent almost the whole of the previous evening digging into her upper arm with a table knife, trying to calm the chaos she could feel building up inside. Now she'd spent less than five minutes watching a different chaos being resolved out on that street.

Lara put in her application the very next day. Two months later she was doing her initial training. Over the next two years she was to realise that far from resolving chaos, her new life seemed to positively embrace it. But by then she'd found a new life to live and new colleagues to live it with, and all her former demons suddenly seemed at one remove.

Lara glanced back at the small collection of papers again.

But they hadn't been left behind completely.

More than a little reluctantly, Lara seated herself at her table, knowing this was something she couldn't put off any longer. She'd known it from the moment Mairead had spoken those words back in that brainstorming session.

– maybe it's been building inside for years –

– she's tried playing the perfect mum –

– being strong for her daughter –

Lara kept looking down at her own characteristically spidery scrawl on the papers in front of her as Mairead's words floated in front of her eyes once again.

– but underneath she was falling apart –

The papers on that table were strictly private, the words even more so. Lara didn't know even why she'd written them down. She'd never kept a diary before and she didn't intend to start now. But for some reason, in the aftermath of the disappearance of Milo's mother on that train, she'd returned home that evening and had just poured it all out onto the page.

My name is Lara Arden. I'm twenty-six years old.

Lara kept reading even though she knew every word by heart.

Twenty years ago my mother vanished on a crowded train.

But maybe the reason Lara was sitting there right now wasn't just down to a few chance remarks in a crowded Serious Incident Room. Maybe it had also been the earlier sight of Ben Turow, alone now in the world aside from his sister, yet another young soul who was going to face life without parents just as Lara and Georgia had been left with none to fend for them all those years before.

And just like Milo himself too, of course, the young boy on the present-day train.

It was another of the strange similarities that had provoked that committal of her own experiences to the page in the first place. Milo also had no immediate relatives. If his mother wasn't found in the next few weeks then his placing in care would become permanent.

Lara looked at the pages in front of her, then looked back out of the window, and for once she didn't see the different sights outside flashing before her eyes.

CHAPTER
EIGHTEEN

THEY CAME *for me in the early morning. A grey car with two people inside, a man and a woman. It parked on the bank. I could see the man check the name of our boat, and nod at the woman. Then they came on board.*

I'd just given Mum her breakfast, but she hadn't touched it. She didn't anymore. A woman from one of the other boats told me she couldn't. Whatever was wrong with her had eaten her away inside.

Before they came down into the cabin, I tried running away through the hatch that led to the cage we used to transport the carcasses of pigs and goats. But the woman was already at the back of the boat while the man guarded the front and they grabbed me, forced me towards the car. I heard my mum whisper my name – Esther – and I tried looking back, but the woman was holding me too tightly and I wasn't able to turn round.

We pulled up outside Kenwood a short time later. The man left me inside the car with the woman while he went to talk to someone. Through the window to my side and high above I could see a boy of about my age, maybe slightly older, looking out at me. He was smiling but I didn't know why. Then I felt the woman touch my braids.

I'd always had the longest jet black hair. It took twice as long to dry as any of the other river girls, but when it was dry came the best bit of all because then my mum would brush it strand by strand, smoothing it, straightening it out. She'd done it just a few days ago even though she barely had the strength to do so.

Then she'd taken small bunches in her hands and started making braids, threading in coloured ribbons, beginning at my scalp and extending all the way down to the tips. She'd scooped the braids behind me, but I moved them back over my shoulders so they hung down at the front and I could see them when I walked.

The man returned and handed the woman a pair of rough shears. The next second I felt the blade hack into the first of my braids, severing them from my scalp. I cried and sobbed but she just held my head tight while she hacked at the rest until she'd cut them all off. All the time too she kept telling me I was dirty, a dirty little river girl, even though my hair was always clean because Mum always made sure it was.

The man turned away, my braids now in his hand, and threw them in a nearby bin. I followed him with my eyes, streaming with tears.

But then I stopped. To his side was what looked like a playground, but it was covered with mounds that looked like giant mole hills. And by the side of one of the outsize mole hills – the most recent given the colour of the newly excavated soil – squatted a small mechanical digger.

Which was when I felt my heart lurch, and I felt so dizzy I thought I was going to faint.

Because now I knew that all the stories we'd heard about this place were true.

That wasn't a playground.

It was a cemetery.

PART TWO

My thoughts are not your thoughts,
nor your ways mine
Isaiah, 55:8

CHAPTER
NINETEEN

MAIREAD SURFACED from the pool of her local health club at eleven minutes past eight the next morning, according to the oversize clock on the wall.

For a moment she luxuriated in the swirling water. Swimming had been her thing for as long as she could remember. Briefly, she contemplated doing just one more lap – which was when she became aware of someone standing in front of the clock. Taking a moment to clear the water from her eyes, she saw the grim face of Lara staring back down at her.

Ten minutes later, Mairead and Lara were heading east. Mairead had planned a day in the Serious Incident Room going through everything that had been collated so far on the Turow family. Now, she was going to spend a day at the seaside instead.

'Chrissie Archer's car's been found.'

Back in the pool, Mairead had stared at her DI. Strictly speaking, the vehicle belonged to Chrissie's boyfriend Kieran and it wasn't a car, it was a Jeep. But the car had been found, that was all she heard.

Meaning the people inside it hadn't.

———

Less than an hour later, Lara and Mairead were standing by a small harbour packed full of working barges and pleasure craft.

Briefly, the location had given Lara a jolt. This was one of the stops their train would have been calling at the day her mum disappeared all those years before. But there were other stops they would have been calling at that day too.

Various cars were dotted around, all with tickets on the windscreens. The Jeep in front of them had a ticket on its windscreen too, but it had expired. Fifteen minutes after its expiry time that transgression had earned the tardy driver a ticket.

The car park in question was patrolled by something of a stickler when it came to that sort of thing. The stickler in question inspected each and every bay at least five times a day, fining any transgressor, be it holidaymaker or local, who dared to park with an expired ticket. Even a very few minutes or so over the allotted period would earn the returning motorist a stern lecture at the least.

The anal ticket dispenser had become something a local joke among the drinkers watching his antics from the large bay window of the local boat club. But even those scoffing drinkers would have had to concede that a full day over the allotted time was pushing it a bit.

This didn't seem to be a tardy visitor sleeping off a holiday hangover. This car seemed to have been abandoned, which was why a report had been filed with the police, who'd logged the vehicle on the police computer. And the electronic flag that had been placed on the registration number provoked an immediate alert.

Lara had begun working her mobile straight away. By the time she'd picked up Mairead, the registration number of Kieran's Jeep had been matched to its chassis and engine number and a local garage had been contacted with the details. When the two officers had arrived in the harbourside car park a mechanic was waiting to meet them with a clone of the electronic key.

Kieran himself had been contacted, but he only had one set of keys, having lost the first set years before. Whether that was true, or whether Kieran had some reason for pretending it was true, was something to be looked at later. All that mattered for now was getting into the vehicle.

Lara pressed a button on the newly supplied remote fob and the indicators of the Jeep flashed. Cautiously, using protective clothing provided by a local scene-of-crime officer, she opened the door and a careful search took place of the interior as well as the boot.

Nothing. No sign of any sort of struggle, no rips or tears in the upholstery or the roof lining. Not even a hint of anything untoward having taken place at all, save for the fact the car was found abandoned miles away from where it was last reported.

And almost as worryingly, there'd been absolutely no flags recorded on its journey over there either. Ordinarily that vehicle would have been spotted and monitored a good few times as it passed various roadside cameras, but nothing had come up. If the Jeep had made that journey inside a covered vehicle transporter of some kind, it meant a great deal of trouble had been taken to get it and its occupants to its present destination, making Lara and Mairead even more fearful now as to what might have happened to them.

It was just before they left that she saw it. Specialist officers were about to do another even more forensic sweep of the interior to see if any prints aside from Chrissie's, Harper's or Kieran's could be lifted, but Lara already doubted it. The elaborate precautions that must have been taken to get the Jeep down to that seaside car park already suggested a more than usually careful hand at work here.

But as the driver's door swung shut in front of her, something – a sudden shaft of sunlight perhaps – illuminated it.

'Open it up again.'

Mairead looked at her, puzzled.

'The driver's door – open it up and keep it open. Bring me a torch.'

Mairead stared at her, now even more bewildered. The sun was directly overhead by now. Why did Lara need a torch?

For the first few moments, her bewilderment only deepened as Lara shone the torch on the cloth interior of the door. But Lara could now see nothing. Maybe it had just been a trick of the light.

But then, as she moved the door slowly, backwards and forwards, Mairead suddenly saw it too.

'There.'

Lara stopped the door in the half-open position. It was only at that angle and with the light playing on it in a certain way that it was visible.

Etched into the fabric was a single word that looked like it had been gouged out by a fingernail.

Help.

CHAPTER
TWENTY

IT HAD BEEN a good haul so far. Three large sea trout were already in Freddie James's poacher's bag. A couple more and he could call it a good night. Any extra and he could call it a great one.

Then Freddie shone his torch into the shallows of a small pool some twenty metres upstream from his last kill, a fallen alder partly covering its surface and started revising his estimate upwards again.

Two large fish, each about nine pounds in weight, were in the pool. The hen fish was preparing the ground, the cock fish beside her. As Freddie watched, the hen fish laid her eggs, the cock fish passing his milt over them, fertilising them immediately. Almost instantly the pink eggs hardened in the water, and as they did so the hen fish covered them with gravel, protecting them from predators.

The largest of those current predators kept staring as the two adult fish righted themselves and rested. And Freddie couldn't help it. He was out tonight on business and he had a family to feed, but even he couldn't help a sense of awed wonder as he witnessed the creation of a new generation.

Freddie took out his three-spronged spear, but then his eyes caught a sudden flash, off to his left. For a moment he stilled.

He'd been careful and canny but the bailiff was careful and canny too, and it was possible he'd tracked him, particularly in the last few moments when his guard had been down.

But the sudden flash of movement to his left that had caught Freddie's eye wasn't the much-feared bailiff. It was a small girl, no more than six or seven years old, by the look of her. She was moving through the woods slowly, almost mechanically, looking neither to the right nor left, seeing nothing, it seemed. Certainly not the poacher who was now only a few metres away.

She made for an extraordinary, if not positively eerie sight, and she didn't even seem to register the cold, which was even more extraordinary as she was also completely naked.

———

Harper sensed rather than saw the flash of the knife. She kept her eyes fixed on the wooden wall of the shack and so she didn't actually see the blade enter her mum's body from behind, digging deep into her neck.

The strange thing was, there was no blood. Just the sound of the knife ripping into flesh. Her mother's flesh. Again and again. And, suddenly, she thought she could hear again that religious service and those voices raised in supplication.

A few hours before, just as she was willing herself to remain asleep, she'd also felt the Jeep tilt as if it was being driven up some sort of hill, but then Harper simply closed down again. When she woke they were in this shack. She still couldn't make out the figure who'd brought them here; it was night by then and the whole place was in darkness. But she could see her mum. And she could see the stab wounds all over her body.

A few moments later Harper was alone. The figure had gone, leaving the door to the shack open. She glimpsed woodland outside, intermittently illuminated by a moon that appeared, then disappeared behind clouds. Her mum was still there, but she wasn't her mum anymore because now she was dead.

Harper herself was unharmed; the attacker hadn't turned to her next as she was convinced they would.

Harper looked down at her clothes, which were splattered with blood, even though no blood seemed to have sprayed out of her mum's wounds.

Then she looked at the open door.

Even at her age Harper knew more horrors had to be waiting for her outside. The person who'd done all this couldn't let her live. If she was allowed to walk out she could tell people what had happened and then that person might be caught.

Harper looked back at the body. But she couldn't stay there either, not with a mother who'd suddenly turned into a corpse.

Harper turned towards the door, and then on an impulse stripped all the blood-splattered clothes from her body. All she could smell around her was an acrid, metallic tang, and she simply couldn't stand it a moment longer.

Then she walked out into a future she couldn't have believed would ever have been permitted to exist.

———

A stunned and disbelieving Freddie followed the apparition, the sea trout in the pool behind him now forgotten.

This wasn't some spectral nightmarish vision; he knew that now. This was actually a small child, around the age of his own small child, in fact, only his child was tucked up in bed, which was where this child should be too, not roaming the woods and definitely not roaming those woods stark naked.

What the hell had happened? And why didn't she even seem to register his presence as he followed her through the under-growth, twigs snapping under their feet?

Freddie called out, but the small figure just kept moving metronome-like, making, so it seemed, for the sea. He could have caught up with her, of course, scooping her small frame up into his arms. Freddie was a large man and could easily have restrained her. It would have been for her own good, after all.

But he didn't, because Freddie was lost right now. All he knew was that this – whatever *this* was – was bad, very bad. And all his instincts told him that someone else had to now take over, too.

Freddie took out his phone, praying for reception even though he knew he was almost guaranteeing himself a short stretch behind bars. It wouldn't take the authorities long to work out what he'd been doing out in those woods that night, and when they did it would be his third conviction for taking fish during the close season. But Freddie could no more leave that wandering naked child in those woods than fly.

———

Harper couldn't work out what she was feeling at first, but then all of a sudden she realised.

She was disappointed. Because she was still walking. Because no one had stopped her. She'd dimly heard a single shout somewhere to her side from among the trees and had assumed that would be the start. The next thing there'd be the flash of that same knife.

Harper just wanted it over. She wanted this nightmare to end. Which was when, from somewhere to her side again, she felt a low rumble begin to hum along the ground.

And a moment or so later she heard the whistle of an approaching train.

———

Freddie had tracked Harper much as he'd track any small animal in those woods. He still hadn't actually approached, that single shout aside, because he simply didn't know what he'd do if she'd stopped and turned his way.

Maybe it was because she was naked. Maybe it was something else. Something he didn't understand and didn't want to.

Freddie kept watching as the small girl moved under a low fence, expecting her to cross over the rails that criss-crossed that part of the woods and then disappear into the undergrowth on the other side. Then he realised she'd turned instead and was actually walking down the middle of the railway track.

At the same time, he heard the second whistle of the train.

Freddie hadn't really registered the first whistle, but he registered the second, probably because it was closer now, a lot closer.

Then he saw the train itself turn a corner some distance ahead and saw its lights begin to pick out the naked girl who was now walking straight towards it.

Which was when Freddie ripped his poacher's bag from his shoulders and hared for the fence. At the same time the driver must have seen the obstruction in front of him, because all of a sudden a warning blast sounded from the train's air horn. Freddie vaulted the fence and ran towards the small figure as she continued to walk down the very centre of the track, the brakes on the train squealing in protest as the driver applied them harder, more blasts sounding from his air horn all the while.

But still the girl kept walking.

And Freddie did his best, he really did. He made up the ground between them as fast as he could, but he was still too far away and all he could do was watch, helpless, as the now-shuddering train kept bearing down on the naked girl, before it stopped.

Just inches away.

Freddie could see the train driver staring out of the window at the small child, and even from metres away he could see that the man was shaking.

The girl herself was now stationary, just staring at the blazing lights in front of her.

Freddie registered more lights sweeping over them from a

police motorbike that had just arrived on one of the woodland paths behind.

Then Freddie and the train driver and the policeman all just stared at the small naked child standing on the rail tracks in front of the train.

CHAPTER
TWENTY-ONE

'WHY HERE?'

Jordan shrugged back.

'Why not? Lots of farms in the area, a big egg packing plant down the road, a couple of slaughter houses nearby.'

He paused, the reference to the slaughterhouse grating on him. Lara looked past the small shack down towards the nearby water and the remains of an old and ruined castle high on a hill.

Jordan took a deep breath and continued.

'If that is how that Jeep got here, in a truck with a container on the back, no one's going to give it a second look. There must be a dozen like that travelling these lanes every day.'

Lara kept looking out over the water. Jordan was right. But something was still wrong about this, very wrong, and it was nothing to do with the slashed body in the shack behind them, currently the subject of an initial on-site inspection by Maisa.

Then Lara looked back at the shack again as Maisa herself now emerged from inside.

Maisa inclined her head, a silent invitation to the two officers. But despite both Lara and Jordan having visited the scenes of countless killings in the past, something still made them hesitate before entering this one. Maybe it was the drained look on

Maisa's face. Maybe it was something else, something both officers could sense in the very air around them. The unmistakable
presence of evil.

The shack was wooden, a store for all sorts of old and rusting
farm implements as well as a temporary shelter. The farmer who
owned the land had accompanied them on their initial trawl of
the area surrounding the rail track, all of which he owned, identifying sites such as this one where a killer might hide out. Or
where a killing might take place. The expression on his face as he
opened the door told Lara all she needed to know right now.

They'd found Chrissie's body.

'The killer used a Bowie knife. At least eight inches long with a
relatively broad blade, around an inch and half to two inches
wide.'

Maisa nodded across at one particular wound, clearly visible
on Chrissie's lower leg.

'This particular knife has a notch on the bottom of the blade
near to the hilt. It's sometimes called a Spanish notch, no one
seems to know why, but it's thought to be there to catch an opponent's blade in a fight.'

Maisa looked again at the body before them, the same
thought in all their minds. Something told them there hadn't
been much of a fight involved here.

'It's also used to strip sinew.'

Maisa moved forward, indicated Chrissie's shoulder where
the sinew had indeed been stripped from the bone.

'On some of the wounds we can also identify a clip point at
the top of the blade, which brings the tip lower than the spine
and in line with the handle.'

'And that's for?'

Lara forced her eyes to keep looking at Chrissie, to absorb
what information she could, to see the murder victim here, not

the woman or the mother. In the long run, Chrissie would be better served that way.

'Better control in any close quarter encounter.'

Maisa indicated Chrissie's exposed chest.

'The other characteristic of the Bowie knife is that it's not only used for killing, it's also used for butchering game.'

Maisa pointed to part of Chrissie's right breast, which was trailing down her stomach, another part of the same breast a short distance away on the earth floor.

'The curved bevel of the blade is used to remove skin from a carcass.'

Maisa looked back at Lara.

'I'll need to get her back to the lab to tell you more. But I can tell you that even though all these wounds seem to have been inflicted post-mortem, she's still been stabbed well over three hundred times.'

Jordan emitted a low whistle.

'Someone must have really hated her.'

Lara kept looking at the eviscerated corpse before them.

'Or really loved her.'

After another moment, Lara turned and headed back outside.

————

Half an hour later, Lara was standing by the ruined castle on the hill that towered over the farmland below. Night was falling again and the castle was bathed in a warm glow from floodlights on the surrounding grass that changed colour every week. This week the ruined structure was cast a pale red.

Lara looked out onto the estuary village below, a niggling thought burrowing away inside her mind.

Two cases.

The Turow family, and now Chrissie and Harper.

In both cases, a witness left behind.

CHAPTER
TWENTY-TWO

THE NEWLY OPENED gym that had caught Lara's eye those few nights before catered for women who were interested in an intense daily work-out to burn off calories and build up stamina, as well as those who wanted to handle themselves competitively in the boxing ring, according to the promotional leaflet handed to her as she signed in.

The gym promised to teach the fundamentals – foot and hand placement, throwing punches, hitting the speed bags as well as heavy bags, and circuit work. All an interested punter had to do was book a personal training session, although spaces, those same interested punters were warned, were always at a premium.

Lara had done this. Returning from the shack in the woods, she'd called and asked if there'd been any cancellations, it being the only way of securing a spot at that sort of notice. There had been, and she was told the gym could fit her in the following afternoon.

Lara met her personal instructor for the session, the gym's female owner and lead trainer. She showered and changed, and a few minutes later, with her hands encased inside fourteen-ounce Lonsdale gloves, was throwing hooks to the heavy bag.

Bam.

Bam.

And just for good measure, Bam again.

On and on she pressed, the lactic acid building in her arms all the time.

———

'Punch from your shoulders, not from your hands.'

The trainer, Andrea Rice, was one of very few female trainers in the country, and she hadn't taken her eyes off Lara from the moment she'd walked in. Even at first glance this one didn't look like the usual sort.

The punters they generally catered for were a cross-section of arsy locals, both male and female, and gone-to-seed heavies looking to cut it in the world of private security, mostly male, but some females too.

The former were usually kids looking to make their mark in a world that had offered them little opportunity up to then.

The latter usually comprised men and women seeking to reverse a decade, if not more, of disastrous over-indulgence.

But this one was different. She was too old to be an arsy kid, and something was already telling Andrea that this particular new recruit rarely indulged in anything, be that disastrous or otherwise. There was just something about her. The same something that was making Andrea warier by the minute.

Everyone expected a boom in female boxing after Nicola Adams's success in the Olympics in 2012, when the Yorkshire flyweight became the first female to win Olympic Gold. As one of the first female boxing trainers in the UK to be awarded a professional licence by the British Boxing Board of Control, Andrea seemed ideally placed to ride that surge of popularity – although her cheeks still burned as she recalled walking into her first licence assessment session, only to be asked by a genuinely bewildered instructor whether she actually realised she was a girl?

Maybe that had given her extra motivation. Andrea sailed through the assessment with a pass mark of ninety-seven per cent. She checked later on that same instructor. He'd only managed ninety-five.

But female boxers were still a rarity, which made Andrea even more determined that any she took on were there for the right reasons.

The odd male maniac didn't matter. They were quickly buried, sometimes literally. Women were different. They made waves. Strange as it might sound, and it sounded strange even to her ears, the last thing Andrea wanted in her line of work was trouble.

Andrea barked out more instructions, but she could already see it was a waste of breath. This one simply wasn't listening. She was away in some world of her own right now, which was her right in any other world apart from Andrea's. In Andrea's world, she was used to being listened to.

———

Lara was forcing out the punches now, feeling that same lactic acid burning through her system, aware of a voice telling her things a short distance away, but she was listening to her own voice instead, the voice that was sounding inside, telling her that these sorts of punches, the ones that were making her heart and lungs work overtime, were the ones that counted. They were the ones that converted themselves into real and lasting strength, and Lara needed that right now.

She had to be strong.

She had to be fit.

Her body could not be permitted to let her down.

Suddenly Lara felt herself being whipped round. She stared into the eyes of the female instructor she'd barely taken any notice of up to that point, but she was going to take notice of her now. The female instructor had her hands over Lara's boxing gloves, her grip like iron, and she was staring straight into her eyes.

Andrea said just the one word.

'Enough.'

Lara looked back into those cool, appraising eyes. She'd stared into many eyes in her time and had faced down most of them, but these eyes were different. These eyes were never going to back down.

Meaning Lara had just found the trainer she'd always been looking for.

At the exact moment that the trainer decided she was one new recruit her gym could very much do without.

CHAPTER
TWENTY-THREE

'I'VE ALREADY TOLD you all this.'

'I know. But please. Tell me again.'

Mairead was with Ben Turow in the small garden of a new safe house. A swing and a slide were rusting in the far corner, a wooden shed to the side. Mairead didn't know what was in it, but suspected there wasn't much in the way of garden tools or implements, given the overgrown lawn. Through a couple of missing slats on the wooden fence that marked off the property from its neighbours, Mairead could see similarly overgrown lawns and weed-infested flowerbeds.

Ben was struggling and no wonder, reflected Mairead. She'd struggle too if she was forced to re-live something like this. But Ben was the only surviving eye witness to a double murder, so she had to keep pressing him.

Behind them, Tony appeared from the kitchen, a jug of water in hand. Ice bobbed in the jug as he put it down on the small table, which was peppered with bird shit. Tony put two glasses down next to the jug, then moved away again. If anyone looked in at the small group through those missing slats in the wooden fence they could be a mum and dad talking to a teenage son about his subject choices for the next school year, not an officer from a Serious Incident Team, a protected persons officer and a badly traumatised witness to a brutal and sadistic double killing.

'What accent did she have?'

'I've told you this too.' Ben flared briefly again, but then subsided once more. He knew what Mairead's answer would be. The same answer he'd been given at the same question and answer sessions that had taken place almost every day since it happened. The same apologetic, but firm insistence that he tell them nonetheless.

What the hell were they trying to do?

Trip him up?

Catch him out?

Get him to say that it had actually been his hand on that trigger all along?

Ben took a deep, deep breath.

'She didn't have an accent. Not really.'

'She wasn't from the island then? She didn't talk like you or your friends?'

'She sounded like she could be from anywhere. I don't know – we didn't exactly talk much.'

Ben paused. The night before, he'd been channel-hopping. Nothing grabbed his attention for more than a few minutes right now so he'd happened on it by chance. It was a game show; he didn't know what it was about – all he saw was a collection of characters in some sort of strange suspension. He didn't know what they were waiting for and he didn't give himself chance to find out, because he turned it off almost straight away.

But it didn't make any difference. All he saw in front of his eyes for the rest of the evening was three figures in the same strange suspension, waiting for two of them to die.

'And is there anything you can add to your description of her?'

Again, Mairead knew this was torture. She was forcing him to recall the one face in the world he wanted to forget right now, but at the moment Ben's description was anodyne to the point of total anonymity.

The woman who killed his parents had no accent. She had no distinguishing features. She was neither very young nor old. Maybe twenties, maybe a little older, he couldn't be sure. He couldn't remember how she was dressed, even whether she wore a skirt or jeans. Everything, it seemed, had been blanked.

Apart from the gun.

Ben remembered that.

Mairead looked down at the notepad in front of her. So far she hadn't written a single word. She turned towards the watching Tony and nodded, a silent signal. Tony turned away, disappearing for a moment. Ben stared out, unseeing, over the unkempt lawn as Mairead remained silent. Then she tensed as Tony, and then Lara and Beth, reappeared in the doorway.

And someone else as well.

For a moment Ben didn't register anything. Then, some instinct at work, he half-turned to see his sister.

––––––

Jools stared back at him from the kitchen door as Lara watched both siblings intently. Tony stood a little apart. Beth stood next to Jools.

There was no reason now why these two should be kept apart. While officially all lines of inquiry remained open, Ben had effectively been all but eliminated as any sort of suspect. CCTV cameras in the vicinity had established a woman being let into the family house before Ben returned home, and leaving twenty or so minutes later.

A large hat concealed her face on both occasions, so further identification was proving impossible for now, but it was yet another corroborating factor, and Jools had been told that, although they didn't know whether the young girl had really taken it in. Or whether all she was still seeing was a gun too, in her brother's hand. The gun that, a few moments before, had killed their parents.

But there was more involved here than a simple reunion. They were hoping this might in some way spur something inside Ben, that the sight of his sister might connect to some hitherto-buried memory, something they could work with. It was cod psychology, and Lara and every officer on the Serious Incident Team knew it. But it was one of the very few options they had left, so they had to pursue it.

The problem was that while Jools was looking at her brother with the same combination of fear, grief and blank bewilderment that had scarred the young girl's eyes ever since she'd walked in on the scene of that still-inexplicable double killing, Ben's eyes were completely blank.

———

Ben's eyes might indeed have been blank but inside he was raging. And one emotion was swamping all others.

Because as Ben kept staring at his sister, all he could feel was the most intense envy. He knew Jools had gone into that sitting room. He knew she'd seen their mum and dad. But she hadn't been in that room when they were killed. She hadn't seen the expression in their eyes as they were murdered.

And then Ben realised it wasn't just envy he was experiencing right now.

He hated her.

Ben actually hated her for not seeing the pictures he saw every time he closed his eyes, the images that would not and, he was already beginning to suspect, could not be erased.

And all he wanted to do right now more than anything in the world was to make her see all he'd seen.

To turn her into him.

CHAPTER
TWENTY-FOUR

LATER THAT SAME DAY, Lara and Jordan were conducting another interview they were trying to disguise as a conversation. They weren't getting the largely silent hostility Mairead had received in bucketfuls from Ben Turow. But they weren't getting much in the way of new information either.

Harper was still in St Mary's. She'd been taken there suffering the double effects of exposure and shock. The former had been treated easily enough and, physically, the small child was now OK. The latter was going to take a lot longer to work through, which was why she was still in the care of the medics.

But she was also in their care because the only responsible adult into whose care she could be committed right now was himself still a suspect, of course, although Lara once again remained doubtful. She'd been there as he'd identified Chrissie's body. His agony as he looked at the woman he'd loved – at the woman he still loved, if the expression in those eyes was anything to go by – was Oscar-winning if it was an act.

But right now it was Harper who was Lara's only focus, and she was asking the small child the same sort of questions Mairead had been asking the older, but no less traumatised Ben Turow.

'What sort of voice did you hear, Harper? Can you describe it for me? Did it sound like anyone you know, maybe a neighbour or a teacher or someone you've talked to in a shop?'

Harper didn't reply. They were in a small play area next to the children's ward, which was equipped with toys and games. A door opposite led to the hospital's own, well-equipped education unit. Lara didn't want to imagine the sort of illness that might condemn some of the patients in the ward next door to that sort of long-term schooling.

'And you're still not sure if it was a man or a woman?'

Harper hesitated, but then she shook her head. Lara looked at the watching Jordan. Finally they'd had a response. But if the officers hoped it might herald any further breakthrough they were to be disappointed. All Harper's simple response seemed to do was drive her further back into herself, and maybe for a good and understandable reason. Like Ben Turow before her, the last thing she wanted to do right now was re-live all that had happened.

Taking her cue from Harper's body language, Lara didn't ask any more questions. She just took some Lego from one of the boxes on the shelves, and for the next ten minutes she and Harper made a small house. Jordan built a treehouse and some swings and slides, arranging them outside to create a small garden.

From time to time Lara stole a glance towards their small charge, but Harper kept her eyes fixed on the Lego as if it was the single most important thing in the world right now, maybe because it was.

———

'So it could have been a woman.'

'What?'

'Chrissie's attacker.'

Jordan looked at Lara, curious; there was something clearly

significant about that. They were heading back along the river. Both officers had felt in need of some fresh air after that impromptu Lego session with the withdrawn Harper.

'The killer of Ben and Jools's mum and dad was a woman too.'

They turned into the nearby park, Lara moving to one of the swings.

'So you think there might be a connection?'

Lara hesitated as Jordan opted for a seat on the nearby climbing frame. In truth the stray thought that had floated through her head standing by that ruined castle seemed now to be just that. A stray thought of no importance. So the two murders had both left innocent young witnesses behind. So did many others. Maybe that stray thought said more about Lara and her situation than either of those two cases.

Still squatting on the climbing frame, Jordan picked away at the new possibility, growing more puzzled as he did so.

'There's nothing to indicate any sort of link. The Turow killer used a gun, Chrissie's used a knife. The Turows were killed at home, Chrissie was driven miles away.' Jordan worried away at it some more. 'OK, they live close to each other —'

Lara cut across. Now it was all being rehearsed out loud it was sounding like even more of a dead end.

'So how about you?'

Jordan looked back at her, momentarily thrown.

'It's not a week yet, I know,' she continued, 'but...'

A wave of irritation surged through him. They might be in a kids' playground right now but the last thing he needed was being checked up on.

But then Lara smiled. And all of a sudden Jordan's irritation vanished. Because this wasn't a senior officer mounting any official investigation. That single smile told him all he needed to know. All this was being said as a friend.

Jordan smiled back. Briefly, the two officers held eye contact. But then Jordan felt himself maintaining that eye contact just that little bit longer than the situation strictly warranted, and suddenly it was like a shutter had slammed down.

Lara nodded back at him briskly, all warmth in her eyes now evaporated.

'Let's get back, shall we?'

————

Driving home later that same day, Jordan was still cursing himself for misreading the signals.

Lara was strict, but fair. The perfect DI, in short. Why had he done it, why had he overstepped the mark like that? No wonder he'd been slapped back in place.

On an impulse, Jordan turned round, driving down to his old house, but he didn't actually get there. At the top of his old street, just before the adjacent waterway hove into view, Jordan braked as he saw Coco, dressed once again for a night doing anything apart from the studying she should be doing right now. And she was climbing into the passenger seat of a bright red Bentley.

The Bentley in question was a Continental GT. It could have been the V8 or the W12 – Jordan didn't register the badge. All he saw was a flash of his daughter's leg as she closed the door of the massively expensive behemoth in front of him and was then wafted away.

Jordan, instinctively, made a mental note of the registration number. But that's all he did. He didn't do what he wanted to do, which was to put on the blues and twos, stop the driver of that upmarket motor and then beat holy shit out of him.

Jordan turned his own much more modest car round instead and headed back to his equally modest flat, where he spent the rest of the night trying not to think about a bright red Bentley.

Or his regular dealer, who he could actually now see across the road from his flat, standing just outside the meat market, and already doing a roaring trade.

CHAPTER
TWENTY-FIVE

'KIERAN WALTERS.'

It didn't sound like a question and it wasn't a statement. It sounded like an opening gambit of some kind, but of exactly what, Lara couldn't decide.

So she decided to treat it as a question anyway.

'We had no reason to keep holding him. There's no evidence to tie him to the abduction and subsequent murder of his girlfriend, and at least three eye witnesses have now placed him at home at the time of Chrissie's murder.'

Besides – and as she'd already reflected to Jordan and to Mairead – Kieran just didn't smell right for something as extreme and calculated as this. His grief seemed too raw, too real, but Lara didn't mention that. She had a feeling olfactory instinct wouldn't exactly impress her current companion.

Across her desk, which was neat, functional and totally devoid of any personal effects, Paula just kept looking at her.

'And if he really wanted to kill his girlfriend, then why stage such an elaborate charade? Why drive Chrissie and her daughter miles away to do it? Why risk Harper identifying his voice? And why, once he'd killed Chrissie, did he let the little girl go?'

Paula stayed silent.

Lara had researched her new senior officer in the last couple of days. Paula had risen through the ranks in unusual circumstances. She had been part of a specialist unit for most of the previous ten years, dedicated to undercover work. Exactly what Paula had been doing for that previous decade wasn't known and never would be, in all probability.

Her unit had been disbanded when a couple of its members had gone rogue, like so many undercover cops back then, unable to reconcile what had become two warring parts of the same life. On the one hand, the cop spying on whatever group they'd infiltrated, at the same time an actual member of that often tight-knit group, forming friendships, forging alliances.

Some cops had done more than that and had begun relationships; one cop, who was now revered and despised in equal measure by both sides of that unbridgeable divide, had even started a family with one of the women he'd been spying on. No one knew the lengths to which Paula had gone in the half-life she'd been living in her missing decade, but she'd clearly been successful. Her present post was testament to that.

Lara hesitated. Later, she'd reflect that maybe she wouldn't have said what she'd said next if it hadn't been for Jordan and that misjudged, lingering look back in the riverside park. She'd probably have talked it through with him instead, much as she'd talked through many cases in the past.

But after that she couldn't get out of the park quickly enough. Lara had replayed the encounter over and over ever since. She was convinced she hadn't sent out any of the wrong sort of signals, meaning Jordan had misread them, which would be worrying in any cop. It could be disastrous in a cop in a unit such as theirs. Add in Jordan's newly acquired drugs habit and it meant her previously trusted sidekick was very much living on borrowed time right now.

'Ben Turow was allowed to leave as well.'

Paula looked back across her desk at her.

'Whoever killed his parents just walked out, according to

him. She gave him that present of the gun that killed them, then just let him walk out into the street, knowing he could identify her.'

Paula kept looking at her.

'It was only by total chance that Harper didn't see her mother's killer. The little girl was so frozen in horror she just closed down. But she could have done – at any point in that journey, Harper could also have seen the killer's face.'

Paula cut across, her question the same as Jordan's. 'So they're connected?'

Lara struggled for a moment. 'We haven't found a connection.'

'Do the families know each other?'

'Not that we're aware of.'

'Do we know if they've ever even crossed paths?'

Lara struggled again. They'd found absolutely no evidence of that so far either.

Paula maintained her stare. Lara expected a cutting dismissal. She expected a reminder that the Serious Incident Unit dealt in facts, the kind that would hold up in a court. She expected an equally cutting reminder that if Paula wanted conspiracy theories, all she had to do was trawl the internet.

But then Paula just turned back to the files on the desk in front of her.

Lara hesitated, then turned away herself. Once again, and much like Paula's initial questions that weren't quite questions, and statements that weren't statements either, this dismissal also felt like the opening gambit of something else.

The problem was that Lara still couldn't work out what.

CHAPTER
TWENTY-SIX

ROLLO REALLY COULD DO without this. But he owed Lara so much he didn't feel he had much choice.

He'd been building up to this visit for days, still convinced he'd screw it up in some way. Forget to get fresh milk. Find that the sandwiches he'd bought in were past their sell-by. Serve gravy granules instead of instant coffee as they'd all once seen in an episode of a TV sit-com whose name he'd forgotten.

They'd watched it together after he'd returned from one of his tours of duty. He'd remembered it as one of the few occasions they'd all laughed together. A rare moment back then, which was probably why it had stuck in his mind.

But none of that had happened. The doorbell had rung; Mum and Dad had stood outside on the doorstep, both smart, but not in what they'd call their Sunday best. Just neat and tidy, as was Rollo, who was freshly shaved, his hair combed. He wouldn't have passed muster in any snap inspection by his old company sergeant major, but he could see in his mum's gratified eyes that he was a million miles removed from the shambles of a man who'd disappeared from their lives those years before.

The promising beginning had continued. They kept the

conversation light, choosing deliberately non-controversial subjects, no politics, no current affairs and definitely no football. Dad was Southampton and Rollo was Pompey.

They talked about neighbours and family friends, retirements and births. Simple stuff. The kind of stuff that would have sounded deathly dull to any other ears; the kind of stuff that would have sounded deathly dull to Rollo all those years before. But now he devoured it much as his dad devoured the cake he'd actually baked, not bought in from the supermarket along with the sandwiches, and which had actually turned out OK.

Then came that second ring on the bell. Which was when the whole afternoon threatened to implode.

'Mr Adams, I'm Caroline Harrington. I'm your new case officer.'

An official accreditation from the island's Social Services department was waved in front of Rollo's eyes, accompanied by a warm, if slightly tired, smile. Rollo glanced behind at his parents, visible in the small sitting room, already clearly intrigued by his visitor.

And his heart sank.

Rollo had endured snap visits from Social Services before. They were all part of his ongoing rehabilitation. Anyone could put on a decent enough act given enough notice, could prepare a face to meet the faces you meet, as an old poem he'd once read in school had put it. Those sorts of scheduled visits didn't give a case officer anything like the information an unannounced call of this kind could provide.

But it wasn't the fact of this particular visit that made his heart sink, and it certainly wasn't the circumstances that were going to present themselves. This case officer wasn't going to find Rollo in the middle of some episode or witness the all-too-obvious signs of one having just taken place – the soiled bedsheets, the smashed furniture, the empty bottles of cheap booze littering the floor of a trashed flat.

Caroline Harrington was going to see tea and cakes and sandwiches instead. In one sense, and like Rollo's parents, she was going to be seeing him at his best.

But that was the point, of course.

Rollo's parents.

They were here. And all of a sudden all that had happened before was going to be out there again, before everyone's eyes. The last few hours of deliberately non-confrontational talk was suddenly going to count for nothing.

But if he blanked her, turned her away, Lara would be the first to know.

Caroline moved on into the sitting room and smiled politely as Rollo made halting introductions. He didn't say what she was there for because he didn't need to. Once he said those two simple words – *case officer* – it was obvious enough.

The next ten minutes were as bad as Rollo feared. Dad seemed to go in on himself. Mum seemed totally at a loss as to how to deal with the arrival of the unexpected stranger too. All the various elephants in that small room began trumpeting at once as the case worker brought the past crashing into a present that was simply too fragile to bear it, and every painful piece of the partial conversation that followed – the traffic problems out on the high street – the unseasonably warm weather they were all currently enjoying/enduring – the recent price rise at all the local petrol stations – just made it worse. This, in short, was fast turning into the disaster Rollo had always feared, and now he was just counting down the moments until it would all be over.

But then, suddenly, his mum started talking. And it wasn't the traffic or the unseasonable sunshine or the recent hike in petrol prices she was talking about.

'We had this little girl in school a month or so ago. Couldn't have been more than ten. Just a little slip of a thing she was and no wonder, because it didn't matter what any of us did, she just wouldn't eat.'

Rollo looked at her, as surprised as everyone else, judging by the look on their faces, at this sudden fork in the formerly stilted conversation. Dimly he remembered she'd started a new job a year before, as a dinner lady. It was one of the few deliberately non-confrontational subjects they hadn't touched on yet.

'I tried my best along with everyone else. All the usual stuff – chips, burgers. Nothing worked, even though you could see in her eyes she was hungry. Then one of the other ladies brought in a marzipan lolly and that was it, she just couldn't stop herself – the minute it was held out in front of her she reached out and took it.'

Caroline smiled politely, clearly still having absolutely no idea where this was going or even why she was listening to it, which made her part of a sizeable majority in Rollo's front room right now.

'And that's when we all saw it. The bruise on her arm. And another one, just a bit further up.'

Rollo's mum hesitated. 'When the teachers looked at her properly, the poor little mite was black and blue. And that's why she wasn't eating in school. Not because she didn't want to, but because she didn't want to risk anyone to seeing her bruises if she did. The ones her dad had given her.'

Then she looked at her son, and for the first time she really looked at him too, making eye contact and maintaining it.

'All this is lovely, Rollo, it really is. The effort you've gone to, we really appreciate it.' She hesitated. 'But...'

She didn't complete what she was struggling to say, They all knew what she meant. They might have been of a different type, but Rollo had bruises too. And his parents didn't want to walk out of their son's flat that afternoon without talking properly about them too. Without talking about him and how he was really doing. And if Caroline's unannounced visit was going to make that possible, then maybe it wasn't going to be such a disaster after all.

Because all of a sudden, it was like a valve had been released. Tensions that Rollo hadn't even been aware of before, tensions hidden beneath neatly cut sandwiches and sponge cakes, suddenly seemed to ebb away.

Caroline was the first to react as she responded to the school anecdote with one of her own regarding a recent visit to a strictly unnamed family on the watch register, where a similar story of abuse had been uncovered via a rusty climbing frame that didn't seem to have been used for years, so why did it have traces of fresh blood down one side of it?

Then the case worker endeared herself even more by offering to make them all a fresh pot of tea so they could talk without a relative stranger listening in. And this time they did what his mother had asked them to do, too – they talked about Rollo and how he was really coping, and they didn't once mention old neighbours or family friends or the price of petrol.

There was one strange moment when Caroline, pouring the new batch of tea she'd just brewed, mentioned his being found that night by Lara. Rollo had tensed, not aware that particular incident had been in his files. But as Caroline disappeared back into the kitchen to collect some more of the cake he'd baked, he relaxed again.

That didn't really matter, not now. If Lara had confided the circumstances of that strange reunion to someone else, so what? All that did matter was that today – a day that had promised so much and had then threatened to deliver so little – had somehow been turned round.

Rollo sipped his tea, at which point he began to realise just what an emotional toll all this had taken on him. How else could he explain suddenly feeling as weak as a kitten? And it wasn't just him – he could see his dad's shoulders almost visibly slump as he too sipped his tea, and his mum's head now seemed to be lolling back on her shoulders as well.

Then Rollo saw Caroline looking at them.

Suddenly, a chill feeling began in the pit of his stomach and he tried to stand, only for some reason his legs wouldn't let him. Then he tried to speak, but he suddenly found he could form no words.

Across the room, Caroline seemed to be studying him now.

Much as a cat studies a prospective kill.

CHAPTER
TWENTY-SEVEN

It WAS the longest of long shots and Lara knew it. She didn't even know how to phrase the search so the latest HOLMES2 software could process the request.

Murders where kids are left behind.

That didn't sound right.

Innocent witnesses to murders involving parents.

That also just led down a blind alley.

All in all Lara thanked God that the office was deserted and the rest of the building empty right now. She really didn't want anyone looking over her shoulder.

As Lara waited for her computer to attempt some part-coherent response to a largely incoherent set of search criteria, she let the rolling type to the side of the screen wash over her.

HOLMES2, so the text informed her, was an acronym for Home Office Large Major Enquiry System and was an investigation system designed to assist law enforcement organisations in their management of the complex process of investigating serious crimes.

More text swam before her eyes.

It enabled those law enforcement organisations to improve effectiveness and productivity, helping to solve crimes more quickly and improve detection rates. Admittedly, it was proving less than useless now, but maybe that said more about the officer accessing the facility and the odd search she was initiating.

Lara raised her eyes from the screen and looked round the empty office. It was getting on for midnight, way past the hour any officer on the Serious Incident Team would be in the building, emergency investigations excepted. Lara looked beyond the door to the open corridor, the security lights dimmed, lending an almost ghostly glow to the world beyond.

What was going on here? She'd separated her own personal story from the dozens of other stories she dealt with year in, year out, or at least she thought she had.

Was this all that was needed? One simple trigger? Stumble across a bewildered child suddenly plunged into an alien world and all of a sudden, Lara was six years old again?

Lara closed down the computer, having failed to find any killer with the sort of M.O. that had destroyed the lives of the teenagers Ben and Jools and the much younger Harper, probably because they didn't exist. This meant that the potential connections she'd seen in all this were something picked up on only by her for reasons of her own. Reasons that, so far, no one else on the Serious Incident Team knew about, because she'd made sure her background had stayed her business. But that wouldn't last long if she kept on like this.

Lara rose and turned towards the corridor, which was when she heard it. A single, short bang, as if a window had just been opened or closed nearby.

She looked at the offices lining the corridor. All were in darkness. She looked round the Serious Incident Room, but all was dark there too, just a single light over her desk, illuminating her computer. Then she heard a second bang. Lara moved quickly down the corridor as a third bang sounded, closer at hand.

Lara pushed open the office door nearest to her. The sound seemed to be coming from in there. As she did so, a fourth bang sounded, really loud this time. For a moment Lara stood in the doorway, disorientated.

Then she saw the open window on the other side of the room, the window banging back and forth as the wind from outside whipped it out, then smashed it back in again.

Lara, relaxing all the while, crossed to the window and pulled it shut. But as she did so she paused. Down in the car park across the road, red lights flared briefly as a car pulled away. Lara kept staring after the car, which she recognised immediately.

Paula had, apparently, just finished work and was driving away. But Paula's office was one door along that same corridor, and her room had been in darkness just like all the others for the last hour at least.

Lara kept watching as the red brake lights flared again, then disappeared as Paula turned the corner and vanished from view.

CHAPTER
TWENTY-EIGHT

ALL ROLLO'S mum could see were dragonflies and beetles.

It had been one of Rollo's favourite games as a small boy. He'd empty his collection of toy bugs into their bed and she'd have to climb in and scream as she saw them. She could still see him jumping up and down by the side of the bed, his eyes shining. No matter how many times he hid them there and no matter how often she'd let out that mock scream, it still provoked the same reaction. He never tired of the game and so neither did she.

This had to be some sort of game too, didn't it? Rollo had always been such a joker – until he'd joined the army anyway and that very different boy had been returned to them. But he was better now, much more like the old Rollo, so this had to be some sort of joke too. Rollo had enlisted some friend of his to play a trick on them. How else could you explain the strange state she seemed to be in right now, sitting in a room in Rollo's small flat, but floating above it somehow. Looking out from a body that just didn't seem to be hers anymore.

Deep down, she knew this was some sort of defence mechanism. She couldn't allow herself to admit something was badly wrong. So she kept concentrating on those plastic dragonflies, conjuring up more species of bugs from that childhood jar as she did so, even though in her heart of hearts she knew that this was no game.

The now-cold eyes of the woman who'd introduced herself as Rollo's case officer, those same cold eyes that were watching them all the time now, were making that all too clear.

———

Rollo's dad wasn't thinking about dragonflies. And he wasn't wasting time in wondering what sort of game this was either.

Yes, he'd been encouraged by the sight of this apparently new Rollo. Yes, he'd been further encouraged by the elaborate preparations he'd made for their tea. He'd seen the cautious hope in his wife's eyes for days now. He'd seen only too clearly how desperate she was to believe that their son had finally turned some sort of corner.

And he'd gone along with it, on the outside at least. He'd smiled and nodded in all the right places as Rollo had greeted them and had even observed to the letter his wife's stern instruction as they'd stood on his doorstep not to talk about football.

But he'd been let down by Rollo too many times in the past to let his guard down completely. The truth was he'd probably always be slightly wary around his only son from now 'til the day he died. He kept telling himself that in time he might get over that, might stop looking out for signs that Rollo hadn't conquered his demons quite so fully as they'd all hoped, but he'd never really believed it.

It wasn't that he didn't want to give his son the benefit of the doubt. He'd just been too scarred by all that had happened between them. And while his wife seemed able to put it all behind her, in his case those scars were going to take time to properly heal.

So this was all too simple in his book. Rollo had fallen foul of some local lowlife. He'd got in over his head with someone, probably drug-related. It had been Rollo's problem for so long now that this had to be more of the same. This woman, whoever she really was, had been sent round to teach Rollo some sort of lesson, and the fact his parents were with him hadn't fazed her at all.

Any minute now the door behind them was going to open, the Trojan Horse in the shape of that young woman was going to leave and some other lowlife villain or villains would come in, and Rollo, incapacitated by whatever she'd slipped into his tea, was going to be taught a painful lesson that they were both going to have to watch.

He'd hoped against hope that all his wife had promised him was true, that Rollo really had turned his life round, but even he didn't expect his darkest fears to be confirmed as quickly as this.

CHAPTER
TWENTY-NINE

IT WAS A RISK, much as putting Jools and Ben Turow together again had been a risk.

The protection agency knew it, Social Services knew it and Lara knew it. But they had to return Harper to something approaching a normal life sometime, even if nothing would ever really be normal for her again.

So bringing the little girl back to her old family home and reuniting her with Kieran was one step at least along a hopefully restorative road.

Kieran had now also been officially dismissed as a suspect. As well as the eye witnesses, various CCTV tapes had shown him in various locations many miles from the scene of Chrissie's murder. This meant that he was definitely no ongoing threat to her, and anyway he seemed desperate to be reunited with his former girlfriend's daughter.

Maybe that was because he wanted to somehow feel close to her mother again. Once again, no one really knew. Decisions still had to be taken on Harper's long-term care, and while Kieran insisted that he could look after her, it was still far too early for that sort of decision to be made. But the success or otherwise of this first visit could go some way to determining whether that might become a possibility in time. He was, after all, one constant at least in a life that possessed precious few others for Harper right now.

Kieran had arrived first. Social Services had already prepared the house, dusting the surfaces, running a hoover over the floor. Flowers had been placed in a bowl on the table, Harper's favourite squash had been sourced and some sticky treats she loved had been laid out on plates. A couple of her favourite comics had been bought in from the local newsagent and placed on the table as well. For his part Kieran just perched on the edge of a chair as if he was hovering on the edge of some kind of precipice. Perhaps he was.

Lara watched him tense as a key was heard turning in the door, and a moment later Harper appeared flanked by a protection officer, another colleague from Social Services and Mairead. For a moment Lara feared that Kieran was going to ruin this from the very start by rushing to the young girl and sweeping his up into her arms, which would have been a clear mistake.

All Harper's body language spoke the same story right now. She was still trying to make sense of a world that felt as alien to her as if she'd suddenly been beamed down from space. The last thing she needed was to have to deal with an adult's grief by proxy.

But Kieran held back. He even managed a smile. He talked about the car she'd come in and showed her some of the sticky treats. He also mentioned a film that had just been released that Harper had been looking forward to seeing. Kieran hadn't seen it himself yet but he'd read about it, and for a moment Harper and the rest of the room were treated to a resume of the story, although he was careful not to include any spoilers.

All the time Harper just stared at him. And when Kieran dried up, Harper transferred that same unblinking stare onto the protection officer, then the woman from Social Services and then onto Lara. Then Harper looked round the room almost as if she was seeing it for the first time.

Lara stepped in, trying to play her part now too. In truth she had no idea how Kieran had managed to keep up that desperate attempt to seem and sound normal, so the very least she could do was help him out. Lara talked about another film a colleague had taken her small daughter to, before the woman from Social Services chipped in with details of a new soft play facility that had just opened up, which she'd taken her own child to over the weekend.

Then everyone stopped talking as Harper suddenly stood. Lara tensed as she moved towards the door, holding out a restraining hand as Kieran stood too, Lara's silent signal clear.

Just let her do what she wants.

At her own pace and in her own time.

Then all the adults kept watching as Harper moved into the hall and climbed the stairs.

Slowly, and moving as casually as she was able, Lara followed. She stayed with the young girl as she went first into her bedroom and looked round at the posters on the walls and at the toys crammed into cupboards and drawers. Then, after a few moments, Harper turned and went into her mother's old bedroom, which hadn't been touched since the murder. Chrissie's make-up was still out on the dressing table, her clothes still in the wardrobe. Once again, Harper just stared at it all before turning and moving out onto the landing and back down the stairs again.

The kitchen was next visited, as was a small back garden, which was already starting to look overgrown. A small table and chairs squatted on a concreted section next to a fence, where presumably Chrissie and Harper used to have their tea on warm evenings.

Again, Harper just looked at it with that same unblinking stare before retracing her steps through the kitchen and making for the sitting room again. But as she did so she paused by a door that opened onto a small cupboard. Harper turned the handle and looked inside, genuine puzzlement creasing her face before she turned round and moved through back into the sitting room, where she picked up one of the comics that had been placed on the table and began to read.

Lara stared at her as she suddenly realised what was happening.

Harper had absolutely no idea where she was. She might have remembered the voice of the person who'd abducted her and killed her mother, but that aside there was nothing.

She had no recollection of her former home and no recollection of Kieran. So far as she was concerned she was in a strange house with people she'd never seen before.

That was why they'd all been treated to those unblinking stares from the moment she'd arrived. Harper wasn't in some near-catatonic state, as Lara had begun to fear.

She simply had no idea what she was doing there.

CHAPTER
THIRTY

I WAKE the next morning in the same place, looking out on the same sights I saw the previous night. I've never known this before. Up to now, every time I've opened my eyes there's been something new to see.

I feel like bursting into tears all over again, but as I look round the dormitory at all the other children, every one of them is smiling. Just like the boy I saw up in that high window last night.

After a breakfast of some thin gruel-like porridge, we're marched into a classroom. Everyone sits at long tables, their heads bowed. I do the same, but one of the boys looks up, maybe as something catches his eye out of the window.

Suddenly, he's yanked up by one of the masters, who's again dressed in a black flowing robe. As the boy stands there, shaking, the master turns to study what looks to be a collection of sticks in a box. He seems to linger over his choice, which is making the boy shake even more. Then the black-robed master turns back, but I've got it wrong because it isn't a stick I can now see in the black-robed man's hand, but a rope.

Swiftly, expertly, he ties the boy's wrists, clamping them together. Then he inserts a large metal hook into the rope. Equally swiftly and equally expertly, he threads the hook onto a pulley I can now see suspended from the ceiling. Three savage tugs propel the now-mewling *boy into space, his small frame wheeling round, legs scrabbling as he does so.*

Then the black-robed man picks up one of the sticks and starts asking questions.

Where is he from?

Where does he live?

Which is a nonsense, of course. He lives anywhere and everywhere, like us all, and he gasps that out, but that only seems to infuriate the master, who then starts hitting him with the stick.

Each blow spins the boy round, giving his attacker fresh territory to attack with each turn. After the third strike the terrified boy soils himself, which only enrages him the more, fresh blows now landing even more savagely, and I have to stop myself retching as I hear one of the boy's bones crack.

I look round but still the rest of the children keep smiling. Across the classroom I see the boy I saw up in that high window last night and he mimes a smile at me too, as if he's telling me to do the same. That's when I realise why they're all smiling like that, because they're all terrified about what will happen if they don't.

Later that night I wake to see the same boy standing by my bed. For a moment I start to panic but the boy – who I later find out is called Finn – just holds his fingers up to his lips.

Then he opens his other hand to show me my braids he's retrieved from the large bin outside, where they'd been thrown.

CHAPTER
THIRTY-ONE

UNLIKE HIS MUM, Rollo wasn't thinking about plastic boyhood bugs. Rollo's eyes kept flicking back to his dad.

Oddly enough the woman who'd orchestrated this strangest of ends to what had always promised to be a strange little tea party didn't feature in his thoughts at all. He had absolutely no idea who she was, although he now knew she wasn't any sort of case officer, not unless Social Services had begun to pioneer some very weird outreach programmes. But what she wanted – and what this crazy charade was all about – was totally beyond him.

Rollo hadn't even considered the possibility that this was some sort of retaliation for some recent misdemeanour on his part, because he hadn't fallen foul of anyone for a long time As for drugs, yes he was still using – but as those drugs were supplied by a well-respected member of Her Majesty's Constabulary, that ruled out a more than usually annoyed lowlife dealer he might have upset too.

He'd lived a totally anonymous and, it had to be said, blameless life since Lara had come into it all those months before, but that didn't stop someone blaming him, as the darting eyes of his father were making only too clear.

As his dad kept glancing across at him, Rollo suddenly

realised that he hadn't actually looked at him for years. Not in the way he used to look at him anyway, and definitely not the way most fathers look at their sons. Easily. Naturally. For as long as Rollo could remember now his old man would stare at a point just to the side of Rollo's head whenever they talked. And his eyes would always glaze over slightly, as if he was trying to work out what his son was really saying rather than listening to the words that were actually coming out of his mouth.

He was always looking for signs, in other words – signs that Rollo was lying about something, concealing something; as if mendacity and manipulation had been Rollo's stock-in-trade for so long it now was all he could see. A walking, talking succession of fuck-ups, and all his dad was doing was waiting for the next one.

And those darting eyes were telling Rollo everything he needed to know now, too. This was it, in his dad's book anyway. On the afternoon of what was supposed to be a brand new chapter for them, the old story was playing out again.

Suddenly, anger surged inside Rollo. And the words were out of his mouth almost before he even had time to realise he was saying them. Just four simple words; the same words he'd yelled so many times before, words that had always fallen flat across the inalienable divide between them. But these words told the plain and simple truth now.

'This isn't my fault.'

Rollo's dad's eyes darted to that same spot just to the side of his head.

And that silent, trademark dismissal only enraged Rollo even further.

'It's not my fucking fault!'

Neither of his parents reacted to his outburst, but something in the way the silent woman in the corner of the room leant forward told Rollo that his words had provoked some kind of response in her.

CHAPTER
THIRTY-TWO

IT WAS late on Sunday evening. Work loomed the next day. Lara stood across the road from a doorway tucked among a row of small shops, lights blazing inside. She could almost smell the sweat.

Lara hadn't been able to get Andrea Rice out of her mind. She'd researched the female trainer after she'd been effectively thrown out of her gym and had cursed herself for their getting off on quite obviously the wrong foot, because Andrea was different.

Special.

Time and again, Lara had debated heading inside and trying to book another session, and tonight she'd travelled to the gym to do that. But here she was, hesitating over making the actual approach.

Lara knew why too, from what had become almost forensic researches. Andrea Rice wasn't the kind who offered second chances, which was exactly the reason Lara wanted one. Boxing was more than exercise to Andrea and it was more than that to Lara. It had become her mainstay at more times in the past than she could remember. Her way of working through all her problems and frustrations.

The problem was that her efforts had been unfocused up to that point, her training unscientific. She knew that if she could push onto the next level she could unlock so much more inside. Take even more control over the demons that still threatened to overwhelm her.

Yet here she was dithering like a school kid trying to pluck up the courage to ask out a first date. It was ridiculous; it was something Lara did not do, and something she would not permit herself to do any longer.

Lara pushed herself away from the wall and crossed the road, heading to the front door of the gym. As she did so that door opened and Andrea herself emerged from inside, dressed in a loose-fitting tracksuit. Lara watched as she pressed the remote fob she was holding, as lights illuminated on a SUV parked nearby, and as she climbed inside. Within moments she was driving away.

But by that time Lara was already heading home.

The body is a complex machine. Multiple organs and systems work together constantly to keep it functioning. But occasionally one or another of them fails, at which point an attempt is made to fix them. Sometimes the organ or organs in question can be fixed, sometimes they can't, but the rest of the body can still keep going.

That isn't due to some kind of divine intervention.

It's due to life support.

At the same time as Lara was hovering outside Andrea Rice's gym, Mairead was looking at her father lying on the bed before her. His life support was of the traditional variety, a ventilator or respirator that maintained oxygen flow by pushing air into the lungs. One end of a tube was fed into his windpipe via his mouth, with the other end attached to a simple electric pump.

Both her father's lungs had originally failed following a blood clot, and the hope had been that they'd recover after a short period of outside help. That short period had lengthened to the point that it could no longer be regarded as anything but extended.

Perhaps even over-extended.

No one had actually said that to her as yet, not the doctors nor any of the nurses. But the silence had started to become deafening

Mairead took her father's unresponsive hand in hers. She'd been on the hospital website every night for the last week, reading the guidelines for patients like him.

Doctors usually advise stopping life support when there is no hope left for recovery, when organs are no longer able to function on their own and there is no prospect that they will do so.

She'd stopped right there on the first night. But the following night she'd gone back to it again.

Choosing to remove life support usually means the patient will die within hours, but the timing depends on the nature of the treatment that's withdrawn.

And then the killer sentence of all, to pardon the pun.

When someone is unconscious or not of sound mind, the medical staff and family members decide between them when life support should stop.

That was where Mairead had given up once more and told herself not to return, but she knew she would.

It's important to remember that it's the underlying condition, not the removal of life support, that actually causes someone to die. Doctors encourage family members to focus on what they think their loved ones would want.

These were fine words and sincerely meant. The problem was that there were no other family members to consult in Mairead's case. For more years than she could remember, and ever since her mother had died in a car crash when Mairead had still been in primary school, it had just been the two of them.

Mairead looked down at her father again.

And when she made the decision she knew she'd have to make – and before much longer too – it would just be the one.

———

The official Home Office Policy on ANPR – Automatic Number Plate Recognition – was simple. It was there to help, detect, deter and disrupt criminality as well as playing its part in tackling organised crime groups and terrorists.

The system itself was simple too. Vehicle movements were recorded by a network of nearly eight thousand cameras capturing between twenty-five and thirty million number plates daily, and those records would then be stored for up to two years in the National ANPR data centre.

They were intended to be accessed, analysed and used as evidence as part of official investigations by the UK law enforcement agencies.

They were not meant to be used on an idle Sunday evening to trace the boyfriend of a teenage girl.

At the same time as Lara was hovering outside the gym and Mairead was maintaining her vigil by the bedside of her father, Jordan was in his small flat overlooking the meat market, staring at the records associated with the driver of the red Bentley he'd seen drive away with Coco.

It was registered to a white male called Kris Winstone. A quick check on all the usual social media sites revealed that Kris Winstone was twenty-five years old and that the brand new Bentley was owned by him outright. His address almost certainly ruled out privilege, meaning that Kris was almost certainly a drugs dealer. He'd obviously managed to evade arrest for what had to have been his many and numerous crimes and misdemeanours up to now, given the car he was driving, but Jordan – still staring at the computer screen – made a man he now knew as Kris Winstone a silent, solemn, promise.

By hook or by crook, by fair means or foul, he wouldn't be escaping the clutches of the law much longer.

CHAPTER
THIRTY-THREE

LARA HEADED BACK into the Serious Incident Room at nine the next morning. Within five minutes a glow of excitement began inside as Paula gave her and the rest of the team an update on the inquiry that had been ongoing for the previous few months, the attacker that had been preying on the local S&M community.

It had been a particularly tricky case to crack, given that all the potential witnesses actually invited the sort of treatment that in any other circumstances would be deemed serious physical assault. It also didn't help that many of the meetings where these assaults took place were shrouded in secrecy. Most of the participants were ordinary Joes and the occasional Josephines in their more traditional lives. The last thing any of them wanted was any kind of exposure.

But now one of their number had broken ranks after his occasional but much-loved boyfriend had become the attacker's latest victim. He'd agreed to feed back to the Unit details of the next meeting, wherever it might take place. This might only have been a small advance, but it was an advance nonetheless.

Then that cautious glow vanished in an extinguished heartbeat.

Or, more accurately, two of them.

———

'Another double killing.'

Jordan stood in front of Lara's desk, the details flashed up from the Comms Room a moment or so before in his hand.

'Uniform have just called it in. A couple in their sixties – looks like it might be down to their son, an ex-squaddie apparently.'

Lara began to still as Jordan shook his head, this not exactly an unfamiliar story these days.

'From what Uniform are telling us, he seems to have just flipped.'

Lara kept staring at him as Jordan pushed the print-out from the Comms Room over her desk.

Then she stared down at the piece of paper, the address screaming up at her.

Almost as loudly as the disbelieving scream that was now reverberating inside her head.

———

Ten minutes later, Lara and Jordan were approaching the scene-of-crime tape marking off Rollo's flat from all other properties to each side. A uniformed PC stood outside the open door while white-coated officers moved in and out.

Lara flashed her warrant card, donned the customary protective overalls and shoes and moved inside.

The first thing she saw were the remnants of the tea Rollo had prepared for his now-dead parents. Cake was still neatly laid out on china plates. Sandwiches, cut into quarters, were laid out on another plate. A large teapot squatted in the middle of the table along with cups and saucers, a small jug of milk resting next to it.

Only one detail spoilt the tableau and that was the dried and jagged streaks of blood that covered it all.

'The suspect is Rory Adams. Twenty-eight, ex-Princess of Wales's.'

Lara didn't reply.

She already knew that.

'He was invalided out of the army a few years ago after a string of disciplinary offences. Probably suffering from PTSD, but slipped through the net like so many of the other walking time-bombs they discharge out onto the street.'

Jordan consulted his notes some more as Lara kept staring at the cakes and sandwiches.

'He's got previous for a couple of minor offences – breach of the peace – threatening behaviour.' He looked up at the blood-stained walls and floor. 'Nothing on this scale though.'

Lara remained silent. The facts seemed simple enough. A neighbour had reported hearing a disturbance. Chairs or tables being kicked against a wall, and then shouts and screams. Uniform had rocked up a short time later and hadn't been able to get in or raise a reply from inside. It was touch and go for a moment whether they went off to attend to another call they'd received since they'd stood on the doorstep of that small flat, but then one of the officers lifted the letterbox and looked inside. He couldn't see anything out of the ordinary initially, but he could smell something that just seemed wrong. Something thin, brittle. He took out his torch and trained it down the hall. When the yellow beam picked out blood streaking one of the far walls he'd kicked in the door.

Jordan's voice was still sounding in Lara's ear.

'Adams was out of it when they got inside. We've no idea yet what he'd taken or whether he'd taken it before, during or after he'd offed his parents, but the hospital are doing tests.'

Lara cut across. 'He didn't.'

Jordan paused, looked at her. It was all his senior officer had said since they'd walked in. 'Didn't what?'

'This wasn't down to him.'

Jordan looked round the small flat, then back at Lara, feeling his way cautiously.

'We've already found drugs on the premises. We've also got a report of a disturbance from a few years before when he'd had to be restrained from attacking his old man.'

Jordan looked at Lara as she didn't respond. All the signs here were clearly pointing to the same thing. A seriously unhinged chancer who'd just gone wild.

Lara kept her face poker still and her emotions hidden.

On the outside, she was alabaster. Inscrutable.

Inside, her mind was racing.

CHAPTER
THIRTY-FOUR

MAISA HAD REQUESTED the report personally. Strictly speaking, it wasn't the living that were her province, but the dead. She gave them life after life itself had ended, allowing their story to be told through her painstaking reconstruction of all that had happened to them.

But she was also interested in the innocent relatives of those she'd only known as bodies on a mortuary slab. Perhaps that was down to her own background and circumstances. Either way, it was why she'd asked to be kept in the loop regarding Harper.

Following that abortive home visit, Harper had been referred to a paediatric psychologist. It was her report, emailed over just an hour or so before, that Maisa was reading on her laptop, and it was clear that all Lara's suspicions as she stood in the hallway of Harper's former home that day had now been confirmed.

Previously, some stray memories had been retained – a voice – the odd whispered instruction – but that had now gone too. Harper had no recollection of the attack on her mother. She had no memory of their abduction. Even more tellingly, she had no memory of her life before that day either. Her home had simply become an alien entity to her, and Kieran nothing more than an alien presence inside it. She had no idea now what part Kieran had formerly played in a life she no longer recognised.

Maisa scanned the initial steps the psychologist had taken to try and overcome this block in the small girl's memory, all of which seemed textbook stuff. Harper had already visited the family home, of course, but then there'd been a second visit, this time focusing on Harper's bedroom and the small garden outside, where, according to neighbours that Harper also didn't remember or recognise, she used to play most of the time. All had been met with the same blank stare.

So a whole collection of family photographs had next been assembled – Harper and Chrissie at birthday parties, day trips out to some attraction or other. But still there'd been nothing. Just a stare from her so wooden you could have knocked on it.

So the paediatric psychologist had next tried EMDR – or Eye Movement Desensitisation Reprocessing, to give the technique its full title. It had first been developed in the 1980s by an American psychologist, Francine Shapiro. Haunted by her own traumatic memories, she was only too aware how the body's natural cognitive and neurological coping mechanisms could easily become overwhelmed. When that occurred, the memory of the trauma was inadequately processed, becoming stored – locked indeed – in an isolated and seemingly inaccessible network inside the brain.

The goal of EMDR is to properly process those traumatic memories, reducing their impact and helping trauma victims develop coping mechanisms. Shapiro had pioneered an eight-phase approach, and Harper had been carefully led through each and every one.

The first two stages were dispensed with fairly quickly. There was little point in asking Harper what specific distress she was experiencing, as she simply didn't know, and the usual relaxation exercises would have been a waste of time as well. But phases three to six promised more.

The paediatric psychologist next attempted to lead Harper

back to the experience that had plunged her into this state in the first place. It was all intended to lead to the seventh phase, which was closure, and then the eighth, which was re-evaluation.

But it was obvious to the psychologist before they'd completed even half the process how this particular exercise was going to end. Harper's memories remained locked. No exercise that was enacted promised even briefly to breach that inner barricade. Harper remained as oblivious to all that had happened at the end of the session as she had been at the start.

She'd quite simply wiped not only all that had happened to her, but even who she was.

———

The paediatric psychologist's report provoked a considerable degree of professional fascination among many of her colleagues.

It provoked a rather more empathetic fascination in Maisa. Displaced souls of whatever hue and persuasion were always going to speak to her.

It provoked a high degree of frustration in Lara. Harper was their sole witness to all that had happened to her mother. To be denied even the sketchiest of testimonies from their only witness was galling, to say the least.

But it provoked a very different reaction in someone else. This totally unauthorised person had intercepted the report as it was emailed from the paediatric psychologist to Maisa and to Lara, much as they'd intercepted many others.

This person read the report at roughly the same time as Maisa and Lara, but this person didn't feel any sort of professional fascination or frustration, empathetic or otherwise. This person felt one emotion and one only.

Plain and simple fury.

CHAPTER
THIRTY-FIVE

Lara, a baseball cap jammed down over her head and covering most of her face, had been walking for most of the night.

Where she'd been walking, she had no idea. If she'd been asked who she'd seen on that walk, it would have provoked the same response. She was in a blind fog and the only thing that registered with her right now was the simple mechanical effort of putting one foot in front of the other. But it was what she needed more than anything, because it drove everything else out of her head.

Rollo.

His parents.

The aftermath of the bloodbath in his flat she'd just witnessed.

Lara was stopped as she cut up from the river. It was just a chance encounter, two young suited and booted professional gents coming out of a coffee shop, takeaway mochas in hand. Lara barged into first one and then the other, and a minuscule amount of liquid spilled from the top of one of the takeaway containers carried by the first of the suits.

It was nothing. The sort of accidental encounter that took place every minute of every day. The yelled protest that followed in its wake was the kind that was heard every minute of every day as well.

What was different this time was the sudden and piercing scream of agony that followed.

Because suddenly Lara snapped. She didn't even see the face of the man who'd just yelled at her. Maybe his well-cut suit forged some unconscious association with the Pimms-quaffing weekend sailors who'd attacked Rollo all those years before. Or maybe that was nothing to do with it at all. Lara turned to face him, initially blasting him with a cursed expletive of her own.

The man with the well-cut suit didn't like it. He grabbed hold of the diminutive woman who'd not only spilled his mocha but had just yelled in his face in place of any kind of apology.

Lara lashed out with a flying high kick to his right forearm, sending the remaining contents of his coffee over his companion. Before it had cascaded back down to the floor, Lara had her aggrieved complainant's wrist trapped in an Akkido joint lock. The man was at least a hundred pounds heavier than Lara and a good six inches taller, but it wouldn't have mattered how much taller or heavier he might have been, he was going down.

As he fell, gasping, onto the floor, Lara chopped him in the throat, not hard, but enough to knock the wind out of him, then she brought her arm back to chop him again – at which point it was as if the mists suddenly cleared.

Lara took in the expression on the face of the suit's badly shocked companion, the equally shocked expressions on the faces of the few bystanders who'd stopped to watch. Then she stared down at the moaning man on the floor.

What was she doing?

What the fuck was she doing?

Lara didn't waste any time answering her own silent question.

Instead, she pulled her baseball cap even further down over her face and moved quickly away.

CHAPTER
THIRTY-SIX

JOOLS, at her own request, had now been separated from Ben.

It wasn't that she harboured any lingering suspicions over his role in the murder of their parents. Even leaving aside those CCTV images of that woman with the hat, she'd never actually had Ben down for a cold-blooded killer anyway. But she still didn't want to live under the same roof as him right now. It wasn't anything he'd said or not said, or anything he'd done or not done. But something about him was still spooking her.

Or maybe, and perhaps understandably, she was just spooked by everything and everyone right now.

So Jools had been moved to a small holiday let the Protection Unit used towards Freshwater, one flat in amongst a small collection of others. Tony had gone with her, drafting in another late thirty-something officer called Ellie to go with them too. Their cover story, in case any friendly holidaymaker tried to make conversation, was that Tony and Ellie were there on a short break with their daughter as a reward for her doing well in her recent exams, but so far none had.

Lara seated herself on the small balcony opposite the quiet Jools. For the last few nights, the young girl had taken to sitting out there. There was a partial glimpse of the sea courtesy of a gap between two larger holiday lets opposite, but something told Lara she wasn't there for the view. Jools was locked inside her own world right now, at the same time as trying to make sense of another world that had suddenly twisted itself inside out, and maybe that was the real reason she wanted to get away from Ben. He was an all-too-painful reminder of all they'd both lost for reasons neither could – and never would – begin to understand.

Lara hadn't cleared this visit with Paula. No one in the Serious Incident Unit knew about it either, because Lara didn't want any awkward questions being asked, such as why she was making this trip in the first place and what she hoped to achieve. The simple fact was that she didn't know.

Lara spread a couple of photos out on the small table in front of them. One was a mother and daughter shot of Chrissie and Harper, the pair of them smiling at the camera, captured by Kieran on a trip out to the theme park at Blackgang.

Next to that photo, Lara placed another one of Harper alone – an individual photo taken in school – and then another photo of Chrissie taken from her passport.

'All I want to know is whether you've come across either this woman or this girl before.'

Jools looked at the photos without a flicker of recognition.

Lara hesitated a moment, then slid another photo across the table, this one of Rollo, taken from his army files. But as Jools looked at that photo her eyes told Lara that Rollo was as much of a stranger as Chrissie and Harper.

'Should I know them?'

Jools looked up at Lara and now her eyes told another story. The same story those eyes had begged of everyone who'd come into any sort of contact with her since the double-killing of her mum and dad.

Please.

Explain all this.

Help me.

Lara shook her head. 'It's just a long shot.'

'What is?'

Jools suddenly leant forward, tapping the photo of Chrissie as she did so.

'The woman – is that her – is she the one who came to our house?'

'No.'

'Then why are you showing me her picture?'

And there it was. That awkward question to which Lara had no answer, making her even more grateful that she was being asked it by a fifteen-year-old girl called Jools Turow and not by a forty-something DCI called Paula Davies.

———

A short time later, Lara was sitting opposite Tony. Jools had gone for a shower. She did that every night and every morning. She'd spend up to an hour in there at a time, just standing under the pummelling water, blotting out the world once again and everything and everyone in it.

'Has anyone been in touch?'

Tony looked at her.

Lara persisted. 'As in friends, family?'

Tony kept looking at her. 'You've read the file?'

'I've read it. I just wondered if it there was any one we might have missed?'

Tony shrugged. 'Doesn't seem to be. These two don't seem to have any sort of family, extended or otherwise. There was just the two of them and their mum and dad. To be honest, the killer couldn't have picked a more isolated pair of kids.'

Lara looked out again beyond the two larger holiday lets opposite at the partial view of the sea.

Another silent thought was now hammering away inside.

CHAPTER
THIRTY-SEVEN

MOST NIGHTS, Jordan was left alone. He made sure of it. None of his work colleagues had ever been invited home, mainly because he wasn't that close to them and also because he'd never really thought of it as any sort of home. Home was the house he'd left, the house still occupied by Edie and Coco.

But sometimes the outside world intruded. Living across the street from the always-busy meat market and a couple of clubs, it was inevitable he'd be disturbed from time to time. So when the buzzer sounded late that night on his intercom he assumed at first it was another pissed reveller leaning against his outside door for support or maybe an opportunist villain chancing his arm. Either way he was about to ignore it.

Until he glanced down from his first floor window to see the unmistakable shape of his detective inspector standing on the doorstep.

Jordan hesitated a moment, then buzzed Lara inside. When she appeared at the top of the stairs a couple of moments later, she held out to him a bottle of wine wrapped in a convenience store bag. Two minutes later the wine was uncorked.

Jordan had no idea why she was there or what she wanted. Briefly – a triumph of hope over experience if there ever was one

– visions of finding out what breakfast cereal she preferred danced before his eyes, but then Lara started talking about Ben and Jools and Harper and the soldier, Rory Adams. And those visions, more than a little regretfully, faded from view.

Lara had arrived to talk business. Business she'd tried to talk about before in that kids' playground in Riverside Park. Business she'd stumbled towards rehearsing with Paula too.

'What you said before – no, there's no connection between the victims. They weren't known to each other despite Chrissie and Harper living only a stone's throw from Phil and Kate Turow.'

Jordan prompted her as Lara hesitated.

'But?'

Lara took a deep breath.

'But they do have one thing in common. It's tenuous, I know. That's the reason I'm saying this to you, rather than saying it tomorrow to the rest of the team.'

'And that is?'

Lara hunched forward.

'Take out Ben and Jools's parents and those two kids have no one. The father had been in care from an early age, which was maybe why he went into childminding in the first place. The one thing he knew about was displaced kids. The mother came from a more conventional home, but her single mum died when she was eighteen. There'd never been a dad in her life and there were no surviving grandparents either. Meaning Ben and Jools are now alone in the world with no other relatives to step in and take charge.'

'And Harper?'

Lara nodded, Jordan clearly ahead of her.

'Same story. Chrissie's husband – Harper's father – is dead. Both her parents and his parents are dead now too. He had no brothers and sisters and neither did she.'

'Chrissie did have a boyfriend, though.'

'But Kieran's not a blood relation. And the relationship with Chrissie has only been going on for a few months. Social Services are going to have to be very sure before they place a vulnerable young girl with a single male she's only known for a matter of months and who's now going through a period of intense mourning himself.'

Lara shook her head before continuing. 'To all intents and purposes, Harper's now as alone in the world as Ben and Jools. And she's facing the same future, in the short term at least. Foster parents or being placed in some sort of care.'

Jordan leant forward, his pulse quickening as it always did when connections started forming. A connection meant some-where to start. The all-important first piece of the jigsaw slotted in place that might in time lead to an actual picture.

'So what about the soldier – Adams?'

'Rollo.'

The nickname was out of her mouth before Lara could stop herself. He'd only been identified in the official reports so far by his Christian name, Rory. But if Jordan noticed the slip he gave no sign.

'He's obviously not a small child like Harper, or a teenager like Ben and Jools,' Lara went on. 'But he's just like them in terms of immediate family once his parents are taken out of the frame. There's no one now, absolutely no one at all. No grandparents, cousins, aunts or uncles.'

Lara paused. Now she'd actually said all this out loud she was even more convinced she was onto something here.

This killer wasn't just in the killing business.

This killer was in the business of creating orphans.

———

An hour later, Lara was back outside Jordan's flat, watching clubbers stream into Fabric. She knew it well, as did every other officer on the island.

The club, founded by two local businessmen, first opened in the last few months of the 1990s. It boasted three separate rooms with independent sound systems, two of which featured stages for live acts, while the third had a vibrating floor, more accurately known as a bodysonic dance floor, with sections attached to transducers emitting bass frequencies of the music being played at the time.

A few years previously, Fabric's licence had been revoked following the drug-related deaths of two clubbers inside, but supporters launched a social media crowdfunding campaign to support its reopening. Over twenty thousand pounds was raised towards a legal fund to fight the council's decision. A short time later Fabric was back in business, but conditions were attached, including the adoption of a new ID system, the installation of a covert surveillance system, a lifetime ban for anyone found dealing or in possession of drugs on the premises, and a blanket ban on anyone under the age of nineteen being allowed in between a Friday evening and a Monday morning.

Lara hadn't realised she knew so much about the place. If anyone had told her all that would float through her mind as she stood opposite it that night she'd have told them they were deluded.

It was displacement activity, of course, stopping her thinking about something else, but it was only postponing the inevitable and she knew it.

All Lara had talked about to Jordan was Ben and Jools, Harper and Rollo. Her focus had been on the different victims of those apparently inexplicable crimes, finally rehearsing with him all she'd attempted to rehearse with Paula.

But she hadn't told him everything. Because all the time she was talking, the same silent thought had been hammering away inside her head.

Ben and Jools, Harper and Rollo might now be members of a macabre club, but they weren't the only ones.

Lara had been talking about them.

She could so easily have been talking about herself.

CHAPTER
THIRTY-EIGHT

As SHE TOLD the later inquiry, Beth, the female protection officer, simply couldn't see any harm in it. In fact, she'd actually encouraged Harper when the girl had first floated the idea.

It had been one of the very first lessons drummed into her when Beth took up her new post in the Protection Unit. So far as possible, everything should be done to make a client, whatever age they might be, feel that life was as normal and as everyday as possible.

Life inside any Protection Unit was a pressure cooker. How could it not be? Wrenched from one reality to a very different reality, one that often resembled no reality at all, clients were always under the most extreme type of strain. All of them without exception were living a life that was no life at all, cut off from all they'd known before, and in most cases totally unable to embrace what they'd been told would be their new existence from that point on.

Every now and again some sort of release had to be found, even for those at the highest level of risk. They weren't the ones in prison, although sometimes it might feel that way.

So when Harper had looked out of the window and seen

some kids bounding eagerly into a nearby park, Beth really couldn't see the problem. Why shouldn't she take her for an hour or so to play on the slides and swings?

Beth had logged the trip with Tony as usual. He wasn't actually in any of the safe houses that day; he was travelling by train to the mainland and then on to Brighton to deal with a Category A who'd gone rogue. The Category A in question was a long-standing client who required lifelong protection, the most difficult category of all to manage, and this one was proving no exception. He'd tried to return to his old home and haunts on more than one occasion in the past, and the recent death of a much-loved aunt was now providing another powerful incentive.

The Category A was adamant he wanted to attend her funeral. Tony and the rest of the Protection Unit had been equally adamant that he shouldn't even think about it. Beth really didn't envy her colleague the confrontation that was inevitably going to ensue. Visions of immovable objects meeting irresistible forces swam before her eyes. All in all she thanked her lucky stars the only tricky decision she had to make today was whether a small child should be allowed to spend an hour or so in a local park.

There'd been no response from Tony to her email, which hadn't surprised her. Maybe that immovable object had already encountered that irresistible force. If so, her senior officer would very definitely have other things on his mind.

Beth escorted the little girl into the park at two that afternoon, and for the first time since she'd entered the protection programme, Harper actually looked like a little girl. A simple, carefree child suddenly replaced the cowed casualty she'd presented up to then.

Within moments she was on a climbing frame constructed to resemble a boat. A minute later she was a pirate on the high seas and Beth had been cast as Captain Hook. Two minutes later Harper had acquired a first mate in the shape of a boy of around three called Lewis, who had quite clearly fallen in love with the older Harper and who would equally clearly now do her every bidding.

The small boy's parents stood some way off, smiling as they watched, the mother trying to engage Beth in conversation in the not unreasonable assumption she was Harper's mum. Beth didn't choke off the approach. That was always guaranteed to provoke the worst sort of response for any officer in the Protection Unit, which was curiosity. But neither did she encourage it. She just moved away as casually and as naturally as she could and plunged herself some more into the make-believe world Harper was currently constructing.

At the small girl's instruction, Beth became a giant ape being transported in the hold of the imaginary plane. Then she became a snake. Having failed to produce a convincing impersonation of a snake, Beth was next commanded to be Thor. Beth had absolutely no idea who Thor was, but then the smiling father enlightened her.

A short time later, Lewis had to go home for his tea and regretful goodbyes were exchanged. Lewis shyly hoped Harper would be in the park again, and Harper, after a quick look at Beth, had promised she would. There was no reason not to visit again, after all. It had been a simple and straightforward couple of hours with all the cares of Harper's current world forgotten.

A happy memory, in fact, but there were to be no more of them.

The single bullet that suddenly blasted into the back of Harper's head made sure of it.

Harper was dead before she even reached the ground, blood pumping from the gaping wound. Beth, her coat splattered by a combination of the small child's blood and brains, stared down at her, frozen for a moment. Across the park, Lewis and his parents kept walking towards the gate, totally unaware of all that had happened behind them, thanks to the silencer that had been fitted to the assassin's gun.

But then, just as they were about to exit out onto the nearby road, they turned.

Because then they heard Beth's scream.

CHAPTER
THIRTY-NINE

I'D NEVER HAD a friend before, as in an always-there, laughing, playing sort of friend.

We'd pass other children as we journeyed the rivers and the canals, not just on the island but on the mainland too, usually as we travelled from the Severn up to Birmingham, and then on down to the Fens and on to Essex. But we were always too busy ferrying carcasses from farms to various abattoirs to stop and talk – and definitely not to stop and play.

Sometimes we'd also see other children when we'd call into boat-yards to pick up oil and dirty vegetables in large sacks, but it was the same story there. We always had to keep moving. It's what we did. River folk always kept one step ahead.

But now I did have a friend and I knew one thing right from the start. Those black-robed masters, and we always called them all masters be they men or women, must never be permitted to know.

We first sneaked out of Kenwood two days later. Just the two of us, when everyone else was at silent prayer or awaiting punishment for whatever misdeeds they'd done that day. The first few times we explored the fields at the back of the house, the ones that bordered onto the railway line, although you could only really hear the passing trains, not see them, thanks to the untamed trees that had been allowed to grow wild, shielding the home from view. We weren't running away. We had nowhere to run to. I couldn't have found my mother now anyway, and Finn had lost touch with his years before. We were just making our own little world for the two of us to play in.

Which was when, out on one of those forbidden excursions away from the home, we found the windmill.

We both stopped and stared at it, unable to believe our eyes. It was an actual windmill with blades that revolved in the wind. Mum had read a story to me once about a knight from years before who'd tilted at them with his sword, and now we were looking at one in real life, although I couldn't see any knights or swords.

As we grew closer, we could see it wasn't quite full size. Then, suddenly, and almost as if it could sense our presence, the blades began to turn. At the same time we heard the distant whoosh of a train as it passed the end of the overgrown garden, the sudden wind fluttering nearby branches, passengers glimpsed briefly inside the carriages, but none of them seemed to take the slightest notice of us as they sped on their oblivious way.

Then the blades settled once again. I reached out and touched the nearest one, which was made of wood like the others, and which was pockmarked with peeling paint.

Was it some sort of abandoned child's playroom? We had no idea, But it cast an irresistible spell. We dashed inside and for the next few minutes explored every inch of that strange space with its basement and two floors. We ran up and down stairs and banged on the walls and poked around in dusty corners, shrieking in hushed terror when tiny spiders crawled across the floor. For those few moments we forgot everything – where we lived – how we lived – even who we were.

Exhausted, we crept back into Kenwood a short time later, unaware of the girl across the room watching us from her bed. Then we climbed into our own beds, unaware of her slipping out of hers.

There were rumours of ice cream the next day for a few lucky souls.

One word in the right ear and she might be one of the favoured few.

PART THREE

Your iniquities have separated you from your God and your sins have hidden His face from you
Isaiah, 59:2

CHAPTER
FORTY

'WHO KNEW?'

It was the fifth time Paula had asked the same question in the last half hour, and it wasn't the last time she was going to ask it.

It was standard police procedure. Keep repeating the same question over and over again in case it provokes a different answer. Even a slightly different response could expose a crack that could be opened up further, but the answer came back the same each and every time.

'No one.'

Albeit with the same immediate qualification. 'But I had logged it. I told you, I followed all the protocols.'

A helpless, wracked Beth paused. 'But apart from that, apart from the Unit, no one else could have known.'

Paula looked across the table at Beth. She'd checked and double-checked all she'd told her. There was an advance record of the trip that day to the park, but so far as Paula could establish, that advance record would indeed have been circulated inside the Protection Unit only.

A message had been left for Tony, telling him to get back from Brighton immediately, if not sooner. When he arrived he'd be grilled along with every member of his Unit regarding who might have had access to Beth's log in his absence. But while each and every member of that Unit would be interviewed, and while each and every one of them would be asked the same questions over and over again too, Paula already had a strong suspicion it wouldn't lead them anywhere.

If the killer really was inside a police unit, why wait 'til Harper was out in that park? They could have picked a dozen alternative locations for what seemed to be another execution-style killing. A park carried all-too-obvious risks, not only witnesses, but also Beth's almost immediate scream. Within seconds of Harper's killing the scene inside the park was mayhem. Everyone would have been looking at everyone else.

This meant that the killer chose that spot because a window of opportunity had arisen and been taken. But who'd handed them that opportunity, and why?

And so, and for the sixth, seventh and eighth time, Paula asked Beth the same question again.

And for the sixth, seventh and eighth time, she received exactly the same answer.

———

At the same time, Lara was interviewing another set of shocked witnesses, the hapless family who'd also been with Harper during what turned out to be the last hour or so of her life.

At the time, it just seemed a simple and innocent encounter, but was it? Was that family a plant, a decoy to keep Beth and Harper in the park while a gangland-style hit could be arranged?

The mother had been swiftly discounted. She'd been the first to dash back after hearing Beth's scream. She'd assumed that Harper must have fallen, maybe from the swing. When she saw the blood, it seemed to confirm her suspicions. She and her husband had taken Lewis, their own little boy, to a soft play centre the month before and he'd suffered a freak accident, tripping on his way into a plastic tunnel, opening up a head wound that had propelled her in a complete blind panic from the nearby table where she'd been laying out a family picnic. They'd stemmed the bleeding quickly enough and the wound was only skin deep, but she could still well understand how Beth might be feeling.

Then she saw the gaping hole where the back of Harper's skull had been. Then she'd seen the blue-grey brains snaking down Beth's blouse.

At this point she'd gone into a state beyond hysteria, which was where she'd remained ever since, clinging to her own small and bewildered child, refusing to be separated from him for even an instant lest the horror that had so obviously stalked the park that day returned to take him too.

One look at her told Lara all she needed to know.

So Lara stared into the eyes of her husband instead.

At the same time, Mairead and Jordan were with the park supervisor, checking through the different CCTV tapes that covered the three entrances and exits. There was another camera covering a small boating lake in case of accidents, but the lake was in the middle of the park and the playground was well away from that.

The two officers concentrated on the half-hour period before the killing and the five or ten minutes immediately after. The park had been locked down shortly after that.

Swiftly, they trawled through the cameras covering the exit nearest to the killing, but no one left via that route during that time. The second camera was similarly checked and then the third, but it was the same story there, meaning either the killer had left the park by some other means, perhaps forcing a way through the thick hedges that surrounded it on all sides.

Or the killer was still in there.

Specialist officers next conducted an inch by inch search. The trajectory of the bullet was quickly established, leading to a small copse of trees just a few metres from the playground. They'd found nothing there, as they'd expected. This killer seemed nothing if not professional.

But that didn't mean there wouldn't be some trace left behind. A tiny scrap of cloth where a sleeve caught on a branch perhaps, a shoe print, something – anything.

All the time updated progress reports were being sent back to Lara and the rest of the team, but all spelt out the same message. So far they'd found nothing.

————

Back in the Serious Incident Unit, Jordan took over the interview with Lewis's father. Again it was standard procedure: mix up the questions and the questioner. And it gave Lara the opportunity to trawl through his phone.

She was searching through all his recent messages, any one of which might seem innocuous enough, but could be an arrangement of some kind. So far she'd found two text messages, one offering him a refund of some insurance premium he might or might not have taken out, incorrectly or otherwise, and a message from a work colleague postponing a trip the next day to a meeting on the mainland. There'd been a problem in the area, some signalling issue apparently, and there was a strong possibility it wouldn't be fixed by the morning.

Lara looked through the one-way window at Jordan, who was now one hour into the interview. As if he sensed her presence, Jordan looked back, his eyes saying it all. Something was already telling Jordan that this interview, and this possible suspect, was a dead end too.

At this point Lara looked down at the father's phone again, an idea suddenly forming. In amongst the apps on the home screen was one for the National Rail Service. Swiftly Lara accessed it, then inputted some journey details. She waited a moment for the app to process the information.

Then she stared at the results on the screen.

———

Twenty minutes later, Lara was leading a break-in. The door was swiftly breached courtesy of some of the station's Ghostbusters, more popularly known as Ghosties, officers with steel battering rams.

Lara moved inside, taking care not to touch anything. The flat was unoccupied, as she'd expected. Donning protective gloves, Lara moved into the bedroom and opened the wardrobe door, where empty shelves mocked her stare. A small, and similarly empty, chest of drawers told the same story. Lara stood in the middle of the bedroom, her mind now running at a thousand miles an hour.

Tony Stone – Beth's immediate senior officer and the man to whom she'd logged the advance notice of her trip to the park with Harper – might have intended to travel to Brighton that day to take care of the rogue Category A, but he hadn't got there by his intended method of ferry and train at least. All trains on the south coast had been cancelled that morning by the signalling problems that had prompted the text to Lewis's father. Tony's car was still parked outside his house. They hadn't been able to reach him on either his work or personal mobile, and now all his clothes seemed to have been cleared from his flat too.

Within hours of the murder of a small and vulnerable girl whose care he'd been overseeing, Tony Stone seemed to have disappeared.

CHAPTER
FORTY-ONE

LARA ARRIVED in work early the next morning, but as she walked into her small office just off the main Serious Incident Room, Paula was already waiting for her.

Instinctively, Lara shot a quick glance towards the window. Paula's car wasn't in the car park opposite. Lara had no idea why that small detail suddenly bothered her, but there wasn't any time to pursue it, as Paula launched onto the offensive almost immediately.

'Media Liaison are having a meltdown.'

Lara stayed silent, imagining the scale of that meltdown only too easily.

'Phil and Kate Turow could have been a burglary that went wrong. That one they could try and spin. The Chrissie killing, we just about managed to keep a lid on. Rory Adams was the easiest of all, a soldier who'd suddenly flipped. Most of the public switch off the minute they hear anything about those poor fuckers.'

Paula nodded at Lara, her face growing grimmer by the moment.

'But a small girl gunned down like that,' she continued. 'That's news. News we can't spin or hush up even if we wanted to. Apart from anything else, one of the scabby red tops has already got to the father of the little boy she was playing with and he's given them chapter and verse.'

With a sinking heart, Lara looked at an early edition of a morning daily as Paula brandished it at her.

The headline screamed in her face.

Murder of an Innocent.

Underneath was the picture of the smiling Harper cropped from the school photograph that Lara herself had shown to Jools. Jools had had no idea who Harper was. Now virtually everyone in the country was going to know exactly who she was.

'I've got a press briefing at ten o'clock. What am I going to give them?'

'We're still searching for Tony Stone.'

'Apart from offering them one of our own.'

Paula hunched closer across Lara's desk, her stare withering. 'Harper's mother was murdered a few days ago. Now Harper's been killed too. Who the hell would have that sort of grudge against this family? And why the hell didn't they just kill Harper along with her mum at the time? That had to be one fuck of a sight easier – and a fuck of a sight safer for the killer – than waiting 'til she decided she wanted to go and play pirates in some park somewhere.'

Paula kept staring at Lara, her eyes basilisk-like. 'Those are just two of the questions that are definitely going to be asked, so I'm asking you again, DI Arden, what the fuck am I going to give them?'

It wasn't an entirely unfair question, and it wasn't an entirely unexpected tactic either. It was the way most things worked, not only in the police but in most other organisations too. Paula would have been bawled out herself by her own senior officer, probably in the early hours when the first edition of that scabby red-top came out. The next call from a panicky Media Liaison officer would only have added to the heat. Now Lara was getting that heat from Paula in turn. Later that morning Lara herself might even turn some of that self-same heat on officers in the Serious Incident Room.

It wasn't just passing the buck. It was also an attempt to keep everyone firing on all cylinders, to keep brains razor-sharp in case one small lead, one tiny piece of vital information slipped through minuscule cracks in tired minds and the killer of an innocent slipped through after it.

Then, suddenly, the door banged open behind them and a breathless Jordan appeared. He didn't look at Paula, didn't even seem to see her.

'We've found him.'

Lara stared back at him.

'Tony Stone. He's been picked up by the border police trying to board a ferry in Hull.'

Paula moved to the door, nodding at Lara as she did so. She now had the main plank in her upcoming statement. A suspect who had to remain nameless for now was about to be taken into custody, where he would be helping police with their inquiries. It wasn't much, but it meant she wouldn't look like a total incompetent.

Lara followed Jordan to the door, but before she did so she shot another quick glance towards the car park, now filling up with vehicles as other officers arrived.

Paula could have arrived by any means that morning, of course. There could be nothing sinister in her car not being there.

Just as there might well be nothing sinister in Lara finding her in her office. She shot a quick look back at her desk as they moved out onto the corridor. So far as she could remember everything was as she'd left it the previous evening. But as they moved down the corridor, Lara couldn't help wondering just how long Paula had been in her office before she'd arrived.

And what she might have been doing in the time she was in there.

CHAPTER
FORTY-TWO

WHENEVER LARA HAD THOUGHT about Hull previously, which admittedly hadn't been that often, the only image she could ever conjure up was of naked men and women. Three thousand, two hundred of them, in fact. This was the number famously assembled by the American artist Spencer Tunick for his *Sea of Hull* art installation.

On one single day a few years previously, and under the artist's personal direction, those three thousand, two hundred soon-to-be-naked men and women had all been corralled into an area circumscribed by Alfred Gelder Street on the one side and the Scale Lane Bridge on the other.

Then, and still under the artist's personal direction, the volunteers had stripped off, before painting their skin with one of four shades of blue body paint, each hue inspired by the city's seafaring heritage. Then those few thousand naked bodies simply lay down.

The intention, according to the artist, was to juxtapose the human form against the public spaces around them, conjuring new textures and shapes, metamorphosing the contours of those bodies into ripples of the sea. The images had been disseminated far and wide. It became a big news story and provided a massive boost to the city's profile as well as the bank balance of its various bars and restaurants.

Driving along that same street, hours after leaving the island, and looking out over that same bridge, Lara didn't see any naked bodies, which she fervently hoped, as she seated herself opposite an already mutinous-looking Tony Stone, was to be the only disappointment of the day.

———

'Why the sudden flight, Tony? Why were you walking out on your job – your flat – your life?'

'I wasn't walking out on anything. I was going on holiday, for fuck's sake.'

'By yourself?'

Lara stayed silent, letting Jordan do the talking, just as she'd done with Mairead and Kieran Walters. Like then, it gave her the chance to watch, to observe.

'I do it a lot. Go on holiday by myself. Check if you like.'

'I do sometimes too. Once I've put in my holiday dates, cleared them with my senior officers, cancelled the milk and the papers – only you hadn't done any of that, had you? You'd just taken off.'

'I don't have a milk delivery. Who does these days, for fuck's sake? And I buy my newspaper from the same shop I collect my milk.'

'The Protection Unit had no idea you were going away.'

'Then there was a cock-up. I filed the dates three weeks ago.'

Tony nodded down at his mobile, an email displayed on the screen, a terse note detailing his holiday start date and the date he'd be returning. It had been accessed by Tony from the sent folder on his server, but there was no record of it ever being received.

Either it was still floating around cyberspace waiting to land or Tony had mocked it up after he'd been detained by the border police. Tony's computer was being looked at by the tecchies back in the Serious Incident Unit, but so far anyway there was nothing to suggest that the email had been added to Tony's outbox after the day it had, apparently, been sent.

'You didn't even tell Beth you were going away.'

'Wrong.'

'OK, you told her you were travelling to talk to a Category A.'

'I never got there. Problem on the trains. I contacted a colleague to meet him instead. Check and you'll find that email too. I sent it before I hired a car at the ferry terminal.'

'You also didn't tell Beth you were planning on travelling to the continent today.'

'No.'

Lara, finally, broke in. 'Why not?'

Tony looked back at her, cool. 'Have you got a boyfriend?'

Lara answered immediately. 'No.'

'Have you ever had one?'

Lara answered immediately again. 'Yes.'

'When you gave him a blowjob, did you swallow or spit?'

By Lara's side, Jordan tensed as Lara herself just eyed him. Tony had made his point. And Lara didn't need to say it, but she said it anyway. For the record.

'Because it was none of her business, right?'

Tony just nodded back.

Lara let it lie.

'You received the email about Harper being taken to the park?'

'Yes.'

'But you didn't respond.'

'Is that a statement or a question?'

'Why didn't you respond?'

'Because I had other things on my mind.'

'Sorting out the Category A? And your holiday?'

'Correct.'

'Your clients – what do you think of them?'

Tony paused, for the first time a question seeming to take him unawares. But he got the point nonetheless.

There were actually very few innocent souls in amongst Tony and Beth's usual clientele. Most of the people they looked after were criminals themselves, often turning Queen's evidence to negotiate a lighter sentence. Venal lowlifes doing deals to put away slightly more venal lowlifes. It would have been a miracle if Tony hadn't felt more than usually jaundiced when it came to most of the clients he had to oversee during the course of a long and more than occasionally trying working day.

'Harper was a sweet little kid. I've no idea what her mum was mixed up in or why she'd have been targeted like that.'

Tony eyed his two interviewers, still seated opposite. 'Maybe we'll find out when her killer does a deal with you lot and us poor bastards are told to look after them.'

Lara studied Tony again, letting the silence stretch as she did so. His fabled bad temper was certainly on view now for all to see. He was gaining zero marks in the charm school stakes too, but they weren't there to warm to his winning personality. They were there to work out whether he could have had anything to do with the hit on Harper.

Harper hadn't positively identified her mother's killer as male or female. It could be, despite all Lara's suspicions, that this killer was a different sicko they now had to nail.

All they did know was that Tony was one of the very few individuals who had prior knowledge of Harper's whereabouts at the time she was killed. There were others, but the combination of his close contact with the murdered girl and his sudden apparent flight in the wake of her death had very definitely put him in prime position in the suspect stakes.

Lara looked out of a nearby window, glimpsing in the distance the same bridge they'd passed just an hour or so before. She still couldn't see any naked bodies. Suddenly her mobile flashed, an incoming call alert. Moving out of the interview room, she took the call, which was from Mairead, who'd been digging into Tony Stone's finances.

It seemed that Tony Stone had been in receipt of several windfalls lately; large sums of money, always paid in cash and all deposited in one or another of what had turned out to be his various savings accounts.

The last such windfall had been credited on the very morning Harper had been killed.

CHAPTER
FORTY-THREE

JORDAN WATCHED as Lara sipped her warm white wine.

They'd made it back from the mainland just in time for what used to be called last orders back in the day. Or at least, back in Jordan's day. These days bars stayed open for ever. He certainly hadn't heard anyone ringing a bell and calling out a ten minute warning for years. The twenty-four/seven lifestyle, as he'd heard it called. More and more time for more and more people to get more and more wrecked.

Not that they'd actually made it to any bar. Despite both officers having been on the road for over fourteen hours, they'd returned to the office to collate all the data they'd managed to assemble so far. But in recognition of a reasonably promising day at least, Lara had cracked open a bottle of wine that had been lurking in the back of one of the now-deserted Serious Incident Room's cupboards.

Tony Stone was still being held by the police in Hull while more investigations were mounted into his unexpectedly inflated finances. Tony had been tasked on the payments himself, but once again they'd just endured a tirade of abuse at what he clearly saw to be an unwarranted intrusion into purely private matters. So he'd been left to cool his heels while they all tried to work out if his response was the justifiable outrage of a totally innocent man or something else.

But one additional discovery had shaded things very much more in the direction of the latter than the former. Because Tony had a prior connection with one of the murder victims. Ben's father, Phil, had been caught up in a crime sting some years before. After his arrest, and with his wife in custody being closely questioned herself, Ben and Jools, then just toddlers, had been taken into the protection programme. It had been a misunderstanding, a mistake; Phil had been cleared of all charges some few days later and the children had been returned. But for those first few days Tony Stone had once again been principal carer to Ben and Jools, the same role he'd also assumed for the now-dead Harper.

All of which had definitely lightened the mood on that long drive back down to the south coast. For the first time in these maddeningly opaque cases there was a lead to pursue, and Lara's suggestion of a drink by way of a nightcap only added to the general good spirits.

That warmer mood and those lightened spirits lasted, so far as Jordan was concerned, exactly for one single sip of white wine.

'So how has it been?'

Jordan looked back at her, momentarily puzzled.

'I wasn't going to say anything...' Lara hesitated. 'To be honest, I haven't needed to. You've looked better these last couple of days than you've looked in the whole of the last few months.'

Lara paused, perhaps reluctant to spoil the mood, but going to spoil it nonetheless. 'Then I came across this.'

Jordan looked down at a print-out taken from Lara's pocket. With a sinking heart he recognised his own warrant number on the top. Printed below were details of the Bentley he'd been checking out, the car he'd watched whisk Coco away those few evenings before.

Jordan looked back at his senior officer. He didn't ask how Lara had come across it. In truth there were any number of ways an inquiry by an officer on her team could have been flagged for her attention.

The point wasn't how, and they both knew it.

The point was, why.

Lara continued. 'The car's registered to a known lowlife who's apparently very much living on borrowed time. Drugs Squad thinks he's going to lead them to a tasty importer they've had their eye on for a while. That certainly makes him of interest to Drugs Squad, but we don't actually have any interest in this individual.'

Lara looked at him, not needing to even frame her next question.

So why was Jordan so interested in him?

'It's not what you think.'

Jordan stopped, Lara's eyes saying it all. She'd really expected better than that.

Jordan paused a moment longer. And then, suddenly, out it came. The whole story.

Himself, Edie and Coco.

And he told Lara the lot too. Edie's determinedly individualistic attitude to parenting. Coco oscillating between the pair of them after their break-up like some kind of teenage shuttlecock.

All those evenings he'd spent parked up metres from the former family home, maintaining an ever more impotent watch on his old front door.

Jordan even told her about Coco's asthma attacks, which had increased in severity and frequency in the last couple of years and would only keep on increasing too, given her current lifestyle.

And he also told her about his equally impotent vigil those few nights before as he watched his only daughter climb into a car that cost more money than he'd be able to save in a lifetime, to be driven away to God knows where, to mix with God knows who, to do only God knew what because Jordan certainly didn't.

Lara stayed silent all the way through, and as Jordan finally ground to a finish he felt a wave of self-recrimination wash over him.

He'd kept quiet about this ever since his break-up with Edie. Now he'd just fed the one person in the Unit with the power to make or break his career with the inside track on the seemingly insoluble mess in which his life was currently mired.

Jordan looked at Lara as she studied him some more. But then the strangest thing happened. He suddenly felt relief.

New options and possibilities started to dance before his eyes. If this was to signal the end of what had become a more than usually testing career, would that be such a disaster? He'd burnt so many bridges lately that maybe this was what he he actually needed right now – to burn them all; and maybe that's why he'd launched so fulsomely into that self-destructive rant to the one person in the world who could comprehensively destroy him, because maybe deep down he simply wanted out.

Which was when the second strangest thing happened. Jordan suddenly realised that while Lara was still staring at him, there was a very different look in her eyes, one he hadn't seen before.

And because Jordan had absolutely no idea how to decode that look, he put down his own glass of warm white wine and went to the toilet.

When he came back, Lara was gone.

———

As she moved out onto the street, Lara knew that Jordan was probably watching from the office window. She knew he'd probably watch her long after she'd turned the corner ahead and hailed the cab that was to take her the few miles home. She could almost see the bewilderment etched into the hunched shape of his shoulders.

Briefly, she'd been tempted to walk all the way to clear her head, but it couldn't be cleared and she knew it, and that was because a very different figure was now swimming before her eyes. Now it wasn't a colleague she'd only known a few years, but who could so easily have just become more than that.

Georgia, her sister, always did this. She always made her appearance at times like these, summoned out of the ether like an invisible witness, a silent, accompanying ghost.

And the moment she did so, Lara was back again to that frightened and lost young girl on a station platform, standing next to another equally frightened and lost young girl, the two of them facing a world that had suddenly turned strange and cold.

Something had crystallised inside Lara and Georgia that day. In Lara's case it led to a determination never to find herself in that position again. And the way to do that was simple, because something closed tight inside her that day too. Trust and belief evaporated. From that moment on she looked at the world through eyes that were forever wary, as if she knew, somehow, it would always let her down.

Maybe these spectral appearances by her sister were her mind's way of reminding her of that silent resolution. A warning to Lara to never fully let down her guard, along with a reminder of what could happen if she did so.

What happened back then hadn't had the same effect on Georgia, and with a jolt Lara suddenly realised she was overdue a visit to a place that had been her sister's home for perhaps too long now. Where Lara had gone inwards, Georgia reached out, to everyone and to everything. She latched onto one relationship after another in much the same way she grasped at one drug after another. She'd continued to believe the world might contain within it the salvation the young Lara had simply ceased to believe existed that day. Somehow Lara had known that from that moment on they were going to be alone in the world, but Georgia had never accepted it.

Lara looked out from the cab window onto the street. She knew Jordan wouldn't understand why she'd left so abruptly after that one single drink. Why she'd moved away just at the time anyone might reasonably have expected the opposite. Maybe he'd already written her off as some kind of inadequate, a woman incapable of reaching out to anyone. He wouldn't understand; how could he? He probably thought he simply didn't count enough to warrant even an explanation, but if he didn't count, she could have stayed with him all night.

But he'd started to, and that was why she hadn't.

CHAPTER
FORTY-FOUR

WE SNUCK out again late the next afternoon when everyone else was at prayer. That strange, half-size windmill was all we'd been able to think about all night.

We left Kenwood separately as always — two children together would have been easy to spot. One child on his or her own could have been sent out into the grounds on some errand or other. We met by a large oak tree with branches that hung down to the ground forming a natural shelter, an enclosed retreat where nothing and no one — hopefully — could intrude. We buried some small keepsakes in a hole in the earth floor — an old skipping rope I'd found, as well as a small ring that Finn had managed to keep, one of his mum's few possessions, and some of my hacked and still-braided black hair. Finn also had a small camera that developed pictures all by itself, and we took some photos of the two of us and buried them too. Then we went on to the windmill and played again, like last time.

After another hour or so the light was beginning to fade and it was time to get back. We turned, reluctantly, towards the door, which was when, suddenly, it opened, and there he was.

One of the black-robed masters.

Looking in on us.

He stared at Finn first and then at me, and then he began to take off his belt. But it wasn't to whip us. We could both see in his eyes he had a very different sort of punishment in mind.

As he kept staring at me, his fleshy lips already starting to pucker, Finn stepped forward, trying to block his path, but the black-robed master just swatted him out of the way much as you'd swat a fly. Finn crashed to the ground, blood pouring from one of his ears, then I lost sight of him because the large bulk of the black-robed master was suddenly all I could see.

He clamped one hand round my unformed breasts, digging in deep and tight until I could hardly breathe. I tried to push him off but I couldn't. He was too strong. All the time he was hissing at me, telling me what we were always told, that I was a dirty river girl and that I had to learn. All the while his other hand was scrabbling inside my skirt, pushing up between my legs, searching for an opening, and when he found it I thought I was going to pass out because then he forced his fist inside.

Outside I could now hear a strange sound, a desperate creaking sound, but that was drowned out by the black-robed master hissing at me again, telling me that I'd thank him for this, that this was a lesson that would last me a lifetime.

Then I heard that strange creaking sound again.

Later, I'd discover that Finn had crept outside, blood still pouring from his ear from the black-robed master's blow, but not to run away. He'd picked up a stray branch from the ground, and, hooking it behind one of the blades, he'd used it as a lever to force the blade forward. Protesting all the time, the wood started to bend. Then, suddenly, the blade separated from its housing and crashed to the ground.

Back inside, the black-robed master was trying to force more and more of his fist inside me, opening me up further and further, but then suddenly he stopped and he fell to the side, choking now and gasping, horribly.

I struggled to a sitting position and stared down at him. He was never going to savage another child as he'd just tried to savage me.

The wooden blade from the windmill that Finn had just driven into his skull was going to make sure of it.

CHAPTER
FORTY-FIVE

OK, it was childish and she knew it.

Not that Coco would ever have admitted it, definitely not to Kris and hardly even to herself. But she just couldn't help it.

The truth was there were lots of things she could have loved about the luxury motor that was currently wafting her along. She could have thrilled to the sensuous touch of the hand-stitched leather or the acres of walnut fascia, all taken from just the one tree, according to the breathless sales pitch her new boyfriend had proudly repeated to her one day.

She could have felt her spirits soar as the power from the twin turbos planted the back wheels firmly down on the tarmac while the bonnet rose, catapulting them past traffic that seemed almost stationary by comparison.

But all she cared about, all she craved indeed when she was out with her brand new boyfriend in his brand new car, were the looks.

The long straight they'd just travelled along had been a chance for the car to flex its muscles, a brief surge of speed made possible by a gap between two speed cameras, powering the sports Bentley from the statutory thirty miles an hour to over a hundred and twenty in almost a literal blink of the eye, but Coco couldn't help it. All she felt was a sense of relief as they paused at a set of traffic lights. Because then she'd be seen again. Then she'd feel those eyes on her once more.

Coco looked round. Turn right and they'd be heading down to Freshwater and, beyond, to the Needles. Turn left and they'd be heading back towards the capital. She debated for a moment, then nodded across at her companion beside her.

'Let's go left.'

Her boyfriend grinned, cancelling the right hand indicator and gunning the car left instead. No one behind them protested the sudden change of mind. If a Ford Mondeo had forced the cars behind to jam on their brakes while a driver cut in front of them there'd have been a dawn chorus of horns. But a Bentley was different, and Coco had realised that the very first time he'd picked her up in it. Different rules of the road seemed to apply. It was all down to those looks again.

Coco settled herself back on her seat. Her eyes stared ahead but her peripheral vision checked every sideways glance, every stare of envious appreciation. This was the kind of car that was noticed, meaning the people inside were noticed too, and she loved it.

'It's a fact. Highest number of cocaine users in the northern hemisphere.'

Kris had been talking for the last ten minutes. He loved his facts and figures. Coco had no idea where he unearthed them, but each journey they'd ever taken was punctuated with stuff he'd either been told or picked up from some online trawl.

'And where does all their piss end up?' Kris gestured out of the window, giving Coco another chance to glance outside too. 'Down in the sewers.'

Which wasn't strictly true, Coco silently observed, as she watched a tramp across the street relieve himself in a boarded up shop doorway. But it was a minor quibble.

'The proportion of coke in the water down there is massive, and you know how they know that?'

The question was rhetorical. Coco was going to be told anyway. Sometimes, she wondered if Kris did this even when there was no one else there. Just him and his car and his facts and figures.

'One of the guys working down in one of the sewers collapsed one day. Heart attack. They got him out, rushed him into hospital, which is when they found all those traces of coke in his system. When he comes round he threatens to sue the hospital – seems he's a religious nut as well as a health freak – his body is a temple and all that, so why the fuck he's poking round in other people's piss and shit all day is something else, but he's still not having it. Who's been pumping him full of all this stuff, he wants to know?'

Kris settled on his seat.

'One week later, the same thing happens to another worker on the same shift. He suddenly collapses too, and they find the same levels of coke in his bloodstream. So then they investigate, take some readings, and that's when they realise. There's more coke down in the sewers than there is in the carsy in Bar Zub.'

Coco drifted again. It had all started when she was small. Her dad had taken her to a dance school in Spring Vale. She really didn't take to it at first. She was shy, one of the reasons Dad thought it might be a good idea. Bring her out of her shell.

Coco skulked around the back of the class for weeks, keeping herself out of the limelight, letting the other girls and the occasional boy grab the plum parts. She was given a role in the chorus for an upcoming show instead, which suited her just fine, but then came the first performance, and the one thing she was totally unprepared for.

The applause.

It hit her like an Exocet. Wave after wave of clapping and cheering and whistles. Everywhere she looked she saw people looking back at her, smiling and laughing, cheering and whistling.

And from that moment it was all she craved. She didn't care

what she did. All she wanted was that one hit at the end. The best, the most potent drug of all. The sound of people clapping.

'Here.'

Coco nodded to her left, indicating a small side road leading down to a row of shops. Kris grinned.

'Knew that'd put you in the mood.'

Once again, Coco didn't contradict him. She'd already forgotten all about sewage workers and heart attacks. But she didn't stop him as he parked the car, the soft burble from the engine evaporating around them. She just watched as he lifted one of the centre consoles and extracted a privacy phone, whatever that was. He'd explained it once, but it had gone in one ear and out the other. Then he carefully opened the phone to reveal a small stash of white powder.

Coco leant back on the ivory leather. Right at that moment, she felt invincible. Almost superhuman. As if all the normal rules ordinary people lived by simply didn't apply. She was wrapped in a cocoon, as if she was up on that stage again, luxuriating in all those admiring stares.

Coco was wrong, of course. She wasn't invincible at all. She was only too human, in fact, and she wasn't wrapped in any sort of cocoon either. The truth was that right at that moment she was in the most extreme danger she'd ever faced in the whole of her short life, but she didn't realise that.

Not until it was way, way, too late.

CHAPTER
FORTY-SIX

THE BRIEFING WAS SCHEDULED for nine the next morning.

There were two items on the agenda. The first was an update on the investigation into the murder of Harper, the second an update on the protection officer, Tony Stone.

There was a third item on the agenda too that morning, but that was a strictly private matter, which was the potentially changed relationship between Lara and Jordan. And how that potentially changed relationship might affect or influence their working relationship inside the Serious Incident Team.

For Lara it was simple. It would not. Walking into the office that morning, she'd know within the next thirty seconds whether the same held true for Jordan. Nothing might have happened that previous night, but they both knew it could. Only Lara knew that maybe it should.

Paula was already in place at the head of the room, papers on a table in front of her, a Media Liaison officer at her side. The brutal and public manner of Harper's execution – there was no other word for it – and so soon after the killing of her mother, had ensured it had stayed a favourite among the red tops for the last day or so and would remain so for at least the next few days to come.

Those of a cynical disposition might have pointed out that Harper was also white and pretty. It shouldn't make a difference, but Lara had been around too many other murder investigations to pretend it didn't. An older kid of a different ethnic type would have been lucky to merit a passing mention at the foot of the classifieds.

Lara felt herself still for a moment as Jordan looked across at her. He was at his usual desk, papers in front of him too. Briefly, Lara felt a flare inside as his gaze settled on her for a second, no more. Certainly nowhere near long enough for anyone else in that room to register anything. Then Jordan went back to studying the papers before him.

This meant that Lara had her answer in even less than thirty seconds. She also had a shrewd suspicion that if she didn't ever refer to the previous night, he wouldn't either. Lara crossed to her desk, unsure whether that made her relieved or depressed. Plenty of time to work it out later.

Paula selected Tony Stone as the first item on the agenda, perhaps because – and somewhat depressingly – there was little to report. The combination of his inside knowledge of Harper's whereabouts and his apparent attempt at flight around the time of the killing had definitely quickened the team's collective pulses. The unexpectedly munificent state of his finances and the connection to Ben and Jools Turow had quickened them even more.

But there'd been little else in the way of excitement since. The tech boys had still not been able to establish whether Tony's email about his holiday had been sent prior to his apparent disappearance as he was claiming, or afterwards in an attempt to cover his tracks. His employment record had also revealed no question marks against his conduct or character.

Tony's intransigence when it came to refusing to answer any questions regarding his private life was also double-edged. It provoked suspicion certainly, but if he knew he was innocent, why waste time and effort convincing anyone else?

But it had given them the perfect reason to keep him in custody while his flat had been visited and his home computer examined. It hadn't yielded anything in the way of leads as yet, but that didn't mean it wouldn't.

'Thoughts?'

Lara was the first to proffer a suggestion. It was something she'd been turning over in her mind all the way in.

That, and Jordan.

'Let him go.'

All eyes swivelled her way, including Jordan's. Fleetingly, Lara registered his stare again. Fleetingly, again, she felt the same flare inside. Keeping her eyes firmly fixed on Paula, Lara rolled on.

'We can't keep him much longer anyway, and if he did have anything to do with Harper's murder he won't be any good to us in custody. If he's back out on the street at least we can monitor his movements, see where he goes, maybe who he contacts.'

Paula nodded back. She'd already come to the same conclusion herself.

Lara continued.

'The tech guys have already put traces on the computer they retrieved from his flat and a remote tracker on his mobile. He's not going to be able to do so much as dial up a pizza in the next few days without us knowing what topping he's ordered. So let him run. He won't get very far, and where he does go might just give us something.'

Mairead cut in, this still clearly a knotty issue for her.

'What about all that money in his account?'

Across the room Paula checked the notes before her.

'It's still largely unaccounted for. Most of the deposits are cash and some of them go back years. There doesn't seem to be any sort of pattern to them and there certainly haven't been any more after the credit on the day of Harper's murder.'

Paula paused.

'Something else we're just going to have to monitor for now.'

She was about to move onto Harper herself when Jordan cut across.

'I've been thinking about Rory Adams.'

All eyes now swivelled his way. If he was aware of Lara's eyes on him now too, he gave no sign.

Paula stared at him, puzzled.

'What's Rory Adams got to do with Harper?'

For a moment, Lara's heart lurched. Was Jordan about to repeat the strictly private theory she'd rehearsed to him?

'Adams has a record as long as my arm. And that record and his files would be accessible to Tony Stone's department as well as to ours. If he is in the frame for Harper, that's only one of six murders on our patch in the last few days.'

Only Lara caught the quick flick of his eyes her way. Or, at least, so she hoped.

'I'm not saying there is a connection. But if there is, then maybe that's how Stone came across Adams as well.'

Paula paused again, then nodded. It was indeed the most tenuous of connections, but it was still probably worth checking out.

For a moment silence settled across the room. Then, and unable to completely hide a small show of reluctance, Paula picked up the next file on the table. What to do about the newly enigmatic protection officer had been relatively easy to decide, and all the leads suggested by that briefing, such as they were, would be followed up.

How to play all they next had to play with Harper was very definitely something else.

'The key question, and the only question the press are asking right now, is timing. That's something they can't get their heads round and something we can't help them with, because, as everyone in this room knows, we can't either. There simply can't be two separate killers here – of Chrissie and her little girl – because frankly that beggars belief. The two murders are obviously related, but if the intention was always to kill Harper then why did the killer, be that Stone or someone working with Stone, let her slip through their fingers when she could so easily have been killed along with her mother when there were no other witnesses around?'

Paula carried on talking, but suddenly Lara wasn't listening.

'Why wait for a chance decision to visit a public park a few days later? Why kill her there when there had to be an infinitely increased chance of the killer being spotted?'

All of sudden, Lara had it. As Paula continued, she knew.

'Is he or she taunting us in some way? Look what I can do? Look how easily I can take someone out from literally under your noses?'

By Paula's side, the Media Liaison officer stepped in.

'That's not just DCI Davies, by the way. That's from a comment column in one of tomorrow's red-tops. And that's the least lurid of the speculation we've managed to access so far.'

But then the officer stopped as Lara suddenly cut across.

'She wasn't of use anymore.'

Now all eyes turned back towards Lara. It was the only possible explanation that made any sort of sense.

'It's nothing to do with timing. It's nothing to do with the killer flexing his or her muscles either. It's Harper. It's all down to her.'

Across the room, Mairead began to still. She'd also witnessed Harper's return to her old family home that day.

'Harper couldn't remember. She couldn't remember her mother, she couldn't remember the murder, she couldn't even remember who she was or where she'd grown up. She'd been wiped blank. So she wasn't any good anymore.'

Paula cut across. 'Any good for what?'

'What this killer wants.'

'Which is?'

This time Mairead cut across.'Legacy.'

Lara nodded back.

'This was a crime that would have stretched down

throughout the rest of Harper's life, maybe down through other lives too. Who could know how badly all this would have twisted her out of shape?'

Lara shook her head and continued. 'But Harper wasn't twisted out of shape because she couldn't remember a single thing about it. So is that what we're missing? Was that why she was let go? The point wasn't the mother, it was the daughter. The killer wanted to create a survivor, but what was the point if the survivor didn't even know she was one?'

Paula looked at Lara for a long, long moment. She didn't look at Mairead at all. And despite the sudden rush of blood that had provoked her outburst, Lara was all too aware there was something in that look she could replay a million times and still not even begin to decode.

The room around Lara remained silent.

And Lara remained silent now too.

CHAPTER
FORTY-SEVEN

EDIE HAD ALWAYS HATED her mum, although maybe hate was too strong a word.

She'd never liked her, that was for sure, and she was certain the feeling was mutual. There was just something in the way her mum always used to look at her. As a child, Edie always felt as if she was a mild disappointment. And as she grew up that disappointment went from mild to overt.

So of course she gravitated towards her dad. Yes, he was a bit rough and ready – a bit more than rough and ready, if truth be told – and in all sorts of ways, including his accent, behaviour and manners. And this only provoked more disappointment on her mum's part, this time directed his way.

Edie always thought it was down to the difference in class. Mum had married a good couple of rungs down the social ladder and never stopped reminding her life partner of that unalterable fact. Little comments about milk cartons being left out on the table, pointed requests not to watch the TV during the evening meal, not to mention constantly referring to that meal as supper and the midday meal as lunch. Coming from good working-class stock, he'd never quite managed to rid himself of his lifetime habit of calling lunch dinner and the evening meal tea.

Just as he'd never been able to stop himself putting the milk in a cup along with the tea bag rather than pouring the water in first.

Edie vowed that would never happen with her kids. And OK, she'd only had the one, but that made it even more important that she never made her feel the object of even the mildest disappointment. So all through her childhood she'd praised Coco, bolstered her, tried to make her feel special, tried to make her feel that her mum was as much a friend to her as a parent.

And it had worked. She could feel herself wafting along on a cloud of mutual adoration as she walked along hand in hand with her precious little girl.

Jordan warned her it couldn't last. He had three younger sisters and he'd watched them run their mum ragged when they'd hit their teens, but Edie again vowed inside that she and Coco wouldn't journey that well-worn path. She knew that she just had to hang on in there, to be the support – and yes, OK, the almost exclusively uncritical support – she'd always been for Coco and then it wouldn't matter if her little girl was three or thirteen.

Even Edie had to acknowledge it was easier when she was closer to the former rather than the latter, but that was still no reason in her book for Jordan to suddenly turn into some kind of Victorian patriarch. And to make Coco's life a misery by his constant lectures and endless questions.

Maybe it was being a copper. Maybe, dealing with the worst that life had to offer all the time, he automatically looked for the worst at home as well. And it hadn't got any easier after he'd moved out from home either.

Jordan usually called at least three or four times a week, and there was always that same note in his voice when she told him Coco was out somewhere. He didn't actually come straight out and demand to know where she was, how long she'd been away and when she'd be getting back, nothing so blunt or blatant, but it was still all he wanted to know.

In the old days – the days immediately following their break-up – those sort of not-so-veiled inquiries often provoked screaming matches. Things had settled since, but they were still both only too aware of the tensions simmering beneath the surface. So if Jordan knew that Coco hadn't come back at all last night, he'd probably have mobilised the SAS.

The first time she'd stayed over at some friend's house and had forgotten to tell her, even Edie had been concerned, she had to admit. But then Coco had waltzed in the next morning, all smiles and gossip about the events of the previous night and Edie knew she'd do exactly the same again now too. Sometime later today, they'd sit down in the kitchen over a cup of coffee and have a lovely giggly update on her latest escapade, the sort of lovely giggly update Edie had always craved with her own mum.

Coco was never going to be met with a torrent of reproach the moment she opened the door, because Edie and her daughter were friends.

Special friends.

And always would be.

———

Coco had come round a few moments before. For a sudden, disorientating instant she had no idea where she was or even who she was. For that sudden and bewildering moment, panic flooded the cracks in her memory.

Then she felt the leather against her back and her eyes adjusted to the polished wood in front of her eyes, and she began to calm.

Coco reached into her pocket, took out her inhaler and breathed in deeply for a few seconds, beginning to calm some more as she pieced together some small details of the previous few hours – that ride around the streets, the silent stares from all those passers by, that single hit courtesy of that stash of coke.

What the hell was in it? She'd never been wiped out like that before.

Coco looked to her side, pausing as she next realised she was actually alone in the car, that Kris wasn't sparked out beside her, marooned in his own coke-induced miasma.

Then Coco stopped as she smelt it.

Something almost metallic.

Coco looked down, which was when she stopped, puzzled. Because everything about Kris's car was exactly as she'd always remembered it, but one detail was now different.

The carpets in that lovely car used to match the seats, which were an ivory shade of cream.

Now those carpets were red, and a bright red at that.

Almost blood red.

CHAPTER
FORTY-EIGHT

ENERGISED BY THAT TEAM BRIEFING, and resolutely ignoring the quizzical look from Paula that had effectively ended it – she was getting used to those by now – Lara had been doing some digging.

And within moments she was positively buzzing. Because what she'd just uncovered might just have ushered in yet another of those all-too-rare moments of euphoria that mark any possible advance in any investigation. The moment a potential pattern begins to emerge.

Then Lara came across something else.

And equally suddenly it was as if a drenching draught of the coldest water had just been emptied over her.

Five minutes previously, Lara had been following up Jordan's remark at that same team briefing, only she wasn't just checking on Rollo's records, she was also checking out Chrissie and Kieran's too.

Jordan himself was doing a house to house on Kieran's neighbours, searching for background. So far they'd uncovered little. Most of Kieran's neighbours couldn't have picked him out of an identity parade, despite a couple of them having lived next door for the last three years. Like most places these days, it was that kind of neighbourhood. Or maybe it was just that kind of time.

Lara had already established that all Jordan had said back in the briefing was correct. Rollo's record was on view to anyone who wanted to access it from inside any police station and associated departments, meaning Tony Stone would certainly have been able to see it any time he wanted.

But Chrissie didn't have a criminal record and neither did Kieran, so Lara started spreading the net wider. And now Lara stared at a printed extract from the file she'd just uncovered.

Chrissie had been involved in a road rage incident about three years before. Some lowlife scroat with too much testosterone and too small a brain decided he didn't like women drivers and cut her up coming out of Newport on her way home.

According to the report in front of Lara, Chrissie had blared her horn at him, and he had stopped his car in front of her and, directly under a CCTV camera, ripped off her driver's door mirror. He was picked up, hauled in and given a ticking off, but it didn't make much difference. Three months later he did it again, different place, different woman, same M.O.

Lara picked up another extract from another file, her pulse rate quickening just as it had done a short time before as she read the name on the front.

Kate Turow.

By that time the lowlife scroat in question had actually crossed paths with quite a few women. He just seemed to have a thing about female drivers. But his crossing with Kate was the final straw. This time he wasn't just given a ticking off, he was flung into the cell for a night and hauled up before the magistrates the next morning. The CPS decided it was worth a punt and contacted Chrissie, asking if she wanted to submit a statement too. She did, as did Kate Turow. The two women had still never actually met so far as Lara could see, but their joint details appeared on that one file.

So now they had yet another connection, and while it still

might not be much, it might lead to the more concrete link Lara was fast becoming convinced was behind these seemingly disparate murders.

Which was when Lara spotted something else.

Police records are digitally stored these days, and to access them leaves a trail. Lara had accessed Rollo's records herself that morning, as well as the ones involving Chrissie and Kate, so a trace could later be put on her activities that morning should anyone be so inclined.

But she could now see that another trail had been created first thing that morning, and this one had been activated by Jordan. For a moment Lara wondered if he'd stolen a march on her, whether – maybe acting again on all she'd said to him – he'd been searching for similar links here as well.

But Jordan hadn't been looking at Chrissie or at Kate or at Rollo. Jordan had been looking at a different case entirely. The puzzling and recent case of a lone boy abandoned on a train.

Lara kept staring at the file Jordan had accessed, the file she herself had placed on the system regarding her latter day counterpart, Milo.

Why Jordan should have taken the time and trouble to access that particular file she had absolutely no idea.

But the fact that he had concerned her.

It concerned her a lot.

CHAPTER
FORTY-NINE

Coco was still alone in the car. Both doors must be deadlocked or something; it didn't matter how many times she tried to open them, the handles moved up and down but the doors remained tight shut. She tried pressing various buttons on the dash too, and on the central panel dividing the passenger seat from the driver's, but nothing happened when she did that either.

Coco looked down. Because she wasn't, strictly speaking, alone, of course. She still had that blood staining those carpets for company.

Which was Kris's blood – it had to be. So what was happening here? Had she become caught up in something he'd done that had gone disastrously wrong and this was the grisly retribution? While Coco was out of it, while her mind was being blasted by whatever the fuck had been in that coke, had Kris been attacked, maybe even killed as she was just lying there in a drugged stupor in the passenger seat beside him?

Coco had no idea. All she did know was that whatever had happened to him, it had definitely happened right here, otherwise how did all that blood get there?

But where was Kris now? And where the hell indeed was

Coco? All she could see out of the window were trees, their dark heavy branches overhanging the car on all sides. She didn't even know if it was night or day at first; the dense foliage was blocking out everything. But then the leaves suddenly fluttered as a stray gust of wind caught them, which spooked her massively at first – she thought someone was actually tapping on the window – before she saw it was just those same branches. Through a small gap in the foliage she could see light, so it was still day. But what time it was and even what day it was she had no idea.

Unaccountably, from nowhere an image of her dad flashed before her. Even more unaccountably, she felt a brief surge of anger flare inside.

Where was he?

Why wasn't he here?

Why wasn't he helping?

Even as the child inside momentarily took over, she knew it was stupid, of course. It wasn't just the fact that he couldn't possibly know where she was – because if she didn't, then how could anyone else? – it was the fact that all she'd done in the last year was push him away. She hadn't let him know even for a moment where she was going at any time or what she was doing.

Previously that had been a point of pride. She'd smirked silently in school as classmates recounted yet another blazing row with total pains of parents, mentally congratulating herself on sidestepping that particular rite of passage. So far as her dad was concerned, she'd frozen him out so completely she barely saw him these days. Yes, she'd catch sight of him now and again, usually parked up in his car a few hundred metres down the street as she left the house, but he never approached. He knew what he'd get if he did.

Only now she wanted him to approach. Now she just wanted him to open that car door, take her out of this expensive prison and take her home. All of sudden she wanted more than anything for him to make her safe.

Coco shifted position on the leather upholstery, keeping her feet on the seat, not wanting any part of her body to have any contact with that blood below.

And what made her current situation even more difficult was the certain knowledge that if she'd very much choked off any sort of rescue attempt on her father's part, she'd totally disqualified any similar attempt from Mum. It had become another point of pride between them that Coco could come and go as she pleased. Not for them any tiresome teenage tantrums – they were beyond all that and always had been. Mum trusted her, even if strictly speaking Coco hadn't ever done very much to earn that trust. The upshot was that if she stayed out for a night or two, or even three, she could just walk back in and there'd be no questions asked.

The corollary of which was Coco's current predicament. Mum would ask no questions and so would seek no answers. Meaning Coco could remain exactly where she was for days before there was even the prospect of any sort of intervention from that quarter.

And for the first time in months, perhaps even years, a totally uncharacteristic and overwhelming emotion surged inside Coco as she actually began to yearn for an affliction that had cursed the lives of so many of her friends. She suddenly began to crave over-protective parents.

Which was when she heard the tapping on the window again. Coco jerked her head to her left, half-expecting again to see some sort of monster peering in, but there was nothing, only that same branch striking the window once more as another stray gust of wind buffeted it against the glass.

But then Coco saw something else. And now she physically blinked, because the sudden apparition was so strange and unexpected. For a moment she thought she must be imagining things, but there it was.

Coco kept staring through the trees at the unmistakable sight of a windmill, its blades moving in the wind. Then the wind stilled, the leaves dropped like a veil in front of her and the windmill was lost from view.

CHAPTER
FIFTY

MAIREAD HATED SURVEILLANCE.

Actually, that was wrong; she didn't hate the actual surveillance. Keeping watch on someone, monitoring them, tracking their movements was fine. The problem was that for the vast majority of most surveillance operations, police officers weren't doing that. They were staring at a locked door instead, much as Mairead was doing right now, staring at Tony Stone's front door from a flat across the street.

The surveillance had been rotating between spy cameras sited in a succession of tradesman's vans parked down the street and officers physically sited in that flat, accessed from a local letting agency. From inside the curtained front room the light from the TV could be seen, flickering as pictures flashed across the screen. Briefly, Mairead tried to guess what Tony might be watching – sport – one of the soaps – but it was a desultory debate. Displacement activity, more designed to distract than anything else.

It was another reason she hated this kind of surveillance. Because it meant there was too much space inside her mind, allowing demons to gather. Nothing to banish the thoughts and concerns that were daily threatening to overwhelm her.

It was all to do with her father, of course. It always was these days.

She'd had a call from his consultant the previous evening. When she saw the name on the display she'd diverted the call to answerphone. The message wasn't alarming in itself. There'd been no significant change in her father's condition or news to report, which was actually more worrying in a sense. If there was no news to report then why was he making the call?

But Mairead already knew the answer. If she'd done what she should have done and returned the call, there'd have been some seemingly innocuous chat for a few moments, then there'd be an apparently casual-sounding request that she call into the hospital to see them sometime soon. Just to talk about things.

Mairead knew what that would mean. They were approaching the end game, the stage of her father's illness when they – meaning her – needed to face facts. When someone – meaning her – had to make a decision. And as she still felt completely unable to even contemplate facing anything like those facts, let alone making any sort of decision, she hadn't returned the consultant's call.

Which was fine for today and tomorrow too, in all probability. The consultant knew she was a busy woman holding down a job that could be all consuming at times. But he was holding down a demanding job as well, with lots of calls on his time and attention. And her father was one of those more and more pressing demands.

Mairead looked across at Tony Stone's flat. Then she looked at the communal front entrance. No one had gone in or out in the last ten minutes, but she still had a niggling unease that something had changed.

Mairead looked again at the front door, at the windows in Tony's flat – and then she realised.

It was the TV. It was still on, but the pictures weren't flickering anymore. Mairead jerked up quickly from her seat. It meant that the TV wasn't on at all – what had been turned on behind those drawn curtains was a pre-programmed security device instead, which was now casting a deep blue glow over the room.

She and the rest of the Serious Incident Team knew all about such devices; they were a useful shop-bought foil designed to fool any passing burglars that there was someone inside, and if Mairead hadn't been so preoccupied by her own concerns in the last ten minutes or so she'd have spotted the switch immediately.

Mairead yelled at her companion, who dashed back from the kitchen. By that time Mairead was already out of the property and was haring down a small alleyway that led from the rear of the flats down to the nearby river.

Ahead, she could now see a figure in the distance dropping down from a walkway onto a communal garden and from there onto a riverside path.

Mairead ran like the wind as the figure ahead of her turned off the path and onto a street that led to a local retail park.

———

Klee Jukes had only been in her job a month. For most of that time she'd trailed round behind an overweight male supervisor who'd pointed out various entrances and exits, as if she couldn't read the signs herself, and who was basically as much use as a chocolate teapot when it came to any sort of hands-on training.

Not that there was too much in the way of hands-on training you could do anyway. Being a security guard in a retail park was pretty much the same as being a security guard anywhere. You kept your eyes peeled for trouble and you tried your best to contain it. So far she'd had two lost kids to contend with, a hen night depositing what remained of their kebabs on the polished tile floor of one of the upmarket stores and a couple of skateboarding teenagers. It had all been a bit tame, in truth, but suddenly all that was about to change.

Klee first saw three girls, all of them Asian but dressed in western clothes, all in their late teens or possibly early twenties, and all carrying large pink holdalls.

Behind them came a small gang of Asian boys of roughly the same age. All were hard-eyed and looked hostile. They were all carrying holdalls too.

Klee, beginning to grow uneasy, took out her radio to liaise with the control room, which was when, and from another entrance she saw about another ten girls and boys – again all in their late teens or early twenties – arriving en masse. Most of them were carrying holdalls too.

Then from the upper floor Klee suddenly saw more new arrivals, another twenty, maybe thirty, coming down towards the lower level, all the same sort of age, and within seconds the whole floor all around her was suddenly taken over.

Klee just had time to bark out an appeal for back-up when music suddenly started up from somewhere. She looked round, trying to identify the source, which was now getting louder and louder.

At the same time a lone female voice started singing, joined a moment later by another voice, also female.

Klee looked up. She could now see two girls moving up one of the escalators leading to the shops on the upper levels. She looked round to see various instruments being unpacked from the holdalls the kids had brought in with them – violins, cellos, even a double bass. At the same time, she became aware of the rest of the new arrivals peeling off their coats and anoraks to reveal the name of a choir emblazoned on identically coloured T-shirts underneath.

Moments later the rest of the kids joined in as the two lead singers, now at the very top of the escalators, completed the first verse of their song and led them into a chorus, by which time the whole scene was being captured on a multitude of different smartphones as dozens of entranced shoppers captured the impromptu flash-mob entertainment.

A couple of those same smartphones also captured a lean, lithe-looking woman sprinting into the retail park.

At least one of them captured the desperate expression on her face as she scanned the different levels, trying to see beyond the massed ranks of faces before her.

None of them captured the look of total defeat on her face as the young woman turned away.

They were too busy enjoying the show.

CHAPTER
FIFTY-ONE

DESPITE ALL HER previous best intentions, Edie was about to cross, albeit tentatively, a personal Rubicon. She was about to check up on Coco.

Edie had her cover story prepared, though. She was going to tell her daughter that there'd been a couple of messages from friends who'd been trying to reach Coco on her mobile, but who kept hitting her answer service, and that was true. But one friend in particular had just given her the opportunity she needed.

There was a big gig on at the weekend over in Freshwater. Some American singer that, to her mortification, Edie had never heard of, but she'd wasted little time in googling her name so she could have something approaching an informed chat with Coco about her when she finally came home. One of Coco's friends had called her on her home landline to say she'd managed to get a couple of tickets and did Coco want to go? If not, she'd pass the ticket on to someone else.

Edie had sent Coco a text to that effect two hours before but hadn't, again, received a reply. So now she was going to call her. Not to ask where she was, or why she hadn't called for the last day and night, nothing so crass. Just to see whether she wanted that ticket.

Edie's fingers hovered over her mobile, mentally rehearsing her opening remarks as she did so, making sure her tone sounded light, casual.

Then came the ring on the bell. Edie closed down the phone immediately and moved to the front door, a sudden spring in her step.

Was this Coco?

Her daughter had a key but she was always losing it.

Then Edie stopped as she saw the unmistakable shape of Jordan through the frosted glass insert in the door.

———

Jordan had learnt his lesson. For once he wasn't going to charge in, and he wasn't going to act the heavy-handed Victorian either, an accusation that had been levelled at him more than once in the last year or so. For this, his first actual home visit in more than two weeks, Jordan had his cover story prepared.

Coco had told them both that she wanted to learn to drive for some time now. Her seventeenth birthday was approaching, the age at which she could legally start, but insuring her on his car was equivalent to raising a king's ransom. Edie had never learnt to drive, had never seen the point. But last night Jordan had looked at Lara's old Mini, had done some research and then done some thinking.

If he invested in a car like that – a car more than forty years old – then there'd be no road tax to pay. Insurance could be done on a limited mileage basis and the rates for classic cars were always lower than for more modern hatches. Even better, if he got the right model and the car was cool, there was actually the chance of selling it for more than he paid for it in a few years' time.

An old Mini like Lara's would be good, although not a Cooper. That was way out of her league. An old Beetle would be fine in the cool stakes too.

An old Rover would probably be less so.

A quick search on a classic car internet site had identified a restored Beetle just outside Yarmouth. Jordan had printed off the details, and it was those details he was holding in his hand, pasting on a smile as the front door of his former home opened and Edie looked out at him.

———

Ten minutes later, both Edie and Jordan were silently congratulating themselves. Neither had been able to speak to the other without shouting for the last few months. But for the last ten minutes, as Edie had looked at the details of the car Jordan had brought along with him, and as he'd explained the thinking behind it, everything had been, if not sweetness and light, then close enough.

And the reason was simple, of course. The car aside, Jordan hadn't directly referred to or asked any questions about Coco.

Edie in turn hadn't stamped down on any stray reference on his part to their daughter. Coco had floated between them all the time, but that was all she'd done. She hadn't done what she'd done so many times in the past, which was fan the flames.

It was only as Jordan was leaving that the brief spectre of something even remotely approaching danger raised its unwelcome head.

'She's in school, yeah?'

Briefly, Edie hesitated, and Jordan hurried on.

'I just wondered what time she was home today, whether I should leave all this for her or call back?'

Edie struggled for a moment. Unaccountably she felt the sudden need to confide what were increasingly becoming actual fears.

Jordan looked at her, beginning to grow curious.

'Edie?'

And in that instant the moment was lost.

'Leave them. I'll make sure she takes a look when she gets in.'

Walking back to his car, which was parked just past the adjacent waterway, and composing a text all the while, Jordan felt a definite spring in his step. Maybe so far as Coco was concerned, he just had to learn to live and let live a little.

Jordan checked the text he'd just composed, then – and now with an even more pronounced spring in his step – pressed *Send*.

———

The ferry set off half an hour later.

Ordinarily Lara would have made the journey alone. The meeting was only routine anyway, an evening update in the main Police HQ on the still-fruitless search for the local S&M attacker.

But the previous day when Jordan, trying to sound casual, had suggested he tag along, Lara, trying to sound just as casual, had agreed. Underneath the coded exchange, they both knew what that suggestion was really all about. It was a chance to talk away from the office, to spend some more time together.

Lara had actually been quite excited about the simple little trip at first. The ghost-like presence of Georgia was still on her shoulder warning her of the dangers of commitment on the one hand, but those silent warnings hadn't always been heeded. Occasionally, Lara had taken the plunge. Up to now none of those relationships had worked out, but that didn't mean one wouldn't.

But Lara's mood had now plummeted, the problem being that it was too late to back out. Jordan was already on his way, as the text she'd just received had made clear.

Once on board, Jordan bought them both coffees and pastries and Lara settled on one of the seats beside him. She spent the next hour looking out at the boats and the sun as it set over the water. What she didn't do, a simple greeting aside, was exchange more than a few words with a puzzled Jordan all the way, and the reason was simple.

Where previously, sitting in their office with those nightcaps in front of them, Lara had seen a man heavily invested in his family, now all she could see was a man who'd baled out, who'd quit. A man who seemed heartbroken over a rupture with a teenage daughter, but who hadn't really done anything about it. And where before Lara couldn't help responding to a man who seemed in genuine torment, now she saw a man who just seemed to have given up; a flawed man, in fact.

Which, in the light of all she'd just discovered about his puzzling checks on a file he had absolutely no reason to access, was making her wonder whether Jordan was flawed in more ways than one.

CHAPTER
FIFTY-TWO

THE INITIAL TRAWL of the CCTV tapes had drawn a blank. A figure resembling Tony Stone was seen heading into that retail park just a few moments before a figure that was very definitely Mairead hared in after him.

Two minutes later the flash mob had descended.

The sudden appearance of that flash mob could have been a fortuitous distraction that had disorientated an already wrong-footed Mairead and handed her quarry the perfect opportunity to slip away undetected, but Lara doubted it. A quick trawl of various social media sites confirmed that the appearance of the flash mob that night had been carefully flagged. Everyone who turned up that evening knew exactly when it was taking place and where. Tony Stone could have accessed that information just as easily as any member of the impromptu choir and could just as easily have timed his exit from his flat a short distance away accordingly.

'There.'

Paula, by Lara's side, pointed at a male figure seen exiting a staircase into one of the underground car parks. The techie in the room with them froze the tape. It was the second sweep of all the available CCTV tapes they'd done, and for the first time Lara felt her breathing quicken. There was a definite resemblance. Lara and Paula watched as the figure skirted the car park, ducking behind parked cars whenever the opportunity presented itself, trying to keep out of range of the cameras as he did so, perhaps.

Then both officers sank back in their seats as a small child ran across the car park towards him, her face a picture of giggly delight before she pounced on the figure rising from behind one of the cars, who was now smiling too, their game of hide and seek over.

Lara glanced quickly at her senior officer. She'd expected a real tongue-lashing when she'd called in Tony's disappearance following her return with Jordan from the mainland. Lara wasn't carrying out the surveillance herself, but losing him like that had still happened on her watch and an officer she'd entrusted with the task had let her down.

So far it hadn't happened, which had surprised her.

That didn't mean it wouldn't.

That wouldn't surprise her at all.

'Lara.'

Jordan burst through the door once again, to the viewing room this time, pausing momentarily as he saw Paula in there too. Exalted DCIs didn't normally concern themselves with those sort of mundane security checks, but these weren't normal times, and the Harper killing wasn't exactly a normal sort of crime.

Jordan ploughed on anyway.

'Tony Stone's just turned his mobile back on.'

_____

This wasn't in the plan.

As in this really wasn't supposed to be happening.

Or to be strictly accurate, something was supposed to be happening and nothing was.

What the fuck was going on? The trap had been set, the bait

prepared – it should have been a case of just sit back and watch all hell break loose.

Instead there'd been silence. An apparent total lack of interest.

The mother's parenting technique was bordering on the laissez-faire, to say the least; that was well known, although this was almost criminal neglect. But what about the father? Hadn't he even noticed his daughter was missing? Didn't he call, phone or visit? Where did he think she was, and why wasn't he trying to find out?

But he wasn't doing any of that. He was doing exactly the same as his estranged wife right now, in fact, which was absolutely nothing at all. He'd made one phone call the previous evening to a local take-out service. To her totally inadequate credit, the mum had tried calling her daughter's phone – once – and left a message that was something to do with a ticket to a gig.

So it didn't look as if there was much choice now.

This was going to have to be hurried along a little.

Lara and Paula were back in the Serious Incident Room looking at an indistinct blob on a screen. That blob was Tony Stone, or at least an indistinct blob they hoped was Tony Stone. It was certainly Tony's phone that was sending out the signal, but it was possible he'd simply palmed that phone onto a totally innocent passer by, slipping it into someone's shopping bag, perhaps. If that was the case they were now tracking an unwitting decoy.

'Moving along The Highway.'

The Highway was one of the main thoroughfares in the area. They could get officers flooding the area in seconds, but there were too many side roads leading off from it. They needed somewhere more contained, with fewer entry and exit points.

'Crossing the road.'

Paula leant closer to the screen. This was now getting more promising. Fewer entrances and definitely fewer exits.

By Paula's side, Lara began to still, but for a different reason.

'Turning down onto—'

Lara cut in, supplying the location before the techie could identify it from the map that was being updated every few seconds on the side of his screen.

'Ocean Way.'

Paula looked at her, but didn't say anything. Then the mobile signal suddenly failed.

For a second, Lara hesitated, totally unable to make any sort of sense of this. Then she looked back at Paula.

'That's outside my flat.'

Paula's eyes never left her face.

'That's where I live.'

CHAPTER
FIFTY-THREE

COCO KNEW she'd been moved again. One moment she was in Kris's Bentley parked up in the middle of some woods somewhere, and the next she was in this weird damp room with no windows, and water almost constantly trickling down the walls.

Of course there couldn't have been just a single moment between the two events, so she must have been drugged.

How that had happened, she didn't know. She remembered feeling sleepy, but that wasn't unusual. She had nothing to do but sleep right now, and anyway it was a relief when she could actually drop off for an hour or so. It meant she didn't have to think. She also vaguely remembered hearing something – a strange clanking noise, like metal grinding up against metal, but what that was she had no idea.

But even though she knew little about anything right now, Coco knew she'd been out for longer than an hour or so when she came round. She felt rested, for one thing, and her body felt almost half-way human for the first time since this had all started.

Coco looked round. There was food there now too, some chocolate and sandwiches and fruit. Momentarily she resisted, but she couldn't hold out for long. Besides, if whoever was behind all this was intent on doing her harm, then starving herself to death was just doing his or her job for them.

So Coco picked up one of the sandwiches and finished it, along with a piece of the fruit. All the time she kept looking round her makeshift prison, searching for a way out, but there was none.

Then, and strangely given her current circumstances, she just felt like she wanted to sleep again.

But as Coco shifted position, turning now onto her side, she suddenly sat bolt upright.

Because maybe whoever was behind all this hadn't been as careful as they thought.

CHAPTER
FIFTY-FOUR

As she fitted her key into the second of the door locks, Lara
hesitated a moment.

It wasn't out of any sudden fear of what she might find on the
other side of the door.

It was just all deeply odd.

On the other side of that door was her space, her private
retreat. She didn't – ever – bring anyone back here. It was how
she lived, everything and everyone in separate compartments. To
have someone else by her side and to have that someone about to
step over her very own personal threshold was massively disorientating. And when that someone was her very own senior officer, it was even more so.

Lara turned the key and led the way, Paula following behind.

At first glance the flat was exactly as she'd left it. Half-read
papers were strewn over the table, an empty and unwashed
coffee cup discarded by their side. Paula had looked instinctively
towards the window as they came into the open plan sitting
room, the never-ending floor show that was life out on the water
immediately catching her eye as it always caught Lara's too,
something she never tired of and hoped she never would.

At this point Lara realised that her flat wasn't exactly as she'd left it that morning. But, and for reasons she didn't immediately understand, she kept that to herself.

Paula nodded at her, silent, indicating that Lara should check out the bedrooms while she took care of the kitchen and one of the bathrooms. It didn't take long, and not just because the flat was small; both officers already knew no one was inside. There was an unmistakable atmosphere in any empty dwelling. Tony Stone might have been in the immediate vicinity of her flat at some point in the very recent past, he might even have approached Lara's front door, but he wasn't there now.

Lara kept her face as poker-still as ever.

But someone had been.

———

Half an hour later, Lara and Paula were back in Paula's office. Paula's door was closed. From the other side of the door came a low constant hum as life in the building continued as normal. Inside Paula's office everything was feeling far from that.

'Why would Tony Stone make for your flat?'

'We don't know he did.'

'His phone placed him right outside.'

'There are other flats in that building.'

'So it was just a coincidence?'

'I didn't say that.'

For a moment Paula just eyed her and Lara stared back. If she'd been in Paula's position, Lara would have been asking the exact same questions. Those questions didn't bother her, as she knew she had nothing to hide, so far as Tony Stone was concerned. Something else was bothering her a lot more, though.

'Have you had any contact with Stone in the past?'

'We've worked together on two, maybe three cases. All those cases are documented in the files.'

'And there's been no personal contact between the two of you aside from those work-related collaborations?'

'None.'

'It's all been strictly professional?'

'I said.'

Paula slid a piece of paper across the table towards her. For a moment Lara just stared at it, bewildered.

'That's the case against the road rage driver, the case that links Kate and Chrissie, the only link we've managed so far to establish between the two women.'

Lara kept staring at it. Mairead had logged her findings as she would have been expected to do. It was still a highly tenuous link, but it was all they had so far that might conceivably have given Tony Stone access to both Kate's and Chrissie's personal background and circumstances.

'There were five requests for that file. One was requested by Tony Stone. The other four were made by officers from this Unit.'

Mairead was there – Lara could see her name and police number clearly displayed. Then she stared as Paula slid another piece of paper across the desk.

'The first of those requests – the one immediately before Tony Stone's – was made by you.'

Lara had absolutely no recollection of requesting that file and no idea why she should have done so. She also knew for a fact that the first she'd heard of these road rage cases was from Mairead herself.

Paula nodded at her as if she could see the thoughts flashing through her mind, which, given their visit to her flat that short time before, Lara fervently hoped wasn't true.

'Don't tell me.'

Lara looked back at her.

'Another coincidence.'

Lara didn't know if that was supposed to be a question or a statement, but it didn't matter anyway.

Either way, she didn't reply.

———

One hour later again, Lara was back home. This time she didn't even give the view outside her floor-to-ceiling window so much as a passing glance. She looked at the far wall instead.

On that wall hung a photo in a frame. It was a simple family shot, a woman and two small girls. The girls were Lara and her sister, Georgia. The woman was their mum. The photo had been taken no more than a few months before she disappeared. And Lara had never, in her life, seen it before, which meant that sometime in the previous few hours, someone had accessed Lara's flat and had hung that photo on her wall. Lara had no idea who would do that. Tony Stone had to be the prime suspect, but why?

Lara kept staring at her mother smiling out at the camera, at herself and Georgia smiling more shyly by her side, neither of them clearly knowing what was about to happen to their otherwise unremarkable family.

Another sudden thought flashed through her mind as she took in the small figure she presented in that photo. It was just another coincidence, it had to be. But Lara had been six when her mother vanished like that.

Which was Harper's age when her mother had been taken from her, too.

Lara stayed in front of the photo for some more moments before she reached out a finger and traced the counters of her mother's face.

Is this really all about her?

CHAPTER
FIFTY-FIVE

COCO STARED at her phone for fully five minutes.

Her initial reaction on feeling it in her pocket was one of massive relief. Whoever was behind all this seemed to have missed it, leaving her with some sort of lifeline at least.

Her next reaction, all too hard on the heels of the first, was to curse her stupidity. Her phone hadn't been there a short time before. She'd have felt it, meaning it had to have been returned to her pocket during one of her drug-induced sleeps.

So was this some sort of trick? Or – another sudden new thought – had her innocent-looking phone been turned into some kind of device? If she turned it on, would it just explode in her hands or something? For a moment or two she actually felt herself shrinking away from it.

But then logic began to re-impose itself, because if anyone wanted to do her that sort of harm right now, they didn't need to stage an elaborate charade involving a mobile phone that wasn't in her pocket one minute, then was suddenly back there the next.

Which only ushered in yet another new thought. Was there something on it, a message perhaps? Coco hesitated, then hit the keys on the keypad, swiftly accessing the message facility as she did so.

First, she accessed the text button, but there was no message there. Email was dead. So she next went into *Settings* and tried accessing a network server, but none showed on the display, so that ruled out access to any social media sites too.

As, of course, did messaging for any sort of help.

Coco looked at the phone, puzzled. She did have mobile connectivity, though.

Which left just one other possibility. Her phone had been returned to her so she could make a call.

Coco flicked on the keypad again but nothing came up. She stared at the screen, nonplussed for a moment. She'd never seen that before; it meant the keypad had to have been disabled in some way, which meant that the only calls she would be able to make would be to numbers in her contacts list.

Then she realised that her own number was also disabled, so if she did manage to call anyone they wouldn't see her name, and the number she was dialling from would be withheld as well.

Coco took a quick deep breath, accessing the contacts list next, only to stop as she saw just the one number displayed. There wasn't a name next to the number but there didn't need to be, because Coco recognised it straight away.

It was Dad's number.

For another minute or so, Coco just stared at the display. For that minute or so, she didn't allow herself to think. Because now she could almost smell the danger.

All this couldn't be about her. That made no sense. So she'd latched onto the only other person caught up in it all and that was Kris. She had thought that she'd become enmeshed in some kind of crazy vendetta, but this was nothing to do with Kris either.

It was all to do with that man whose number was currently almost screaming out at her from her phone.

This was all to do with her father.

So what would happen if she called that number? Would she

lead him into some sort of trap, the same trap she seemed to be caught in right now?

The problem was that this remarkably cool and calm thought, given the circumstances, sprang from the rational part of her brain, but at heart Coco wasn't feeling cool or calm or rational at all right now.

Deep down she was still just a half-formed entity, despite her looks and attitude, caught between two worlds, that of adult and child.

And then the child in her pressed the number on the screen, because all of a sudden – and once again – Coco just wanted her dad.

———

The Serious Incident Room was quiet. Lara was away and so was Mairead. Jordan had been checking and re-checking various surveillance leads for the last hour but was getting absolutely nowhere.

Then his mobile rang. Jordan looked at the phone, puzzled for a moment. The number wasn't in his contacts list, so no name was coming up on his display. He hesitated a moment longer; the last thing he wanted to do right now was field some cold call from a call centre. But then he answered anyway.

Jordan remained where he was for a moment or two, listening to the voice on the other end of the line, feeling his heartbeat increase exponentially.

Then he stood and, with his mobile still in his hand, strode towards the door.

One of his underworld snouts had just come through.

Jordan had received a lead on Tony Stone.

———

A few miles away, Edie felt the most enormous wave of relief wash over her.

She'd just let herself back into the house. She hadn't called Coco all the time she was out, but she knew she wouldn't be able to get through the evening without doing so. Or, and this would be worse, much worse, calling Jordan and finally letting him know exactly what was happening.

Or what was not happening, which was their daughter not returning any of hers, or her friends' calls.

Walking up to the front door she'd paused as she saw a strange looking boat moored on the adjacent waterway. Most boats moored there were weekend pleasure crafts, all gleaming paintwork and faux-brass fittings. This one was scarred by peeling paint and streaked in mould. But when she opened the door and walked back into the house she forgot all about rundown boats as she suddenly smelt it. The special shampoo that Coco used. She could smell it in the air and she could hear water running upstairs from the shower as well.

Edie closed her eyes, dropping her bags to the floor as she did so. She kept them closed a moment longer, telling herself to stay calm, stay cool and not do what she actually wanted to do, which was to totally blow her top. The nightmare was over. That was all that mattered.

Then Edie opened her eyes as she heard a footstep on the stairs.

And realised that, far from being over, this nightmare had only just begun.

CHAPTER
FIFTY-SIX

MAIREAD WATCHED as the man tethered his captive to the chair using thick leather straps.

Once secured, another man handed him sheets that had been soaked under the tap for the last half hour.

The temperature in the room and the heat from the captive's body meant the moisture in the sheet started to evaporate the moment they were wrapped around his legs and arms, causing the material to visibly tighten before Mairead's eyes. Then the final touch: heavy duty black duct tape was wound around both the straps and those fast-drying sheets.

The captive was now helpless, totally at the mercy of others, and the expression on his face said it all.

He absolutely loved it.

Mairead looked round the room, letting her attention wander from the floor show unfolding before her. She'd screwed up at the worst possible time and she knew it. Just when they were all under maximum pressure – herself, Lara, Jordan, even that tight-arsed DCI that had been foisted on them lately – she'd taken her eye off the ball and Tony Stone had slipped from their grasp.

Or, as that tight-arsed DCI herself had made all too clear without really needing to say anything at all, Tony Stone had slipped from Mairead's grasp. That stunt with the security light shouldn't have fooled a child of five, let alone an officer with her sort of experience.

Mairead had offered up nothing by way of a defence because there was nothing she could say. She'd fucked up. Simple as that.

There were reasons, of course. She had issues to deal with, other things on her mind, and she could just imagine what Paula would have said had she bleated that lame attempt at a half-justification. Welcome to the human race.

. Briefly, she looked towards the captive again, still tethered to his chair as his persecutor moved in closer, the whole room tensing as he did so. What would come first – a kiss – a kick – a blow – or would that same persecutor extract the penis everyone could see was straining for release inside the captive's jeans and would they all witness a blow job, perhaps by way of a warm-up for some more serious action to come?

Mairead's mind drifted again back to the abortive surveillance. It didn't help that the issues that had so distracted her had only become more pressing in the hours that followed. Those answerphone messages from the hospital had increased in number, and for the first time a direct reference to the elephant in the room had been made. The doctor needed to talk to Mairead about the future, he'd explained. Her father's future. And what they should do. They wanted to discuss all options with her, but Mairead already knew that they wanted to discuss just the one option. Which was turning off the machine that had sustained his life for these past few weeks and letting him die.

Across the room, the bound captive started to mumble a few words, pleading with the persecutor to put him out of this agony of uncertainty, but that persecutor remained cool and calm. He just stood over him, watching, waiting, making the captive wait even longer in turn.

Mairead wasn't there in any private capacity. This wasn't her way of letting off steam. She found everything that happened in that club repulsive, and maybe Paula knew that. Maybe this was another way of punishing her for all that had happened with Stone. But maybe that was just paranoia on the currently perennially edgy Mairead's part. Someone had to do it, after all.

This was the next meeting of the members of the local S&M club. Mairead had no idea which of the masked attendees their mole might be, but that didn't matter. All that did was that this club might be harbouring a psychopath, and the Serious Incident Unit now had an officer on the inside.

The persecutor in front of her had to be one of their chief suspects. So far his identity had been concealed behind a gimp mask, but the night's dubious entertainment had only just started. At some point in the proceedings Mairead was hopeful he'd let his mask slip. And even if he didn't, there was going to be all sorts of DNA that Mairead would be able to surreptitiously collect as the evening's activity continued – fingerprints, samples of hair and the like.

There'd be semen at some point too, probably.

Mairead didn't even want to think how she might collect that.

She stared at the far wall as the extended tease being enacted in front of her played out some more, and as she kept watching, another thought began running through her head, and, mercifully for once, it wasn't anything to do with her father.

Was this going to be her working life from now on? Poking around – literally sometimes – in a human cesspit? The Serious Incident Team equivalent of being sent to book illegally parked cars?

She'd tried talking to Jordan about it. Not to unburden herself, just to see if he'd picked up any soundings. He'd always seemed closer to Lara somehow, but he'd surprised her. A world-weary expression had stolen into his eyes, before he made a strange and cutting reference to their joint senior officer, telling her there were so many things about Lara that none of them knew. She'd tried probing further, but then he'd just clammed up.

But then, suddenly, something happened that wrenched her

back to the present, something that took not only Mairead but the whole room by surprise. Because the persecutor suddenly struggled out of his mask and howled; there was no other word for it. A low, guttural scream rose in intensity and pitch until it was almost bouncing off the fetid walls. Everyone in the audience stared at him, unsure what was going on.

Was this part of the act? Or the precursor to something really spectacular?

But Mairead didn't even hear the scream. All she was looking at was the distorted face of one of the men whose actions she'd been sent to monitor that night.

Kieran Walters didn't see Mairead. He wouldn't have recognised her anyway, hidden as she was behind her mask. And given the state he was quite clearly in right now, he might not have recognised her even without the mask.

Mairead kept looking at Chrissie's former boyfriend, the man she'd last seen almost paralysed by grief at the death of his lover.

CHAPTER
FIFTY-SEVEN

SHE CUT the strangest of figures in a lobby filled with footballers.

Her back was curved, a time-honoured combination of age and arthritis, her hair almost pure white. One hand grasped an outsize bag that could have contained most people's worldly possessions, while the other clung onto a stick that tapped across the polished tiled floor. Every time Lara saw her, which wasn't usually much more than once a year these days, her first new sight of the increasingly enfeebled June came as a shock.

June was the guard from the train all those years before. The kindly woman who'd looked after Lara and Georgia while they'd searched for a mother who'd vanished before their eyes. She was also the woman who'd alighted from the train with them at that first stop and stayed with them until a representative from Social Services arrived and had taken them under her wing in turn.

June had kept in touch with them via Social Services, not just for the rest of that year, but for all the years they were growing up, probably because what had happened on that train that day had haunted her as much as Lara and Georgia. Every train journey she took after that she saw them again, and it had its perhaps-inevitable effect. She'd left her job and the rail company almost exactly a year after that strangest of days when a family of three got on a train, but only two disembarked. Since then she'd remained a constant presence in the two girls' lives, never missing a birthday or Christmas, when cards would always appear. And once a year at least, the girls and June would meet up.

But recently it had been just Lara and June. Georgia tolerated her sister's visits to her new home, but she'd placed a blanket ban on any others, including from June. The old lady hadn't made any sort of fuss – she never did. She merely smiled, just as she was smiling now as she approached Lara through a press of testosterone, that smile as warm and gentle as ever.

Lara glanced around the lobby and nodded a wry apology.

'And I picked this place because it's quiet.'

June smiled knowingly as Lara leant closer and kissed her on the cheek.

'Never on a Friday before a game.' She cast an appraising eye around the room. 'They all use this place. The coach has got his own special seat, just over there.'

Lara looked at the young men now beginning to file out to a coach that had just pulled up outside.

'Should be honours even today, but it's not going to save that coach, though – he'll be out by the end of the weekend, you mark my words.'

Then June paused as she looked up at Lara, her eyes creasing in puzzlement as she registered Lara's stare.

'What?'

And Lara simply couldn't help it.

She burst out laughing.

———

One hour later, Lara wasn't in quite such good spirits.

June and Lara were in the middle of the high tea for which the hotel was justly renowned. But over the finger sandwiches and cupcakes it had become increasingly obvious that it wasn't just June's body bearing testimony to the passing years. June might have possessed an unexpectedly photographic memory when it came to local footballers, but in just the last half hour she'd stumbled over Lara's name twice, had forgotten Georgia's entire existence, and on at least one other occasion had also forgotten where she was and what she and her young companion were doing there in the first place.

She'd even forgotten what Lara did for a living.

'The police?'

Lara smiled back politely as the old lady digested that apparent bombshell.

'And how long have you been working for them, dear?'

Lara hesitated, but before she could reply, June's mind had veered off on yet another tangent.

'I never thought you'd make a success of that other thing, you know.'

Lara looked at her, but June had turned back to the food and was now excavating a miniature Victoria sponge.

'What other thing?'

June looked up as a waiter, attentive as ever, arrived to top up their cups.

'What?'

Lara prompted her. 'That other thing?'

June's eyes clouded. 'What other thing?'

The kindly waiter flashed Lara a quick, sympathetic smile as June turned her attention to the filling in one of the sandwiches.

Lara hesitated, then leant forward. Because this wasn't just another routine reunion, this was more, much more.

'Has anything happened lately, June?'

'Happened, dear?'

The old lady stared at a thin slice of cucumber decorating a smear of cream cheese.

'Has anyone contacted you? From your old place of work, maybe? Any old colleagues or friends?'

Lara knew she should probably have just come straight out

and asked what was really on her mind, but what was she supposed to say? Had a mother who'd vanished twenty years ago suddenly re-appeared? Rehearsing it in her own mind sounded weird enough. She didn't want to be the second soul on that small table to suffer the indignity of pitying glances from passing waiters. It just seemed safer to roam round that general period in the past and see if it sparked anything.

But it didn't.

―――――

Another hour later Lara was helping June into her taxi, the hotel's equally attentive doorman holding open the door. Lara was about to wave her off, but then on an impulse she climbed in and told her she'd see her home.

Lara travelled with June to her small ground floor flat in Shanklin. There, surreptitiously and hating herself for it all the while, she trawled through a selection of old letters she knew June kept in a file in a small chest of drawers and also accessed her phone records. But there were almost no letters in that small chest of drawers save a very few bills, and the only calls she'd received – Lara's aside – were from cold callers. At any other time Lara would have felt more than a pang of sorrow for the lid it lifted on the kindly old lady's world right now, but she had other matters on her mind and so she kept on with a search that was to prove fruitless. June hadn't been visited by any ghost from the past.

Lara paused in her search, seeing once again that rogue posed photo on her sitting room wall.

CHAPTER
FIFTY-EIGHT

WE'VE no idea where we're going. All we do know is we have to get as far away from Kenwood as we can.

For the rest of the evening we keep moving, praying we aren't wheeling round in some giant circle. We stick to country lanes, and if any cars approach, or we see anyone, we shrink back behind trees or dive into nearby fields. As night falls we feast on fruit picked from trees and hedgerows and drink from streams. Then we fall asleep, our arms entwined around each other, desperate for comfort and warmth.

When dawn breaks, we set off again, but now we have some sort of plan at least. We're going to try and get onto a ferry and from there travel to the mainland. What we'll do when we get there we don't know, but the island's too small – we're bound to be found if we stay here too long.

Around the bend in the next lane and across the field we glimpse a farmhouse. For a few minutes we debate whether we can slip inside to see if we can find some food.

Then we hear the voice behind us.

At first we can't believe what we're hearing. Because it's our names being called over and over again, but it sounds distorted as if whoever's calling is using a loudhailer. I stare, panicked, at Finn, who stares back at me, neither of us knowing what to do for a moment. The voice calls *again, telling us not to worry if we're listening, that we're safe, which has to be some sort of a joke. Blindly, we set off, running away from whoever's out there and is calling out our names like that.*

Half an hour later the storm begins. Within moments the new lane we're walking along becomes a river, but then we come across an actual river and it's wide and it's in full flood, and across it, over a distant few fields, we catch our first glimpse of the sea.

Which is when we hear the voice again.

We look at each other, even more panicked now. We have to get across that river. Once we do, we'll be at the coast in just a few more minutes, and then we'll be within striking distance of one of the ferries at least. But how?

Finn looks at me. And now I read something in his eyes.

I stare at the raging river in front of us, then I look back at him, this boy who retrieved my braids, who saved me from that black-robed master, and then I nod as Finn keeps staring at me, because I know what he's saying to me. We can do this. Together. Together nothing can stop us.

Then, and without saying a single word and without thinking, because if we hesitate even for an instant we may never do it, the two of us plunge into the water.

Finn's yelling in my ear as the torrent takes us, although maybe it's my own panicked yells I can hear, I hardly know anymore; it's impossible to work out where his voice begins and mine ends.

Then suddenly we're floating through air.

For a moment I've absolutely no idea what's happening. Our yells still as we're launched, upwards. For that moment it's almost as if we've been catapulted off the very edge of the world. But then, and just as suddenly, we crash back down into the water, meaning we must have shot over the side of some waterfall, submerging into the depths before we surface again, still miraculously holding onto each other somehow, still entwined,

The river's carrying us ever faster now as it hurtles downstream, and we're crashing into more rocks as the water twists and turns us first one way and then another, smashing our limbs down onto the river bed and then back up again. But Finn keeps hold of me, his arms still encircle me and I know, as an unalterable fact, that he won't let me go.

Still we roll and crash and tumble. Still the water takes us. And, suddenly, I'm slipping, not from Finn – his grip is as strong as ever, but I'm feeling my own resolve weaken. All of a sudden I'm feeling as if I just want to sleep, only it won't be sleep and I know it, but I can't help it.

Still clinging onto Finn, who's clinging onto me, I close my eyes. A new sense of peace, impossible to resist, seeps through me.

And I keep my eyes closed and I don't expect, in this life at least, to ever open them again.

PART FOUR

If they speak not according to this word,
it is because there is no light in them
Isaiah, 8:20

CHAPTER
FIFTY-NINE

'SHE NEVER KNEW. NO ONE DID.'

Kieran Walters tailed off. He'd done a lot of that in the last hour. Stumbled through sentences only to leave them unfinished. Half-explanations dying in mid-air.

Mairead looked at him. Kieran was still clothed in the same outfit he was wearing as he'd stood before the captive in that fetid room and let out that almost-primal scream. But while his face might have been distorted back then and the setting he now inhabited was different, something was still very much the same. In both incarnations, Kieran Walters looked haunted.

'Chrissie found something in the house once – a magazine. I thought I'd thrown everything out – I didn't want any of them, not after meeting her. I made an excuse, told her it must have been something a mate had planted on me as a joke. She never thought anything about it. I think she found them funny, what the hell made people dress up, do things like that?'

Kieran stared, unseeing, at a far wall behind Mairead, the activities of his fellow clubbers still going on, if the sounds coming from the other side of that wall were anything to go by.

'No secrets, that's what they always say. Don't hold anything back, because it'll always come out, and once it does that's when they'll start to wonder, what else is there?'

Kieran turned pleading eyes back onto Mairead, but he wasn't looking at her. What he was saying now was all he'd so obviously wanted to say to Chrissie.

'But it wasn't a secret, because it stopped the moment I met her. I never went near these sorts of places from that day on because I never wanted to.' Kieran shook his head. 'I was lost before she came along. I didn't even know what I was doing, and all of a sudden I met her and I wasn't lost anymore.'

Mairead remained silent. She'd been so sure in the instant it had happened. That chance sighting in the crowded cellar on the other side of the wall seemed to have promised a game changer in the search for Chrissie's killer, and maybe the killer of those other innocents too.

And, if she was honest, like Jordan before her, it promised something of a game changer for her too. The memory of Tony Stone slipping through a net she'd been personally overseeing was still all too recent and raw.

There was just one problem, and that was the now-broken figure of Kieran Walters before her.

'And now Chrissie's not here no more. And Harper...'

Mairead kept staring at him. Either Kieran Walters really was a consummate actor as well as a cold-blooded killer, or he was a man totally adrift, as he was now claiming to have been before Chrissie came into his life. For the sake of what had become a suddenly troubled career, Mairead still desperately wanted it to be the former. Every instinct, instincts developed and honed by her time spent working with Lara, was beginning to tell her it was the latter.

Suddenly he turned and moved quickly towards the door.

CHAPTER
SIXTY

JORDAN KNEW he should have logged the call. As with any potential sighting of a person of interest, to use the well-worn phrase, there were procedures to follow, protocols to observe.

But there was also a potential killer to catch, and as Lara had drummed into them all on more than one occasion, when it came to catching a killer or following protocol, then fuck the Ps and Qs.

Besides, the memory of that ferry ride still rankled. The unexpected icy atmosphere. He'd still no idea what that was all about, but he did know that he wanted the ice maiden to melt. And what better way of doing that than single-handedly bringing in their main quarry right now?

If he'd paused, even for a moment, to think about it, he'd have had to admit there was more than an element of the schoolboy handing over an apple here. But Jordan didn't. He just swung into action mode instead.

Less than an hour after leaving the Serious Incident Unit, he was looking out over the same harbour that Lara and Mairead had visited those few days before. The abandoned Jeep driven by Chrissie had been found there, making him even more convinced he was onto something.

The harbour in front of him was packed with working barges and pleasure craft. The pleasure craft were taken out for weekend jaunts. But many of the barges were also permanent homes, as evidenced by the hanging baskets and pot plants decorating the decks. Even with the extortionate mooring fees, the cost of life on this stretch of water was still dwarfed by life in the towns that crowded it.

But some were short-term lets, rented out to visitors who wanted a different kind of base for a period, and this was where Jordan's snout had come in.

In return for staying out of prison, Micky Jarrett had fed through to Jordan details of girls, all of whom would have claimed they were of legal age when they called him in his role of internet pornographer, but many of whom weren't.

For the ones who were of legal age, Micky used the occasional services of a short-let provider to secure accommodation. One such provider had told him about a recent let in this very harbour. Payment had been taken in cash and a deposit had been paid, but that had been in cash too. As a precaution the letting agent had requested a credit card, but he'd been fobbed off. The client's card had recently been stolen and he was awaiting a replacement, he'd been told.

The wily letting agent had picked the client's pocket before leaving, finding a credit card that seemed to have miraculously re-surfaced, and had copied down the details, just in case his new tenant made off with the fixtures, fittings or even his whole boat.

The card was registered to a name Jordan had circulated not only to Micky, but to the rest of his snouts. Tony Stone. Meaning Stone might not only be a rogue cop, but also be operating a lucrative little sideline trafficking some of the more vulnerable girls in what was increasingly looking like his dubious care.

Jordan dropped down onto the deck. There was no sound from inside. He moved across to the hatch leading down to the living accommodation, which was unlocked.

It was the last thing he remembered.

———

Jordan came round an hour or so later and just stared for a moment at new and unfamiliar surroundings.

Then, as his eyes slowly adjusted to the gloom, he could see he was in some sort of holding cell, albeit one of the most primitive he'd ever seen. There were no windows and didn't even seem to be any kind of flap in the door. And all he could smell was damp.

Briefly, his mind ranged over that email message from his tame snout, which he now realised couldn't have actually come from his tame snout at all, meaning his computer must have been hacked. Or that tame snout had been pressurised – or, knowing Micky – bribed to send it.

Briefly too, he also remembered that no one knew anything about what had clearly turned into a fool's mission that day, which was when he began to appreciate the point, the value indeed, of those Ps and Qs.

Then, in the gloom at the far end of that makeshift cell, he saw two pairs of eyes looking back at him.

Coco looked out of it, totally adrift.

But Edie was staring straight back at him.

CHAPTER
SIXTY-ONE

ANDREA RICE WASN'T much of a public speaker. She preferred to do her communicating in the boxing ring.

But she was also, as her long-suffering accountant frequently informed her, a businesswoman with rent to pay. So every now and again she left the gym she'd founded and made a lunchtime speech to some local organisation or other.

Usually the whole thing was a waste of time. She'd suffer through a pile of inedible stodge as she sipped at some luke-warm tap water before standing up in front of a room packed to the brim with pissed and overweight men, who'd never in a million lifetimes dream of coming anywhere near the training facility she'd pioneered.

But occasionally one or other of them gave it a go, or recommended her to some friend or contact. It meant that sometimes the business cards she'd leave behind at the end of those functions paid some sort of dividend, so she gritted her teeth and accepted each and every one of the invitations that floated in.

It was why she was now standing in the function room of a chain hotel asking for questions from the floor at the end of a thirty minute talk on how she came to be one of the UK's leading female boxing trainers.

Andrea braced herself for the inevitable feebly sexist questions that usually followed such an invitation. But today was to be different, because the first question didn't come from one of the boozed-up men on the tables grouped around her, but from a woman at the back of the room.

'Mike Tyson famously avoided the weight room for most of his career. Do you think lifting weights helps or hinders a boxer's development?'

A surprised Andrea focused on the questioner, but the overhead lights of the function room were casting her in shadow and her outline was hazy. And Andrea wasn't only surprised, she was impressed. That was an actual boxing question, posed by someone who sounded as if they knew what they were talking about. A rare treat, in other words, and Andrea responded.

'Power in a boxer is defined as force times distance plus time. The point about Tyson was that he was blessed with exceptional genetics. He stood five foot ten inches tall and weighed two hundred and thirty pounds for most of his career, but most of that mass was muscle. Because of those exceptional genetics he didn't feel any need to lift weights until late in his professional life.

'So he's an exception?'

Andrea still couldn't quite make out her questioner.

'You're either blessed with natural strength or you have to develop it. But where most boxers go wrong is allowing the weights to slow them down. They need to move fast so the exercise can activate their muscle fibres properly.'

The female questioner moved out of the shadows at the rear of the room, and now Andrea recognised her. She was the young woman Andrea had thrown out of her gym, the same woman she'd seen seemingly keeping watch from across the road. Briefly, Andrea had wondered if she'd collected herself a stalker.

'And do you recommend the use of dumbbells when shadowboxing or would you prefer a bench press?'

Andrea responded promptly again.

'I've seen a lot of fighters shadowbox with one to two kilo dumbbells. I've even seen Joshua do it. But I don't like it. That type of exercise places stress on the shoulders and even the lumbar spine. Stick to general exercise with the bench press is my advice.'

A hush had fallen over the room. Several of the men who'd clearly been contemplating asking one of the usual piss-take questions were starting to look intimidated.

'Last question. What about energy intakes just before a fight?'

Once again, Andrea responded promptly.

'Nutrition's one of the most neglected parts of a fighter's training. Sometimes what they do is just plain wrong. A common misconception is that a fighter needs sugar before training or competing. I actually saw a trainer once give a boxer a slice of cake before he stepped into a ring for a title fight. He won, but he didn't perform well, because it sapped his energy. So far as food's concerned it's simple. You get out what you put in.'

Lara nodded down at her largely untouched plate of food on the table in front of her. She'd made a connection and it was a connection she really needed right now. She needed an edge and she knew Andrea could provide it.

'So, as far as a fighter's concerned, you wouldn't recommend this shit?'

A smile started at the corner of Andrea's mouth as she glanced down at the largely untouched plate of food in front of her as well.

She shook her head.

'I wouldn't recommend this shit, no.'

Across the room, Paula Davies, who'd organised this latest regular charity event on behalf of NARPO – the National Association of Retired Police Officers – didn't look even remotely amused.

CHAPTER
SIXTY-TWO

TWO HOURS LATER, Lara walked down the empty corridor leading to the Serious Incident Team office and looked across at Jordan's desk, but Jordan wasn't there. Then she looked across at Mairead's desk, but Mairead wasn't there either.

Lara looked back towards the empty corridor, at those two empty desks again, then wheeled round as a voice cut in from behind.

'Where the fuck have you been?'

Lara turned to see Peggy O'Riordan and stared back at her. She would never have tolerated that from any officer on her watch. She would have vehemently protested if it had come from any senior officer as well. Rank, no matter how exalted, had never equalled treating others like a doormat in her book.

But this wasn't a junior or a senior officer, this was the legendary Peggy, the much loved and much prized office tea lady who'd survived myriad attempts to replace her with a whole variety of vending machines over the years, and who'd even managed to live side by side with the moka pot. In her thirty years patrolling the corridors of that one single building she'd acted as friend, confidante, comforter and, on one never to be forgotten occasion with a female DC now retired, midwife.

She looked out for everyone and had everyone's back, which was one of the main reasons she was much loved and much prized.

And right now, and despite her characteristically unusual way of announcing it, she had Lara's back too.

Peggy nodded towards the corridor and Paula's office, keeping her voice low.

'It's all she's been saying for the last ten minutes.'

Which was when a shadow fell across the room, literally and metaphorically. Looking behind Peggy, Lara saw Paula herself standing in the doorway. Peggy shot a quick sympathetic glance at Lara before wheeling away her trolley, her attempt to forewarn Lara that touch too little, too late.

For a moment neither officer spoke. When Paula did, Lara wondered briefly if she'd been listening as she now replicated what Peggy had said just those few moments before.

'Where the fuck have you been?'

Normally Lara would have protested at being addressed like some sort of doormat.

This time she just followed Paula back to her office as Paula led the way.

————

Briefly, as Lara followed her into her office and stood by her senior officer's desk, she wondered at Paula's thin skin.

Had she really taken such offence at Lara's innocent wind-up in that charity lunch those couple of hours before? But even as she posed the question she knew, if only from the expression on Paula's face, that this was nothing to do with that.

'What did you want to tell me when we came back from your flat?'

For a moment a wrong-footed Lara just stared back at her.

'There was something. I could see it in your eyes.'

In truth, she should have expected this. Paula hadn't risen to her present rank without being an exceptional copper. And exceptional coppers always know when someone's keeping something back.

Paula leant forward across the desk, her tone cajoling now, almost conciliatory.

'We can work together, Lara. We both know that. You've every quality I want in an officer on my watch. You're committed, you're bright and you're not afraid to tell it like it is, whether that's to officers under you in the Unit or to me. You also don't care if I like you or not, which I appreciate. From what I've seen of you so far, it's pretty clear that only one thing matters to you as regards the people you work with, and that's respect.'

Lara kept staring at her silently, but her mind was spinning inside. What the hell was she supposed to do now? Tell Paula all about the strange apparition that had suddenly appeared on her sitting room wall, which would obviously mean then telling her all about her own very fucked-up history?

But that wasn't all that was holding her back; there was something else as well. Something she was still trying to work out.

Paula continued in the same honeyed tone.

'What matters is whether you respect the person in front of you. And whether they respect you.'

Lara remained silent. Paula's tactics were clear, but none the less effective for that. She knew that if she put Lara on the spot too early, she'd risk her junior officer retreating into a shell. So she kept talking, even if she was just using different words to say exactly the same thing. Paula also knew full well that Lara was only listening with half an ear to what she was actually saying right now. The other half was listening to her own voice inside her own head conducting its own inner debate.

But then Paula began to tighten the screw.

'I think we understand each other. And I think you know exactly what I'm talking about, and I don't expect you to insult my intelligence by pretending otherwise.'

Paula leant closer still.

'So what's it to be? Can we work together, or not?'

Lara looked back at her. She hadn't spoken a word since she'd followed Paula into her office and she knew that Paula herself wasn't now going to say another word until Lara answered.

Which was when Lara's mobile pulsed with an incoming call, Mairead's name on the screen.

CHAPTER
SIXTY-THREE

St Mary the Virgin is a Church of England parish church in Cowes. The first church on the site was built in 1657, and John Nash designed the west tower, which was added in 1816 in a Greek Revival style, according to leaflets left by the door that Mairead had dashed through a minute previously.

It was her first time in the church and had Mairead the eyes to see it at the time, she'd have had to acknowledge that the building and its setting were simply breathtaking, and she wouldn't have been the only one to think that. The poet T.S. Eliot, no less, had celebrated the church's spiritual and architectural importance, and a biographer of Eliot also noted that while, at first, he enjoyed the building aesthetically for its splendour, he later appreciated it more when he visited as a sinner. And it was a sinner that Mairead was very much interested in right now.

Had she been fed a line after all? Was that why Kieran had suddenly run like that? Had history repeated itself, first Tony Stone and now Kieran? Had not one man, but two, been taking the piss out of her: Tony with a trick that shouldn't have fooled a child and Kieran with a sob story that bought him just about enough time to get the hell away?

But not completely away, and a totally fired up Mairead was determined he wouldn't be getting any further.

She caught a movement out of the corner of the eye and saw Kieran himself heading down a nave. For a moment Mairead thought he was making for one of the exits that led out onto the street, then she realised he was actually heading for a stone stair-case that led up to a gantry and a further, smaller stone staircase leading up onto the roof.

At this point she saw the arriving Lara.

Swiftly, Maired updated her senior officer, grateful beyond words for her swift response.

———

'I don't understand it, you don't understand it. It makes no sense to you, it makes even less sense to me. You don't see any reason to go on, and if I were you I'd probably feel the same.'

Now up on the roof with him, Lara leant closer to the staring Kieran, a dizzying drop below them both.

'And it's not the first time you've felt that way, and that's even more reason to let go, because it feels like just one more blow at a time you've taken too many already.'

On the same roof, a few metres away from the two hunched figures before her, Mairead stole a nervous glance down at the drop below.

Lara rolled on.

'But Chrissie wasn't the end of the process, she was the start. Harper was the real point. Whoever did that to Chrissie wasn't interested in a simple killing. The point was to inflict even more pain on those left behind – that's what they really get off on, the idea that somewhere, sometime, the after-shocks work their way through.'

Something in Kieran's eyes stirred. For the first time since the two officers had followed him up to the top of that tower, Mairead could see that something seemed to be getting through.

But then Kieran stood and moved closer to the edge.

Lara's tone didn't change. If she registered an even greater level of clear and present danger, she gave no sign.

'From now to when Harper would become an adult and beyond they would have been watching. When would it happen? When would the pressure get too great? And what would she do then? With Harper gone, they have to be now watching you.'

Lara paused and then continued, a new note – a note Mairead couldn't place –creeping into her voice.

'We all live with shadows, Kieran. I do too, and I know how they can eclipse you. How they can take over 'til there's nothing else there, nothing of you left to hang onto, but it doesn't have to be that way.'

Maired kept looking at her, a new window opening on a senior officer she thought she knew quite well.

But then Kieran moved closer still to the edge, and Mairead could see it. In his mind, he was already falling. Worse, he was already relishing the sensation.

The sudden drop.

The certain knowledge that everything would then be over.

'You do this and you do exactly what Chrissie's killer wants.'

Kieran actually looked at Lara for the first time since she'd joined him on that narrow edge.

Then he turned back to that dizzying drop below.

And took another step towards oblivion.

———

Five minutes later it was all over.

Mairead was sitting next to Lara on a patch of grass outside the main entrance to the church.

A paramedic had just placed blankets around both their shoulders, the same paramedic who was currently helping Kieran into a nearby ambulance, Kieran having taken a step away from that steep drop those few minutes before.

Mairead watched the ambulance as it drove him away. Then she looked back at Lara, as for the first time since they'd returned to the safety of the ground, Lara spoke.

'I need you to help me.'

Mairead kept looking at her.

'I'm on the thinnest, the very thinnest of ice. If Paula cuts me loose, I'm going to need someone on the inside.'

Lara was already moving on from Kieran, moving on too from that strange confessional she'd just shared with him. She always moved on from everything; Mairead had seen it before. Probably, it was one of the reasons she'd risen so quickly at such a young age. It was one of the reasons Mairead probably never would.

Mairead hesitated, but only for a moment. She had no idea what Lara was talking about, but she already knew what her answer would be.

Mairead nodded back.

———

Miles away, perhaps still close to that harbour, perhaps not, he didn't know, Jordan had now checked every inch of that makeshift cell. If there was a way out, he hadn't found it. So he turned back to his two fellow captives instead.

Coco was totally out of it, a combination of shock and fear. In truth he was hoping she'd stay that way until something or someone delivered them all from this fetid hell-hole.

But Edie was still just staring at him and he was trying – *trying* – to stumble his way towards some sort of explanation for all this.

'We don't know who's behind it – we still don't...'

Then Jordan stopped and looked at her, sudden hope flaring inside. Had she seen anyone?

But Edie just kept staring back.

Jordan took a deep breath and ploughed on.

'The first one happened a couple of weeks ago. It was crazy, even more then usually crazy – a kid and his mum and dad. The parents were killed, but he walked free. Then there was a second, another kid – younger, a lot younger this time – and there was only the mum involved this time, but it was the same M.O. She was killed, the kid walked away. The third happened a couple of days ago – same set-up as the first. Two parents and a son. This one was older, a lot older, but now they're dead and he's not.'

Jordan looked at her. Was any of this going in? Was she beginning to even remotely understand what he was trying to say to her?

'It's the same set-up all over again. Lara knew there had to be a connection almost from the start and she was right – it's all about the kids.'

But Edie just maintained her unblinking stare.

Jordan looked towards the door as water appeared at the top before trickling down and draining away, although where it had come from, and where it was going to, he had no idea.

Then he just stayed silent, two thoughts now racing through his mind.

For the last couple of years all they'd done was fall out and fall apart. Jordan looked across at his still-silent wife and daughter again.

They had to be the last – the very last – family this should be happening to.

CHAPTER SIXTY-FOUR

BEN DIDN'T LOOK as if he belonged in this world.

Jools looked as if she didn't want to.

Both teenagers followed the two coffins into the small crematorium with the same expression that had been on Kieran Walters's face up on that high church tower, at least until that very last moment when he finally decided to choose life.

The two teenagers looked as if they'd have given anything to swap places with their parents. Anything had to be better than the living hell they were enduring right now. At least in death there was an end; what end was there in sight for these two? And, as Lara had already rehearsed with Kieran, what damage would they inflict on each other and anyone else they came across along the way?

Lara bent to examine the CCTV tape for the sixth time in as many hours. Phil and Kate Turow had never been religious. They'd made wills when they had Ben, making it clear that in the event of either of their deaths each of them wanted a humanist funeral. Neither could possibly have expected their wishes to be respected so quickly. Like most couples they'd probably have speculated in private moments which one might go first and how the one left behind would cope. Neither could have anticipated either how cruelly redundant that speculation would prove.

The service was led by a celebrant. The term seemed incongruous in the circumstances, but he did his best. There was little to celebrate in any of this, and little comfort to be found in lives cut short. But he managed to source a couple of warm anecdotes from some friends, although not family. There was none in attendance apart from Ben and Jools, because there was none, of course. Which, as the watching Lara once again silently reflected, was probably exactly the point.

Lara would normally have chosen Jordan to be at her side for this kind of forensic trawl. He'd proved adept in the past at spotting things she might have missed, but Jordan was missing himself. There'd been a brief flurry of alarm at his initially unexplained absence, but then Lara had received a one-word text from him, which was was simple and to the point.

Sorry.

What exactly Jordan was sorry for and where he was right now had been swiftly consigned to the back of her mind. Lara indeed was already mentally clearing his desk. Later, when there was time, she might reflect on yet another promising career destined to be unfulfilled, but Jordan wasn't the first and wouldn't be the last to buckle under the pressure of the job and seek solace elsewhere.

Later still, she might reflect on yet another possible relationship that seemed to have fallen at the first hurdle, but it wasn't the first either and it wouldn't be the last.

Lara, with Mairead at her side, hunched closer over the monitor. The camera was discreet, just one step up from a spy camera. It had to be, not only out of respect for the bereaved teenagers, but so as not to scare anyone away. A plain clothes DC from the unit dressed in a dark suit and tie had been among the mourners, his tie fastened with a thin pin. In the middle of the pin was a small ornamental gemstone, and inside the gemstone was the camera. All he had to do was make sure he faced all the arriving mourners at least once and their image would be captured and fed back to the Serious Incident Team.

'Detail, detail, detail – anything, that's what we're looking for. Something that stands out, something that's wrong even if it doesn't look wrong, something that burrows inside your head so softly you don't even notice it at first, but once it's there it won't let go.'

Lara paused in her mini-briefing as a memory suddenly claimed her.

'When I first started out we had a misper. Man in his forties. His wife swore he'd just gone to the shops and hadn't come back. We drew a blank on everything, CCTV, phone records, credit cards – he just seemed to have vanished. There was nothing on her either, no previous, anything.'

Lara shook her head and continued. 'She could barely speak at the start, she was so upset. She took to wearing one of his scarves all the time, wouldn't take it off, and a bracelet she was going to give him on his birthday, just to feel close to him, I suppose. As the days ticked by, you could see it in her eyes. The longer it went on the more likely it was he was only coming back in a box.'

Mairead looked at her senior officer, a memory stirring for her too. Had she heard this story when she'd first joined the Unit, one of the many war stories about Lara that had been bandied about among the team?

'A week went by. I went to give her the regular update, which basically was no update at all. How many ways can you say, no fucking clue? It was the first time I'd done it by myself too – maybe my DI was getting bored by then. Before I left, she did what she always did. She reached out her hand, like she'd always done to my DI too. She was old school, manners at all times, even times like that. And the minute she shook my hand, I could feel it.'

Lara paused, her eyes still that lifetime away.

'Her hand was warm. But the bracelet was cold. It was weird. Why was that? I went back, talked to one of the tech guys and he explained. Put on any piece of jewellery and it takes time to become as warm as the skin around it, which seemed obvious enough. What wasn't so obvious was why an apparently distraught wife should have taken her husband's bracelet off in the first place and then put in on again a few moments before a visit from a police officer.'

And, suddenly, Mairead had it.

'The body in the septic tank.'

Lara nodded.

'We found him in the tank in the garden a day later. Another week and he'd have totally decomposed.'

Lara kept watching the monitor before them. That one little detail, that one tiny little niggle, and it cracked that case wide open.

Then Lara stilled. The young DC was now following the mourners out at the end of the service. For a moment the bowed heads of Ben and Jools Turow filled the frame, and suddenly, looking at them together, she remembered that there were two years between Ben and his sister. The same age gap as between herself and Georgia.

But then Ben and Jools were lost as the camera washed across the exit, and a woman Lara hadn't noticed before was now briefly visible, her face partly hidden by the flowers she was carrying.

Lara scrolled back the recording, froze the frame and looked at her again.

And kept on looking.

———

There were dozens of apps that Lara could have used. *AgeMe*, *MakeMyDay*, *In25years* were just three she'd found from one single trawl on the net. Unable to choose between them she'd downloaded and used the same technique on each of the sites to come up with the image she wanted.

All she had to do was upload a full-face photo, add the gender, the desired age increase and also, bizarrely in the case of one of the apps, declare whether the subject was a drugs user or not. The parameters, esoteric or not, hardly seemed to matter, though. In each case, and with each app, the results were remarkably similar.

Lara looked at the different pictures of the woman in front of her. Then she looked back at the donor photo, the one she'd chosen to age using all three apps, the smiling woman in the photograph that had been left on the wall of her flat.

Then Lara stared at the face seen, all too briefly, in that crematorium. The woman aged via those different apps bore more than a passing resemblance to her, but it was impossible, surely.

That could not be her mother.

Could it?

CHAPTER
SIXTY-FIVE

GEORGIA MOVED ROUND THE ROOM, a tense Lara following. Both sisters were balancing plates of microwaved food, placing one or the other in front of uncomprehending souls who stared back at them blankly. Lasagne or breaded fish was today's choice.

Occasionally, eyes betrayed some sort of tenuous grasp on the outside world, but it was an outside world as alien now as if they'd just landed on Mars.

The nursing home had been intended as a bed for the night for Georgia. She wasn't even meant to see any of the other usual inhabitants, octogenarians for the most part, some nonagenarians even, as well as a couple of old ladies who'd just received the traditional good wishes from the Queen.

But there'd been a delay processing Georgia's paperwork. The rehab clinic to which she'd been assigned following her latest suicide bid had no record of her impending admission and, even worse, had been forwarded none of her medical records. So while she waited for officialdom to crank into what passed for action, Georgia wandered through the home.

When the lunch gong sounded, another nod to the bygone age most of the residents also still inhabited, Georgia instinctively picked up a plate and followed one of the carers in handing out food. No one stopped her; any sort of help was welcome. By the time the paperwork had been sorted out it was teatime and Georgia had helped out with that as well. The activity was repetitive and mechanical, and it seemed to be exactly what she needed right now, according to the waiting woman from Social Services who'd been watching her closely for those previous few hours.

Strictly as an experiment, she was allowed to stay and help out the next day too. By the time that extra day had turned into a week and a week into a month, her stay in the care home had been made permanent. Strictly speaking she was neither resident nor staff, and it wasn't any sort of conventional rehabilitation either, but she seemed to have found some sort of meaning in a simple routine, and for now that was all that mattered.

Lara occasionally wondered what exactly the perennially harassed woman from Social Services actually reported back to her overseers. Georgia was getting increasingly adept at balancing several plates of hot food at the same time? Was that progress? Maybe it was compared to trying to inject herself with whatever she could lay her hands on.

But speculation such as that was displacement activity on Lara's part and she knew it.

The truth was she had no idea how to start talking about the face she saw last thing before she went to sleep and first thing the next morning. It was like she came out of a sleep that was no sleep at all with that same face before her. Nothing to mark the transition.

The photograph left on her wall certainly bore a resemblance to that figure glimpsed briefly in the funeral, but did that say more about Lara than anything else? Was she now starting to see in everyone she came across the woman who'd disappeared from her and Georgia's lives all those years before, the woman she'd be searching for in all probability 'til the day she died?

Lara looked at the concentrating Georgia again, a familiar half-vacant smile on her face as she handed out the food. Lara was too young to remember a lot about her mother, but Georgia was older.

Which was when, suddenly, she came out wth it.

'Do you ever think about her?'

Georgia turned, the same half-vacant smile on her face.

'Who?'

'Mum.'

Georgia's smile began to fade and Lara hurried on.'Maybe you don't want to. Maybe I don't want to either. I don't know.'

Georgia's smile was fast being replaced by something else, something almost hunted.

'But now and again I can't help it. Suddenly there she is, only if I actually try and think about her, how she used to look, how she used to dress, nothing's there. I see a face now and again, but then I realise it's someone I've seen on TV the day before or out on the street and I can't seem to bring her back at all.'

Lara hesitated. 'Can you?'

Georgia hesitated a moment herself, then nodded across the room.

'Emma.'

Lara stared back at her.

'Emma and her friend.'

Lara followed her look to a small girl also helping with the meals, a smaller acolyte with her.

'When I look at them, sometimes I see her.'

Georgia's half-smile widened as a memory began to form.

'Mum had a friend when she was little. It was the only friend she ever talked about.' She paused. 'I think that's who we were going to see that day.'

Georgia nodded across at them again, fondly, while Lara just stared at her, rocked by what her sister had said.

'Looking at them sometimes, I see her,' Georgia said again.

Lara kept staring. 'Are you serious?'

'What?'

'Mum? That's why we were on that train? We were going to meet someone?'

'I don't know, not for sure.'

'You still could have said!'

'We never even got there, so what would have been the point?'

Then Georgia stopped as a bell sounded from the kitchen, and she moved away to bring out that day's choice of dessert, which was apple pie or ice cream.

Lara looked across at Emma again. She was the daughter of one of the care workers and also helped out, in her case during the downtime between arriving from school and her mum being released from her shift.

Lara hesitated a moment longer, then put that not-so-little bombshell out of her mind and approached. Emma was asking an old lady what she wanted for dessert. The lady was a stick-thin ballerina type who always seated herself on a small sofa in the entrance and always took at least five minutes to make up her mind.

'Has anyone been to see Georgia lately, Emma?'

'Anyone?'

The small child's eyes swept round the crowded room, puzzled.

'From outside?'

Emma shook her head, then paused as she remembered. There had been one caller.

'A woman did come to see her.'

Lara half-stilled, but then she reminded herself of Georgia's frequent visits from the social worker.

'Apart from one of the doctors or the woman from Social Services?'

Emma looked puzzled.

'A friend, you mean? I didn't know she had any friends.'

'She hasn't, not really.'

'So how could any of them visit her?'

Which was, as Lara reflected, unanswerable logic. But then Emma's lips tightened.

'The dinner gong went and she still kept talking to her.'

And now the young girl's eyes creased in injured protest. 'All the food was ready to be put out. They were waiting for us to take it round but she kept talking, so I walked past and knocked against her chair, and her bag fell off the table and everything in it went everywhere.'

Emma grinned. 'Then she left and we started. It was ham salad or fish.'

Lara glanced down the hallway, Georgia now nowhere to be seen. By their side the stick-thin ballerina-type lady was still agonising over her simple choices.

'Was this her?'

Lara took out a small, cropped print of the artificially aged image that had obsessed her those last few nights. Emma took less than a second to answer with a decisive shake of the head.

Lara looked round. Across the room, a couple of the residents were already filing out for some of their daily check-ups. Growing ever more desperate, she tried again.

'So this woman was a new doctor or something?'

Emma stared back, quizzical again.

'She couldn't be both, could she?'

'Both what?'

'A policewoman and a doctor.'

Emma grinned again, cheekily. 'When her bag fell onto the floor, a card fell out. Her picture was on it. It said Police on the top.'

Lara looked at Emma for a long moment.

'Did you see the name on the card?'

Emma shook her head. 'She picked it up straight away.'

Lara hesitated, even more puzzled now. The stick-thin ballerina-type seemed to be finally inching towards a decision. And then, once again and out of nowhere it came, another question Lara didn't even know was in her mind before she asked it.

'Was this her?'

Lara reached into her bag and showed Emma another photo.

———

Ten minutes later, Lara was driving away. The stick-thin ballerina-type had made her decision. It was ice cream.

Lara looked out of her windscreen at a couple of residents greeting two others as they returned from a walk in the nearby small copse of woods. Then she drove on, operating now on auto-pilot, barely seeing the road ahead.

Even though she didn't know her name, Emma had had no problem picking out the woman who'd visited Georgia in the group photo Lara had just shown her.

The photo was a staff shot of all the officers in the Serious Incident Team.

The woman in question was the most senior.

Lara kept on driving, registering less and less of the road ahead as she negotiated the various bends and junctions. Paula Davies had visited Georgia, of that there was no doubt. Why on earth she should even begin to think of doing that was a totally different matter.

But then a call from Mairead flashed up on Lara's mobile.

Rollo had come round.

CHAPTER
SIXTY-SIX

PHYSICALLY, the ex-squaddie had been patched up. He was now aware of his surroundings and able to hold a conversation.

Mentally he was in a worse state than the night those weekend sailors had turned him into a public urinal.

At least there was the prospect of recovery back then. Lara looked at the shambling figure seated opposite herself and Mairead in a side room of the psychiatric clinic to which he'd been committed after his discharge from St Mary's. Now he seemed to have shrunk in on himself, almost as if his body was apologising for the space it was occupying.

Lara was also well aware that the last thing Rollo wanted to do was go back to that room, to the scene of the double killing of his parents, and re-live all that had happened. As a friend – and she and Rollo had become good friends over the past couple of years – it was the last place she would have wanted to take him. But as a police officer, Lara had no choice. Rollo was one more piece in a puzzle, and a vital one too. Ben Turow was still too young and shocked to even begin to absorb all that had happened to him, and they weren't going to extract from him anything that hadn't been excavated already. Maybe in years to come some fresh details might emerge, but for now his brain had simply closed down.

That sort of self-defence mechanism wasn't available to Rollo. He'd already been through too much as a soldier for it to even have a hope of working.

'How old was she?'

Rollo looked back at Lara across the low table, a stab of pain almost visible in his eyes. They'd already been through this, but Rollo didn't protest. He was beyond that now, too.

'Youngish. Late twenties. Maybe a bit younger, maybe a bit older.'

'And she showed you ID?'

'She showed something. Could have been a library card, I don't know. I wasn't taking much notice – all I could think was that Mum and Dad were there.'

Rollo stopped abruptly and stared at the far wall for a moment.

'Why now, that's all I was thinking. Why today?'

As Lara reflected, this was precisely the sort of distracted state the killer was banking on, meaning she had to have known how important that simple afternoon tea was to the now-broken man before her, and how desperate he was that it all go well. In the distracted state he'd have presented that afternoon, he'd have been a virtual babe in arms.

'And she seemed to know all about you?'

Mairead remained silent. This time the roles were reversed. This time it was Lara asking the questions, Mairead maintaining the watching brief.

'Of course she did. She had my fucking file, or what looked my file anyway.'

Rollo's voice, little more than a hoarse whisper as it was, now cracked.

'A lot of the stuff she said...'

He looked at Lara as he tailed off, and for the first time since the two officers had walked in something latent, dangerous, flashed in his eyes.

'Where had she got it from? She had dates – hospital appointments – sessions with the shrinks – case notes...'

Then Rollo paused. 'And she had our first meeting.'

Lara didn't reply.

'She actually said it – not what happened, she didn't need to. She was just looking through the file and out it came. Mum and Dad didn't know what she was talking about, but I did – it was there in the file, why I'd been taken into hospital in the first place.'

Then suddenly it happened, without any warning. One moment Lara, Mairead and Rollo were sitting on opposite sides of a small table. The next moment the table was in pieces, smashed against a wall where Rollo had kicked it.

The papers Lara had brought with her, papers that had formerly been lying on the small table, were floating down from the ceiling, but before they'd hit the ground Lara was on the floor too, Rollo's fingers around her neck, scrabbling for grip on her windpipe, trying to choke the life out of her. It lasted no more than seconds before Mairead, along with a couple of orderlies alerted by the commotion, wrenched Rollo away from the struggling Lara and bundled him into a corner where he yelled back at her, impotent.

'Only you! Only you fucking knew all that, so how did she?'

More and more spittle was flecking Rollo's lips all the while.

'Who fucking told her?'

Lara just looked back at Rollo as he yelled at her.

'Who?'

CHAPTER
SIXTY-SEVEN

AN HOUR LATER, Lara was back in front of a computer screen, trying to banish the image before her eyes of Rollo in as extreme a state as she'd seen him in years, trying to concentrate on the screen instead.

Lara had fed that staff shot of Paula into a face recognition system half an hour before. It was one of several biometric identification systems they used, all with the same end in view. They all examined physical features in an attempt to uniquely distinguish one person from another, often taking a single image in an attempt to match that image to existing entries in a database. Sometimes the process is easy. An employee trying to get into a restricted area, for example, looks directly at the camera in proper lighting to make things optimal for the software analysis. A face picked out in a crowd left more room for error.

For that last thirty minutes, Lara had been trawling every police site she could think of, looking for matches, but there'd been remarkably few. Occasionally a press photograph captured Paula at some scene of crime or some press conference or appeal for information, but little else.

What the fuck was she up to? Why had she visited Georgia? Ever since she'd joined the Unit, Lara had sensed an agenda of some sort on Paula's part, but what? And how the hell did that connect – if it connected at all – to their ongoing search for a killer?

Lara felt as if she was back in that same old fog again. They had appeared initially to have a particularly sadistic lone female assassin on their hands. They might still have that lone assassin on their hands, they didn't know. Who she was and why she was doing it they still didn't know either. How Tony Stone might fit into it all was a mystery too.

The only link between the killings they'd managed to establish so far was that they made orphans of the sons and daughters left behind. Lara did have her own strictly private musings on some possible connection to her still-missing mother, but that could easily lead to another dead end.

Which was when, as she was waiting for the program to conclude its search, another image, seemingly out of nowhere, flashed in front of her eyes.

Once again, Lara saw those two residents in Georgia's care home greeting those two others on the front lawn as they returned from their walk. She hadn't thought anything about it at the time. Georgia was supposed to be in a secure unit. But she wasn't, she was in the care home and it suited her and seemed to make her happy. Yet that didn't alter the fact that if she wanted to she could actually walk out of that place at any time. No one was going to stop her, and so long as she returned within a reasonable time, no one was going to worry either.

Georgia could actually go anywhere.

Such as to Lara's flat.

And do anything.

Such as hang a rogue photo on her wall.

Then a new alert flashed up onto the screen in front of her. This wasn't from a police site; this image of Paula had been linked from a different source. A puzzled Lara looked at a wedding party celebrating in the grounds of some country hoteptl. Scanning the guests she drew a blank. Paula wasn't among them. For a moment she thought there'd been some kind of malfunction, but then she realised the face recognition system had zoned in on a face behind the celebrants, a figure walking by an ornamental lake in the distance.

Lara zoomed in on the image, which she could now see was of a couple walking together, and there she was.

Paula.

Lara next zoomed in on her companion, then stopped dead. She didn't need any software gizmo to identify him.

Lara remained stock still in front of her computer looking at Paula Davies and Tony Stone huddled together as they walked side by side.

————

Another hour later, Lara was back at Tony Stone's flat.

The crime scene tape had long been taken down. While the property had been visited in the aftermath of his disappearance, with the occupant still evading the police there'd been no forensic search of the place. There'd been no need to do one and no reason for any officers to remain.

Up to an hour ago Lara couldn't imagine why she would want to be there either. But having discovered clear evidence of a previous relationship between her newly appointed DCI and a man her home unit very much wanted to speak to in relation to the killing of an innocent child, she now very much wanted to be there.

Lara wasn't looking for any clue to his disappearance the previous search team might have missed. She was looking for more evidence of links between him and Paula. Links that might throw more light on the nature of a relationship Paula hadn't even alluded to up to that point. Why, was something else Lara was now keen to establish.

Lara moved through all the ground floor rooms, finding nothing of interest in any of the living room drawers or units.

She drew the same blank in the bedrooms. The loft space was similarly empty and the house didn't possess a cellar.

Lara stared round the empty flat in a mounting agony of frustration and impatience. All her instincts told her that somewhere here was the key to unlocking all this – the murders of Phil and Kate Turow – the murders of Chrissie and Harper – the mystery behind what happened to Rollo – maybe even Milo and his missing mum.

Lara moved outside to a small garden shed, but that was empty too. But then, heading back to the house, she paused as she looked at a skylight set in the roof of the empty loft she'd just searched.

And saw a second skylight just next to it.

CHAPTER
SIXTY-EIGHT

EDIE HAD ALWAYS HATED LIARS.

Which was all down to her mum again. She'd spent her whole life in denial about her feelings towards Edie, as well as being jealous of the relationship Edie shared with her dad. Nothing was ever said, which was only another form of denial. A refusal to even acknowledge there was a problem, and so deal with it. If they'd all done that then maybe it wouldn't have festered in the way it had all those years.

One memory always stuck in Edie's mind. She and her dad used to go to the local library on a Saturday morning; it was a cherished ritual. She'd spend half an hour or so wandering around the children's section while he moved on to the record library, another cherished ritual, although one very much of his own.

He never took anything out, be that a CD or one of the dwindling stock of cassettes. Vinyl hadn't made its comeback by then, so there were no LPs. But there were two listening stations where a borrower could sample the wares before making their choice, and it was where she'd always find him when she finally came looking, her own books in hand. Headphones on, his eyes closed more often than not, listening to some opera or choir.

It was the sort of music no one would ever have associated with him, which was maybe why he always looked as if he'd been caught out or something. As if it was something to be ashamed of, which was another form of denial, of course, if she'd stopped to think about it at the time, but she hadn't. She just wanted to get home to start reading whatever books she'd chosen that week.

But one Saturday there was an atmosphere before they left for their weekly trip. She didn't know why. Breakfast had been eaten in near silence and they'd collected their books in that same silence. And then, just before they'd left the house, her dad turned to Edie and suggested she ask her mum if she'd like to come with them today.

Edie was more amused than anything else. Mum was in the same room. Why was Dad asking her a question he could easily have asked Mum himself?

But even then some instinct must have been in play. Even at that early age she must have been aware of some game playing out even if she didn't understand the rules. So Edie turned to her mum and asked the question she'd been asked in turn, which was when something even stranger happened. Her mum didn't answer directly, she just answered with a question of her own as she stared at a point somewhere behind Edie's ear and asked what she would like her to do.

Would Edie like her to come with them that morning?

And all of a sudden Edie felt as if she couldn't breathe. If she was amused before she wasn't now, and if this had felt like some sort of game before it felt like no game now. The air in the room suddenly seemed a hundred times heavier. And all she could see were two pairs of eyes staring at her while trying to pretend they weren't looking at anything at all.

Edie was no more than eight years old. And she felt as if the whole future of the world was suddenly hanging on her answer.

She'd never told anyone about that moment as she stood there, holding a bag with her books in her hand. And she'd never told anyone because it sounded trivial, but it wasn't. It was one of the key memories of her early childhood; the first time she felt something shift in her own personal universe. And one of the first times she could remember when she knew there was a before, and an after.

Up to then things had been simple. She'd been asked questions and she'd answered, because those questions and answers had been easy. Did she want beans or eggs for tea? Did she want toast or cereal for breakfast? Did she want to go and play in the park or go swimming in the local pool?

But this wasn't simple, even though all she had to say again was yes or no. But something in the way her mum and dad weren't looking at anything or anyone right now was already telling her that this was the hardest question she'd ever been asked in her life, and that same something was also telling her she was now going to upset one of them whatever she said, and what was even worse was that she wasn't going to understand why.

Before that day, there was one life, one set of relationships. Afterwards, there was a different life and a different set of relationships. And all it was going to take to move from one to the other were just a few words.

Briefly, now sitting in that holding cell, water streaming down the walls and the door, Edie felt tears sting her eyes. If Jordan or Coco had been looking at her at that moment they'd have put it down to the fear they were all feeling right now, but it wasn't. It was a piercing stab of sympathy for a small child at the mercy of forces she couldn't possibly have understood and who was going to be damned whatever she did.

Edie had taken a moment before she'd finally answered; she remembered that. She'd looked at her dad, searching for help, but he'd kept his eyes fixed on the far wall. She'd looked back at her mum, but she was now looking at the floor. And so Edie said the only thing she could think of.

'It's up to you.'

For a moment no one moved. It was almost as if neither of her parents had heard her. Then there was a quick sideways glance from her dad to her mum, a meeting of eyes that were just as quickly averted. Then Mum stood and told them briskly that she'd be fixing the usual for their lunch, a casserole. It was in the slow cooker but that didn't mean it could cook for ever, so don't be late, and he'd nodded back and promised they wouldn't be.

And then they'd left. They walked out of the house and drove the short distance to the library in the old car he was always tinkering with back in those days, and they never talked about that strange moment that Edie already felt had changed things for them all.

For a few years afterwards, Edie wondered what would have happened if she'd just answered with a simple yes. Would that have marked some sort of turning point? For those same few years she'd beat herself up for hesitating like that, for not coming down on one side or the other.

But then as she grew older, anger began to replace self-recrimination. As she began to understand more about the way relationships worked, she began to understand in turn that she'd been cast in the guise of an unlikely go-between that day. On her answer hung a trio heading out to the local library instead of the previous pairing of her and her dad. And maybe then she'd have found him introducing her mum to the world of that strange sounding music that seemed to so entrance him at that listening station and maybe things might have worked out differently.

This was when the anger really kicked in. Because how dare they load all that onto a small child's shoulders? How dare they foist on her the sort of choice they should have been making themselves?

No wonder she'd always hated liars, and not just out and out liars who spout blatant untruths. Edie looked across at Jordan, her misting of tears gone, her eyes now clear. She especially hated liars who said one thing when all the time they were concealing something else.

Edie kept eyeing the oblivious Jordan. She knew what this was all about. It was painfully obvious. She'd only taken in about one word in every two he'd said those few moments before, but she hadn't needed to hear any more anyway.

Jordan had obviously upset someone. In the early days of their relationship he used to regale her with some of the exploits of the more seriously deranged weirdos he'd come across. Now one of those weirdos had taken their revenge, only she and Coco had been dragged into it all as well. It was probably some extra little twist. The icing on the cake.

He was lying to them, pure and simple, just like her mum and dad all those years ago on that strangest of Saturdays when a simple trip to a local library created a war that turned ever colder as the years went by.

Edie kept looking at Jordan, hate building in her eyes. He was just being what he always had been, only she'd been too stupid to see it at the time.

A bastard.

Then Edie looked across at her daughter, who was just staring at the floor right now, frozen. And then Edie stilled.

Because suddenly she could see it, all the tell-tale signs – the hollow expression that had begun to creep into Coco's eyes – the intense concentration that would suddenly still her body – even years before when she was too young to begin to understand all that was starting to happen to her.

Coco was about to have a full-blown asthma attack.

Edie was the first to act but Jordan, also well attuned to all the same warning signs, was close behind. Jordan scrabbled in Coco's discarded jacket for her pump. Edie searched the pockets of her jeans, only for them both to stop dead as they realised Coco's precious inhaler wasn't there.

CHAPTER
SIXTY-NINE

THE EMAIL she'd just received specified a time and a place. The place she knew well. The time was in just over an hour.

Paula stared at it, disbelieving at first, but then she couldn't help it. She felt that all-too-familiar glow begin deep inside.

The meeting point was a local park they'd used before. All human life tended to pass through, meaning an anonymous woman and an equally anonymous man taking the afternoon sun on one of its benches wouldn't attract too much attention, but Paula still made all the usual checks, just in case. It was simple trademark, ingrained during her initial training, and had become almost second nature by now.

So before she made for the park she first visited a nearby mall. In the middle of the mall were switchback escalators, the windows of the shops on either side acting as mirrors stretching from the basement to the roof. Paula rode the escalator to the second floor and then on up to the third. The fact that those escalators were sited in the middle of the building permitted another seemingly innocent check to be made, as on at least two occasions she was able to make an apparent wrong turn into one of the shops only to double back as she realised her mistake, allowing her to check at the same time for any potential tail.

All the time her mind was racing, as it had been ever since Mairead had let Tony slip from her grasp like that. What the hell had happened – had he simply flipped? Had the pressure of his old life, their old lives, finally taken its toll as it had on so many of their former colleagues and friends? But if it had, why just run like that? And why hadn't he said anything to her of all people?

Those strange and seemingly random windfalls in his account had been cleared up quickly enough. They were pay-offs. Sweeteners from a police hierarchy that did not want claims from damaged former undercover officers. But that still left a hell of a lot of other questions in its wake.

Including, for Paula, the biggest one of all.

She was only human. The carapace that cocooned her didn't totally define her. Even she needed a release valve now and again, which was why he'd become so important to her these last few years, personally as well as professionally. And while up to now no line had been crossed, that didn't mean she hadn't occasionally wondered if it might.

Paula cleared her mind as she finally seated herself on the park bench, making sure to smile indulgently, as all adults are supposed to do, while watching some children playing around her. A moment later she kept her eyes fixed straight ahead as she sensed the approach. Seconds later, she felt the bench tense slightly as another presence seated itself at the far end.

Paula kept her eyes on the playing children for a moment longer, her peripheral vision checking for any faces she might have seen before, much as she'd also done on those mirrored escalators and inside the shops.

Then, and only then, did Paula turn to face Tony, her face freezing instantly, her soft half-smile dying on her lips, as she saw Lara sitting there instead.

CHAPTER
SEVENTY

FOR A MOMENT, as she saw the shambling figure shuffle in, exchanging greetings with one person and then another, the young Emma's mind raced back to Georgia's visitor that day or so before and her question.

Had anyone been to see her sister lately? Had any visitor called?

Briefly, Emma wondered if she should have mentioned this visitor as well as the policewoman, but then she dismissed it. Georgia's sister was talking about strangers and this visitor wasn't a stranger.

She was anything but.

———

As she always did, the old lady made a beeline for the near-comatose man, dribbling into his beaker at the far end of the room where the staff always seemed to seat him.

The old man was out of the way there and it seemed to suit him, although as he never spoke to anyone, no one could really know for sure. Maybe the truth was it suited the staff to seat him out of direct eyeline. He wasn't obstructing the view to the television there either.

The old lady had made her first appearance a few days after her brother had been admitted. She was upset at the time. The last she'd heard he was still in the local hospital – someone really should have told her he'd been moved. This was true, but hardly unheard of. Bed blocking was an acute problem in all the local hospitals, so when a place came up in a home like this, the hospital administrators moved fast, knowing that if they didn't other administrators in other hospitals would grab the place instead. Along the way, simple protocols such as informing the next of kin often fell by the wayside.

She came at least once a week and always spent a good few hours with her uncomprehending sibling, usually spanning meal times too, which meant she also shouldered the often-arduous task of trying to get him to eat and drink.

And if the old lady also drifted around the room at times, talking to different residents as she did so, that was understandable. She obviously loved her brother; she'd hardly make that regular trek to visit if she didn't. But to sit for hours on end in virtually total silence, manfully trying to keep up a one-sided conversation all the while, would try the patience of a saint. Small excursions around the room, for variety if nothing else, were to be expected.

Most of the other residents just stared back at her, uncomprehending too, but occasionally there was a connection. Like the one she'd made with Georgia. From the first time she'd approached her, on one of her early trawls around that residents' sitting room, the old lady and the younger-than-usual resident just seemed to hit it off.

Initially she had wondered if there'd be any sort of checks made on her, some independent effort to verify who she claimed to be. But the moment she'd rung the front door bell of the crumbling Victorian renovation, any niggling fears vanished.

A harassed-looking Thai care worker just smiled a perfunctory greeting. She waved her on into the sitting room, where she'd stood for a moment before finally picking out her quarry. She didn't actually know the old man from the proverbial Adam, as they'd only crossed paths the once. She'd come across him in the hospital, where she also put in the occasional shift as a volunteer and had established from the start that he seemed to have no relatives or dependents. He certainly never had any visitors. Once she discovered he'd been sent to this one home among several that could have taken him, she'd acted quickly. Within a day or so she was making her first visit, her aggrieved cover story prepared.

She didn't make the approach she actually had in mind on that first visit. She'd simply kept the dribbling old man company, occasionally speaking to him if any of the staff looked their way, now and again reading him some items from a newspaper, although she might as well have been reciting the telephone directory.

But as she did so, her eyes flicked around the room. For the first hour or so she battled to quell a rising sense of panic as all she saw were a near-constant procession of OAPs. But then the lunch gong sounded and finally she saw her, moving from resident to resident as if she was one of the home's care workers, but she wasn't, the old lady knew that. She knew exactly who she was.

She'd made her actual approach on her third visit. Just a smile and a simple hello, much as she'd smiled and exchanged similar greetings with a few of the other residents and staff. By now she'd become something of a familiar face, and she received what seemed to be a trademark, slightly vacant smile by way of a response, which wasn't much, but the first contact had been made, the ice broken.

On the next visit there was a little more in the way of conversation. And on the next, as the lunch service ended, she actually instigated a proper exchange. Nothing too heavy, a light reference to the meal her so-called brother had just enjoyed, in his own way at least. A brief discussion about the weather.

It didn't matter what they talked about. The actual words didn't matter; it was what was going on underneath that was important to her.

She was never going to get close to the other sister. She knew there was no point in even trying to broker any sort of contact there. There was a wariness in her that was absent in this one.

But there was always one more task to perform on these visits too.

The drugs trolleys were almost as much of a fixture as the different food trolleys, and there was usually a plentiful supply of the medication she was looking for on them. Temazepam was the number one choice, being the most commonly prescribed benzodiazepine, but today there was something new, a nonben-zodiazepine, Zaleplon, and she felt her heart quicken as she spotted it. According to her always-forensic online researches, that could sedate a patient in moments.

The old lady shuffled towards the door, keeping a weather eye out every step of the way. One of the drugs trolleys was now encamped outside the door of a bedridden old lady who punctu-ated the life of the nursing home with constant guttural growls, and she headed for it with an alacrity that would not only have surprised a casual on-looker, but would have led some to wonder – and with good cause – if the lady in question was quite as frail or as old as she presented?

A moment later fresh supplies of Temazepam and Zaleplon were transferred from the trolley into an open pocket of her bag, harmless placebos being substituted in their place.

But there were no casual, or not so casual on-lookers, and no reason for anyone to look at her suspiciously either. The old lady was just another sweet old soul, visiting yet another of the care home's walking wounded, probably destined to become one herself before too long.

CHAPTER
SEVENTY-ONE

LARA SEATED herself in front of the floor-to-ceiling window in the lobby of the same upmarket hotel where she'd entertained June.

A pleasure cruiser was moving past out on the straits, a pounding bass note drumming across the water as it washed against the wharves. Partygoers packed each of the decks, drinks in hand, most of them already drunk, all of them destined to become so by the end of their mini-cruise. For a moment, Lara envied them their absorption in nothing but the moment.

'It was all about you.'

Lara stared at Paula, seated next to her.

'It's why I was sent here.' Paula looked back at her. 'Why I was appointed in the first place.'

A few hours earlier, all Lara's suspicions had been confirmed. The loft above Tony Stone's flat was communal, divided into makeshift sections by thin plasterboard sheets. Most had just been crudely tacked in place. It was the work of only a few moments to prise open first one and then another. Lara didn't find what she was looking for in the loft next to Tony's, or the one next to that.

But in the third one along she found a large holdall.

Back in the upmarket hotel, Lara watched a light aircraft

overhead making for the airport at Southampton. Paula didn't miss a beat.

'Ben and Jools Turow. Chrissie Harper. That soldier you befriended – Adams, Rory Adams. You said it yourself, or as good as. The ages were different, but they all had one thing in common.'

Overhead, the light aircraft began to disappear from view as it banked for landing.

'A child – or children – left behind.'

Paula hesitated. 'What happened to you and to your sister, that's been on file since you started on the force, but it's hardly common knowledge. There was never any reason it should be. But it's there. And then when all this first kicked off...'

Lara looked back at her as she shrugged.

'It's every cop's worst nightmare. A rogue officer leading an investigation into murders he or she might actually be committing themselves.'

Lara cut across, in total disbelief now.

'You thought this might be down to me?'

Paula shook her head, closing that one down straight away.

'If we had, you'd be somewhere very far away by now.'

She paused, looking out of the floor-to-ceiling window herself. The party boat was waiting for two sailboats to ease past on either side, the music pounding ever louder.

'It's something to do with you, though. It has to be. All these type of killings, all on your patch and all under your watch – whoever's doing all this seems to have you in their sights somehow. Keeping you out there seemed the best way of trying to work out how and why.'

Lara looked out of the window again. Those few hours earlier she'd unzipped the holdall to reveal Tony Stone's body encased in heavy-duty clingfilm. Whether that had been wrapped around his body after he was killed, or whether that was how he was killed, would be a matter for Maisa.

Lara turned back to Paula.

'So all the time I've been leading this investigation, I've been investigated too?'

'No, you've been monitored.'

Lara was reeling all the more now.

'We still don't know how it's connected,' Paula continued. 'We still don't know why. All we do know is you're part of the picture.'

Lara had told Paula about Tony back in the park. The look on Paula's face as she did so told Lara all she needed to know about the relationship between her senior officer and the protection officer, which was perhaps to be expected. Maybe working undercover all those years, Paula was always going to be attracted to a man from the same kind of background and who now constructed lies for a living. Before he became the latest victim of the killer, so far still unidentified, who'd also killed Phil and Kate Turow, Chrissie and her small daughter, Harper.

Lara could now see on her face the effort it was costing Paula to concentrate on all she was saying right now, and for a moment regretted the subterfuge of her email summoning her senior officer to that park ostensibly to meet him.

Paula, still struggling, hesitated.

'Tony...' She stopped, then ploughed on. 'Tony was a prickly fucker. Maybe it was all that time doing the things he did. He never helped himself, with anyone...'

Paula paused, struggling again.

'But he helped his killer even if he never knew it. They must have got into his work files, and that's how they've been tracking everything we've been doing; that must be how they knew about the park, and Harper.'

Lara kept looking at her, more and more unanswered questions spilling out.

'So what has Georgia got to do with this? Why did you go and see her?'

'I went to see her counsellor, but yes, I did talk to her too.'

Paula reached into her bag. 'I wanted these.'

She slid photocopies of CCTV images across the table of Georgia in a room with two white-coated doctors.

'As you can see from the date and time stamps, Georgia was in the middle of regular sessions with her counsellors at the time of the Phil and Kate Turow killing and also the murder of Harper.'

Lara tore her eyes away from the print-outs. 'You couldn't seriously have suspected...?'

She tailed off, feeling more and more as if she was inhabiting some kind of parallel universe.

'It was more a process of elimination. We'd already ruled you out of the frame. Once we saw these, Georgia was ruled out too.'

Lara stilled.

Take two daughters out of the frame and that only left one name remaining, didn't it?

Was that what Paula was about to say? Maybe because she didn't want to hear it, Lara fixed on yet another inexplicable part of this ever-expanding puzzle.

'But you were already here when Phil and Kate Turow were killed. You started virtually the same day. So were there more killings before that?'

'Not a killing.'

Lara was already cursing herself for her stupidity; the answer to her own question was already all too obvious.

'Milo.'

'Not just Milo.'

Lara looked at her as Paula paused again.

'The same day Milo's mother disappeared, we got a call. At first we thought it must be a hoax, but the woman who made the call knew so much about what happened, not only to Milo, but to you all those years ago too – the train you were on – where you and your sister were going—'

Lara broke in, couldn't stop herself. 'A woman?'

'Like I said, it could have been a hoax. Your details, your back story – that's not something just anyone could access, but it doesn't mean they couldn't have found out if they did a little digging.'

Briefly, an image of Jordan and his still-unexplained download of the Milo file flashed before Lara's eyes.

'But then we found something else.'

'What?'

'DNA. It was discovered on a knife discarded in the woods near to where Chrissie's body was found. It was the knife used to inflict the original injury to the brain that killed her. Given the care the killer had taken up to that point, it seems strange to say the least that it should have just been thrown away near to where a full-scale investigation would be taking place, so it must have been deliberate. That knife – and the DNA that was on it – was intended to be found.'

Lara kept staring at her.

'As I said, we'd eliminated you, then Georgia. So then we cross-checked the DNA with swabs taken from your old home at the time by officers investigating your mother's disappearance.'

Paula nodded back at her.

'It's a match.'

CHAPTER
SEVENTY-TWO

I COME ROUND on the riverbank. I've no idea how much time has passed or how long I've been unconscious, but I can still hear the water pounding close by, meaning it must still be in full flood.

I struggle up, which is when I see Finn, who's not moving. He's lying on his side, face away from me. I keep staring, convinced he's dead, and my stomach lurches and I feel as if my heart's about to stop.

Then, from behind, I hear voices again, but more than one this time, and all calling my name and calling Finn's name again, but they're not distorted this time, so whoever's following us aren't using loudhailers anymore, meaning they must be closer, a lot closer. One of them – a woman this time – calls Finn's name again, and he stirs.

I dash to him, taking him in my arms, brushing his hair from his face as his eyes slowly focus on me. Then I freeze as, further down the bank, I now see them. The men and women who've been following us. The police.

There are three, maybe four, and they're all in uniform and they spot us at the same time. But they don't approach – they just stand there, all holding up their hands as if they're surrendering or something, which makes no sense.

Finn's eyes flash wide in panic as he sees them and he struggles to his feet, looking round wildly all the while as one of them, the woman I heard a few moments before, steps forward.

Finn hisses at me to run but I don't. I just stand there as the woman starts calling out to us, telling us that they know about Kenwood, that they were called there, that they found the children, children like us, river children, and that they're all safe now and out of harm's way, and that's what they want for us now, to be safe and out of harm's way too.

Finn hisses at me again, telling me it's a trick, that it's the black-robed masters in disguise. The woman can't hear him, not from that distance, but she seems to sense what he's saying because now she's telling us that none of what happened was our fault, that the man we attacked was the one at fault, that he's not dead anyway, he survived, but he's the one who's in trouble, now, not us.

Finn is shaking his head, telling me not to listen, telling me that we have to go, while we can. But still I don't move, still I just look back at the woman with the other officers at her side.

Which is when I see her. I see my mother's face before me, smiling as she always used to smile.

I turn back to Finn, and he can see it in my eyes. He knows even before I do and he's right. Some instinct inside is telling me these aren't like the ones who came for me, they're not like the ones in Kenwood — they can be trusted. And as Finn looks at me I feel as if my heart's going to stop again, because it's as if something's opened up inside, some wound I can almost now see, because I'm going to do what everyone else has always done and he knows it. I'm going to leave him too, but this is worse, because he expected everyone else to leave him, but he never expected me to do the same.

Just once, and softly, he whispers my name.

'Esther—'

Trembling, I reach out to him, but now he's looking behind me because the woman has finally started to approach.

Finn looks back at me, one last time, pleading, desperate, but I can't do it, I can't go to him, and all of a sudden it's like a light goes out in his eyes, but just before it does I see something else there too. I see a wild concoction of love – and hate.

Then he turns and runs.

'Finn—!'

I call out to him, but he just keeps on running. I keep staring after him as the woman comes up to me and I don't even feel the shawl she puts round my shoulders. I just yell after Finn that I'm sorry, and that we'll see each other again, but he keeps running and I keep staring after him until he's lost.

PART FIVE

I will create new heavens and a new earth.
Former things will not be remembered
Isaiah, 65:17

CHAPTER
SEVENTY-THREE

LARA REALLY NEEDED THIS. Andrea Rice could see that from the start.

They'd begun with two minutes on the speed bag, a simple warm-up, then press-ups, then it had been straight onto the heavy bag. After five minutes she was drenched in sweat. She'd be dripping in another ten. It was why she was there.

It was all about pushing her body until it felt like there was no oxygen left in her lungs, and to keep on pushing until she found reserves she didn't know existed; that extra reservoir of air – or energy – or will – that seems to be stored for emergencies.

Lara had arrived at the gym half an hour before, sports bag in hand. Andrea had been standing by the reception desk. The two women just stared at each other, and for that moment Lara feared a repetition of the curt dismissal she'd endured the last time.

But they had made a connection at that charity lunch and both women knew it. And, after staring at her for a moment longer, Andrea nodded towards a small office just off the reception area, indicating for Lara to follow.

———

'Boxing isn't about hurting people. It's about control.'

From across the other side of a desk that was in a total state of chaos, Andrea eyed her.

'I didn't know what you did before. For a living, I mean. When you walked in here that first time I wasn't interested, but now I do and I am.'

Lara just looked back at her. Right now, she had no idea what was in the mind of the trainer seated on the other side of that gratifyingly messed-up desk and less idea where this was going.

'You're right on the edge. Right on that line. I saw it that first night and I can see it now. And I'd hate to see what would happen if you suddenly tipped over.'

Andrea kept looking at her, but Lara remained silent. All Andrea's first instincts about this one were correct. She was trouble. But at least she possessed the good sense to keep quiet right now. Which wasn't much, but it was tipping those fragile scales ever so slightly back in her favour again.

Andrea struggled a moment longer, then she nodded behind Lara towards a corridor that led down towards the changing rooms.

'Don't let me down.'

———

'Slip and rip.'

Lara threw a jab against the pad Andrea was holding, before moving her head out of the path of the right cross the trainer snaked out in turn. Then Lara threw a right upper cut against Andrea's right pad, before repeating the drill.

Lara knew that fighting with fists just seems to come naturally to humans, whether it's kids scrapping for fun, or adults brawling in anger. Most will instinctively protect themselves by holding their fists in front of the face, or attack by punching with them. It's an activity that's always been controversial. Some see it as exciting and challenging, a true test of a person's physical strength, mental alertness and courage. Detractors see it as a brutal and dangerous activity that should be banned.

She'd read book after book on the history of the sport that had absorbed her from her early teens, but that was all about the how. Few of them touched on the why. Why did all those men and women, and boys and girls, feel compelled to put on those gloves and to enter the ring in the first place?

Lara still didn't really know herself. Maybe it was because everything else was driven from her mind when she was in the ring. There was just her and her opponent, and one slip of concentration, one momentary lapse and she'd be on the canvas.

But that wasn't the whole picture either, because it wasn't just about blotting everything out, it was about letting something in as well. Lara didn't know exactly what. All she did know was that after a long session in the ring or an even longer session training, she'd sometimes walk out having made a decision she'd hadn't even been aware she was debating. Something happened inside.

But not this time. Standing before one of the very best trainers in the country, her body drenched in sweat, Lara still had no idea what she had to do next.

———

Andrea watched as Lara made for the door, sports bag over her shoulder.

There was another reason she'd been reluctant to take her on. Yes, she'd been wary of taking on a potential loose cannon who looked as if she might explode at any moment. Yes, she wanted to be absolutely sure that any female boxer that passed through her gym wasn't going to damn it by association.

But it was only partly a business decision.

There was something else going on here too.

CHAPTER
SEVENTY-FOUR

Despite all Paula had said, or maybe because of it, Lara was still unable to see any way forward.

So she went back.

All the way back to a train.

'Just try and remember.'

Lara hunched closer to the bewildered child as Milo just stared back at her.

'Just one more time, that's all I'm asking. Just in case.'

Milo kept looking at her, blank. It was an expression Lara knew only too well, and she knew only too well what was behind it, too.

He'd got on a train with his mum. He'd got off the train with a complete stranger. He'd remained with other strangers ever since.

No wonder everything just seemed blank right now.

Lara hunched closer again, trying not to crowd him, but desperate to make some sort of connection as she led him through each stage of the journey. A cross-check with Google maps had identified various landmarks along the way the young Milo might have seen – a water park – a football ground – a newly constructed mosque – each one a potential trigger, something that might spark an associated memory, but each time she was greeted by the same blank stare. There was only one sight Milo was interested in and that wasn't anything he might glimpse out of the window of a train. All Milo had wanted to see from roughly ten minutes into that journey had been his mother.

Lara persisted.

'Do you remember anything happening when she got up? Did she talk to anyone, did anyone talk to her?'

But it was hopeless, and this just about summed up the small boy himself right now too. He was yet another lost soul increasingly without hope of any semblance of a normal life again. As for Lara, she was just another alien presence talking to him about things he couldn't understand.

'Did the guard come round maybe, checking the tickets? Did he or she talk to you at all?'

Which was when all of a sudden, something happened. Out of nowhere, something struggled to the front of the young boy's brain.

Almost despite himself, Milo saw again the guard as he approached. He saw his mother reach into her bag for their tickets, just before she'd left him to go to the buffet or to the toilet, he still couldn't remember. And he saw again something he'd completely forgotten 'til that very moment.

He'd only glimpsed it for a moment as she stood up. Maybe it was that image of her about to head away for what he thought would be just a few moments, but which turned into something a lot, lot longer. Maybe it had suddenly been unlocked, that fleeting glimpse of something distant, revealed in a momentary gap through the trees that lined one of the adjoining banks.

What Milo said next would have made no sense and struck absolutely no chord for anyone else.

But it struck a chord for Lara.

———

Half an hour later she was back in her waterside flat, hunting through a small box of childhood keepsakes.

Lara lifted them out, one by one, until she came across the one she was looking for. It was one of a pair of toys given to her and Georgia by her mother when they were both small, one each. Whether Georgia still had hers, Lara had no idea, but Lara had always kept everything.

Lara looked at the toy windmill in front of her. A scaled down version of the same sight that Milo had just remembered seeing out of the window as the train sped by.

Lara leant back in her chair and looked out over the water again.

CHAPTER
SEVENTY-FIVE

COCO'S ATTACK hadn't been as bad as Jordan and Edie first feared. And she hadn't had another one for the last half hour. For now – mercifully – her body remained still, but her breathing was far from normal, meaning it was a strictly temporary respite.

'Tell me.'

Jordan looked back at Edie. They were almost the first words she'd said to him since he'd come round. Across the room, Coco's eyes were now closing. She was desperate for sleep to claim her, but they knew her body would soon have other ideas.

'What you were saying – what you started to say then stopped...'

Edie stared at him. Was there some truth in all that after all? And if there was, could it make any kind of sense out of all this? Anything that might help Coco?

Edie hissed at him again. 'What the fuck is this?'

And Jordan told her. He told her everything he'd tried to say before when she hadn't been listening. Much as with Lara in that deserted Serious Incident Office, everything came spilling out, maybe because he was now trying to make sense of it all too.

Keeping his voice low, he told her all about Ben and Jools Turow, about Harper, and about Rory Adams. He gave her chapter and verse on all those macabre killings, all of which were different and all of which involved different victims, but of which all were related, they had to be, because they all seemed to have just the one end in view.

Jordan looked across at the oblivious Coco.

But this time it could be different, of course.

Because this time it might not be the parents who were destined to die.

CHAPTER
SEVENTY-SIX

THE NEEDLES ARE three jagged stacks of chalk that jut out from the sea at the most western end of the island. There was a fourth stack at one time, but that collapsed during a ferocious storm back in the eighteenth century. The chalk spine actually continues under the sea floor to emerge again at Dorset's Isle of Purbeck, and standing at the top of either site, it's possible to see how the two were once connected.

It was Lara's favourite spot. Her strictly private retreat. A place she returned to time and again, especially at times like these when she was also trying to find hidden connections.

But right now she was trying to do it again, trying to conjure her up once more, trying to see the face that seemed to be fading from her memory all the time: the face of her mum. And she was starting with the image she'd also urged Milo to remember, that last time she saw her as she leant close to them that day, whispered that she was going to get them some squash and crisps.

But this time, almost as if she was having some strange out-of-body experience, she saw the two of them instead; she saw herself and Georgia hunched over their colouring books.

Lara had once dated an officer from the national police force of Greenland. Like all relationships in her life it had been short-lived, but one thing had endured. She remembered that at key moments in her former boyfriend's life, at key times in his various investigations, he'd simply stopped investigating, stopped researching, stopped everything. Instead he'd surrendered himself to a process that had no name in the country of Lara's birth but which did have a name in Greenland: *qarrtsiluni*. The closest translation that Lara had been able to find was, *waiting for something to burst*.

It described the moment a thought hovered just on the edge of consciousness. At one time, her former boyfriend told her, he would pursue that thought like a hunter stalking a kill, only for it to recede ever further into the mist. So he'd learnt to wait, sometimes travelling as he did so, letting the thought come to him instead, well aware from past experience that it would remain obstinately out of reach if he dared approach it head-on.

So Lara just looked out over the sea and let her mind take her where it would. She let it wander over the last few weeks instead, beginning again with that other child abandoned on a train, Milo, before summoning up two other siblings in Ben and Jools Turow.

Then Lara turned and trod up the steep path towards the multi-coloured cliffs as Harper next swam before her eyes.

Lara gazed across the water at the hidden line of chalk as Rollo came into focus, which was when she began to tense, and her breath suddenly started coming quicker, deeper.

Lara kept gazing across the water. She'd made the individual links before, of course. But now she'd put all those faces almost in a line she could see that the choice of victim had been circling ever closer all the time.

Ever closer to her.

Milo was some sort of message; he had to be. What happened to him was so close to what had happened to herself and Georgia it couldn't be anything else.

Then there was Ben and Jools, two children separated by the same age gap as herself and her sister.

Then came Harper, a child the exact same age as she had been.

Next there was Rollo, a man who'd become one of her closest friends over the previous few years.

Lara kept pacing the cliffs. It wasn't just the fact of becoming newly created orphans that linked them. There was another link to her in all those killings too, more allusive maybe, but still clear.

Lara paced some more. It meant that if she was right, if the pattern was to be repeated, then the next one had to be closer still, and Lara knew, if she knew little else right now, that there would be a next one.

So – who? If she could work that out, then for the first time she might actually be ahead of this most twisted of persecutors for once.

Then Lara stilled again, because the answer was once more already staring her in the face. And now she cursed her stupidity in doing what she'd always warned her team against doing: taking things on face value.

CHAPTER
SEVENTY-SEVEN

OVER THE YEARS Esther had met many lost souls. She'd been one herself after being wrenched from her old life and taken to Kenwood. And she'd become one again just a few years ago after her loser of a lover walked out on her and left her with two young girls to bring up single-handed.

He said he'd keep in touch, help out, but of course he hadn't. But in a way it had been a blessing. At least Lara and Georgia had known from early on that they weren't going to have a dad around. Not that he'd ever intended his desertion as any act of charity.

On the second Christmas after he left there'd been a single card addressed to the girls. It was delivered three days late, and the sticker marking it down as reduced price was still in place on the back. It went straight into the bin. Since then there'd been nothing, but she still trawled through the post before each girl's birthday and before each Christmas just in case. So far he'd more than exceeded her expectations. That single, probably drink or drug-fuelled attempt to make contact hadn't been replicated and she was pretty sure that it never would.

Esther looked at her two girls, heads bent in studied concentration over their colouring books. Briefly, an image flashed before her eyes of the classroom at Kenwood and those massed ranks of other children also keeping their heads down.

Esther looked out of the window as the countryside flashed past. Could you ever repair that kind of damage?

Or were you forever cursed to repeat the same old mistakes, fall into the same old traps?

Just as she had with Lara and Georgia's dad?

CHAPTER
SEVENTY-EIGHT

MAIREAD COULD HEAR the intense exchange from the top of the stairs.

'It doesn't actually need to be him who signs, I keep telling you – it can be anybody.'

An impatient-looking delivery driver, a courier company's logo stencilled on the epaulettes on his shirt, was facing off against a small, wiry man, a nameplate identifying him as the caretaker for the flats. The caretaker tapped a package in his hand, hard.

'To be signed for by the recipient. That's what it says on the docket. Do I look six foot three and black? Yeah, I can scrawl something that looks like his signature, and the next time one of your lot come knocking and he's not in I can do it again.'

Mairead, being totally ignored by the two rutting stags before her, looked at Jordan's front door

'And the next time – when he's not in and I'm not in – well, someone else signed last time, didn't they? That's what you'll think – someone else can sign this time, only now it won't be him and it won't be me, it'll be one of your lot who scrawls their name instead.'

Years before, Mairead's dad had encouraged her to take an

Ancient History module in school. It had been a passion of his from his own schooldays and he hoped it would spark a similar passion for her. It didn't, but one quote from the Roman senator Cicero had always stayed with her. Sometimes, the orator had said, if you find yourself landlocked in the middle of something, just start a fight. Even if you have no idea how you'll win it, just start – because it's only when everything is suddenly happening all around you that you can even begin to hope to see your way through.

Mairead took a few paces forward, then lashed out with her foot, the door crashing in as her heel drove into it, smashing it back onto the floor. Then she held up her warrant card to the stunned and staring delivery driver and caretaker.

'Police.'

———

Meanwhile, Paula was setting up a press conference.

She'd wanted Lara there too, but her junior officer wasn't answering her pager or her calls. There'd be time later to find out why. For now all that mattered was making a direct appeal to the woman who'd vanished from Lara's life some twenty years before. The woman who Paula was convinced was behind all this.

Even leaving aside the DNA found on that discarded knife, there was simply no other rational explanation for all that was happening, even if why was still a complete mystery.

But press conferences were risky because they came with an occupational hazard. The crazies simply crawled out of the woodwork.

At least fifty per cent of the calls that came in would claim to be from Lara's missing mum herself, which meant her junior officer would have gone in almost the literal blink of an eye from having no mother to having hundreds. Of the remaining calls most would claim certain knowledge of that mother's whereabouts, as they'd served her in their local superstore or petrol station, or, as had happened in the case of one caller following an earlier appeal, because the caller was actually cutting her hair at the same time in a local salon.

There'd also be a significant proportion of calls that would claim to know exactly what had happened on the original train that day, either because they'd been on that train themselves, or because they had the ability to imagine themselves so completely into any situation, it was as if they were there. Another steady stream of callers would have no idea what Paula's appearance on TV was all about, but felt, from the way she looked at them and them alone, that they shared a special connection.

A few more would simply suggest they meet Paula for the sex she quite clearly needed, judging by her tell-tale body language.

The increasingly harassed responders would listen to each and every call with the same practised politeness. The more obviously lunatic callers would be swiftly, but still politely cut off or diverted to more junior responders who dutifully, if reluctantly, recorded their details.

But Paula pressed on nonetheless, even though, barely twenty minutes into the appeal, all her deepest fears were fast becoming realised, with all manner, variety and types of weirdos calling in.

But then someone else called in too.

———

Inside Jordan's first floor flat, Mairead checked his laptop, all the while trying to keep her eyes averted from the sight she could now see outside his window, the constant procession of bloodied pieces of carcass being transported into the meat market just metres away.

Lara had called her twenty minutes before. All she'd said was that Jordan could be in danger and that his note to the Unit explaining his absence could be a fake. Mairead's task was to find out.

Mairead stared at a copy of a message stored on Jordan's hard drive. And she had. She took out her phone.

Less than ten minutes later, a local beat copper, acting on Mairead's instructions, began also trying to get a response, this time from Jordan's ex-wife. A fruitless period of banging on Edie's front door led to another unofficial forced entry – again at Mairead's insistence – via the rear of the property. He called Mairead thirty seconds later.

And as she listened to the message, she began to wish she'd acted on Cicero's advice even earlier.

———

Back in Police HQ, Paula seated herself opposite a young man called Tom Yorke.

Tom had been just one of those who'd called the police hotline. But unlike those other callers, he was now sitting in the Serious Incident Team Office after a patrol car had been swiftly dispatched to pick him up.

Tom had a similar story to Lara's in that his mother had vanished from his life in unusual circumstances. But unlike Lara he knew exactly what had happened to her. Tom's mother had been murdered when he was just eight years old.

Before her death, Tom's mother had been about to begin work on the trains as a customer services host. She'd been almost childishly excited about it, but she never completed even just the one journey. As she'd set off for her very first shift the following morning she'd been intercepted by a person or persons still unknown, and killed for reasons also still unknown, because the murderer or murderers had never been brought to book.

'Have you a picture of her?'

Tom nodded, reaching into his pocket. Paula looked at a photo of an early middle-aged woman that meant absolutely nothing to her.

'She took me into the depot the afternoon before, asked one of the cleaning crew to take a picture of the train she'd be joining.'

The picture almost broke Paula's heart. Tom and his mother were standing by the train, both smiling out at the camera. To their side was one of the large catering trolleys about to be loaded onto that same train, the type of catering trolley his mum would have hauled its length and breadth the very next day. And as Paula stared at it she realised she might have just stumbled across a possible means whereby Lara's own mother could have been spirited off that train that day.

Then she looked at the date scrawled on the back of the photo. It matched exactly.

'I never heard from anyone from the company. I suppose after Mum didn't turn up for work they just assumed she'd fallen sick or something.'

'And there was no one else?'

Tom looked back at her, puzzled for a moment.

'It was just you and your mum, you've no brothers or sisters?'

Tom hesitated for a moment, then shook his head.

'There'd only ever been me and her.' He smiled briefly, a smile that was no smile at all.

Paula kept looking at him. So whoever killed his mother that day had also, and not for the last time, created an orphan.

CHAPTER
SEVENTY-NINE

IT WASN'T the same train of course; that particular rolling stock had long since been taken out of service. The journey wasn't taking place at exactly the same time either – countless timetable changes over the intervening years had seen to that. But it was the closest Lara could manage.

Lara had only travelled this route once before, on the day her mother disappeared. When she'd taken charge of Milo, the train had already come to a stop and her only task that day had been to walk him up and down in as equally fruitless a search for his mother as she'd endured all those years before. Until now she'd seen no earthly reason why she would ever want to recreate a journey that had blighted both her and Georgia's lives. But that, like so much else, had changed.

The journey that day had clearly been special for Lara's mum. How and in what way was still a mystery, and Georgia's stray, chance remark hadn't exactly cast much light on that. But did the journey itself hold some sort of key? Could it provide the answer Lara had been searching for ever since?

The train jerked, slightly, then began to move. The few other people in the same carriage were already absorbed in papers and laptops, but Lara kept her eyes firmly glued on the landscape now passing the window. For the next hour of this strangest of return journeys, every single moment had to count.

Lara had received the panicked call from Mairead regarding Jordan, Edie and Coco an hour or so before. It wasn't just the message Jordan hadn't logged that had rung alarm bells, and which now looked sinister in the extreme. Edie's house also bore evidence of a considerable struggle, and Coco hadn't been seen by any friends or in school for the last two days, which was the same time Jordan had been missing.

But Lara hadn't returned to the Serious Incident Unit to direct the hunt for him; she knew Paula and Mairead were more than capable of that. Lara had pored over Google Maps instead. She had no idea where Jordan and his family might be right now, but – and like Paula – she knew this had to be connected to her mother. If she could find out how, maybe she'd find them.

The problem was that all she had so far was a young boy's stray sighting of a windmill – something that had remained obstinately hidden from her view for the whole of her journey so far. Nothing had been revealed by any internet search either.

Briefly, Lara allowed doubt to assail her. Was her conviction that Milo's sighting meant something just a desperate hope on her part? She could almost hear Paula's voice in her ear, pointing out that the only thing she seemed to have to go on right now was the testimony of one small child and two long forgotten children's toys.

———

One hour later, and with her journey still yielding absolutely nothing in the way of new leads or insights, Lara was standing by a small cottage, bordering a patch of woods on one side, an open field leading down to a river on the other, and in the distance the rooftop of what looked like an old manor house.

A few moments before she'd knocked on the door of the

cottage and had spoken to the current occupants, short-term tenants – according to her online checks with a local letting agent – who'd only moved in a month or so before, and who looked at her as if she'd just landed from Mars.

In truth, Lara couldn't blame them.

She was looking for a what?

Not that the initially obliging and friendly short-term tenants actually said a word. They didn't need to – the wary glances they shot her way said it all. Their new home squatted on the fringe of a small village just visible across the nearby river, and they were clearly wondering if they'd just encountered the local idiot.

Lara struck off across the field towards the old house she could still see in the distance, fronting what looked like a now little-used road. Maybe whoever lived there could help, but as she drew closer Lara's heart sank even more. As more and more of the property came into view she could see that it was virtually derelict. The roof had collapsed in places, the windows were rotten and there were great gaps in the outside render leaving the underlying and decaying brickwork exposed underneath. An old house sign, *Kenwood*, was also visible in the undergrowth.

Lara stopped, distant bells now ringing. She'd heard of the place before; she was sure she had. But when – and why – eluded her for now.

Which was when, all of a sudden, she heard it. Something borne on the wind. A faint but distinct high-pitched whistling sound, which then speeded up before it slowed again, then suddenly stopped.

Lara stared at a nearby copse of dense trees. The sound, which had now started up again, seemed to be coming from behind them. Lara hesitated a moment longer, a nameless fear taking over momentarily. But then she took a quick deep breath and struggled her way through the dense outcrop ahead, the sound of the nearby and fast-flowing river growing louder all the while.

A moment or so later she was in some sort of clearing. But

then, and from the direction of the derelict house behind, she suddenly heard a loud banging.

As if someone was hitting something, desperate to be let out.

CHAPTER
EIGHTY

WAS IT JUST THE BETRAYAL? Was that why this latest failed relationship had played on her so acutely? Or was it something else, something that had driven Esther back to Kenwood in the first place?

Because Lara and Georgia's dad wasn't the only one who'd abandoned a soul in need, was he? They were totally different circumstances and the two situations couldn't be compared, but back then she'd been Finn's only friend in the world, and she'd abandoned him too. And not a day had gone by when she hadn't thought about that.

The first trip had been a strictly solo affair. There was no one now in that strange and rambling old house, which had fallen into disrepair and which was unlikely to ever be any sort of house or home again. Too many hushed scare stories about what had taken place there had seen to that. But the moment she walked out into the grounds and saw again that strange old windmill, which had to be some sort of playhouse even if probably only two children had ever played there, she felt as if the years had slipped away. As if she herself was a small child all over again.

And then she saw it. Something she'd actually forgotten about 'til that very moment. That small patch of earth where they'd buried all those keepsakes.

She'd probably have left well alone if it hadn't been for the fact that *it had obviously been recently disturbed. Someone seemed to have dug down to whatever was still there, and sometime in the last few weeks or months too, given the surrounding grass and weeds hadn't had time to grow back.*

She began scraping away at the loose earth to find one of the boxes she and Finn had buried. The lock was broken, but as she lifted the lid, she found it still bulging with the items they'd placed inside.

She stared at them all for a moment – the skipping rope – her own decayed braids.

Then, on an impulse, she took a piece of paper out of her pocket and scrawled one word.

Finn?

Then she buried it in the same box. One week later she travelled back again and found her note had gone with a new one in its place. It comprised just one word again.

Her name this time in place of his.

There'd been other notes since. And it had taken time to move onto this next stage, to arrange an actual meeting. But today was the day it was happening, and she was taking her two children along. She knew from his notes that he was in the darkest of places right now and had been for too long. Briefly, as she read all he had to tell her, the same fears assailed her. Could they ever really become like everyone else, find a place in the world, find peace?

But then she'd looked at Lara and Georgia and her doubts began to ease. And taking them along today was her way of showing him – and maybe herself – that despite the strangest of beginnings – and they'd both had the strangest, the cruellest of those – a life, a proper life that meant something, could still be within their grasp.

She looked at her two small daughters, their heads still bent over their colouring books, and smiled.

Then she leant close and whispered that she was just going to the buffet to get them some squash and crisps.

CHAPTER
EIGHTY-ONE

LARA BURST through the outer ring of trees, pausing as the derelict manor house came into full view. Now she was closer she could hear it even more clearly. A definite, almost rhythmic banging sounding from somewhere inside.

Jordan?

Desperately, she scanned the ground floor, stopping as she saw one of the rotten window frames actually leaning away from the brickwork. She put her hands behind it and pulled it away, sending up a small plume of choking dust. Ignoring the hundreds of wood beetles now scurrying for cover at her feet, Lara hopped up onto the sill, praying it wasn't as rotten as the frame it had attempted to support. It wasn't, and a moment later she was standing inside a downstairs room, the banging now even louder.

She knew she should be mobilising a specialist unit for a search like this. Leaving aside what she might find inside, this was a large house with multiple entrances and exits. It was impossible for one officer to cover them all. But in the time it would have taken to sanction, let alone organise such an operation, what the hell would be happening to whoever it was sending up that wordless cry for help? It couldn't be just a loose window rattling in the wind; the banging was too regular for that, and the wind had dropped now anyway.

Then Lara stopped. Unless it was some sort of trap, of course. And if it was, then Lara was plunging headlong into it with every step. But then she pressed on, it was too late to worry about that now.

She moved quickly through the ground floor rooms, eliminating each one along the way. Most peeled off a central entrance hall, the focal point of which was a still-impressive wooden staircase leading up to the first floor. The doors of most of the ground floor rooms were either open or had fallen in, so she could see into most of them the moment she stepped into the hallway, but she checked each one just in case.

Nothing, and no one, presented themselves. And the thick layers of undisturbed dust covering the rooms – including one that seemed to have served as some sort of classroom if the few remaining desks in there were anything to go by – told her that nothing and no one had been in that part of the property at least for some time too.

Lara trod up the staircase, which still seemed firm and stable, the banging getting louder all the time. As she reached the first floor landing she could see four corridors leading away from that central point. Lara moved down the nearest of the corridors and smashed open a door ahead, which led into a bedroom. In the centre of the room was a child's cot, caked in cobwebs. Lara steeled herself to look inside, but there was just a small family of spiders, scurrying for cover much as the wood beetles outside had done, spooked by the sudden presence in a room that had clearly seen no human presence for a long time.

She turned back and swiftly eliminated more bedrooms, but still the banging sounded, and Lara returned to the top of the staircase, wheeling round in complete confusion now.

Which was when she saw the loft ladder.

Lara's eyes travelled up to an opening in the ceiling. At one time there might have been some sort of trap door there, but now the loft ladder simply ascended into darkness. And the banging seemed to increase in volume and intensity. As if whoever was making that noise could now see her somehow, and was urging her on.

Lara began to climb. Less than a minute later, as her eyes began to acclimatise to the gloom, a blast of air thundered against her suddenly panicked eyes. A moment later, and across the loft, she saw the large seagull trapped under the far eaves.

The outsize bird took up what had obviously become its residence in a spot directly underneath a skylight, where it started on the glass once more with its wings, sending up that regular, almost rhythmic banging Lara had heard from down on the ground.

Moving cautiously, Lara crossed the loft space. Ignoring the extended claws of the bird, she tried to open the skylight, but it wouldn't give an inch; years of dirt and dust had glued the glass to the frame. Taking off and twisting her jacket into a rolled up ball, Lara hit the glass with the makeshift jimmy, sending smashed shards down onto the wooden slats under her feet as the seagull retreated – panicked again – across the loft behind her.

Carefully removing the last of the slivers from the now-open frame, Lara stood back, affording the trapped seagull an uninterrupted view of the scudding clouds above. Realising that far from being a threat she was actually some kind of saviour, the bird hesitated before flying past her and out.

Lara stared after the bird as it swooped and dived, luxuriating in its sudden freedom, then she looked down at the trees below.

Then she stopped again.

Because from her new vantage point she could now see something else.

CHAPTER
EIGHTY-TWO

A SPECIALIST POLICE escort ensured Paula and Mairead made the journey across the island in record time.

An hour earlier, a techie had taken Jordan's laptop apart. Tracking the URL attached to the message uncovered by Mairead, she highlighted an address. It meant nothing to her, but it meant something to Mairead, snouts being something everyone in the Serious Incident Team shared.

Less than twenty minutes later, Mairead found a dead Micky Jarrett slumped over his own laptop in his office. A single message was still displayed on the screen before him, addressed to Jordan, but very definitely not from Micky, summoning Jordan in turn across to a location she recognised immediately.

It was where they'd found Kieran Walters's abandoned Jeep.

With that scrawled message inside, presumably from Chrissie, pleading for help.

Now they were at the harbour. Their quarry was one specific boat referred to in that rogue message from the dead Micky, but exactly which boat they didn't know. That information, deliberately or otherwise, had been wiped from the screen.

A massively frustrated Mairead stood in the harbour, staring as dozens of boats bobbed up and down in front of them. And that, as an equally frustrated Paula pointed out, was leaving aside all the boats that might have left via the locks at the inlet to that harbour in the couple of days Jordan and his family had been missing.

Paula took out her mobile and started calling in just about every available officer from every available nick in the area. It was the longest of long shots that they might still be on one of the boats before them, but they had no other shots anyway, long, short or otherwise.

If Jordan, Edie and Coco weren't there, then they really had just hit a brick wall.

CHAPTER
EIGHTY-THREE

NOW BACK ON THE GROUND, Lara stood by the patch of earth she'd seen from the vantage point of that loft skylight. It wasn't obvious from ground level, but from up above it was quite clearly coloured differently to the rest.

For a moment she felt her insides turn to ice. Had she just found a burial site? Despite the DNA evidence Paula claimed to have uncovered, had Lara just stumbled across her mother's grave?

Because could she really believe anything Paula might say, given the game she'd been playing? Lara still distrusted the so-called evidence of that road rage file she was supposed to have accessed; more evidence of game playing on her senior officer's part, perhaps.

But then calmer counsels began to prevail. If her mother really was buried down there, she was looking at a grave that had to be twenty years old. Everything would surely have grown over in that time, any disturbed earth long ago merged and matched with its surroundings.

But there was still something different about the earth she was looking at right now. The floor of the clearing all around her was covered in bluebells. The patch of ground Lara was staring at was covered by the same blue carpet, but the colour was brighter here, more intense.

Dimly, from a couple of years before, she remembered a murder case she'd dealt with, a killing that had taken place in a car. The killer had used a small mechanical digger to excavate a grave not only for the victim but for the vehicle too. Both had been buried together and would have probably remained undetected forever, the body rotting inside its makeshift tomb.

But the car rotted too, of course, and as it did so iron sulphate seeped into the earth, imparting to the plants above it a distinctive tell-tale sheen. Lara stared again at the differently coloured patch of earth before her. She didn't expect to find a car. But there was definitely something down there.

Lara tried using her bare hands to attempt an excavation, but the ground was rocky, and within minutes her fingers were sore, blisters beginning to form. She looked round. The air was still, and she could no longer hear the whistling sound from earlier. Across the clearing were a couple of fallen branches, and Lara crossed to them, picking up the stronger-looking of the pair.

Smashing it against the trunk of a stout oak tree she broke it in two, producing a jagged spike. Lara returned to the partly excavated patch of earth and drove the spike down into it. A couple of rocks put up an unequal struggle but then shifted in the soft earth and Lara drove down further. Within another few minutes she hit something, and, using her hands to clear the rest of the soil away, she uncovered a metal box with a lid. Using the jagged branch as a lever she managed to get one end of the box partly raised out of the ground before turning to the other, hacking away at the soil underneath it to lever that side of the box up too.

Which was when, suddenly, something whipped past her head and Lara dropped the jagged branch with a scream. For a moment she wondered if the seagull might have returned for some reason, but then she saw a small kestrel nestling in the trees and staring back at her, deeply suspicious of this new presence in what was obviously its own formerly happy hunting ground.

Lara looked across at the kestrel for a moment, trying to return her breathing to normal. She held up an acknowledging hand, hoping to reassure the creature she posed no threat. And as she was allowed to resume her excavation, she guessed some sort of understanding must have been reached.

Briefly, as Lara reached down to manoeuvre her chapped and cracked fingers under the lid of the box, she did wonder once again about the usual protocols. She had no idea what she was about to find, but whatever it was she'd well and truly contaminated the scene of any crime now. She squeezed her fingers into the thin grooves at each end and prised off the lid.

Lara peered inside. At first she couldn't see anything save a few cobwebs and some scurrying insects alarmed by the sudden and unexpected light. Then she saw a roll of cloth, presumably some sort of protective covering for whatever had been hidden underneath. More gingerly this time, Lara lifted it.

The first thing she saw was a skipping rope and some strands of what looked like hair. But then something else at the bottom caught her eye and Lara lifted out a thin plastic envelope. She opened the flap to reveal a selection of photos. Some were close-ups, some were pictures taken from a distance. Almost all featured the same small boy and girl. Who the boy was, Lara had no idea. But the girl was her mum.

Across the clearing the kestrel was now scanning the bed of the clearing for any small mice or bugs. Lara put down the photographs and stared at the metal box that had housed them. It was some sort of time capsule; that much was obvious. A series of mementoes from a happier time. But why they should be buried like this, Lara had no idea.

Suddenly, the whistling sound from earlier started again. Lara looked round as a gust of wind disturbed the branches of another set of tightly grouped trees across the clearing.

Then she forgot all about long-buried children's keepsakes, as through the gap in the trees she finally saw it.

Lara saw the windmill.

CHAPTER
EIGHTY-FOUR

WITH A SINKING HEART, Mairead recognised the harbourmaster. It was the anal attendant who'd patrolled the nearby car park, the human stickler who'd first reported the abandoned Jeep.

First impressions of the multi-tasker hadn't been favourable then, and they were swiftly reinforced now. Procedure and protocol were clearly everything. Even the additional pressure an exalted DCI could bring to bear had only reluctantly prised the keys to the boats under his care from his small office at the rear of the yacht club. He held them in trust for the owners who lived away, as he told them over and over again, and it was clear he regarded it as something of a holy charge.

In light of the delay in instituting the search for the still-missing Jordan and his wife and daughter, it was a further delay that was sorely testing the patience of the recently arrived officers. Each of those officers would have happily tossed that anal harbourmaster who doubled as a car park attendant into the lock that fed that small harbour, opened the lock gates and washed him out to sea.

Mairead looked across the harbour as one by one different officers emerged from a whole variety of boats, the same grim expression on each of their faces telling her they'd drawn yet another blank.

From behind came the sound of a train heading towards a nearby station, the growl of its engine an eerie echo of the frustrated scream sounding inside her head.

Mairead looked back at the harbourmaster, still maintaining his disapproving watching brief as the search continued.

Then again, they might just toss him in that lock anyway.

CHAPTER
EIGHTY-FIVE

LARA STARED AT THE APPARITION, now just a metre or so in front of her.

The windmill wasn't full-size. It looked more like some sort of child's playhouse now she was closer, but it was clearly in working order because the blades were still revolving freely in the sudden wind.

For a moment she simply didn't know what to do. And for that same moment too, she felt as if she'd actually seen it before, even though she couldn't recall when or how. It was something atavistic somehow, reaching back into a part of her life to which at present she had no access.

And then, suddenly, as she kept staring at the scaled-down windmill in among that overgrown patch of woods, something inside Lara snapped and she started banging on the walls.

The reason was all too obvious, of course. Maybe, just maybe, she might finally be close to a mother she hadn't seen for twenty years, a mother she'd never expected in her life to see again. And if Lara could have torn that strange structure apart, wooden slat by wooden slat, right there and then, she would have done.

And there was something else too. Something she hadn't been able to properly acknowledge even to herself. The all-consuming fear that at the end of this quest she'd find a monster. A woman who'd abandoned her children only to return years later to initiate the most twisted of seemingly senseless vendettas.

But then she paused, her brain finally beginning to impose some sort of order on her raging emotions. Lara looked round the small clearing, assessing and dismissing a whole array of branches that presented themselves. They weren't going to make much of an impression on those interlocking slats in front of her. The jagged spike she'd just created from that other broken branch wouldn't help her here either.

Then a fresh gust of wind blew and Lara looked up at the blades on the windmill. For the first time she could see that one was missing, as if at some time it had been broken off.

Lara climbed up behind another of the revolving blades. She waited for the wind to die down and the blades to stop moving, then she braced herself, her back against the outside wall of the building, and jammed her foot down on it, concentrating on the point at which it attached to the motor by a couple of bolts. The bolts wouldn't give and Lara knew that, but the blade might, just as the missing one seemed to have done at some point in the past.

Lara braced herself against the building some more, then pushed with all her might. The next moment she felt the blade buckle a little, but that was all. It was slightly out of alignment, but there wasn't even the hint of any sort of crack.

Then she spotted another sturdier branch on the ground, and she dropped down and picked it up. Hooking the branch behind the now-slightly misaligned blade, she used it as a lever to force it forward, and slowly it began to move. Protesting all the time, the blade began to screech as it started to bend. Lara paused, then reversed the branch so it was now on the outside of the blade, pushing it back, then forward, then back again, working on the crease that was now beginning to appear at its base.

Suddenly, the crease began to widen. Lara, energised, worked the blade faster and faster, then the blade separated from the motor housing and crashed to the floor.

Gasping now, she lowered herself back to the ground and picked it up. She turned the blade round in her hands for a moment. Then she eyed the interlocking wooden slats before her and drove it, tip first, into the point at which one slat overlapped the other. For another moment nothing happened. Then the wood began to splinter.

Lara drove the blade into the fast-splintering wood again and again. A hole in the structure appeared, little more than a pin prick at first, but she drove the blade at it and the small hole widened, the wood to either side cracking more and more as it did so.

She threw the blade down on the grass, then peered inside. For a moment she could see nothing, just blackness, but then, slowly, as she widened the hole again, her eyes began to adjust to the gloom

Struggling inside, Lara retched as the smell hit her, but it wasn't just the urine and faeces she could now see littering the floor. It was something else, something even more insidious, terrifying. She'd sensed it in that shack with Chrissie's dead body and she was sensing it now: the stench of evil that seemed to permeate the very pores of the building.

Lara moved down a dim corridor illuminated only by the odd skylight let into the roof. Leaves and debris from the over-hanging trees had stained the glass a mildewed green, permitting only a ghostly sheen to penetrate. Then, suddenly, she stopped. Because behind the door now nearest to her she heard a sound, the faintest – the very faintest – of cries.

Lara moved to the door, then hesitated for a moment, feeling it give a little as she put her hand up against it. Taking another deep breath, she pushed it open.

Then she stopped dead as she looked inside.

CHAPTER
EIGHTY-SIX

EMMA WAS IN A WHIRL.

A couple of hours previously, she'd been handing round the lunchtime meal when a face flashed up on the TV. No one else seemed to have seen it, but then again no one ever really watched the TV anyway. It was on constantly, of course – pictures of people and places flashed before the residents every minute of every hour of each and every day, but it all just washed over them.

But this picture didn't wash over Emma, because it was a face she'd seen many times before, in a frame shut away in Georgia's bedside drawer.

Emma had taken the photo out a few times when she knew Georgia was at some appointment somewhere and wasn't going to catch her snooping. She'd look at the two smiling girls on either side of the woman whose face she was now watching on the TV across the room, and wonder who she was. And why did she never come to visit? And why did Georgia keep that photo closed away in her drawer? Why didn't she put it out on display like all the other residents did?

Someone was on screen talking about the picture that could still be seen behind her. The sound was down low and Emma couldn't hear what she was saying, so she looked across at Georgia, which was when the young girl stopped, because Georgia was staring at the screen now too, and she had the strangest expression on her face.

Emma couldn't work it out at first. But then, slowly, she began to realise what she was seeing on her older friend's face.

She was seeing fear.

CHAPTER
EIGHTY-SEVEN

HER OWN SON wouldn't have recognised her right now.

But Lara knew exactly who she was.

Lara stared at the frantic, pleading eyes of Milo's mother as she looked back at her from across that darkened room. Lara could almost hear the questions that were all too obviously hammering away inside the brain of that wasted, already badly emaciated figure those few metres away.

Who was she?

What was she?

Saviour or saint?

Persecutor or protector?

The end of one nightmare, or just the beginning of another?

Lara just stared back at her for a moment, then looked round at the tiny, fetid space. Had she really been here ever since she'd disappeared from that train? Lara kept looking round, searching for food, water, knowing already – if only by the state of the woman in front of her – that she was going to find precious little of either.

But then, suddenly, and still staring at her from across the floor, the woman's body slumped. Because now she knew Lara was no saint. Now she knew she was no protector, that this was indeed just the beginning of yet another nightmare. She had to be – the figure that had just appeared behind her new visitor was the all-too-obvious confirmation.

Just look at them. They might not have been peas in a pod, but they weren't far off.

Lara wheeled round. And, for the second time in as many moments, she knew exactly who was standing there.

Lara stared at a pair of female eyes looking back at her.

The eyes she'd wanted to see for long.

Her mother's eyes.

But this wasn't her mother.

CHAPTER
EIGHTY-EIGHT

IT WAS like time had slipped away again.

But I wasn't in Kenwood this time, with my only friend in the world. With Finn, who'd returned to me my braids; Finn, who'd played with me in that strange windmill; Finn, who'd rescued me from that savage attack by that black-robed master; Finn, who'd kept me safe as we hurtled down that river in full flood; Finn, who'd nearly killed for me.

I was back on that riverbank, the police behind us, the open country in front. I was listening to Finn begging me to go with him, saying that we couldn't let them do it, couldn't let them tear us apart. And I was seeing again that look on his face. I was staring once more at that open wound I had inflicted as I remained where I was.

But then I saw something else as he stared at me, all those years later, with my daughters out of sight in the next carriage. He didn't say it. In fact he'd hardly said anything since his first approach, but he didn't need to, I could see it in his eyes.

I could still see that old concoction of love and hate, and I saw something else as well.

I'd got away from him once.

I wasn't going to get away again.

CHAPTER
EIGHTY-NINE

LARA STARED AT THE SMALL, slight figure, who was just watching her from the door.

Behind, Milo's mum had now slumped to the floor, cradling herself in her arms, a low keening sounding from her lips as she awaited whatever fresh torment the gods seemed to have ordained for her.

But Georgia was all Lara could now see. The figure wasn't Georgia either, but there was still something about the mouth, the set of the shoulders.

Lara kept staring. There was so much she needed to know, so much she had to try to understand. But somewhere, deep down, deep inside, she already knew the answers. They were there in the eyes of the girl still standing those few metres away, a girl who could only have been in her late teens, but who looked so calm, so controlled.

It wasn't just the physical resemblance, to Georgia, and to herself.

They were tied and she knew it, one to the other.

They were blood.

Then Lara felt her shoulders start to sag. She took a quick, deep breath; this was no time for her body to let her down. She felt her shoulders sag again, and all of a sudden she realised why they were waiting like this.

Her whole body began to droop, and this time there was nothing she could do to stop herself sinking down into a bottomless black hole.

The last thing Lara saw before the whole world turned black were the young girl's eyes looking at her.

CHAPTER
NINETY

No ONE TOOK any notice of her.

She was just another traveller, maybe a holidaymaker heading for the ferry. More and more were arriving onto that station platform all the time, flooding every available inch of space as if there was no tomorrow, which was quite appropriate in one sense. Because for one person on that station platform right now, there wasn't going to be a tomorrow.

The drug was one she'd sourced, as everything else, from Georgia's care home. She'd flirted briefly with some of the so-called date rape substances, but all they did was render the subject more or less comatose. This new refinement was much better. It allowed the subject to retain some sort of control over their basic motor functions – movement, sensation and the like – while robbing them at the same time of any semblance of free will. The subject would obey any command, unthinkingly, in much the same way a helpless drunk might allow his or her actions to be determined by a more sober companion.

So she'd look just like she was intended to look. An all-too-willing casualty of an extended late lunch, perhaps. There were always plenty of ladies who lunched around these parts.

Mairead kept looking on, her face as grim as Paula's, as yet more searches by yet more officers drew more blanks.

At the head of the small inlet a small line of boats, all of which had already been searched and cleared, were now bobbing up and down impatiently, their occupants waiting for these sudden and mysterious checks by this small swarm of police officers to finish. They still hadn't been told what it was all about and weren't particularly interested, not with the lure of the open sea on the other side of those gates and a fast-disappearing window of opportunity to get out there thanks to a fast-receding tide.

Mairead stared out over the harbour. The message on that computer could easily have been a deliberate misdirection on the part of the assassin they were tracing, the prelude to what would turn out to be a total wild goose chase.

And yet...

She stared across the water at the line of boats continuing to bob up and down on the wash created by yet another boat now joining them from behind.

Something was telling her that Jordan was here.

Actually it wasn't strictly true that no one on that station platform had noticed Lara.

A female station guard did register the young woman being practically held up by her companion, and something about her did ring bells. She'd seen her before, she was sure of it.

But then again she saw dozens of people every single day. Why she would suddenly pick this one woman out she had no idea.

Besides, she and the rest of the station staff had enough to cope with now as the crush of people on the platform was beginning to pose a real hazard.

Edie hadn't said anything for the last ten minutes, and if Jordan was honest that suited him just fine. It meant he could concentrate on Coco.

An asthma attack can't be quelled by willpower alone. But conditions can be created that make an attack less serious, and that's what Jordan was focusing on now. Creating as calm an environment as he was able to, anyway, in this God-forsaken damp prison with water now almost continually running down the walls.

Dimly, from somewhere outside, he heard a noise. It sounded like some sort of machinery cranking into life, but he ignored it. All his attention was on Coco.

Had he the time and space to think about Edie right now, he'd have assumed that some kind of information overload must have taken place, that she simply hadn't been able to absorb all he'd told her.

But Edie had been able to take everything in. And something else was happening now, something she couldn't share with Jordan, and definitely could never have shared with Coco.

It was faint. Half-formed. But alone of the three people in that makeshift cell, Edie was beginning to see a way out of all this.

The driver of the incoming train would have much preferred to slow to a crawl as he approached the station.

His friend and fellow driver, the one who'd almost mown down that small child those few weeks before, had still not returned to work. He'd visited his old colleague a couple of times and could see for himself the damage that near-miss had wreaked. All it needed was for him to hear the whistle of a train in the distance, the rumble of wheels on a track, and he'd retreat back into the shell he'd almost constructed around himself ever since it happened.

But slowing to a crawl at each and every station simply wasn't an option, and that wasn't just because in the modern railway world, even on this small island, the timetable was king – there was also the safety aspect. Paradoxically a slowing train could actually be more dangerous, as no matter how many times the tannoy might announce that the train was not stopping at that station, the fact that it was slowing caused many to believe it was.

This meant that many of them would then begin to push forward impatiently, desperate to be among the first to board and grab a seat.

And then…

And the driver was so absorbed by the sudden and involuntary images he was now conjuring up inside, he was only dimly aware of the now-swaying woman standing on the very edge of the platform.

CHAPTER
NINETY-ONE

IT WAS JUST one of the many places she'd been imprisoned. Each was preceded by the sound of metal clanking against metal, which meant they were on the move again, just as she and her mum used to move around before Kenwood, transporting animal carcasses in makeshift cages. The same kind of cage that now transported her instead.

If she'd stopped, even for a moment, before she embarked on all this, she'd have realised she was never going to return to find the same soul she'd known all those years before. All that had happened to him had to have taken its toll. Maybe it already had, but she didn't have the eyes to see it at the time. Esther looked round the small space that had been her prison for more days than she could bear to count. But she had the eyes to see everything now.

Suddenly, the door opened again, only a few moments after he'd left her that last time, and briefly she allowed herself to feel a flicker of hope. She'd seen an old lady with him in the last day or so; Finn's mother, she assumed. Maybe the woman had done what she herself had failed to do – maybe she'd talked sense into her son; maybe he was now, finally, going to do what she'd herself demanded he do and let her go back to her girls; maybe this madness they'd both endured was about to end.

But the way Finn was looking at her was different. Up to now he'd been cajoling, supplicatory even, as he tried to convince her, just as he had back on that riverbank, as if they were children once more, that this was ordained, that this was their destiny, and why couldn't she see that?

But this look, which was now sweeping over the whole of her body, was already turning her to concrete.

Because, and like the black-robed master before him, it was now only too obvious that he'd thought of another way of making her bend to his will.

CHAPTER
NINETY-TWO

'ARE THERE ALWAYS SO MANY?'

Mairead joined the harbourmaster as he watched the first of the boats finally approaching the lock that led out to the open sea.

'So many what?'

Mairead nodded towards the first of the departing vessels.

'Boats putting out to sea?'

The harbourmaster shook his head, his mouth setting in a thin line as he eyed Mairead and the rest of the officers balefully. It had been that sort of week, positively rammed with hassle and stress. And this lot weren't exactly doing too much to ease his weighty burden.

'We don't usually have more than half a dozen a day putting out.'

Mairead looked back at him, puzzled.

'The trouble is, no one's been able to go anywhere for the last couple of days.' He took another deep breath as the sound of the lock filling up across the inlet became ever louder. Sometimes his job really would try the patience of a saint.

'Vandals attacked the lock gates a couple of nights ago. Made a right mess they did too.'

Mairead looked out towards the line of waiting boats again as water continued to cascade into the currently empty lock. When it was level with the water in the harbour, the first of those boats could sail out to the waiting sea.

The harbourmaster shook his head again.

'And then you lot show up. Some of these'll be lucky to get back on the next tide now.'

But Mairead just kept looking across at the gates.

————

The noise of the machinery was louder, and something else was happening now too. Jordan was sure more water was coming in underneath the door, where previously it had just streamed down the inside of the walls.

Moving as casually as he could, he positioned himself between Coco and the door, blocking her view, but that meant he was now in direct eyeline of Edie.

And in direct eyeline of something else too.

The thin wisps of what looked like blood mixing with the water as it began to pool around her.

————

Back on the station platform, and trying to keep the press of people behind the marked yellow lines, the female train guard suddenly placed the woman, clearly the worse the wear for drink, she'd seen a few moments before moving past with a friend on the platform.

She was the police officer from all those weeks ago. The officer who'd taken over when that poor boy's mother had disappeared like that and who'd led the ultimately fruitless search for her. Every day, the guard had wondered what had happened, whether the mother had been found, and how they could all have missed her. She'd asked several of her colleagues but no one seemed to know.

The police officer had put it all behind her, though. She must have done. She'd obviously been having one hell of a good time today.

CHAPTER
NINETY-THREE

ESTHER HAD WATCHED as Finn loosened his belt, then moved towards her.

A short time later, bruised and sore, torn inside from his fumbling, manic attentions, she really thought things couldn't get any worse.

But one month on when her period, which was always as regular as clockwork, failed to materialise, she realised that it was another thing she'd got wrong.

Things could get worse.

A lot worse.

And they just had.

CHAPTER
NINETY-FOUR

CHAPTER
NINETY-THREE

ESTHER DIDN'T REMEMBER her namesake, the woman she was named after.

Occasionally, Finn would show her pictures, particularly as the years passed and something she did – the way she moved – the way a certain expression would creep over her face – would send him scurrying for a box of keepsakes, and then she'd see what he'd just seen. She was indeed turning into the very embodiment of the woman who'd borne her.

But that was all she had. Pictures. The woman herself was long gone, but that was no problem, because she had Finn and he had her. He'd told her himself, time and again, that they didn't need anyone else, and he was right.

She'd asked questions, of course, and what she imagined were the usual, natural, sort of questions too. Who was she? Where had she come from?

And he'd told her everything. He'd told her how her mother had run out on them, first on Finn all those years before and then on her too by trying to get away like that, leaving him no choice in the end, because what would have happened if she'd gone and he'd been taken away in turn? What would have happened to her?

———

Esther tensed as she sensed rather than saw the train begin its final approach.

Her dad had told her the story of that day in every detail. And while it wasn't the same train as all those years ago and it wasn't exactly the same time, it was close enough.

Esther looked at Lara, still by her side. Then, slowly, casually, steered her even closer to the platform edge.

CHAPTER
NINETY-FIVE

'WHAT THE FUCK HAVE YOU DONE?'

The water was now rising all the time but Edie, ignoring the pain from her hacked and bleeding wrists, just hissed back at him. 'You said it yourself.'

Jordan stared, as Edie continued.

'This isn't about us, it's about her. She's not going to get hurt; it's just us they want, then they'll let her go.'

Behind them, Coco was trying to find a safe place away from the water, which was now beginning to cascade in under the locked door. But Jordan, increasingly appalled, just kept staring at Edie, not seeing what she was seeing right now, some sort of noble sacrifice.

He was just seeing another life about to be needlessly lost.

———

The harbourmaster couldn't work out what she was doing at first.

The crazed woman was actually now up on the lock wall – while the lock below her was filling with water, which was strictly forbidden. And what she was yelling at him all the while made no sense either.

The harbourmaster stared at her, as the other officer – the older one – now joined them.

'What do you mean, what's out there?'

Mairead stared beyond the churning cauldron below her, scanning the distant horizon. It couldn't have been a coincidence; that just beggared belief. Those lock gates had been out of action for two days and nights, which was exactly the time that Jordan had been missing. Someone must have wanted to stop all boats leaving in that time, but why?

By his side, Paula snapped at the harbourmaster as Mairead kept scanning the seemingly featureless horizon ahead.

'Just answer the fucking question.'

The harbourmaster bristled.

'There's nothing. Look. Just the sea.'

A frustrated Mairead, still spotting absolutely nothing, stared down into the lock itself, ignoring the harbourmaster whose bad week had just turned a whole lot worse. Then Mairead stopped as she spotted what looked like a break in one of the lock walls.

'What's that?'

The harbourmaster glanced at Paula again and, having no wish to risk another outburst – and in strict contravention of the bye-laws he himself had helped devise – hauled himself up onto the lock wall too.

The harbourmaster followed Mairead's outstretched, pointed figure.

'That's the run-off.

'What does that mean?'

'It's a safety valve. In case the lock gates get jammed open. Any excess water runs into there and out to sea.'

'So it's just a drain?'

The harbourmaster hesitated.

'There's nothing else?'

The harbourmaster hesitated a moment longer, keenly aware of two pairs of eyes now boring into him. 'And the sluice room.'

Mairead looked back at Paula, who looked back at Mairead in turn.

'But that's not been used for years.'

———

Lara was now right at the very edge of the platform.

The platform itself was around fifty metres long. But for that day's macabre purpose it didn't really matter where Lara was standing. The approaching train would sweep along the whole of its length, and within the next few moments too – everyone could feel it. There was a sudden change in the atmosphere, a subtle alteration in the way the currents in the air were rearranging themselves as the engine powered its way, inexorably, towards them.

And there was a change of atmosphere inside the station too; some among the crowd were already beginning to move away from the platform edge, instinctively registering the onset of danger, their movement setting a whole series of mini-surges and eddies.

Which was when, suddenly, the female guard saw her again. The woman, the police officer. At the same time, the train could be heard making its final approach, a warning whistle sounding as another tannoy announcement from the station manager himself this time, not the usual recorded voice, urged all passengers to stand back from the platform edge, reiterating the message that the approaching train was not stopping.

Then another sea of faces swam into view as people surged all around her again and the female guard lost the woman once more.

———

Now the harbourmaster felt as if he really was inhabiting a parallel universe.

What the two officers were yelling at him was clear enough. Stop it, stop the lock filling with water, but they couldn't, not 'til the levels had equalled themselves out, and they could start emptying it again.

He tried explaining all that as patiently as he could, but the younger officer just didn't want to know.

Before his disbelieving eyes she now dived straight into the water below.

———

Lara was operating at some level just above consciousness and just below awareness. She could move, she could put one foot in front of the other, she could stand unsupported, even if her posture was shaky and her movements even more so. But she was being directed and was powerless to resist. Like a child, she was being carried along by the will of another.

Which was comforting in a sense. Just to be taken. Not to have to think.

What wasn't so comforting was being led, step by step, to the edge of a station platform and then falling in front of a fast-approaching train, but by the time that thought had penetrated the drug-induced fog swirling around inside her brain it was already too late.

———

Holding her breath under the frothing water and just about managing to keep her eyes open and focused, Mairead could see what looked like some sort of door ahead.

And an iron bar securing that door from the outside.

Mairead stretched out her hands, her lungs already feeling as if they could burst. If she could reach it she was sure she could lift the bar out of the way – it only looked to be slotted into place.

But then a fresh surge of water blasted down on top of her, and with it a large piece of wood washed through from the now-open lock. Mairead didn't see it clearly. But she felt it strike her full on the head.

———

The female guard was the first to see Lara fall.

And for a moment she just stood there, rooted to the platform. Because there was absolutely nothing she or anyone could do now and she knew it. Even if the driver immediately applied the emergency brake there was no possibility of stopping in time. Modern trains were a lot more efficient in the braking department than their steam-driven forebears, but not even this modern incarnation could stop on what would be the rail equivalent of a sixpence.

———

Dazed as she was, Mairead could see that the water was higher now; the run off and that abandoned sluice room was almost completely covered.

Mairead took the deepest of deep breaths.

It was now or never.

Plunging down again, she focused once more on the iron bar in front of her. Kicking out with her flailing legs she felt it move, only to slot back in place a second later as the weight of water pressed down on it, securing it again.

Mairead kicked out again, and then again, her lungs already feeling as if they were on fire, and even though the iron bar jerked upright, it stayed where it was, half on and half off the door.

Every instinct inside Mairead told her to get out of there, get back to the surface; she knew she was about to black out again, and this time maybe her body wouldn't rise to the surface as it had the last time.

Then Mairead looked at the iron bar and steadied herself for one final, desperate kick.

———

By some extraordinary chance, Lara missed the live rail as she fell, although it was scant consolation given that the train, its horn now blaring, was bearing down on her at what looked like massive speed. She might have been spared death by one means but she wasn't going to be spared it by any other.

She could feel the ground vibrating beneath her now, the rails screaming at what seemed the highest possible pitch. She could hear shouting too, from the platform, indistinct and incoherent yells of useless warning and even more impotent instruction.

She also saw her mother.

And she saw Georgia.

All of which was impossible, and Lara knew it. They weren't suddenly there as an actual physical presence before her eyes. And there was no supernatural spring by them either, levitating her from that track, some celestial miracle rescuing her from imminent oblivion.

But something of a miracle still took place that day.

It was something in both their eyes, a message in her mother's eyes in particular. A message only she could read.

Once again Lara saw her stand and head down that train carriage. For the first time – and now she didn't know if this had actually happened or if it was just her imagination – she saw her mother turn at the door and look back. And there was something in that look, a recognition perhaps that in her moment of greatest danger she'd frozen, had allowed herself to fall into the hands of evil and had allowed it to prevail.

And in that moment Lara determined that she would not do the same.

Fighting the drug that was still incapacitating her, fighting the voice inside that was telling her to just lie there, to close her eyes, to will all this to be over as it must be in just a mercifully short second or so, she opened her eyes, and now she saw another face, the face of the train driver this time as he stared from his cab down at the figure on the tracks. This was when Lara twisted her body towards the adjacent track.

She felt her head go to one side of that track, and for a moment, as the train horn sounded even louder and the tracks drummed to a decibel-busting beat, she was convinced that all she'd done was simply choose decapitation instead of being crushed.

But then she managed to get her legs over the rail, and an arm, and then there was a roar and a blare overhead and she heard a scream, a terrible scream that sounded more animal than human. Then she realised it was her voice, her scream.

A whirling vortex seemed to be ripping at her clothes, and then there was something warm, almost comforting somehow, spraying seemingly uncontrollably over her face.

Finally there was silence as Lara lost consciousness.

EPILOGUE

I will not cause pain, without allowing something new to be born
Isaiah, 66:9

CHAPTER
NINETY-SIX

THE DIG HAD BEEN in progress for over an hour.

It was a four-man operation watched by two other pairs of eyes.

And after everything that had happened, those watching pairs of eyes, and the four other officers actually conducting the dig, were all desperately hoping this was going to turn out to be a total waste of time.

———

She'd waited a long time for her to appear.

One day, then two, and then a third.

For most of that time a variety of junkers had meandered past, most piled high with scrap metal or bags of coal. Whole families had looked out at her through cracked or smashed windows. A couple of the ramshackle boats had been decorated, improbably, with random unfurled flags, and on the decks of most were upturned beer crates serving as makeshift seats.

On the decks of some of the barges had been large traps – cage-like structures commonly used to transport animal carcasses from slaughterhouses to canal-side markets. Large traps that could transport humans too.

In company with the river police she'd enlisted to help her, she'd stopped a few of the passing boats, but it was always the same story. Hooded eyes stared back at her, wary, suspicious, silently assessing, and in each and every case those eyes clearly found her and her questions wanting.

When they were asked where they were going, most just replied, south.

When they were asked where they'd come from and who else they'd seen on their travels, she didn't even get a response.

Then those boats, those families and those hooded, silently assessing eyes moved on.

But suddenly everything changed as another boat rounded the bend in the water ahead, a woman at the helm who looked to be well over eighty, but maybe that's what life out on the river in all seasons did for you. Or maybe it was something else.

A few moments later, Lara seated herself opposite the woman on the thin strip of deck. Unlike the other river travellers she'd stopped, this woman had barely made eye contact since Lara had flagged her down and boarded her craft. There was just one single, sideways glance flashed her way, but there was something in that solitary look, a distant flash of recognition, even though Lara knew for a fact they'd never met. Then the woman cast down her eyes again.

'You must have known?'

The old woman looked at the small, slight figure before her. She wasn't the near body double that her sister presented, but there was still something unmistakable in the way she talked, the way she moved, the incline of her head. She was the woman she'd last seen all those years before, the woman abducted and then imprisoned by her son.

'Why not go to the police, tell them...?' Lara broke off, help-less. 'I don't even know her name...'

The she stopped. Because she suddenly realised she did. It

was the only name Finn would ever have given her. The name of the girl he'd spent a lifetime trying to replace.

Esther.

Finn's mother stole another quick glance at Lara.

She could have said all sorts to her right now. She could have told her that river people weren't like other people, that they didn't possess the comforting certainties others possessed. That they didn't go to priests or the police in the same way that they didn't use mirrors or like to be away from the water too long. Look what happened when they were. Look what had happened to Finn.

And, staring back at her, Lara could see it was hopeless. But she'd always known it would be. She was going to get nothing out of this old woman about the young girl or about Finn. But that wasn't the only reason Lara had tracked her down that day.

'What happened to her?'

The old woman had turned away, but now she stopped at Lara's appeal.

'What happened to my mother?'

The old woman hesitated for a moment. But then, and just before she started the engine and moved away, she looked back at her.

————

Back at the dig, Lara looked down at her arm hanging limp and useless at her side.

The surgeon was still putting the chances of saving it at fifty-fifty, which were significantly better odds than she'd given herself as that train had borne down on her. The possible loss of an arm seemed to be the very least she was facing then.

Lara looked towards the nearby river where the tide was turning, the water beginning to flow back to the sea. Then she tensed as one of the diggers paused and gave them a signal. They'd just hit something.

Lara, Georgia by her side, watched as a new and thinner layer of earth was excavated using smaller spades and then brushes. Then another metal box, a lot bigger than the one that housed those keepsakes, was exposed to view.

For a moment there was silence. They didn't need to do any more digging, although they would. But they all already knew.

Lara and Georgia had just had the confirmation they really did not want that their mother was dead.

CHAPTER
NINETY-SEVEN

JORDAN HAD ANTICIPATED all sorts in the wake of Coco moving out of the former family home and moving in with him.

Staying at the former home wasn't an option now anyway. They'd all nearly drowned and would have done had it not been for the heroic efforts of Mairead. But by that time Edie had suffered massive blood loss and associated major organ damage too, so it was now going to be a long convalescence in a succession of hospitals for her.

So Coco moved in with her father. The day she did so Jordan had half-expected her to make her way across to the dealers openly plying their trade at the entrance to the meat market. Replace Kris – whose body had now been found – with a new supplier. Or plunge headlong into the never-ending night-life proffered by the ever multiplying proliferation of local clubs.

What he didn't expect her to do was walk across to a local rescue centre and bring back a dog.

Jordan didn't know if it was something she'd planned for a while, or just some spur of the moment thing, but he signed all the necessary papers on the spot. He'd hardly had more than three or four words out of her since they'd both been discharged from hospital with a more or less clean bill of health, physically at least. As the consultant psychiatrist made clear, the emotional and mental scars they'd both suffered might take rather longer to heal. Finn's daughter might not have visited on Coco's head the legacy she'd intended, but she'd delivered scars, of that there was no doubt. Their nature, and reach, was something they were just going to have to deal with.

But for now what they had to deal with was more immediate, in the shape of various domestic accidents as Coco's new companion tried and failed to control his bowel movements. They also had to deal with dog food sprayed over and around the floor as the enthusiastic hound picked up his bowl in his teeth and trotted round the flat proudly displaying its contents. And they had to deal with various half-eaten shoes as he decided they were far more use in his mouth than on any human foot.

What redeemed it all was the laughter. Something Jordan feared he'd never see or hear again as he left that hospital with his silent and incommunicative daughter a week or so before. His daughter actually laughing again.

They hadn't talked about the new addition to the family. Coco hadn't even named him yet, or if she had she hadn't shared it. All she'd done was take the deliriously delighted puppy out for walks, put her aghast new charge in the bath when he rolled in a vat of bloodied bones awaiting collection outside the meat market and charged round the flat after him in a perennially doomed attempt to retrieve items of clothing before they were shredded.

Coco also hadn't talked about what had happened to them. Jordan had tried, but Coco had frozen, and Jordan quickly abandoned the attempt. Since then, all they'd ever talked about was Coco's dog.

Jordan was no psychologist, but he didn't need to be to know that this new pet – as well as being a wrecker of footwear on a near-industrial scale – was pure and simple therapy. Coco was losing herself in the most uncomplicated relationship she could right now. That could turn out to be another form of withdrawal or it could be a first step in re-engaging with the world. Once again, Jordan didn't know.

As for his own re-engagement with his former world, he was going back to the front line of the Serious Incident Unit, but he was very much taking a back seat so far as Lara was concerned. The little he'd discovered about her courtesy of some illicit research in some supposedly closed file had told him she was carrying around more than her fair share of usually weighty baggage.

Jordan looked across at Coco, playing with her puppy. And they had more than their fair share of that too at home.

CHAPTER
NINETY-EIGHT

MAIREAD HAD RECEIVED the call the day before.

Despite all she had to deal with right now, Lara had actually offered to be there with her. But, albeit gratefully, Mairead had declined.

She didn't know why at first. But then she realised it simply felt right that at the end there was just the one person in the world there that really mattered to him, and that was his sole surviving child. Anyone else would have been a distraction, but a distraction from exactly what was a question she hadn't been able to answer.

Mairead had done her characteristically full research beforehand. She knew that while all drips would be withdrawn, the medical staff could still order a narcotic drip to be inserted, usually morphine or fentanyl, in case her father suffered any pain in his final moments. All she had to do was watch out for any of the obvious tell-tale signs and summon help.

Mairead was also aware that once the breathing tube was removed, he could be given something that would dry up any secretions, but she'd declined that offer too. It wouldn't distress her if her father drooled at the end.

But the rest of what she now faced was very much down to each individual case. Most commonly respiration would slow and oxygen saturations would drop, as would the heart rate. Her father would also stop breathing for several minutes before his heart ceased to function.

Inevitably, she'd come across horror stories. One young woman's mother had been ill for a long time after a car accident. She'd reached a point where she obviously wasn't going to get better and the decision was made to turn off the machine that sustained her. They were expecting all sorts when they did, but what they weren't expecting was for her to take an unaided breath, and then another, and another. And she continued to breathe on her own, even though she was still unconscious for the next four years. Her daughter was insistent that it was harder than if she'd actually died.

But most of the time, when that tube is pulled out, the patient may gasp, may cough, but then – usually – there's just a slow decline.

Mairead stood by her father's bed for a moment, then nodded across at the doctor, who simply pulled the plug on the ventilator much as you might unplug a toaster. Then he put his hand on her shoulder, holding it there for just a moment, and walked out as she'd requested, leaving her alone.

Mairead took her father's hand in hers and continued to hold it as his breathing rumbled a little and then settled. She stayed there, still holding his hand, while her mind went back over the last few days and the case that had dominated their efforts and thoughts for more days than that.

Then she looked back at him. His head was now leaning back, sightless eyes looking up at the ceiling. From her position – and she hoped this wasn't just wishful thinking on her part – it looked like he was welcoming what was now his imminent release.

And then he died. Simply and painlessly and without fuss.

He slipped away, with Mairead continuing to hold his hand long after his soul had departed his now-lifeless body.

Mairead kept looking at him. Her father looked at peace for the first time in months, which was when she realised.

Sometimes it is possible to kill through love.

CHAPTER
NINETY-NINE

ESTHER KNEW they'd be looking for her. But they wouldn't find her.

Leaving aside the fact that she was something of a master when it came to disguise, it was in her DNA. Her father, Finn, could have told them. River people had always been adept at melding into the background. Passing through without leaving a trace.

But now she had work to do.

She'd scoured the bank for stones and rocks for the past couple of hours. Carrying the selection she'd found back to the boat, she packed them into the pockets of his favourite large coat, which would now, and finally, be his funeral shroud. She heaved him up from the large chest freezer. Then she steered him towards the edge of the deck.

She waited for a moment. Not to say any sort of prayer – she already knew to count on no help from that quarter. Just to have a moment's communion.

Then she let go and his body hit the water.

The man she'd always known as Finn – she'd never called him Dad or Father – floated for a moment on the surface, then slowly began to sink into the depths.

———

At the same time, two other souls were also saying their goodbyes.

Lara and Georgia stood on another windswept cliff overlooking the sea. They were the only mourners aside from the officiating priest. That sparse attendance might have been sad in any other circumstances. But not these, because they weren't souls adrift anymore, unsure what had happened to them or even who they were.

All that previous uncertainty had been lifted from their shoulders.

They now knew that their mother had not simply walked out on them.

———

Finn didn't have any choice; Esther knew that. The illness that had savaged him these last few years had seen to that. He hadn't left her – not like her mother had left them.

Esther looked towards the bank as she blinked away sudden tears. But she hadn't left all her children, had she? They might have felt as if she had, but there was only one who'd been lashed by that sting.

In those early days, just after Finn died, she thought she was going to go mad. She hadn't even been able to say goodbye. She'd just stored him, like they used to store the carcasses of animals they'd collect on their travels. Then she'd sit beside him, just like they used to. Which was when all those old demons returned to haunt her, with no one, now, to keep them at bay.

Why did she leave us?

And then Lara and Georgia would appear before her eyes.

Why did she love them, and not me?

And it had helped, that strange community she'd built. Those kindred souls. Somewhere out there were people just like her, souls who'd understand what she was feeling, what she was going through, because they were going through the same. She'd managed to do what she craved above everything else right now. She'd turned others into her.

Esther looked out over the water again.

The question being, was it ever going to be enough?

———

Back on the clifftop, the service was nearing its conclusion, the priest reaching the end of the prayers.

Lara looked out over the sea as the bearers moved forward to take the coffin. Then she held out her hand, much as she'd held out her hand that day when two sisters were led off the train together into a future neither of them could possibly have imagined.

Georgia took it, just as she'd taken Lara's hand that day too, as the coffin was finally laid into the consecrated ground.

Their hands gripped each other's even more tightly as the priest intoned the final blessing.

And they didn't let go until long after the service was over and their mother was buried with dignity at last.

ACKNOWLEDGMENTS

With grateful thanks to Sue Davison, Adrian Hobart and Rebecca Collins.

ABOUT THE AUTHOR

Rob Gittins is a screenwriter and novelist. Rob's written for almost all the top-rated UK network TV dramas from the last thirty years, including *Casualty*, *EastEnders*, *The Bill*, *Heartbeat* and *Vera*, as well as over thirty original radio plays for BBC Radio 4.

He's previously had six novels published by Y Lolfa to high critical acclaim. This is Rob's first novel for Hobeck and is the first in a new series to be set on the idyllic, if occasionally sinister and disturbing, Isle of Wight. Rob's second novel for Hobeck is *The Devil's Bridge Affair*, a standalone psychological thriller.

Visit Rob's website at: www.robgittins.com

THE DEVIL'S BRIDGE AFFAIR

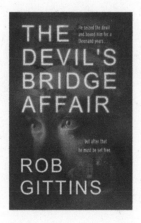

The Devil's Bridge Affair is set in a small town of the same name.

The name derives from a local legend, telling the story behind a bridge that was built for the town by the devil himself centuries before. But there was a price. He would return at different times and in different guises with dark consequences for those who live in the bridge's shadow.

Most in the town believe it to be just a colourful local story; a flight of fancy. Dark deeds can happen anywhere – and there's no such thing as the devil anyway. But when a massive scandal, involving a schoolboy and his English teacher, hits the community, even the most die-hard of sceptics begin to wonder if a devil-like figure is walking in their midst.

CRIME AND THRILLERS BY ROB GITTINS

A crime series set in the hidden world of witness protection.

Gimme Shelter
Secret Shelter
Shelter Me

What's a wife, husband or partner like when you're not watching? A psychological thriller exploring the dangers waiting to ensnare those who try to find out.

Investigating Mr Wakefield

PRAISE FOR ROB GITTINS

'Rob Gittins is a highly acclaimed dramatist whose work has been enjoyed by millions in TV and radio dramas.'
Nicholas Rhea – author of the Constable series, adapted for TV as *Heartbeat*

'Visceral, strongly visual and beautifully structured... powerful, quirky characters.'
Andrew Taylor – Winner, Crime Writers' Association Cartier Diamond Dagger

'Gittins introduces the reader to a dangerous and troubled part of society, and his murky, damaged and at times violent characters are as vividly (and disturbingly) portrayed as those of Elmore Leonard.'
Susanna Gregory – crime author

'Unflinching... as vicious and full of twists as a tiger in a trap.'
Russell James – crime author

'The definitive interpretation of 'page turnability' ... characters that step effortlessly off the page and into the memory.'
Katherine John – crime author

'TV writer Rob Gittins . . hits hard from the start.'
Iain McDowall – crime author

'Visceral realism doesn't come much better than this. Brilliant.'
Sally Spedding – crime author

'Noir at its most shocking.'
Rebecca Tope – crime author

'Terrifying and suspenseful, non-stop jeopardy. Just be glad you're only reading it and not in it.'
Tony Garnett – TV Drama Producer, *Kes*, *Cathy Come Home*, *This Life*

'Gittins is an experienced and successful scriptwriter for screen and radio ... startling and original.'
Crime Fiction Lover

'Well-plotted and superbly written.'
Linda Wilson, *Crime Review*

'Full of intrigue and narrative twists ... powerfully written and uncompromising in its style.'
Dufour Editions

'Corrosive psychological consequences which match those in the best Nicci French thrillers.'
Morning Star

'If there's one thing you can be sure of when it comes to Rob Gittins's literary output, it is that he's not afraid of a scintillating pace ... this has all the hallmarks of a cult classic and I couldn't recommend it highly enough.'
Jack Clothier, Gwales

'Well-drawn characters and sophisticated storytelling.'
Publishers Weekly

'Unputdownable ... this deserves every one of the five stars. I would have given it more if I could have.'
Review on Amazon.com

"Uncomfortable, taut, brutal, it will hold you gripped right to the end. A wonderful piece of writing.'
Cambria

'Fast action, convincing dialogue, meticulously plotted throughout. Every twist ratchets up the sense of danger and disorientation.'
Caroline Clark, Gwales

'Thrilling ... bloodthirsty.'
Buzz

'Gripping and exciting, fast-paced. There is something a bit
different about Gittins's writing that I haven't come across
before.'
Nudge

HOBECK BOOKS – THE HOME OF GREAT STORIES

We hope you've enjoyed reading this novel by Rob Gittins. To keep up to date on Rob's writing please do look out for him on Twitter or check out his website: **www.robgittins.com**.

Hobeck Books offers a number of short stories and novellas, free for subscribers in the compilation *Crime Bites*.

- *Echo Rock* by Robert Daws
- *Old Dogs, Old Tricks* by AB Morgan

- *The Silence of the Rabbit* by Wendy Turbin
- *Never Mind the Baubles: An Anthology of Twisted Winter Tales* by the Hobeck Team (including many of the Hobeck authors and Hobeck's two publishers)
- *The Clarice Cliff Vase* by Linda Huber
- *Here She Lies* by Kerena Swan
- *The Macnab Principle* by R.D. Nixon
- *Fatal Beginnings* by Brian Price
- *A Defining Moment* by Lin Le Versha
- *Saviour* by Jennie Ensor
- *You Can't Trust Anyone These Days* by Maureen Myant

Also please visit the Hobeck Books website for details of our other superb authors and their books, and if you would like to get in touch, we would love to hear from you.

Hobeck Books also presents a weekly podcast, the Hobcast, where founders Adrian Hobart and Rebecca Collins discuss all things book related, key issues from each week, including the ups and downs of running a creative business. Each episode includes an interview with one of the people who make Hobeck possible: the editors, the authors, the cover designers. These are the people who help Hobeck bring great stories to life. Without them, Hobeck wouldn't exist. The Hobcast can be listened to from all the usual platforms but it can also be found on the Hobeck website: **www.hobeck.net/hobcast**.

OTHER HOBECK BOOKS TO EXPLORE

Her Deadly Friend

The Suspect
Bullied by Steph Lewis at school, then betrayed by her lover, Amy Ashby still seethes with fury. Despite the decades-old resentment, she's on the hunt for a new man and a fresh start. This time for keeps.

The Stalker
When both women are stalked by a figure from their shared past, danger threatens.

The Detective
Now Detective Inspector, Steph follows a tip-off to her old rival. After quarrels exploded beyond the playground and changed lives forever, she vowed never to see Amy again. But that was then.

The Deaths

Murder rocks the city. First one, then another. The body count reaches five, and all Steph's leads point to Amy. But is Steph obsessed with a schoolgirl vendetta or closing in on a deadly killer?

Blood Notes

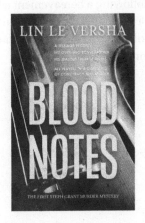

WINNER OF A 2022 CHILL WITH A BOOK PREMIER READERS' AWARD!

'A wonderful, witty, colourful, debut 'Whodunnit', with a gripping modern twist set in the dark shadows of a Suffolk town.'
Emma Freud

Edmund Fitzgerald is different.

Sheltered by an over-protective mother, he's a musical prodigy.

Now, against his mother's wishes, he's about to enter formal education for the first time aged sixteen.

Everything is alien to Edmund: teenage style, language and relationships are impossible to understand.

Then there's the searing jealousy his talent inspires, especially when the sixth form college's Head of Music, turns her back on her other students and begins to teach Edmund exclusively.

Observing events is Steph, a former police detective who is rebuilding her life following a bereavement as the college's receptionist. When a student is found dead in the music block, Steph's sleuthing skills help to unravel the dark events engulfing the college community.

Lightning Source UK Ltd.
Milton Keynes UK
UKHW042132061022
410063UK00004B/393